SUSPECT

OTHER BOOKS AND AUDIOBOOKS

BY CLAIR M. POULSON:

SUSPECT

a suspense novel

CLAIR M. POULSON

Covenant Communications, Inc.

Published by Covenant Communications, Inc.
American Fork, Utah

Printed in the United States of America
First Printing: March 2018

10 9 8 7 6 5 4 3 2

ISBN-13: 978-1-52440-504-5

To Tim and Leesa Wall

PROLOGUE

SOMEWHERE IN THE DEEP FOG of her mind, Ellerie heard the smoke alarm in the living room. She struggled to make sense of what she was smelling. Burnt chicken? There was a pounding on her door. Ellerie became more aware of the smoke as she coughed, and she heard someone calling her name. The door opened, and smoke poured out. Not fully in control of her faculties, she feared it was her husband coming back; she remembered his mandate about having dinner ready. She whimpered in pain and fear and pushed herself into a sitting position, but she only rocked there for a moment before sliding back to lie on the floor.

"Ellerie, are you in here?" a panicked voice called into the house. Ellerie couldn't make her mouth utter a response. After a moment, as footsteps approached, she tried to look up. Through a blur of tears and pain, she recognized her elderly neighbor, Pamela Mavey, holding her apron over her mouth and peering down at her.

Mrs. Mavey's plump face was filled with concern. "Ellerie, whatever in the world happened? Who did this to you?" she asked, her voice muffled by the apron.

Ellerie shook her head, attempting to clear it. Just then a sharp spasm of pain struck Ellerie in her swollen belly, and she cried out, "My baby!"

"You poor dear. Help is on the way. I called 911 to report smoke and told them you were hurt," Pamela said. Ellerie watched as her neighbor moved toward the source of the smoke. "Whatever you had in your frying pan is burned, but I shut the stove off." Pamela dropped to her knees beside Ellerie.

"Ooh," Ellerie moaned. "I was fixing dinner for my husband."

Pamela's round, wrinkled face darkened. "Did your husband do this to you, dear?"

Ellerie remembered his last words to her. *You blame me for this and, so help me, you'll regret it.* If she told anyone he did this to her, he'd be back, and he would hurt her and the baby even worse. So she said nothing about the attack.

"Let me get a cold cloth for your face," Pamela said as she sadly shook her head and rose to her feet.

Overwhelming fear of the man she had been warned not to marry filled Ellerie's anguished soul. Increasing pain in her stomach made her cry out again. She could hear sirens outside. Sobbing, she endured the pain and let her eyes close, determined not to admit to anyone what had happened that day. She would say that a burglar did this to her. Yes, that's what she'd do. A burglar broke in and beat her when he couldn't find money to steal.

Mrs. Mavey placed the cool cloth on her forehead and made soothing, sympathetic sounds. Slowly, Ellerie relaxed and, finally, merciful blackness again enfolded her.

When she awoke, it was light, and a worried face peered down at her. "Ellerie," Pamela Mavey said with a weak smile. "You are awake. Do you feel better now? You are in the hospital, and they are taking good care of you. I've been so worried about you."

"My baby?" Ellerie asked, closing her eyes again.

Pamela patted Ellerie's stomach and said, "The baby is still in there. You were lucky, dear."

"Yes, I guess I was," she responded even as she wondered if her baby would survive Darien's next attack. And she knew there would be more, just like she knew she didn't have the courage to leave him.

"The police have been here. They will be back in a while to talk to you. Ellerie, you must tell them what happened and who did this to you."

Ellerie struggled with a response, her mind replaying what had happened. Her visiting teachers had come. They'd stayed a little too long, and she'd been late starting dinner. Finally, she lied. "I don't know who it was." Mrs. Mavey shook her head, and from the look in her eyes, Ellerie had a feeling she didn't believe it. But she had to stick with her story. Her life and the life of her baby depended on it.

The next visitor to Ellerie's room was her husband. He came in carrying a single red rose in a vase. Pamela stepped back as he placed it on the stand next to Ellerie's bed, smiled at her, and said, "My love, I am so sorry I wasn't home in time to protect you from the creep who did this to you."

Mrs. Mavey, from her position behind but slightly to the side of Darien, watched Ellerie carefully. Ellerie knew her face was swollen, but she couldn't keep the spark of anger—or was it hatred?—from her expression. Mrs. Mavey said, "I'd better leave you two. I hope you get better soon, Ellerie." And she went out the door, slowly shaking her head.

"I'm glad that busybody neighbor of ours is gone," Darien said, the fake concern in his voice replaced with anger. "Now we can talk frankly. You better be careful what you say to that old woman."

Ellerie stared at him for a moment, and then she said, "Don't worry. I won't say anything about what you did to me."

"That's my girl," Darien said as a slow smile creased his face, a smile that failed to reach his dangerous green eyes. "The police talked to me. I told them I had no idea who did it, that if I did, I'd see that they never did it again."

Ellerie kept her emotions in check, choking back a snort of derision. She wisely said nothing.

"Have they talked to you?" he asked.

She slowly shook her head, wincing with pain as she did so. She still didn't speak.

"When they do, here is what you'll tell them," he said firmly. She listened as anger burned in her heart, anger that bordered on a desire for revenge. "Someone entered by the back door, which was unlocked. It was a tall person—at least two inches taller than me. He told you to give him all the money in the house. You told him there wasn't any, and he slapped you. You ran into the kitchen, hoping to get a knife to defend yourself with, but he followed you and beat you up. He took your purse, and then he left."

Against her better judgement, she said, "My purse is in the coat closet."

He smirked. "You think so?"

With a sinking heart she said, "Darien, you didn't."

"You had a couple hundred dollars in your purse, plus your credit card and a debit card," he went on. "I took the money and told the cops there wasn't any. Oh, and I also told them I canceled the cards."

"Darien, I need them," she said as her anger continued to simmer. "And I need my driver's license."

"Why? You won't be leaving the house unless you are with me. You're afraid to," he suggested with that infuriating smirk of his firmly in place.

"They won't believe me about the burglar," she said tentatively. "They'll look for fingerprints, and there won't be any."

"Of course not. You'll tell them he was wearing gloves. And you can't tell them what he looks like because he had a hood pulled over his face." Darien leaned down until she could smell last night's alcohol on his breath. "Don't you veer from the story, or so help me, I will kill you and the baby," he hissed. He stood back up and, looking directly into her eyes, he said, "Call me when they are ready to let you go home, and I'll come get you." Then he issued another directive, one he spoke each time he abused her. "You and I are a couple, and no one is going to change that. You will not leave me. Not ever!" With that, he left the room.

Ellerie shivered, and tears filled her eyes. She was trapped. As badly as she wanted to, she feared she didn't have the courage to leave him. Even if she did, he'd find her, and that would be the end. She didn't know how she would support herself if she did by some miracle manage to escape and successfully hide from him, especially with a baby on the way. She had no choice. She would just have to be more careful not to anger him.

Two uniformed Vernal City Police officers came to see her shortly after that. She stuck to the false narrative Darien had crafted for her. They asked her a few questions and finally left, with a promise to look for the person who did this to her. She had a feeling they both knew they would never find anyone, but at least they were kind enough not to say so.

A day later, Darien took her home, but he didn't stick around long, reminding her that he would expect dinner at six. "And don't let it burn again," he added. "This house still stinks because you were so careless with dinner the last time."

After he was gone, she busied herself with housework, fighting back the tears of desperation that threatened to overwhelm her. She began dinner in plenty of time. Darien was late, but she didn't mention it to him, even when he complained that the casserole wasn't very hot. As they ate, silence reigned. She had nothing to say to him.

Late that night, she woke up alone in her bed, a sharp pain in her stomach. Was the baby really okay? It had better be. If she lost the baby, she could never forgive Darien. Never!

CHAPTER ONE

FOR A FAIRLY SMALL TOWN, and a rural one at that, it seemed like Vernal, Utah, had a lot of crime. Of course, I wasn't that familiar with crime in other towns, as I had been born and raised in Vernal and took my first and only police job here. I liked Vernal, and I had the utopian view that I could make a difference if I worked hard at my job.

My hard work had paid off for me personally, although I don't know that I've made the kind of difference in the community that I used to tell myself I would. I made detective after four years on the force—a goal I'd made when I began. Altogether, I'd been working for the city for almost eight years now. I loved my job. I just worried that there seemed to be more cases for me to work than I could handle. And I was by no means the only officer who felt that way.

I spent my days off caring for my seven-year-old son, Tommy, who had been born a short time after I joined the force. Among other things, we went fishing, hiking, and camping in the summer. In the winter, we spent most of our time in the house, playing games, watching movies, and reading. Tommy never knew his mother, nor had I ever shown him a picture of her, but I did the best I could to make up for her absence in our lives. She'd left us only a few months after Tommy's birth. I'd thought I had a solid marriage. I had loved her and believed she loved me in return. I was wrong. I found my screaming infant son alone in our apartment when I got home from work one evening. His diaper was badly soiled, and he was howling in hunger. My wife had left a note telling me she did not want our baby or me.

She eventually made contact with me through a Salt Lake attorney, giving me notice of her intent to divorce me. Within just a few months, our divorce was final. Not once during that time did I ever see or talk to her. It was devastating to me. I had finally come to grips with the reality of her desertion, but I never knew why she left me. I had convinced myself that it was something I had done; I just didn't have a clue what it might have been.

My parents constantly worried that I had not remarried, but I was in no hurry. The wound of desertion was deep, and I didn't want to experience it again. I didn't trust myself to get involved with anyone else. My worst fear was that if I married again, I might do or say something to cause another wife to leave me. It had been a little more than six years now, and when I was pressed by others about my continued single status, I spoke the simple truth: I wasn't interested now but maybe someday.

Most recently, my dad took me aside on my thirtieth birthday and told me it was time—that I was running out of *somedays*. He argued that my son needed a mother. I admit that after our little talk I started paying more attention to the single ladies and even dated a little from time to time. Trouble was, I didn't ever find anyone I felt comfortable with. Perhaps, I argued to myself, all the women who met my standards were taken. After failing once, I had to admit that my standards were unrealistic. But my dad had started me thinking. I was concerned not so much for me but for Tommy.

I was deep in thought about this very issue after dropping a young lady off at her apartment and driving to my parents' home to pick up Tommy. Yes, I might be single, but I owned my own home, or at least the finance company and I did. I hoped that someday the perfect woman would come along and that, when she did, I'd be prepared with a nice house and yard. I used that to counter subtle reminders my caring family threw at me. "I'm thinking ahead," I'd say. "That's why I bought a house." But I wasn't really serious. I was scared and emotionally scarred, although I admitted that to no one but myself.

The young lady I'd spent this evening with was pretty, had a nice personality, was faithful in the Church, and had all the other things I looked for in a potential wife, all the things I thought I'd found in my first marriage. But I just didn't feel the elusive connection I was looking for. On the other hand, she both acted and talked like she wanted to get serious with someone. As I stepped into my parents' house, I was thinking I probably would not ask her out again. Before I got that thought firmly set in my mind, my cell phone vibrated.

"I'd better take this, Mom," I said as she greeted me with a hug.

"There's a body, Royce," Connie Bost said. She was a dispatcher from Central Dispatch who I'd taken out a few weeks ago. "A couple of uniformed officers are at the scene. They said to call you—that it looks like it might be a homicide."

"I thought Mike was working tonight," I said.

"He went home sick. It's yours, Royce," Connie informed me. "Can you find someone to take care of Tommy?"

"My parents will help me," I said as I caught my mother's eye and she nodded.

SUSPECT7

"Then you might want to go now," Connie said.

"I'm on it," I responded. "What's the location?"

She rattled it off and then added in a slightly seductive voice, "Stop by my place when you get a minute, Royce. There's something I'd like to talk to you about."

I didn't respond to that, as I had no intention of stopping by. Thank goodness Connie hadn't said it on the radio. I could only imagine the snickers that would cause. Connie was an attractive woman in her mid-twenties, and she was someone who would probably marry me tomorrow if I asked her to. But that was about as likely to happen as me buying a fifty-foot yacht to launch at Lake Powell. I simply had no interest in either.

I rushed home, quickly changed clothes, and hopped into my gray unmarked sheriff SUV. The officers at the scene met me at the edge of a vacant lot near the city limits. A little farther and it would have been a county case instead of mine. Not that it mattered. I was okay working a homicide, if that's what it was. It was a challenge I welcomed.

"Has to be murder, Royce," Sergeant Randall Merten said.

"Can't tell what killed him yet, Detective Fleming," Officer Kolton Henderson added. "But there's no way he killed himself and then dumped his body in the bushes like we found him." He chuckled at his own morbid humor. I forced a weak smile.

"Any idea who it is?" I asked the two of them as I pulled my camera bag from my car and slung it over my shoulder.

"Nope. He's lying faceup, but I didn't recognize him," Sergeant Merten said. "But we figured you wouldn't want us to touch the body until you got here. So we don't know if he has ID on him or not. It's this way." He headed back into the weedy, vacant area.

"It's a male for sure?" I asked.

"Yep," Officer Henderson said. "It's a man all right."

"No signs of a wound?"

"Unless it's in his back, there isn't," the young officer said.

"And I suppose it could be," his sergeant added. "I think his hands must be tied behind his back, because they are under him."

"How did you find him?" I asked. "I can't imagine anyone wandering around here this late at night."

Sergeant Merten pointed at the nearest home. "That guy's dog was making quite a fuss. He said after a half hour he got tired of the barking and went out to see what was upsetting the dog. It was running back and forth along his fence, so he turned the dog out of the yard, thinking there must be a raccoon in the area. His dog led him to the body. He called us on his cell and waited by the street until we got here."

"I'll need to talk to him. Where is he now?"

"He's in his house. He said he'd stay up until we told him it was okay to go to sleep."

"I assume you got his name?" I asked.

"Stu Goldman. He's a widower and lives alone."

A moment later, we reached the body. I shined my light around the corpse before stepping a little closer. "What are you looking for?" Officer Henderson asked.

"Whatever's here . . . or isn't," I said.

He gave me a puzzled look, but I didn't expound. I wasn't inclined to take the time to give him a lesson in crime scene preservation and evidence collection. Instead I said, "You explain to him, Sergeant."

Merten took a minute to hit the finer points and concluded with, "There might be evidence we could inadvertently destroy. That's why I had us stay back when we first got here."

"You mean like cigarette butts or candy wrappers or something like that?"

"Or footprints," I said as I squatted and shined my light on one I had just spotted. "Not too large. It looks like it was made by a small tennis shoe of some kind. There's another one. It's either a really small man or a woman. It could be from Mr. Goldman."

"He says he didn't get this close," Sergeant Merten informed me. "He says he shined a light from about twenty feet away and then called his dog and stayed back while he called 911."

"A woman wouldn't have done something like this," Officer Henderson said skeptically as I continued to examine the print that was about ten feet from the body.

"Maybe, maybe not. We've got to keep an open mind," I said as I continued to search. "Ah, there are bigger ones here. Looks like boots made these prints." I glanced at the body. "Could be the victim's, although I don't know for sure. The body wasn't dragged here." I stood up and reached into my camera bag. "I'll need some pictures. While I take them, Sergeant, would one of you go speak to Mr. Goldman? I'd like to see the shoes he was wearing."

"He's not a small man, but it would pay to check them anyway," the sergeant said.

I took several shots of the shoe and boot prints and the body from several feet back. Other officers had arrived by the time I felt I could approach the body more closely. At that point, Officer Henderson returned carrying a pair of work boots. One look at them told me that they did not match the prints on the ground. I approached the body and took some close-up shots and then, with the help of Sergeant Merten, I turned the body on its side. There was a collective gasp from all of us as the victim's arms appeared. They were tied together behind his back with a small rope, just above the wrists.

"I hope he has ID on him," I mumbled as I viewed the bloody hands. "Unless his fingers are lying around here, we can't use fingerprints."

Three fingers on his right hand had been cut off, and both hands had been badly burned in some way, the fingerprints indefinable. "I suppose he could have bled to death," Sergeant Merten said. "There's a lot of blood."

"I hope his fingers weren't cut off while he was still alive, the poor guy," Officer Henderson said. "This is making me sick." To prove his point, he walked a short distance away and threw up. He came back wiping his mouth with a handkerchief. "I hope I don't do this every time I see something like this."

"It gets easier," I assured him as I continued to study the disfigured hands and the rope that bound the victim's wrists. He had a rag tied as a gag through his open mouth and around the back of his head. I examined a nasty wound on the back of his head just above where the gag was knotted. I looked closer at the ground, and it appeared that his head had struck a jagged rock when he fell. "He may have died from this head wound," I said as I shined a light on it. "He was probably shoved by whoever hated him badly enough to do this to his hands."

As I feared, there was no identification on the body. We searched the entire area for the three missing fingers but came up with nothing. In addition to the large pool of blood beneath his head, we found several spots of what looked like blood on the grass and weeds. I photographed what we found.

Officer Henderson commented, "You were right. He must have walked here, but not until after his hands were disfigured and his arms tied behind his back." I glanced at him and saw that he was still looking ill. "This is horrible, Detective."

I agreed with him as I continued to search for more blood. What I found was that large boot prints, probably the victim's, which were hard to see in the weeds, were in line with the small spots of blood. The small tennis shoe prints were slightly off to one side of those. It took almost an hour, but I was eventually able to follow the faint trail with my flashlight to the street near where the police cars were parked.

After we finished at the scene, I allowed the body to be removed to the medical examiner's office in Salt Lake City. Cause of death would be determined by the autopsy, but I was pretty sure it was the horrible wound on the back of his head that was responsible.

By the time I was finally able to sit down at my desk at the police department well into Sunday morning, I was both physically and emotionally drained. But I didn't have time to rest. I began to organize a report while I considered what I should do next. The first thing that had to be accomplished was to establish the victim's identity. Fingerprints were not possible, as badly burned as the hands were.

With the aid of other officers, we looked up missing person reports. We were searching for a male Caucasian between the ages of twenty-five and forty, which is as near as I dared narrow the age. The search was statewide at first, and then, when we came up with nothing, we expanded it to surrounding states. While that effort was ongoing, I released information to the press that we were trying to establish the identity of a man involved in a crime, without revealing that there had been a homicide. We wanted to keep the crime from the public as long as we could. I gave them the best description I could of the body: about six feet tall, around two hundred pounds, with shaggy brown hair and green eyes. I described what he was wearing when the body was found: blue jeans, cowboy boots, and a blue polo shirt. I let people make their own assumptions, but I was pretty sure most of them would think it was someone we were trying to locate and possibly arrest.

I worked past noon on Sunday, and I missed church because of the murder, but Tommy attended with his grandparents. This was one of those times my job interfered with what I really wanted to do. But it came with the territory. By two in the afternoon, I could hardly keep my eyes open, and I decided to go home and try to sleep for a few hours and then go back to work on the case. But just as I was approaching my front door, I was called back to the station. I was informed that a woman wanted to meet with me, that she might have some information about the man I was trying to identify, and that she would wait for me at the police station.

CHAPTER TWO

TEN MINUTES LATER, A YOUNG woman was escorted back to my cubicle. She was limping and holding her stomach as if she were in pain. Several other things about her captured my attention. First, what was probably normally a very attractive face was bruised and battered. Second, though dark purple surrounded her eyes, the color of her irises struck me immediately. I had never seen eyes that color. Amber was the closest I could come to describing it. She was quite small, maybe five-four and a hundred pounds. Her very long brown hair was in a ratty ponytail that fell to her waist. One hand was still pressing on her stomach, which was slightly bulged. *Perhaps,* I thought, *she is in the early stage of a pregnancy.* She was dressed in plain green slacks and a yellow blouse that were both wrinkled, having the appearance of having been either slept in or worn for a prolonged period of time. She had nothing on her feet but a pair of sandals. I judged her to be in her mid-twenties. Finally, what struck me the most was how somber she was.

I stood and held out a hand, inviting her to approach my desk. "I'm Detective Fleming. How can I help you?" I asked.

"I don't know where my husband is," she said in a static voice as her hand took mine. It was small and slightly moist, and her grip resembled a wet dishrag. "I understand you are trying to identify someone. Is it someone you have arrested?"

Her words caught my interest, and I invited her to sit down. After she was seated on a chair directly in front of my desk, I moved my chair to the side of the desk, where I could easily see her hands and eyes, and where the desk would not be a barrier between us. I had a feeling she had something important to say. I wanted to both hear her words and observe her body language.

"What is your name?" I asked, trying to be gentle, as she appeared quite apprehensive.

Those startling eyes looked first left and then right before they finally settled on mine. "I am Ellerie Pearson," she said in a trembling voice.

"Do you live here in Vernal?"

She nodded and looked away from me. Her hands were busy in her lap. A plain gold band was on her ring finger, and with her right hand she continually twisted it around. She did not look back at me, nor did she say anything more. Her eyes settled on her nervous hands, and she calmed them but then began to rub her pudgy stomach. All the time, her right foot tapped nervously on the floor.

"You mentioned your husband," I prompted after an uncomfortable period of strained silence.

She began wringing her hands, but she finally looked up at me. Tears brimmed in her eyes, and she rubbed them. Finally, after nervously clearing her throat, she said, "He left yesterday evening after putting my . . . my . . ." She began to sob, unable to finish her sentence.

I waited. The verbal silence became deafening. I handed her a tissue but said nothing. I'd learned that many times, a witness was likely to continue after a long period of silence, that constant prodding by an interrogator didn't help. So I waited.

And I waited. Her tears were getting to me. I felt like I needed to say something, to try to comfort her in whatever distress she was suffering. I felt the urge to reach out and touch her shoulder, but I did not. Her sobs were making me feel bad for her. But still I waited. She finally quit sobbing. She gently rubbed her eyes again, wincing from what I was sure was inner agony in addition to outer pain. Then she looked up at me again.

Still no words came, so I tried smiling. That brought a tiny shake of her head. But a moment later she said, as if there had been no break in her response to my earlier prodding, "My baby . . . in a box."

For a moment, I was too shocked to respond. That was the last thing I had expected. She began to sob again, but she quickly regained control, and when she did, there was anger in her fiery eyes, and she said, "Darien killed my baby. He killed my precious baby girl. And now he's gone. I hope he never comes back. I hope you have him in jail. I hate him!" Her hands covered her eyes and she cried, her entire body shaking with emotion.

Two pressing things struck me from that appalling statement. First, there was a dead baby. I needed to find it. And second, my murder victim could be her missing husband. Then a third thought entered my mind. Perhaps she killed him herself and was only pretending she thought we were trying to identify someone we had arrested.

I thought about that. She was too small. She didn't strike me as a killer, despite the anger she was showing. But if he really did kill her baby, she had motive. Someone could have helped her. I set those disturbing thoughts aside and concentrated on Ellerie.

"Mrs. Pearson," I began. She looked up at me.

"Please, call me Ellerie. Pearson is *his* name."

I got the message. "Ellerie, where is the baby now?"

"In a blanket on my bed," she said. "I couldn't leave her outside in a box." Fresh sobs began. "And I couldn't bury her in the backyard like Darien told me to."

"That was wise. Let's go see her," I said, rising to my feet. "Is your car outside in the parking lot?"

She stood, stifled the tears, and said, "No. I walked. I don't know what Darien did with my keys. He wouldn't let me have them. I had to leave my house unlocked because the house key is with my car keys. We've got to hurry. I don't want anything to happen to my baby. If you don't have him in jail, he might come back."

I led the distraught woman to my vehicle. Her house was quite a ways from the police department. She'd had a long walk, and from the look of her condition, a painful one. As we rode, I watched her from the corner of my eye. She was wringing her hands and twisting that wedding band. I pulled up in front of a white frame house with a small but tidy yard. Flowers bloomed in a small flower bed beside the front door. There wasn't much grass, but it looked like it had been cut in the past few days. "When did your husband cut the grass?" I asked as I pulled into the driveway behind a tan, older-model Dodge Neon that was parked under a carport.

"Darien? He never lifts a finger around our place. I cut the grass several days ago. He doesn't care about anything but himself."

I ushered Ellerie through the door. Unlike the tidy yard, the inside of the house was a mess. Chairs were tipped over and broken dishes were on the floor of the kitchen.

"Did this happen after you left?" I asked Ellerie.

"Oh, no. Darien did it. He beat me in the kitchen. A lot of times," she revealed with a sad face. "I haven't felt like cleaning it up this time. My baby is back here."

I followed her down the hallway, glancing into the living room. An end table was on its side, and a lamp was on the floor, broken. "He chased me into the living room and hit me with that lamp," she said. "But when I fell, he kicked me. The baby couldn't take it anymore. I think he wanted the baby to die. He resented my pregnancy. He said it made me ugly."

I waited for her to say more, but she simply took hold of my shirtsleeve and tugged. "Back here," she said. "I brought her inside and got her out of the shoebox."

I didn't know for sure what I expected to see, but a premature baby wasn't it. The tiny form had been wrapped in a small pink blanket and was lying in the center of a queen-sized bed. Soon I understood what had happened. The premature birth and death of Ellerie's baby was the fault of her husband and his violence against her, not to mention his demands for Ellerie's physical labor. As I watched her break down again, my anger at her husband was intense while my sympathy for her was almost enough to bring me to tears. What kind of person could do what he had done?

I summoned other officers to Ellerie's house to help me collect evidence, and I got so busy with the investigation of the baby's death and Ellerie's grief that I had to put my murder case on a back burner. But after the investigation at Ellerie's house came to a conclusion, I finally thought about what Ellerie had told me when she came to the police department. She'd said her husband was missing and that she had come in to report his disappearance in response to the information I had released to the press.

I took her aside after most of the other officers had left and the little body had been removed. "Ellerie, your husband deserves to be charged with murder for what he's done. But right now, why don't you tell me why you wondered if he might be the person whose identity I am trying to establish."

She was near the point of collapse. I hated to put her through this, but I did have to identify the body. "Do you have a picture of Darien?" I asked.

She silently rose, went back into the bedroom, and opened a closet door. I followed her into the room and watched as she reached toward a shelf and pulled a framed picture down. She handed it to me. "This is a picture of us when we were married," she explained.

I studied the picture. I was taken by Ellerie's attractiveness and radiance, a far cry from the way she looked now. Darien Pearson was about six feet tall, towering over his bride by eight inches. He was a handsome man with green eyes, slightly shaggy brown hair, and a broad smile. I studied his picture while mentally comparing it to the man in the vacant lot. I couldn't be sure, but it could be him.

"It's him, isn't it?" Ellerie asked as she watched my face. "Please tell me he's in jail. I can't have him coming after me again."

"It could be him. The build and height are right," I said. "So is the hair."

It was time to let her know we had a body, not an unidentified prisoner. "Ellerie, the man we are trying to identify is not in jail. He's dead."

Shock registered on her face. "Dead?" she asked.

"Yes, he's dead—murdered," I said, watching her reaction very carefully.

Her eyes narrowed, and she pursed her lips. "I hope it's him," she said. It was not spoken with venom, but softly, wistfully perhaps. "If it is him, then I can quit worrying about him coming after me. And I won't have to testify against him for what he's done to me and my baby."

"Ellerie, if I showed you a picture of the victim's face, do you think you could tell me for sure if it is Darien?" I asked.

She nodded. "I think so."

"Would you mind coming back to the police station with me? I have the pictures on my computer there."

"Okay," she said wearily and followed me outside.

An elderly woman was standing just beyond the yellow police tape. When Ellerie and I ducked under it, she threw her arms around Ellerie. "Oh, my dear girl. All this time he's been beating you, hasn't he? I knew it. You should have reported him."

"I couldn't," she said tearfully. "He would have killed me."

"But now he's killed your baby," the woman said.

"Yes, he has," Ellerie responded with a catch in her voice.

The elderly lady sobbed and then looked up at Ellerie. "The police will get him now," she said fiercely as she stepped back.

"Mrs. Mavey, this is Detective Royce Fleming. He's helping me," Ellerie said. Then she addressed me. "This is my wonderful neighbor, Pamela Mavey. She knew what Darien was doing to me, but I wouldn't admit it. I didn't dare. But now I think I should have. Maybe my baby would be alive if I had reported what he'd done."

"Ellerie, don't you go blaming yourself. What happened to your baby is his fault, not yours. Now, when you are through talking to Detective Fleming, you come back to my house and stay with me for a few days," the elderly lady said.

"I'd like that," Ellerie said with relief on her face. "Thank you."

"Mrs. Mavey," I said at that point. "How did you know about Ellerie's baby?"

The woman squared her shoulders and said, "I saw Darien carry it outside on the porch and put the baby in a box."

"How did you know it was a baby, and where were you when you saw him do that?"

"I was over there, in my flower garden," she said, pointing across a short fence. "I'd heard him shouting at Ellerie, and then the door slammed. I looked up, and he was standing on the porch, holding the baby in one hand and a shoebox in the other one."

"You are sure you saw a baby?" I asked.

"Well, it was tiny, and it was sort of pink. I suppose it could have been a doll. But what would Ellerie and Darien have a doll for?" the old lady asked pointedly.

"And you watched him put it in the box?" I asked her.

"Yes, he lifted the lid, put the baby in, and slammed the lid back down before storming back into the house."

"Did he see you?" I asked.

"I ducked real low before he turned around. I don't think he saw me," she said. "I hope he didn't."

"Do you know where the baby was when I first saw it?" I asked.

"It was probably in the house. After Darien left, I saw Ellerie come outside. She looked around like she was searching for something. She picked up the box, opened the top, and looked in. She reached inside, and when she brought her hands out, she was holding the little one. She held it against her breast for a moment, and then she ran into the house with it, sobbing and limping," Mrs. Mavey explained.

"Did you go over and talk to Ellerie about it?" I asked, looking sternly at her.

"No," she admitted, dropping her eyes. "I was afraid to. I was afraid he would come back and catch me there."

"And you were afraid he would hurt you?" I asked.

"I guess, but mostly I was afraid he would do something terrible to his wife." She glanced at Ellerie. "I'm sorry, dear. I should have come over right then."

"I'll need to talk to you again," I told the elderly lady. "But first, I need to speak with Ellerie at the police station."

The two women hugged again, and then Ellerie accompanied me to my SUV. On the ride back to the office, she explained that she'd been listening to the radio on a local station in an attempt to distract herself when she heard about the unidentified man.

Once we were back in my cubicle, I turned on my computer and showed her a picture of the victim's face. Her face went very white, and she began to tremble. "That's him," she said softly.

"Ellerie, I need to record our conversation now. There are several things I need to ask you," I said. "Is that okay with you?"

"It is," she agreed.

I led her to a private interview room and shut the door while I went in search of Sergeant Merten. I found him and told him what was happening, that I believed I might have the wife of the murder victim in the interview room. Then I joined Ellerie. Once the recorder was on, I identified myself, my location, and the time. Then I said, "With me is Mrs. Ellerie Pearson. Ellerie, you understand that our interview is being recorded, is that right?"

"Yes," she said.

"You came to me today to report that you hadn't seen your husband for more than thirty-six hours, is that also right?"

"Yes."

"Then you told me he had killed your baby. Why don't you tell me how he did that?" I said.

She slowly nodded her head and, without looking at me, she said, "He has been beating me a lot lately. A few days ago, Mrs. Mavey called 911, and I was taken to the hospital." She went on to explain to me how Darien had come into her hospital room carrying a red rose and how he'd told her what to tell the police. She explained that he took her home the next day and threatened that she'd regret it if she didn't have dinner ready for him when he came home later.

"And did you have dinner ready?" I asked.

"Yes, of course. I knew what he would do to me if I didn't."

"Has he physically abused you since the day you were in the hospital?" I asked.

"Yes, but the worst was the night before last," she said as she began to sob quietly. I gave her a tissue and she wiped her eyes. "He didn't like what I had fixed for dinner," she continued.

I asked her to explain in some detail what he'd done. It was horrific, and I found myself thinking that his death, whoever caused it, was a blessing to her. She explained that after he'd hit her with the lamp in the living room and kicked her, he had left. She said that within an hour, she had miscarried her baby. She'd been sitting on the floor, rocking it when Darien had come home.

"What did he do?" I asked.

"He saw the baby, and he asked me what it was, *as if he didn't know.* I told him she was my baby. He stormed to the bedroom and came out with a shoebox and then took my baby from me and ran outside onto the porch. When he came back in, he didn't have either. I asked him what he'd done with her; he said she was in a shoebox and that after he left I was to bury her in the backyard."

"What happened then?" I asked.

"He told me to shower and then go to bed after I had buried the baby."

"Did you?"

"Did I shower and go to bed? Of course," she said.

"But did you bury the baby?" I pressed, even though I knew she hadn't.

"No, I couldn't do that."

"Ellerie, tell me what you were thinking then and what, if anything, you said to your husband."

"I told him I wished he were dead. I know that was an awful thing to say, but it was how I felt. Can you blame me?" she asked. "He destroyed me in more ways than one. I don't know how I can ever be happy again."

Honestly, I *could* understand why she might feel like that, but the thought crossed my mind that maybe she more than *wished* he were dead. I had to keep an open mind.

I didn't answer her question. Instead, I asked her, "What time did Darien leave that last time?"

"It was maybe seven o'clock in the evening. We hadn't even eaten dinner," she said. "I was so upset that there was no way I could eat a single bite."

"What kind of car did Darien drive, and what color was it?" I asked.

"He drove a pickup, a Dodge. It's light blue. It's about seven or eight years old and has a few dings in it," she responded. "Was it near where you found him?"

"No, and I don't know where it is, Ellerie. Do you happen to know the license plate number?" She shook her head. "That's okay. I'll find that out and see if we can locate it. What was he wearing when you saw him last?"

She scrunched her eyes. "This may sound crazy, but I don't know for sure. He may have been wearing cowboy boots. And he usually wore blue jeans. He had lots of shirts, but I have no idea which one he had on. I'm sorry."

"No, that's okay. Did he usually wear western shirts?" I asked.

"No, he didn't have any western shirts, but he had lots of other ones."

"Can you tell me what some of them looked like?"

She was thoughtful for a moment. "Well, he liked polo shirts the most. He had a bunch of them. He figured they showed off his muscles. He liked to show off. He thought he was really tough."

"Was he?" I asked.

"Oh yeah. I should know. He hit and kicked and threw me around enough," she said with a bite to her voice. "Of course, I'm not very big. He could have hurt me even if he wasn't tough."

"Ellerie, do you have any idea where he might have gone when he left your house?" I asked next.

"Probably to a bar," she said. "He drank a lot."

"Was he only abusive when he'd been drinking?" I asked.

"Oh, no. He was violent even when he was sober, like when he came home from work."

"Okay, we'll check at the bars. Can you tell me who his close friends were? Maybe he went to one of their houses," I said.

She looked at me, her eyes glistening. "You probably think I'm a real idiot. But honestly, I didn't know his friends. Maybe some of the guys he worked with? I don't know. Or just some of the guys he drank with. I don't know who they were either."

"Where did he work?" I asked.

"He works—worked—for an oil company. He didn't work on the rigs, although he used to. He did something else, but I'm not sure what." She thought again for a moment. "I'm trying to think of the name of the company."

"I suppose he has check stubs somewhere?"

She shook her head. "He was paid by direct deposit. I'm not even sure how much he made."

"I can find that out," I told her just as I was interrupted by the intercom.

It was Sergeant Randall Merten. "Detective, I know you're in an interview, but can you break free for a minute? There's someone here I think you need to talk to."

"I'll be right out," I told him and then turned to Ellerie. "I'm sorry. I'll be right back, and then we can finish this." Then I spoke the time into the recorder and shut it off.

I closed the door behind me after I left the interview room and walked up the hallway. I was greeted by a stunning young woman with long black hair. She was wearing tight pants, an equally tight, low-cut blouse, and high-heeled shoes. "Are you Detective Fleming?" she asked before Sergeant Merten could introduce her. "My boyfriend is missing," she said angrily, pointing a finger in my face as if to suggest that I had somehow misplaced him. Then she took a deep breath, and said, "You better find him."

CHAPTER THREE

I HELD MY HANDS OUT as she crowded closer to me, the strong perfume she was wearing threatening to choke me. "Ma'am, you need to tell me who your boyfriend is and why you are looking for him," I said as I backed away, trying to regain my personal space before I started coughing from the power of her perfume.

"I heard you're looking for a missing man. That's why I'm here. Darien is missing. Find him," she demanded.

"Darien Pearson?" I asked, glancing back toward the door where I had just left Darien's wife . . . or widow, if he was in fact my murder victim.

She crowded me again, and I backed up more. My eyes caught Sergeant Merten's. "Sergeant," I said. "I'll need you to take a statement from this young lady. I have an interview to finish. The sergeant will help you," I said to her and fled for the room where I'd left Ellerie.

But the girl was apparently intent on speaking with me and no one else, for she followed me. I turned at the door and said, "If you'd like to wait for a few minutes, I'll speak with you. For now, please go with Sergeant Merten."

"I must speak with you as soon as possible," she insisted as tears filled her eyes.

"What is your name?" I asked as I thought about the broken-hearted woman beyond the door to the interview room.

"I am Kallie Briggs," she said. "Please hurry with whatever you're doing. I need you to find Darien soon."

I wanted to tell her that I was pretty sure he was already found, but I resisted the temptation. Merten coaxed her away from me. As they started up the hallway, I opened the door, but I had not yet shut it when Kallie dashed back. She spotted Ellerie and demanded, "What does *that* woman want?"

"This is a police matter. Please, go with the sergeant. I'll speak with you later." This time, Merten took her arm and more or less dragged her up the hallway.

I was able to get the door shut before there were any further interruptions and said to Ellerie, "I'm sorry about that," as I flipped my recorder on and sat down.

"Who was that girl?" she asked before I had even formally resumed the interview for purposes of my recording.

I did that before responding to her question. "Someone whose boyfriend is missing," I said. "Now, where were we?"

"Detective, please, tell me who that . . . that . . . woman is," she said, her striking eyes burning with intensity.

"Have you seen her before?" I asked.

She shook her head. "No. But she must know who I am. What's her name?"

"Kallie Briggs."

"Who is her boyfriend?" Ellerie asked.

"Let's talk about your situation, Ellerie," I said firmly. "We were speaking about your husband's employment. I suppose we can call the bank and find out who makes the deposits."

"I don't know what bank he uses," she said. "I used my credit card, my debit card, and cash. He never seemed to want me to know anything about our finances. He made the mortgage payments. I bought the groceries."

I leaned forward and looked directly into her eyes. "Ellerie, are you saying you have a source of income of your own?"

She nodded. "I work part time as a bookkeeper. I do all the work at home on my computer. My boss pays by direct deposit to my bank account. That way Darien couldn't take my check. That's all the money I have. And a few days ago, Darien took my credit and debit cards, my checkbook, and what cash I had in my purse. I've had no money since then. My next check is due in a couple of days, but Darien canceled my cards."

"Don't you have access to your checking account online?" I asked.

"I tried that once, but he made me cancel it. He didn't want me doing things like that on my computer. I think he thought he could keep better track of what I was doing with my money if I did it the old way. He even made me take the app off my phone so I couldn't use my phone to do my finances."

"I'm sorry," I said. And I really was. This young woman, it appeared to me, had endured a lot of hardship and pain. "Who do you work for?" I asked.

"His name is Ted Franklin. He owns a small computer business in Salt Lake, where he lives," she said.

"How did you come to work for him?" I asked.

"I was working for him at his place of business when I made the biggest mistake of my life," she said.

"And that was?" I asked.

"Marrying Darien," she said with a hiss.

"Oh," I said.

Before I could fully formulate another question, Ellerie answered what I would probably have asked her anyway. "Ted liked my work, and he liked me," she said with one of the few smiles I had seen from her. "When he found out I'd be moving to Vernal, he told me I could still do what I'd been doing. He even provided me with a computer. It's been nice because I can work when I want to. And Ted pays me quite well. If it wasn't for him, I don't know what I would have done, because Darien didn't figure he should pay for much of anything."

"I'd like to speak with Ted," I said.

"Of course," she responded. She recited his phone number and the address of his business, Better Computer Ideas, as well as his home address. As I was writing it all down, she was slowly shaking her head and pressing on her stomach.

"Are you okay, Ellerie? Do we need to continue this later?"

"I'm just tired, and I hurt really badly," she responded. She began to sob. "I lost my baby, my dear, precious baby girl."

"Ellerie, have you seen a doctor since you lost the baby?" I asked in sudden concern.

She stopped crying and looked up. "I had no way to get there," she said. "Remember, I told you before that Darien took my keys."

"Yes, I do remember. And you walked here to talk to me even though I can tell from your limp that you are in pain. Why didn't you just walk to the hospital? You could have called me from there. In fact, they would have called once a doctor saw the condition you are in."

"I've been hurt before," she said, ducking her eyes. I think she knew it sounded lame.

"You need a doctor," I said firmly. "I'm going to take you to the emergency room and find out what kind of relief they can give you. We can finish this later. Do you have your cell phone with you?"

"No, didn't I tell you that he took it too?"

"No, but maybe we can trace it," I said. "But that can wait. Right now, we are off to the emergency room." I expected her to argue, but she didn't. I closed the interview, shut off the little recorder, and put it in the pocket of my sports coat.

"I can call my neighbor. She'll take me to the hospital," Ellerie said, still trying to choke back some sobs. "You have too much to do."

"No, I'll take you," I insisted firmly. "Let's go."

She followed me into the hallway and toward the rear exit of the building. I realized that I'd made a tactical mistake when a shrill voice called out, "Detective Fleming. I will talk to you now."

Sergeant Merten shouted, "Just a moment, Miss Briggs." But she was already into the hallway, with him hustling behind her. "Please, Detective Fleming is very busy right now."

But the girl ignored him and ran straight for me and grabbed my arm. "You've got to help me find Darien."

"I can't right now," I said as I saw Ellerie's face go pasty white.

"You've got to. I don't know what this . . . this woman's problem is, but I'm the one who needs your help. You can go now," she said directly to Ellerie. "My boyfriend is missing, and I need Detective Fleming to find him for me."

I had made it a practice to be nice to people, even when they pushed the outer limits of proper decorum, but this girl had managed to get under my skin. "I don't have time now. I have to go. Come on, Ellerie," I said, shaking free of Kallie and taking Ellerie by the arm.

There was a moment of shock on the face of Kallie Briggs. Then anger shot from her eyes. "You!" she screamed, launching herself at Ellerie. "You are the one who was destroying my Darien. You couldn't leave him alone, could you? He told me about how you were chasing him. I ought to just—"

Before she could finish whatever threat she had been about to make, I stepped between her and Ellerie as Sergeant Merten grabbed her arm and pulled her back. I said very firmly, "That will be all, Miss Briggs. Sergeant, take care of her." I again began to usher Ellerie ahead of me toward the exit.

The young woman began to shout and swear, but by the time a very shaken Ellerie and I reached the door, Sergeant Merten and three other officers had the other woman under control. As soon as we got outside, Ellerie pulled away from me, stepped to the wall, and leaned heavily against it.

"Ellerie," I began. "Are you okay? I'm sorry about that scene in there."

She was breathing heavily, her eyes wide and her skin as pale as it could possibly get. "She . . ." Ellerie finally managed. "She said Darien. I can't believe it. As if it wasn't bad enough already . . ." She put her hands over her mouth. "He . . . he had a girlfriend. He . . . he said no one else could ever have me. But someone else had him!" Anger was taking over now, and she spat the next words out. "I'm glad he's dead!"

"Ellerie, don't give her a second thought. She's not worth it," I said.

But her anger was still on the rise. "I want to go back in," she shouted, reaching for the door. "I want to slap her face. That's the least I can do. She deserves it. I could . . . I could just k—" She stopped short, and the anger seemed to leave her like air from a balloon, and the next thing I knew, she had fallen against me and thrown her arms around me for support. "I'm sorry. I'm sorry. I shouldn't have said those things," she said after sobbing for a moment, her tears falling on my chest. "I'm not that kind of person. You probably don't believe me, but I'm a good person."

I didn't even know this girl, but as I attempted to console her, I considered the very thing she had just threatened. Someone should slap that other girl's makeup-caked face until she got some sense. But I banished the angry thought. After all, for all I knew, Ellerie could have had something to do with the death of her husband. I gently pushed her away from me. "The hospital," I said. I took her arm again and directed her to the parking lot. Her limp seemed more pronounced, and she kept stumbling. If I hadn't been holding her arm, she would have fallen.

"You must think I'm horrible," she said as we drove to the hospital. "And I am. I'm worthless. Darien should have just killed me along with my baby. I don't have a reason to live anymore."

That kind of talk concerned me. *Surely she wouldn't try to commit suicide*, I thought. To her I said, "Ellerie, you have every reason to live. You can start your life over now. You can put the past behind you. You must. Then things will begin to go your way again."

She shot me a hard look. "You don't know that," she said angrily.

"No, I guess I don't. But I think it. Please, let me help you. I'll find who killed your husband, and then it really will be over." I was babbling, I supposed. But this young woman, this victim of terrible abuse and tragedy, had somehow struck a soft spot in my heart. I wanted her to be okay. I wanted someone other than her to be responsible for killing her creep of a husband. I vowed to do everything in my power to find that person.

By the time I had driven to the emergency room, she had become very subdued. She said nothing when I helped her from my SUV. I took her arm again and led her inside. A nurse took one look at her and said, "Oh my goodness!"

I stayed in the waiting room while they were examining Ellerie. After a few minutes, Sergeant Merten called me. "She left, *finally*," he said. I knew he was talking about Kallie Briggs. "She says the woman with you was trying to steal her boyfriend."

"Did you tell her Ellerie was not just a girlfriend but that she was his wife?" I asked.

"That's why she left," he said with a little chuckle. "She blew up when I told her that she was apparently the one trying to steal Darien. She didn't like what I told her, but I think she believed me. At any rate, I thought you needed to know what she said after I told her that. She said that if anything had happened to Darien, it would be because of Ellerie. She even said that if Ellerie got the chance, Kallie thought Ellerie would murder him."

"So she doesn't know he might be dead already?" I asked.

"I didn't tell her. And she still insists we look for him," Merten told me. "I got her contact information and told her you would get back with her."

"Thanks. I'll do that," I said. "But first I'd better get a search warrant for Ellerie's phone, if we find it, her computer, bank account, credit and debit card accounts, and so on. I'm quite sure she didn't kill her husband, but I need to make sure she didn't have someone do it for her. She certainly has motive."

I honestly couldn't imagine that she had decided to avenge her baby that way, and if she truly didn't have access to her bank account or money in some other way, she couldn't have hired anyone, especially in so short a time. But I had to make certain. I also wondered if I should do the same concerning Kallie. Perhaps she should also be considered a suspect. She had already demonstrated that she had a temper. And she'd used the word *murder*.

Ellerie came into the waiting room a few minutes later, walking with a cane. "The doctor wanted to admit me, but I wouldn't let him," she said. "I just want to go home. I have work to do for Ted, and I need to clean up my house. I'm sorry I have caused you so much trouble. Will you take me home now?"

After the drive, I walked her to her door. I was worried about her state of mind. I was relieved when her neighbor Pamela Mavey came out of her house and scurried toward us. She took Ellerie by the arm and said, looking at me, "I'll comfort and take care of her now, Officer. And if I see her husband, I'll call 911. I will not stand by and see that horrid man treat her so badly ever again."

Before I could stop her, Ellerie blurted, "Darien's dead. Someone killed him. He won't be bothering me anymore."

I would have preferred that she not tell Mrs. Mavey about Darien's likely demise, but it was done, so I decided to let it go. Mrs. Mavey, on the other hand, after removing her hand from her mouth, said, "He's dead?"

This time, before blurting out anything more, Ellerie looked to me for direction. So I said, "We don't know for sure, but Ellerie thinks it might be him. We do have a murder on our hands."

Ellerie, looking directly into my eyes, implored, "Won't you please let her see the pictures you have of the dead man? She can tell you it's him. Then you'll have the word of two of us, and you can look for his killer."

I looked from the young woman to the elderly one and then nodded. "I guess I could do that. It would mean another trip to the police station, though."

Mrs. Mavey, having recovered sufficiently from her shock, said, "Let's do it. It would be a great comfort to me to know Ellerie is no longer in danger."

"And you haven't finished your interview with me," Ellerie reminded me. I did remember, but I was hoping to talk to her again when she wasn't hurting so badly.

So the three of us piled into my unmarked police SUV, and I drove back to the police station. Mrs. Mavey, who had been quite animated on the drive, suddenly became very sober as she walked inside. Police departments had that effect on a lot of people. In my cubicle a minute later, I woke up my computer. When the first picture came up, Ellerie looked away and Mrs. Mavey audibly gasped. Once again, her hand flew to her mouth.

"Take your time. Then tell me what you think," I said.

She studied the grisly photograph for a moment, nodding ever so slightly. I brought up another one and didn't say a word. I just waited. She finally said, "Yes, Detective, that is Darien Pearson."

"You are sure?" I asked.

"Yes, even though he has that cloth in his mouth, I can tell it's him," she said. Then she turned to Ellerie, whose back was still to us, and put an arm on her shoulder. "I'm so sorry, dear. What a horrible thing."

Ellerie sniffled and then asked, "Can we go home now, or do you need to talk to me some more?"

"I think I should. It won't take long," I said. "First let me print some copies of these pictures." After completing that, I said, "Mrs. Mavey, you may come into the interview room with us if you'd like, or you can wait out in the lobby."

"I'll come with you."

For the next few minutes, we talked. When I had finished with the interview, Ellerie was totally drained. I had learned nothing new. Unfortunately, she had no one who could prove she was at home when Darien was killed, although I honestly couldn't see her mutilating her husband's hands, walking him through an abandoned field, and leaving him to die.

On the way back to her home, she asked what she could do about getting keys to her car. "I need to be able to drive. I need to go to the bank. I need new credit and debit cards. And I need to buy groceries."

"I'm sure we can arrange to get you a key from the dealer," I said.

"I'll help you with that, Ellerie. We can use my car for now," her neighbor offered. As I pulled into her driveway a minute later, I thought of something else. Although I was pretty sure of the identity of the victim, there was a way to be positive: DNA. "Ellerie, to confirm what you two ladies have told me, there is something that would be helpful."

"What can I do?" she asked, her voice shaky and her weary body trembling.

"I need something with Darien's DNA on it. A comb, a toothbrush, or something like that."

"Sure, I can get that, but doesn't it take a long time to get results on DNA back?" she asked.

"Yes, but I need to do it anyway." The three of us exited the SUV and walked toward her door.

"Why can't you just check his fingerprints?" she asked. "I'm sure his prints are on file."

Oh, boy. Now what was I to do? I thought for a moment. I cleared my throat and said, "I'm afraid I can't do that. I'll need the DNA."

She stopped at her door and looked at me with a puzzled expression on her face. "You can take a dead person's fingerprints, can't you?"

"Normally, but not in this case," I said.

"Why not?" she asked, glaring at me.

Before I could answer, my cell phone began to ring. I looked at the screen, saw that it was Sergeant Merten, and said, "I need to take this," and turned back to my SUV.

"We'll go in, and I'll get you his toothbrush and comb," Ellerie said in a subdued, very sad voice. I had narrowly escaped having to tell her about the damaged hands.

I answered my phone. "This is Detective Fleming," I said.

"Royce, this is Randall. I think I know where Darien Fleming's truck is."

"Great. That's going to be a big help. Where is it? I'll come in a few minutes," I told him.

"I'm not sure it's his, but it's the right color—light blue—and it's a Dodge. The license plates are missing, but we can run the serial number and then we'll know for sure," he said. He gave me the location, and after mentally reviewing the significance of that location, I told him I'd be there in a few minutes.

The door to Ellerie's house was hanging open as I approached it a moment later. She and Mrs. Mavey were standing just inside. They both turned very slowly and looked at me. I could tell from their faces that something was not as it should be.

"Somebody's been in here," Mrs. Mavey said, her wrinkled face quite pale.

CHAPTER FOUR

INDEED, SOMEONE HAD BEEN INSIDE the Pearson house since we had finished there earlier. Scrawled in red on the living room wall were large letters that read, *Killer! Ellerie, you will pay.* We stepped closer, and Ellerie sank onto her sofa, her head in her hands. The writing had been done with spray paint, but as I searched the house for the can, I could not find it. As near as Ellerie could tell, there was nothing missing, and there had been no other damage done. The door had been unlocked because Ellerie had no key and didn't want to lock herself out.

I was baffled. We had not yet released that there had been a murder. So who knew and had done this awful thing?

Mrs. Mavey sat next to Ellerie, with an arm around her shaking shoulders. "Come, dear. Let's get you a few things, and we'll go to my house. I'll fix you something nice to eat and then you can stay with me for as long as you need to. You need rest, and I'll make sure you get it."

"I'm afraid I'll need to speak with you again, Ellerie," I said as Mrs. Mavey helped her to her feet.

"Not today, you don't!" the elderly lady told me in no uncertain terms. "She's had all she can bear for one day."

I knew Mrs. Mavey was right, although I did need to find out who Ellerie thought might have left the accusing message. Ellerie stood and faced me on shaking legs, even as Mrs. Mavey tugged on her arm. "I didn't kill my baby," she sobbed. "Why would someone write a terrible thing like that?"

After considering for a moment, I decided not to tell her what I was thinking—that the graffiti on her living room wall referred to her husband, not her baby. And yet, maybe that was what it was. But again, few knew about the baby's death. All I said was, "Before you two get some things together, would you give me something of your husband's that would contain his DNA?"

I left a moment later with a toothbrush and a comb. My heart was heavy. Could this seemingly nice woman, this victim of such violence as she had endured, be a killer? I had to consider it. And I had to find out who hated her badly enough to write those toxic words on her wall. Even as I considered that, I drove toward the apartment complex where Sergeant Merten awaited me, the complex where Kallie Briggs lived.

The blue Dodge Ram was parked near the west end of the parking lot behind the apartments. I realized as I parked behind Sergeant Merten's patrol car that I had not mentioned to Ellerie that we may have located her husband's truck. That could wait. Clearly I needed to speak to both Ellerie and Miss Briggs again, especially Miss Briggs. She had some explaining to do.

"Is Kallie at home?" I asked as I walked over to where Randall and another officer were standing beside the truck.

"I don't know. I haven't checked. We got a call at the station from the apartment manager that a truck was parked in someone's slot and that he needed to have it towed," Sergeant Merten explained.

"Any idea how long it's been here?" I asked.

"No. The guy whose spot it's parked in has been out of town for a couple of days. He went straight to the apartment manager when he discovered it here."

"Has anyone touched it?" I asked.

"Not unless the manager or the complainant did," he responded.

"I don't suppose the keys are in the truck," I said.

"Nope," he answered. "I looked through the window, and they are not in the ignition."

"We'll need to have it impounded and searched. To be on the safe side, I think I'll do a search warrant, but let's get it towed first. If you two will take care of that, I'll see if Miss Briggs is at home, speak with her, and then work on getting the warrant."

I checked at the apartment number she had given Sergeant Merten earlier. I knocked, rang the bell, and knocked again. When I got no response, I went to the office of the manager, a Mr. Andy Hanger. The older man that answered was not tall, but he had a huge belly and drooping jowls. The top of his head was shiny and bald with longish white hair wrapped around his head just above his ears, like a damaged halo that had been crammed over his head. "Are you Mr. Hanger?" I asked when he answered the door.

"Andy Hanger," he said brusquely. "What do you need?"

I produced my detective shield. "I'm Detective Royce Fleming. I need to speak with you for a moment."

He looked at me with one of those sneering scowls police officers often get from people who don't like cops. I smiled at him, hoping to break the ice before I began to question him. I received no smile in return. "What's it about, that pickup that somebody parked in my lot? Darn nuisance. People think this is public parking. But it ain't."

"Did you by any chance notice who parked it there?" I asked, pretty sure what his answer would be.

"If I had, I wouldn't have called the cops. I hope you got it towed by now. My tenant needs his spot back."

"It'll be gone within a few minutes. You have a renter here by the name of Kallie Briggs," I said.

"Yeah, real good-looking gal. Too cute for her own good," he said. "I had to tell her to tell that latest guy to stay away."

"Oh yeah? What guy would that be?" I asked.

"You just as well come in and get out of the heat," he said, finally holding the door wide.

I stepped into a room that smelled of cigars, coffee, and body odor. I honestly would have preferred to stand out in the heat. But I thanked him, and he waved me to a chair. I sat, and he did the same before I asked, "What kind of car does Kallie Briggs drive?"

"It's a sporty little yellow thing. It looks very expensive. I think her parents must have bought it for her," he replied. "No way could a young gal like her afford a car like that."

I made a note on a small notebook I'd pulled out of my pocket. "Do you have the make and the license number?" I asked.

He shook his head with a disagreeable scowl before hefting his heavy frame from his chair. He disappeared into another room. When he came back, he had a three-by-five card in his hand. "Says here it's a Mazda," he said. He read off the license number. I noted both.

"Thanks. Now, about her latest boyfriend. His name was Darien?"

"Yep, that's what the chick called him. Didn't hear no last name."

"When did you last see him?"

"Night before last. He was coming out of Kallie's room. I think he'd been staying there. I confronted him in front of her apartment and reminded both of them that he wasn't allowed here anymore. She said something not very nice and went back into the apartment, slamming the door. He walked away, pushing me aside as he passed me. If I wasn't so old, I'd have decked him," he said.

"Why did you ban him from coming here?" I asked.

"He got in a fight two or three nights ago with one of my tenants."

That caught my interest. "Did you call the police?"

"No, I didn't need the cops here. The two of them broke it up when I told them to," he said.

"What is the tenant's name who Darien was fighting with?" I asked. "And what apartment does he live in?"

"Listen, Officer, I don't know what you want to know that for. I handled the fight myself. If I'd have wanted the cops involved, I'd have called them. All I want now is for that truck to be moved. Does it happen to belong to this Darien guy?" he asked as he shoved the card into his shirt pocket and lowered his ample frame into his chair again.

"I think so," I said. "But I'm not sure. The plates are gone."

The manager shook his head, sending his whiskery jowls swinging. "That's strange. But I still don't see what that has to do with Max."

"Max who?" I asked.

"Hermo," he answered with a frown. "You tricked me into giving you his name. But you don't need to bother him. He didn't want the cops called after this Darien guy was fighting him. I told him I wouldn't call them, and I didn't, and that's the end of that."

"Actually, I do need to speak with him," I said very firmly. "You see, Darien was reported missing by Miss Briggs today."

The manager cocked his head slightly and peered at me for a moment before saying, "You don't say. I wonder why he left his truck."

"If it is his truck," I said. "We don't know that for sure. Do you have any idea what the fight was about?" I asked.

"Of course I do. It was about Miss Briggs. Max didn't appreciate this Darien guy coming around to see her."

"And why is that?" I asked.

"She's his gal, that's why. And he didn't like someone else stepping in and trying to steal her from him."

"I thought you said lots of guys came around."

"Well, a few, but it didn't take Hermo long to send them packing. This Darien guy didn't get the message, so they had their little fight," Andy Hanger said.

"Who won?" I asked.

The old guy chuckled. "Hermo was winning when I put an end to it. He's not someone a smart guy crosses. I think he was a professional fighter before he came to Vernal. At least that's what I've heard. He's one tough cookie."

"So did Darien leave after he got beat up?" I asked.

"Course he did, but he said he'd be back and Hermo would wish he hadn't touched him. Hermo said he'd kill him if he came back. I still can't figure why he left his truck here."

"If it's Darien's," I reminded him once more. But I had a suspicion just then. Darien had come back, because the manager had seen him and reminded him that he wasn't supposed to come around. Perhaps he'd come back again later last night, and, when he did, Hermo might have carried out his threat. Max Hermo rose to the top of my suspect list, above both Kallie and Ellerie—way above Ellerie. She was barely clinging to the very bottom of the list so precariously that she could drop off at any time.

"I will need to talk to Max Hermo," I reiterated.

"You think he may have had something to do with this Darien character coming up missing?" he asked shrewdly.

I nodded. "I need to ask him about it."

Andy reluctantly gave me the apartment number, and I asked him for the guy's vehicle information as well. That required another difficult heft from his chair, and he didn't say a word as he waddled out of the room again. He came back in with another card and read from it. "He drives a black Dodge Durango." He gave me the year and the license plate number.

I thanked him for his time and headed to Max Hermo's apartment. No one answered. I searched the parking lot for the Durango but did not find it. But I did spot Kallie's sporty yellow Mazda, so I returned to her apartment.

As I waited at the door again, I wondered if the small tracks at the murder scene might be Kallie's. Perhaps she and Max were working together, although I could not imagine why Kallie would report Darien missing if she had anything to do with his murder. Unless, of course, Max insisted that she do it. I shrugged my shoulders.

The door opened, and the striking girl I'd seen at the station stood there. "It's you," she said, brightening, her purple lips curling into a big smile. "Come in. We need to talk."

"Sorry I didn't have time earlier," I said lamely. I really wasn't sorry at all, but things had changed in the past few minutes. She was now a suspect.

"Have you found Darien?" she asked after offering me a cup of coffee, which I politely declined.

"I think we found his truck," I said in a deliberate non-response to her question.

"Where?" she asked.

"I think you already know where." I gave her my sternest police officer look.

Her face went red, and she smiled a guilty smile. "Yeah, it's in the parking lot." The smile departed abruptly and she frowned as she said, "But I don't know why he would have left it. So where is he? Don't you see? That's why I'm so worried. His truck is here, but he isn't."

"Why didn't you tell Sergeant Merten about the truck?" I asked.

For a moment, she didn't say anything. I waited for a response. When it came it was, "Because I wanted to talk to you, not that sergeant guy. I was going to tell you, but you wouldn't talk to me. You would only talk to that . . . that . . . Well, you know who I mean."

"Yes, Darien's *wife*. What else were you going to tell me?" I asked as I pulled my small digital recorder out. "I'd like to record this conversation. Is that all right with you?"

"Of course it is," she responded. "I only want my lover found."

I spent a moment introducing myself and Kallie for the recording, and then I said, "Okay, now you can tell me what else you had to say to me earlier today. Maybe you could begin by telling me when you saw Darien last."

"I didn't know he was married. He should have told me that. But it's me he loves, not that woman, if she even is his wife. Anyway, he was here for a few minutes early last evening. When he left, he told me there was something he had to do but that he'd be back in a little while. The manager, Mr. Hanger—he told Darien he couldn't come back, and he didn't, but I know that's not why he didn't. Andy Hanger can't tell me who can visit and who can't. I tried to call Darien several times. But each time I did, his phone went to voicemail. It wasn't until this morning that I saw his truck out there. That was also when I heard you wanted information on any missing men anyone knew about," she explained. "That's why I came to the station to talk to you. He is definitely missing."

"He gave you no indication of where he was going or what he was going to do?" I pressed.

"No, but that wasn't unusual," she said. "Why are you wondering who knows of any missing men, anyway? Did you arrest someone who won't tell you who he is?"

I ignored her question. I took the pictures from my pocket of the dead face of the man I believed to be Darien. I figured now would be a good time to show them to Kallie and see what kind of reaction I got. I unfolded them and held one of them toward her. I said, "Can you tell me who this man is?"

Kallie's reaction was as genuine as any I'd ever seen. Her face went pale. She began to tremble. Her head began to go back and forth, and then she simply slumped forward, slid off her chair, and landed on the floor. I quickly knelt beside her. She was out cold but had a strong heartbeat and was breathing well. I verbally made a note of what had happened for the purpose of my recording. Then I went into her kitchen and found a cloth, which I wet with cold water.

When I pressed it gently to her forehead, she stirred, and a moment later she came to and, with my help, sat up on the floor, leaning forward against her knees and moaning. It was a minute before she was able to speak. When she did, she said, "He's dead. Why didn't you tell me sooner?"

"I needed to be sure it was him," I explained. "He had no identification on him."

She reached for my hand, and I helped her stand up and then sit in her chair again. I put the pictures back in my jacket pocket. "Kallie, after Darien Pearson left here last night, what did you do?"

"I didn't kill him," she said. "He was murdered, wasn't he?"

"Yes, he was, Kallie. I'm not accusing you of doing it, but I do need to know where you were last night from about the time he left here until ten or so. It's just a formality. I will be asking everyone the same question. I need to eliminate anyone who had seen him recently so that I can narrow my search for his killer."

"It was probably his . . . you know, that woman," she hissed. "She probably found out he didn't love her, that he loved me, so she killed him."

I didn't respond to that, but instead I said firmly, "Where were you last night, Kallie?"

"I was right here. I waited, thinking he would come back. We were going to go out, but he left when Mr. Hanger harassed him, like I already told you. I watched TV until about one o'clock, and then I went to bed."

"Can anyone verify that you didn't go out?" I asked.

"I don't know. My neighbors, maybe?" She was talking slowly and was very nervous and upset. I frankly didn't believe her. I would have to check with the neighbors.

I then threw another question at her. "Were you with Max Hermo last night?"

Anger crossed her face, and sparks flew from her pretty hazel eyes. "Not even!" she said with venom in her voice. "He's a pig. He and Darien had a fight. Darien told him not to bother me again. Max thinks I'm his girlfriend, but that's a lie."

"Kallie, isn't it true that he had been your boyfriend until recently?" I asked.

"Sort of, but not really," she said evasively. Suddenly her face lit like she'd had an epiphany, and she raised a fist in the air and shook it. "That's who killed him. I'll bet it was him. Max hated Darien because Darien loved me." I certainly was considering that, but I didn't tell Kallie that.

We talked more about Max and how he was strong, a former semi-professional fighter, and a man with a bad temper. Finally, I asked, "Can you think of anyone else who might have been angry with Darien?"

"Not really. He was a great guy," she said.

I didn't agree with that, but I kept my thoughts to myself. "Did he mention to you anyone besides Max, who he might have had an argument with?"

"Nope," she said.

"Kallie, I need a favor. I'd like to take pictures of the soles of all of your shoes," I said a moment later.

"Why do you want to do that?" she demanded.

"Again, Kallie, it is to eliminate you as a suspect. If you don't want me to do it now, then I'll come back with a search warrant later and do it anyway. It would be easier if we take care of it right now."

"Oh, okay. If it'll help catch whoever did this to my boyfriend, I'll let you see my shoes. I have a lot of them." She began to sob, but she soon had a stack of shoes for me to photograph. I eliminated most of them without having to do anything but examine them. She had three pairs of sneakers that I did photograph for comparison with the pictures I had taken of the footprints at the scene of the murder, including the ones she was wearing. When that was done, I thanked her for her time, gave her my card, and said, "If you think of anything that might help me find the killer, give me a call."

She was sobbing again when I left.

CHAPTER FIVE

My phone began to ring before I made it back to my vehicle. I answered and heard a familiar voice on the other end. "Detective Fleming, it's Ellerie Pearson."

I thought she'd be sleeping by now, or at least resting in Mrs. Mavey's house. "Hi, Ellerie," I said. "What can I do for you?"

"I need to see you," she said between sobs.

What now? I wondered. "Are you at your neighbor's house?" I asked.

"Yes, please come. I just received an email from Darien," she said with a catch in her voice.

My head jerked. That was the last thing I'd expected to hear from Ellerie. She was waiting for me on the front porch of Mrs. Mavey's house, leaning on her cane, when I got there. The older lady was standing with her. Both of them looked like they'd seen a ghost. I suppose getting communication on the Internet from a dead man was similar to seeing a ghost. It would certainly be an unnerving experience.

"Tell me about this email you received," I said.

"It's on my computer," Pamela Mavey said, gesturing for me to go inside. "It's in the living room."

"I borrowed her computer to check my messages," Ellerie said. "I couldn't sleep, and I need to keep myself busy until I can."

The screen was open to the message. I sat at the computer and silently read.

Ellerie,

I'm sorry I had to leave on such short notice. I'm in Los Angeles right now. I have a chance for a really good job. I'm almost sure to get it, and when I do, we'll be moving here. We can make a new start. I love you, and I know you love me. You might want to start packing. I'll see you in a few days.

Darien

I sat back and stared at the computer screen. Finally, I stood up and looked at Ellerie. "Are you sure the dead man is Darien?"

She nodded but looked a little unsure. I looked over at Pamela. She still seemed to be in shock. Finally, I said rather sternly, "Ellerie, what aren't you telling me?"

She sniffled, looked at her feet, and finally said in a soft voice, "He has a twin brother."

I hesitated while I digested that stunning revelation. Finally I said, "I take it they look alike."

"Oh yeah, they do," she said. "But I haven't seen him since before we moved to Vernal."

"Let's sit down," I suggested. "We need to talk about this."

After we were seated, Mrs. Mavey said, "I'll go into the other room so you two can discuss this, ah, this astonishing thing."

"You didn't know Darien had a brother?" I asked Pamela.

She said she didn't and scurried from the room. I looked at Ellerie, shaking my head. "May I record this?" I asked.

"Of course," she said, her voice still shaky and her hands trembling. I wished I didn't have to do this. But it was important, so I moved ahead.

I gave the introductions I needed for the recording, and then I said, "Okay, Ellerie, let's talk about Darien's brother. Begin by telling me his name and where he lives."

She rubbed her eyes with her hands. I could see the intense fatigue and pain there. She looked at me after a moment, her amber eyes shining with tears, and said, "Donald lives in Los Angeles."

"What does he do?"

"He's a movie stuntman. Detective, I don't know him well at all. He and Darien didn't really get along," she said.

"Do you know who he works for?" I pressed.

She shook her head. "I think he did stunts for a lot of different film production companies, but I'm not sure of that."

"Do you have an address for him?" I asked.

"There might be something on Darien's cell phone, if you can find it. I don't know it."

"What about an email address? Would there be one on your computer, or did Darien communicate with his brother at all?"

"I don't know if he did," she replied. "I don't even know how to get into Darien's email."

"I'll worry about that later," I told her. "Now, has Darien spoken about him lately?"

"I'm sorry. Darien and I didn't talk about much of anything," she said. "He only came home to eat and then later to sleep. We didn't have a marriage anymore."

I nodded. "Could the dead man be Donald?"

Her eyes grew wide. "I suppose it could, but I don't think so. The shirt Darien had on in the picture you showed me was one he wore a lot. I checked before Mrs. Mavey and I came over here. It was not in his closet or in the dirty clothes hamper. It has to be him." She paused, rubbing her head for a moment. "But if he's in Los Angeles now, it couldn't be him. Maybe Donald has a shirt like that."

Or, I thought to myself, *Donald was wearing Darien's shirt for some reason.* "What about scars or marks or tattoos, Ellerie? Did Darien have anything like that that would help identify him?"

"Yes, he had a tattoo of an eagle's head on his left shoulder."

"Great. That does it. My victim has that tattoo," I said.

"But so does his brother," she said. "They got them together back when they still got along, before I ever met Darien."

"Goodness," I said, deflated. "What about scars?"

She shook her head, but then suddenly she looked hopefully at me. "Wait, Darien had a scar about an inch long on the back of his left hand. And I can identify his ring and his watch. He didn't wear his wedding band, but he had a turquoise ring that he wore on his right ring finger. I don't know where he got it, because he had it when I first met him. I can describe it to you. He never took it off. And his wristwatch, it has his initials engraved on the back. I don't know why I didn't think of this sooner. He had those on him, didn't he?"

I guess the time had arrived to tell her the gory news of the missing fingers from his right hand. "I'm afraid that won't help either," I said. "I'm sorry to have to tell you this, but the reason we can't use his fingerprints or the things you just told me about is his hands have been mutilated—we wouldn't be able to see the scar. Three fingers on his right hand are missing. And we didn't find a watch or a ring."

For a second, I thought she was going to pull a Kallie Briggs on me and pass out, but she recovered before she reached that point. For a minute or two she sat hunched over with her head in her hands, sobbing. Finally, she looked up and said coldly, "Somebody must have hated him worse than I did. Although, frankly, I can't say he didn't deserve it."

I could feel anger in her voice now, and I could see it in her eyes. I chose not to comment on what Darien did or didn't deserve. But I said, "Until we get DNA results back, we won't know if the victim is Darien or Donald. Of course, we will know if we can locate one of them alive right away. I'll get busy and see if I can have someone check on Donald in LA. We should be able to find out where he lives and works."

"But the email was from Darien," Ellerie said doubtfully. I could tell she had reservations about that.

"Someone else could have used his account," I suggested. "Unless you hear from him on the phone or in person, we can't assume he wrote the email. So for now, don't worry about it, but let me know if you get another email or a call or any other kind of communication."

"Okay," she said softly.

"Ellerie, you need to rest. Even if you have a hard time falling asleep, at least you can rest. Will you do that?"

She nodded, and I called out to Mrs. Mavey, who then came back in. I told her that it was important that Ellerie rest. I gave her the same instructions I had just given Ellerie about contacting me, and then I left.

I had to go home and rest that night. I was so tired that I wasn't able to spend much time with my son. I felt bad about that, and so did he.

It was the next morning before I was able to determine that Donald did in fact live in the Los Angeles area. I learned that Donald was employed by an agency that trained individuals to do movies stunts and then contracted with movie companies to use their employees. I talked to Donald's employer, the head of the agency, Felipe Salvagi, who told me that Donald had left work almost two weeks before, saying that he was taking a couple of days off. He had far exceeded the two days and had not reported in since then. The employer told me he'd tried to call Donald repeatedly, that he was badly needed for a stunt; all he'd gotten was voicemail, and none of his calls had been returned.

On the positive side, I was able to confirm that the Dodge truck left at the apartment complex was Darien's. Inside of it, I'd found Ellerie's purse, with the keys to her car and her credit and debit cards, driver's license, and even her cell phone. What I didn't find were the same sorts of items of Darien's that I'd hoped would be there. I checked the items for fingerprints without success. I guessed that Darien must have been wearing gloves when he handled the items, or else that he had wiped them down. Shortly after noon, I finally found time to drive to Pamela Mavey's house so I could return the items to Ellerie, all but the cell phone. Since she was technically a suspect in the murder, I needed to get a warrant and search the phone. I did take it with me to Mrs. Mavey's, however, as I was hoping Ellerie would look for any messages or calls from her husband before I sent it to a lab.

As I waited for someone to answer the door to Mrs. Mavey's house, a voice called to me from next door. It was Pamela. "We're over here," she said. "We're cleaning and straightening things up. Her visiting teachers are helping."

"Ellerie is up to that?" I asked as Mrs. Mavey and I walked the few steps to her house, passing a car that I didn't recognize parked out front, probably the visiting teachers. I hadn't known that Ellerie was a Latter-day Saint.

"She's a different woman today, Detective. Food and a lot of rest did her some good. She says her leg feels better too. She isn't even using the cane. She is anxious to get all this behind her and get on with her life. I was so glad she finally fell asleep last night; she slept for more than twelve hours," Pamela reported.

"That's great," I said. "I need to visit with her for a little bit."

"Well, come in. I'll get her," Pamela volunteered. "You'll be surprised when you see her."

I waited in the living room, which had been cleaned and straightened up. I could hear women talking in another room. I was still looking around when Ellerie came in. When I saw her, it shocked me. She still had her dark eyes and bruises, but she'd applied makeup and hidden much of the bruising. Her waist-length brown hair was neatly brushed and tied back in a long ponytail. Her eyes shone with light that I hadn't seen so much as a hint of the day before. And when she smiled, it was very nice.

She was an attractive young woman. She wore some blue jeans that fit her figure nicely, except that she was still pudgy around the waist. She had a pale-pink blouse on. And she walked with only a hint of the limp she'd had when I last saw her the evening before.

"Hi, Detective," she said.

"Hi," I said in return. "You look nice."

She blushed and said, "Thank you. I'm through feeling sorry for myself. What's done is done. I will grieve for my baby for a long, long time, but I have to put the loss of her behind me the best I can and get on with my life after she is buried."

"That's great, Ellerie," I said sincerely. "The medical examiner should release her body soon, and you can take care of burying her."

"My bishop is getting me a burial plot. I don't know what I'd have done without his help. I don't have any money. The bank told me that I can now access my account but someone used my debit card and cleaned me out."

"I suppose that comes as no surprise at this point," I said.

"Yeah. It was probably Darien. But I will have money deposited by my boss soon. I'm just glad there is a place to put my baby's body," she said, and suddenly her composure slipped and she began to sob.

I wanted to comfort her, but I simply sat there and let her grieve. Finally, she wiped her eyes and her cheeks with a tissue and said, "I'm sorry, you must have something to tell me. Please sit down."

We both sat down, and then I said, "There are some things we need to go over."

"About Donald? Was he in LA?" she asked.

"I talked to his boss. Donald hasn't been seen for a few days, and he has been unable to make contact with him," I said.

The sparkle went out of her eyes and a shadow crossed her face. "So it could be him who's dead. Darien might still come back." Her voice trembled as she spoke.

"I'm sorry, but we do have to consider that," I said. "Although, I really believe that it is Darien who's dead. I wonder, though, if Donald may have killed him." I didn't mention that someone with small feet was involved, probably a woman. In my mind, I was looking for two killers—a man and a woman.

"You'd better stay at my house until the police find out for sure which one is dead, dear," Mrs. Mavey said, putting an arm around Ellerie's shoulders.

Ellerie nodded her agreement. Then she said, "When will the DNA tests be finished? Then we'll know for sure which one it is."

"Possibly," I said.

"What do you mean, possibly? Isn't DNA conclusive?" Ellerie asked.

"That's true, except in the case of identical twins. If Donald and Darien are identical, all the DNA tests will tell us is that it's one of them, and we already know that much."

"So the only way to know for sure is to find the one who's still alive," Ellerie stated dejectedly.

"There is another way," I said. "I need to get Darien's dental records. That is the best chance we have now."

She heaved a sigh. "I don't know if he has any. I know he hasn't been to a dentist since we were married. He has really good teeth."

"That's too bad. I was hopeful for a quick determination. Perhaps we can find out if Donald has any history of dental work. That will take more work and a lot of time, but we may have to do that."

Ellerie ran her hand over her face and sighed, looking quite worried. "If Darien is in California and he comes back for me, I'm not going with him," she said firmly. "He'll just have to kill me first." She was thoughtful for a moment while I tried to think what to say to that drastic statement. Then she brightened a little bit. "But it has to be him, Detective. He didn't take his truck. He'd never go without his truck. It is his truck, the one you found at the apartments where that . . . that other girl lives?"

"Yes, it is his truck. Speaking of which, I have your purse, cards, license, and keys," I said. "I'm sorry. I left them in my car. I'll run and get them for you."

I returned with them a moment later and handed her the purse, the keys, and her cards. "Thanks, Detective," she said. "I can't use the cards now. The bank is issuing me new ones as a precaution. But you didn't find my cell phone?"

"Actually, I did. It's right here." I pulled it from a pocket of my sports coat. "This is yours, isn't it?"

"Yes, that's it," she said brightly, reaching for it.

I drew it back. "I'm sorry, but I'm afraid I can't return this to you yet. I have to get a search warrant and go through it. There may be something in it that tells us more about Darien and his activities for the past few days."

Ellerie looked puzzled. "Why do you think that?" she asked. Then her face grew dark, and anger shot from those unique eyes of hers. "You think I might have something to do with the murder, don't you?"

"Ellerie, I don't for one minute suspect you, but who knows if he might have used your phone and, if so, who he might have called. And maybe there are text messages from him to someone else."

The anger in her eyes faded a little. "Oh, I see. I guess that makes sense. But you don't need a search warrant for that. I'll let you look. I'll even give you my permission in writing. It's my phone, after all."

"I was hoping you would check for some calls that you don't recognize and any messages, but that won't be enough. I have to go by the book. If there is damaging evidence against Darien or Donald or someone else, a search warrant is best."

"I don't see why," she said, her eyes flashing again.

"You've never had to deal with defense attorneys, Ellerie. One might argue that since it was not in your possession when something damaging was said or written, that your permission is not sufficient. I'm sorry, but that's just how it is."

The fire again faded. "Okay, I guess you're right. But can we look and see if there are any messages that I need first?"

"That's what I planned," I said.

We sat side by side as she opened her phone, logged in, and began first by checking her messages. "Did Darien know the password to your phone?"

"He made me give it to him, so yes, he could have used it, and I'm sure it was him who used my cards."

She found several text messages, including some from her boss, Ted Franklin. Ted wondered why he hadn't heard from her for a couple of days and asked her to call him when she could. I handed her my phone. "Call him on this phone," I said. "I don't want to do anything with yours other than look. And after you talk to him, let me speak with him too."

Ellerie called Ted and explained what was happening, but she assured him that she would get her work caught up. Then I spoke to him and told him I needed to see him. "I can come to Salt Lake in the next day or two, if that will help," I said.

"There's no need for that," Ted said. "It sounds like you have too much to do as it is. I think I'll come to Vernal. I know Ellerie could use some moral support. Will tomorrow be okay?"

"That will be great. Call me at this number when you get in town, and we'll meet," I told him.

"Ted's coming here?" Ellerie asked brightly as soon as I'd ended the call.

"Tomorrow," I said.

"He's such a wonderful man. I was afraid he might be upset with me, but I should know better. He and his wife are really good people. He's in the presidency in his stake, and his wife teaches Primary." She fidgeted with her phone in her hands. "Now, did you want me to check recent calls? There are no other messages for me, and I don't think Darien sent any from my phone," she said.

"Do you recognize these phone numbers?" I asked as she opened her iPhone to recent calls.

She slowly scrolled through them. "That's Pamela's phone," she said, pointing to one number. She looked over at her neighbor. "You tried me several times," she said with a weak smile.

"You weren't answering your landline," Mrs. Mavey said. "I was worried about you. For good reason too."

"Thank you," Ellerie said with genuine affection in her voice. "You are the best neighbor a girl could possibly have. I don't recognize the others," she said to me. "Darien must have been using my phone after all. I wonder why he wasn't using his."

"Who knows?" I said. Of course, there was nothing conclusive about him having used her phone. Others may have had access to it. "I'll find out about the rest of these numbers. I'm sorry I have to leave you without a phone."

"As soon as I get paid, I can use my new debit card," she said. "I'll buy a cheap one to get me by. I'll be okay until then."

"I'll loan you the money to get a phone, dear," Pamela said. "And you won't have to pay me back until you get on your feet again."

"Thank you. That's so kind," Ellerie told her. "Now that I have my keys, I have a car to drive again." She sighed, and she smiled at me as she added, "You have no idea how helpless it feels not to have a car or a cell phone."

I smiled back and excused myself to continue my work. I worked the remainder of the day and well into the evening on search warrants and interviewing tenants in the apartment complex where the truck had been located, as well as residents in the neighborhood where the body had been found. A couple of other detectives were helping me, so it made my task a little lighter, and we got a lot done. We also canvased the local bars, but we didn't learn much until I entered a bar on the outskirts of town at about nine o'clock that night.

Many of the patrons had seen Darien there quite often. That was true of the other bars in town as well. Some said he'd come in several times in the past few days with a very pretty girl he called Kallie. She was described as barely old enough to enter a bar or to drink.

It was a fellow by the name of Johnny Torella who made the long hours of tedious detective work worthwhile. He was seated at the bar when I came in and addressed the bartender. When I mentioned Darien's name and showed a picture to him that I had obtained from Ellerie, the fellow at the bar turned toward me and said, "I know him. Can't say I like him, though."

"Why not?" I asked.

"He just strikes me wrong. Thinks he's hot stuff. He parades that pretty little gal around like she was a model or something. Course, she is mighty easy on the eyes." He smiled at that.

"When did you see him in here last, Johnny?" I asked as I looked him over. He was only maybe an inch taller than my five-ten. But he was muscular and solid and looked very strong. He had black hair that hung over his ears and collar and a well-trimmed, short black beard. His eyes were set wide apart beneath a broad forehead. He had bushy eyebrows and was missing one front tooth. He looked tough and mean.

"Can't say for sure, Officer," Johnny said. "It was maybe three nights ago." He grinned, displaying his missing tooth, and said, "The girl wasn't with him, but there were *two* of him that night."

That caught my immediate attention. "What do you mean by that?"

"The guy with him was his twin brother. Identical. They even combed their hair the same way and wore similar clothes. Looked like the brother had money, though, because that night he pulled some bills off a money clip that was pretty thick. That's something I don't think Darien has a lot of. My buddy Andrew and I shot a round of pool with them. The brother—Donald, I think he said his name was—cleaned me and Andrew's plows. Darien wasn't too happy because he cleaned his plow too."

"Did they say much while you were playing with them?"

"Not a lot. I got the feeling Darien wasn't happy that his brother was in town. In fact, if I had to guess, I'd say the two dislike each other. About the time his brother finished the first game, collected from all three of us, and offered to play another game, Darien said something to Donald about how he ought to just head back to California, that he wasn't wanted here."

"What did Donald say to that?" I asked.

Johnny smiled. "He said, 'When you give me what you owe me, I'll leave.'"

"How did Darien react to that?"

"He said a couple of words that weren't too nice, and then he said, 'I ought to kill you and feed you to the catfish in the Green River.'" Johnny paused for a minute, and then he added, "Then Donald said something like, 'I'll meet you at your house, and we'll explain to your missus what you owe me and why. And don't ever threaten me again, or you will end up in the Green River yourself.' With that, he dropped his pool cue on the table, downed the last of his drink, and walked out."

"What did Darien do?" I asked.

"He told me, 'I really could kill him,' and he followed him out. Haven't seen either one of them since then," Johnny said.

I processed this and continued my questions. "So Darien owes his brother money?"

"Sounds like it. But he ain't the only one. I think he owes a lot of people money. For that matter, he owes me a couple hundred and Andrew some too, but I don't know how much. I would have reminded him that night, but I decided to let him have it out with his brother, and then I could deal with him another day," he said with a grin. "I really don't like the guy."

I had been careful not to mention that one of the brothers had been murdered. With the exception of the cops, Ellerie and her neighbor, the unknown person who had sprayed graffiti on Ellerie's wall, Ted and Fiona Franklin, Kallie Briggs, and Stu Goldman, the man who'd found the body, I didn't believe any others of the public knew. And I had instructed everyone to keep it quiet, including Mr. Goldman. I spoke to a few other patrons. A couple of them confirmed that they'd seen the twins playing pool with Johnny Torella and Andrew Hutchins. But they couldn't tell me more than that.

I got the bartender's attention before I left and learned that Andrew was a shorter guy who often came in with Johnny. He'd left right after the Pearson brothers had. I made a note to find and speak with Andrew Hutchins.

CHAPTER SIX

I DECIDED TO CALL IT a night after the other officers and I compared notes at the station. I was the only one who had learned anything of value. I shared what I'd learned with them and headed for my parents' house shortly after ten.

The second I walked in, a very tired little Tommy ran to me and threw his arms around my waist. Oh, how I loved that kid. "You should have been in bed by now," I told him. "I would have carried you to my car."

"He refused to go to bed tonight," my mother said. "I'm sorry."

"I wanted to see you, Dad," Tommy said. Then he thrust a dagger at me with his eyes narrowed. "Why are you always working now? Don't you love me anymore?"

I picked him up and hugged him. "Of course I love you, but I have a lot of work to do right now, and it's very important. I'm sorry, Tommy, but don't ever think I don't love you. You are the most important person in the world to me."

"Really, Dad?"

"Yeah, really," I said as I let him back to the floor.

Even though it was late, Tommy and I stayed up and played games, read stories, and just enjoyed one another until midnight. As I spent such special time with Tommy, my thoughts kept drifting to Ellerie. Saddened, I thought of how she would never be able to enjoy time with her child the way I could with mine. I thought of the horror she had gone through. And I prayed I would find that she was totally innocent.

I dropped Tommy off at my folks' house the next morning at about nine and headed back to the office. As soon as I entered the building, our receptionist told me to go to the chief's office. I had spoken with him only briefly about the case, but I suspected pressure was about to be applied.

Chief Brian Collins was in his early fifties. I found him just a bit intimidating, although he was the one who had appointed me as a detective. He was taller than me, slender, and had thick brown hair that was flecked with gray. But it was his intense green eyes and his commanding presence that made me shrink before him.

As he waved me to a chair in his office, he looked rather grim. "I understand you've been working some long hours," he said. "But I guess you expected that when you accepted the appointment as a detective."

"Of course," I said. "I don't mind."

"Royce," he said. "I am getting some pressure from the mayor. Word is out that an unidentified man was found murdered over by Stu Goldman's place. We need to know who it is and find the killer as quickly as possible. Is there a reason we shouldn't release the name now?"

"How is word getting out?" I asked. "I've tried to keep it quiet."

"It happens. I don't know how. One of the officers may have told his wife, and she might have told her friends—you know how it goes. It's impossible to keep a lid on things like this for very long. But don't you think we should release the victim's name now and let the public know of the murder?"

"It's okay if we let people know there is a murder, but we can't release the identity because we don't know for sure who it is," I said.

Chief Collins raised an eyebrow. "I thought it was a guy by the name of Darien Pearson. I understood that his wife identified him by his picture."

"Well, sort of," I said. Then I proceeded to tell him about the twin brother and that he had been seen in town in a bar with Darien.

"That is a problem," Chief Collins said. "You need to get dental records right away."

"No luck there, either," I said. "Mrs. Pearson doesn't know of any dentist her husband has seen. She says he had perfect teeth. I would suspect the same is true of the brother."

"Don't just assume that, Royce. Check in California on the brother. Does he have a wife?"

"He doesn't. The only contact I have down there is his boss. I'll call him again," I said.

I brought the chief up to date on the interviews I'd done and who I had on my list of possible suspects. "If the victim is Darien Pearson, then I would say the wife is the one you really need to focus on," Chief Collins said. "Revenge is a very strong motive for murder. Have you collected her shoes to examine against the prints from the empty lot?"

I pounded my head. "I did with Kallie Briggs, the girlfriend, but not Mrs. Pearson."

"She's the most likely suspect you have. Get over to her house right now and get that done. You should have done that already. I hope she hasn't gotten rid of them," he said.

The chief didn't know Ellerie, but I wasn't about to argue with him. He was not happy with me, and I didn't need that. "I'll take care of it," I said, trying not to let him hear reluctance in my voice. "Is there anything else?"

"That's it for now. I want to see some progress right away, Detective. Now get going," he ordered.

I wasn't thrilled about having to ask Ellerie for her shoes, but I knew I should have already done that. I left his office red-faced and sweating. When I pulled up in front of the Pearson house, there was a strange car there, a black Cadillac sedan. Ellerie's tan car was in her driveway. I parked in front of Pamela Mavey's house and got out.

Pamela answered the door. "If you're looking for Ellerie," she said, "she is at her house with her boss and his wife right now. Mr. Franklin wanted to put an update on her computer. It was something about heightened security."

"How is she this morning?" I asked.

"She's doing as well as can be expected. It cheered her up to see Mr. and Mrs. Franklin. They are very supportive, wonderful people," Pamela said.

A minute later, Ellerie answered the door and greeted me with a pretty smile. I returned a tight smile, not anxious to upset what appeared to be a reasonably good day for her. She invited me in. She was looking amazing. Only a slight limp was manifest as she walked back into the room ahead of me. I followed her with my eyes as she led me into her home office, where a well-dressed couple was standing near her computer.

"Ted, Fiona," she said. They looked up. "This is Detective Royce Fleming. He's investigating the, uh, the murder."

They both greeted me warmly. "She's been telling us all about you," Fiona said with a charming smile. "She is very impressed with you."

I felt myself blush. "Well, I'm impressed with how strong she is," I said as my eyes met Ellerie's.

She gave a demure smile that made my throat constrict. "I hope you have good news this morning, Royce," she said. Her use of my first name wasn't lost on me.

"Donald has been seen in town," I said.

A shadow crossed her face. "When?"

I explained about Johnny Torello and what he had told me in the bar. After I had finished, Ted said, "So Donald threatened Darien?"

"Yes, but Darien also threatened Donald," I explained.

"So you're no closer to knowing which one was killed," Ted said with a frown.

"I'm afraid not, but I have more suspects to look at now," I said. I dreaded asking about Ellerie's shoes. But I had to do it. "I met with my boss, Police Chief Brian Collins, a few minutes ago."

"Were you just reporting to him?" Ted asked.

"Not exactly. I did give him an update, but he wanted to know why I hadn't asked to look at Ellerie's shoes. He ordered me to come here now," I said, lamely trying to deflect blame for what I was about to do.

Ellerie's eyes narrowed. "Why do you need to look at my shoes? Surely you don't think I had anything to do with the murder."

"I don't, but the chief reminded me that you have motive and that most murders in domestic violence cases are committed by a mate," I said.

"Why my shoes?" Ellerie demanded. She was getting angry, and frankly, I didn't blame her.

"I have to compare the shoes of anyone who could even remotely have had anything to do with it to tracks that I found and photographed near the body," I said.

"My shoes are small," she shot at me. She held up a sneaker-clad foot. "As . . . you . . . can . . . see."

"Yes, I know. So are Kallie's. I took pictures of her shoes," I said. I didn't tell her that a quick look at the pictures from the scene and those of Kallie's shoes didn't match. Not that she couldn't have gotten rid of the ones at the scene of the murder if she was involved.

"And now you want mine. Why? You can see how small my feet are," she said, fuming now.

"This does seem a little overboard," Fiona Franklin said with a shake of her head.

"Why, if the prints at the scene were large, would you want to look at small shoes?" Ted asked.

I cleared my throat as my stomach clenched. "Actually, the only prints there besides the victim's were made by small sneakers," I said.

"You do suspect me!" Ellerie said with a hiss as her face turned a dark shade of red. "Well, it wasn't me! You can look at all my shoes. Starting with these," she said, taking one off and slamming it into my chest.

"Ellerie, that won't help," Ted Franklin said, touching her shoulder.

She shrugged his hand off and hit me with the other shoe. "There, take them. I'll go barefoot," she said.

She started from the room, but Ted stopped her by taking hold of her arm. "Ellerie, calm down. Detective Fleming is only doing his job. This will prove you had nothing to do with it." She again shook his hand off and stormed from the room. "Where are you going?" Ted called after her.

"I'm getting him the rest of my shoes. I won't need them when he arrests me. I think they provide shoes in jail," she shouted back.

That went well.

"I'm sorry, Detective. That creep she married has hurt her so badly. I hope you can forgive her for acting out today."

"Of course I can. I honestly don't think she had anything to do with it. But the chief insisted, and like you said, it will be in her favor."

She stomped back a moment later with four more pairs of shoes. She shoved them into my chest and let them drop to the floor. She said nothing— just flounced to a chair and sat down. I knelt beside the shoes and eliminated two pairs very quickly. The others were sneakers. To my profound relief, neither of them looked even close to how I remembered the ones from the murder scene. But to be positive, I opened my phone and pulled up the clearest shot I had of the prints I had taken at the scene. Not even close.

"Well, that takes care of that," I said. "They're not a match." I showed the pictures to the Franklins. They agreed that it couldn't have been Ellerie's shoes that made the prints at the scene.

"Satisfied, are you?" Ellerie hissed as she got up and stepped toward me, reaching for my phone. I let her look, and she said, "I told you."

"Thanks, Ellerie," I said. "This is all of your shoes, then?"

That brought a dark cloud into the room. "No, it's not," she said in a quiet, strained voice. "I threw away the ones I was wearing when I killed my husband. So do I get to go to jail now?" And with that, she leaped at me and started pounding her fists into my chest.

"Don't do this, Ellerie," Mrs. Franklin said sternly. "It doesn't help."

Ellerie ignored her and continued to pound on me. I offered no resistance. Ted reached for her again. "Ellerie, it is a felony to assault a police officer. Don't do this." She threw a fist at him, striking his shoulder, and then continued her attack on me.

Then, as suddenly as it had started, her attack ended, and she fell against my chest, sobbing violently. I put my arms awkwardly around her. For a couple of minutes, she cried into my chest. Finally, she pulled back, looked up at me, and said, "I'm so sorry. This isn't your fault. I'm no better than Darien." Once more she placed her head against my chest. Then she finally drew away and stepped back. "Are you going to have to arrest me now for hitting you? I understand if you are."

"No, Ellerie, of course not. I am so terribly sorry for all you're going through," I said as I gazed into those sad eyes of hers. Just looking at the pain on her face broke my heart. I felt as if a stone—a rough, nasty one—had found a home in my stomach.

The anger was gone from her eyes. There was nothing there now but a dull yellow glow. "I'll get to the bottom of this, Ellerie. I promise," I said as I stepped back.

"I know you will. Thank you. If you aren't going to arrest me, then I think you should go now," she said softly and turned away from me, tearing at my heart as she did so. Fiona Franklin took her in her arms and was holding her as Ted followed me from the room.

"Can you meet me at the police department?" I asked him. "I don't want to cause her any more hurt by talking to you here."

"Detective, don't you think you should take pictures of her shoes first? I'm sure your chief will want to see the proof."

"Oh my!" I said with a catch in my voice. "Will you get them for me? I don't want to upset her any worse."

He came out with the sneakers a moment later. I took the pictures and set a time for him to meet me at the department.

He walked me to the front door, but before I got outside, Ellerie came back into the room, looked at me, and then left again without saying a single word. As I drove back to the station, I tried to sort out my feelings. All I came up with was that I couldn't help but like Ellerie and that it broke my heart to see her hurting so badly.

I was once again told to go to the chief's office when I entered the building, so I went straight there. He invited me to sit down again and then said, "What's the verdict?"

"Her shoes don't even come close to matching," I said.

"Was she upset by you asking?"

"That would be an understatement," I said darkly.

"I expected as much. Don't count her out," Chief Collins said sternly.

I had my phone in my hand. "Would you like to see the pictures?" I asked.

"No, that won't be necessary. I trust your judgement, Royce. There is one more thing. I assume you got pictures of the note that was written on her wall with red paint?"

That was in my preliminary report, so I wasn't surprised that he brought it up. "I did," I responded.

"Have you considered that she could have done it herself?" he asked.

I shook my head, almost stupefied. "That's not possible," I said, trying not to show any anger, although it did make me mad that he'd even asked. "She was with me from the time I first picked her up and brought her in for questioning. I took her to the hospital, and then I brought the neighbor Pamela Mavey here to look at the pictures of the victim as well. I interviewed Mrs. Pearson again before I took the two women home. The message was written during that time."

"Okay. That's all I needed to know. Sounds like you are on top of things. Go ahead and get back to work. But remember, don't take the wife off your list."

"I won't," I said as I exited his office. But I told myself I would write it in invisible ink at the very bottom of that list. I honestly didn't believe she was capable of such a thing.

Ted Franklin came to the department a few minutes later. He was shaking his head as he sat at my desk. "That girl is hurting," he said. "Please don't hold this morning's outburst against her. I am just sick over what she's been through. If I'd had any idea that her husband was abusing her, I'd have come out here and taken her back to Salt Lake. She could have stayed with Fiona and me until she could get a divorce. But she didn't ever so much as hint at what he was doing. I honestly thought her marriage was going okay, despite the fact that I didn't like the guy."

"It's so sad for her," I said. "I've got to get to the bottom of all this. Maybe that would give her some relief. Tell me about her."

"I would be glad to. She is one of the sweetest girls I've ever known. Ellerie is bright, efficient, and totally loyal to me and my company. She is like a daughter to Fiona and me. We never had a daughter of our own—just boys," he said. "We are very fond of her."

"I can see the good in her," I said. "She's lucky to have you two on her side."

"We tried to talk her out of marrying Darien. I had a bad feeling about him from the first time I met him, and when she announced that she was marrying him even though he couldn't take her to the temple, it was like a knife in my heart," he said. "But Darien was charming, handsome, and full of promises about how she just needed to give him a little time and they would go to the temple. Fiona and I doubted it, but Ellerie believed him. He'd blinded her."

"What about her family?" I asked.

"That's not good. She has a brother," Ted revealed. "He adores her, but he's a wild one himself. Her parents divorced years ago. She and her brother were both victims of that divorce. The parents fought over them. They ended up being split up. Her brother—I think his name is Rico—is a couple of years older than she is. He lived with their father. Ellerie lived with their mother. They had visits that allowed the two of them to spend a weekend together once a month or so, but other than that, they were kept apart."

"That's got to be rough," I said, thinking of how close I'd always been to my brother and two sisters. Even though none of them lived in Vernal now, we still kept in touch, although I envied them of their successful marriages. But they treated me like I was okay, despite my failed marriage. Ellerie didn't have that.

Ted went on with his sad tale. "When Rico got out of high school, he left his father's home and went to work in some dead-end job. Then, according to Ellerie, he got into trouble. He's been in and out of jail ever since then. As far as I know, he's never married. I don't know if Ellerie is still in touch with him. But if she is, he wouldn't be a good influence on her. At least, I don't see how he could be. You'll have to ask her about him."

I shook my head. "I don't think she will talk to me after today."

He smiled. "You don't know that girl like I do, Detective. She has her troubles, but she has a heart of gold. I think she will talk to you again, but let me take the lead on that. I'll talk to her and let you know what I find out about Rico."

I talked to Ted for a while longer, and then he finally stood and said, "I'd better go. I think Fiona will have Ellerie calmed down by now."

After he left, I made some notes and added to my growing report while I considered my next move. On a whim, until I could learn more about Ellerie's brother, Rico, I added his name to my persons-of-interest list. I wondered about her parents. I had to find a way to talk to Ellerie again. I felt like I should find out where her parents were and if she was still in touch with either of them. Her mother had raised her, so it seemed likely that she was still in contact with her. It was a stretch, but if her dad or her brother knew what Darien had been doing to Ellerie, would they have avenged her? I didn't like that thought, but I had to consider it.

I was thinking about that as I decided to try to locate Andrew Hutchins. I needed to get his take on the relationship between the Pearson brothers and, for that matter, between him and Johnny Torello and Darien.

I got up and was putting on my sports coat when I got a call on my cell. "Royce, you've got to come over right now." It was my mother, and her voice was frantic.

"What's the matter, Mom? Is Tommy hurt?" I asked as my chest constricted.

"It's Mayra," she said. "She's here. She says she's taking Tommy. Your dad is out of state with his work and won't be back until at least tomorrow. Can you come?"

CHAPTER SEVEN

I EXPLODED FROM MY DESK and ran to my car, my heart in my throat. I hadn't heard from my ex-wife since our divorce was finalized and even then not directly—it had all been through her attorney. She hadn't wanted Tommy back then and had given me complete custody. She hadn't requested visitation rights and hadn't seen him since he was a few months old. She was a total stranger to him. What in the world was she doing now?

I raced up to the house and parked behind a flashy silver Mercedes. I leaped from my SUV and ran to the front door, opened it, and charged in. My ex was holding Tommy in her arms. He was crying, and when he saw me, he shouted, "Daddy, help me. This lady is trying to steal me."

My mother was very upset, and she was staring at Mayra with anger unlike any I'd ever seen her display. I stepped past her to Mayra, held my arms out to my son, and said, "No one is taking you, Tommy."

He reached for me, but Mayra restrained him and turned her back to me. I didn't want to have to tear my boy from her arms, but it looked like I might have to unless I could talk some sense into her. "Tommy," Mayra was saying. "I am your mommy. You are going to have a new daddy. You will be coming with me now."

"Mayra," I said with clenched teeth. "Put him down, and then you and I will talk."

I was trying to stay calm for Tommy's sake. He was already upset and scared, and I didn't want to make it worse. "Mom, take him downstairs while Mayra and I discuss this."

My mother eyed me warily. "Royce, you can't let her take him, not even for an hour. You've got to stop this." She was really worked up.

I smiled at her and said, "Mom, don't worry. Mayra and I just need to talk about this." I turned toward Mayra, who was still turned away from me. "Mayra, put him down."

Just then she screamed, and Tommy fell from her arms and hit the floor, scrambling to get away from her. My mother scooped him into her arms and fled from the room.

I didn't know what had happened until Mayra, fire in her blue eyes, turned back to me and held up her arm. It was bleeding. "That little brat just bit me," she said angrily. "That just shows what a horrible father you are, teaching him to do things like that."

I couldn't help but chuckle. "He is a smart kid. I didn't have to teach him that. He just knew he had to do something to get away from you, and he did."

She glared and spluttered as she looked at her wound. "I'll teach him better manners," she finally said hotly. "I'm going to go get him, and you'd better not try to stop me, or I'll have you thrown in jail."

I stepped in front of her, blocking her path to the doorway my mother had taken Tommy through. "If you take him out of this house, I'll personally arrest you for kidnapping. In case you have forgotten, which I'm sure you haven't, you gave up all claim to him. You forfeited your parental rights in our divorce proceedings. I suggest you leave now; go back to wherever you came from, and forget this nonsense."

Mayra ran a hand through her short blonde hair and then pointed a finger at me. "Royce, you knew I was coming and that you had to let him go with me."

I shook my head. I had no idea what she was talking about. "I haven't heard from you in more than six years, Mayra. I was told by my attorney when you remarried a few years ago, back when the alimony ended, that I should never hear from you again. And I haven't until now."

A sly smile crossed her delicate features. "Speaking of attorneys, mine filed for a return of my parental rights and for me to take full custody of Tommy. If you'd bothered to show up at the hearing, you'd know all that. But since you didn't, the judge gave me custody, and you will be paying me child support."

"Hearing?" I asked. "What hearing? I wasn't told about any hearing." My heart began to pound, and I felt like I might pass out. I steadied myself against the wall.

"You were served. My attorney told me so. Don't try to deny it. And he also gave you a copy of the court's order. My son is going with me."

"I did not receive notice of a hearing," I said, wondering what she had done as I fought to regain my equilibrium. "Nor did I receive a copy of the order."

"You can lie all you want, but the law is on my side. If I hadn't been so emotionally upset at the time of our divorce, I would never have let him stay with you. My attorney convinced the judge of that."

"Mayra, you left him, left both of us when he was just a few months old. That was a decision you made. You can't change what happened." I was almost shouting I was so upset.

"I already have," she said snottily.

My mind was whirling. Something was going on, and I had to get to the bottom of it before Tommy was torn away from me and emotionally damaged for life. I came up with a quick plan, and I asked, "What is the judge's name?"

She told me. Then I asked for the name of her lawyer. She shared that as well. Then I said, "Okay, Mayra. I'm going to go tell Tommy what's happening and ask him to cooperate. That's the least I can do for him. But don't think for a minute that this is the last of it. Wait here," I said.

"I knew you'd see it my way," she said with a triumphant sneer on her face. "I'll tell you where to send the five hundred dollars each month, when you bring him back upstairs."

That gave me pause, but I gathered my wits about me again. She'd mentioned child support a moment before, but five hundred a month was nuts. I tried not to let her see how upset I was. She thought I was caving in. For now, I was okay with her thinking that, but that wasn't going to be the case, not now—not ever. I would fight for Tommy to the bitter end. But I let her think I had bought her crazy claim. I exited the room and went into the basement. Tommy was calmed down now, and my mother was holding him protectively in her lap. "What is that woman thinking?" she asked me, trying to keep her voice even. "She gave him up."

"I will get to the bottom of this, Mom. Mayra claims she has a court order to take custody of him, that I didn't bother to go to a hearing I knew nothing about. She thinks I came down here to explain to Tommy that he had to go with her. She assumes she's won," I explained.

"What are you going to do?" my mother asked.

"I told her I'd explain to Tommy what's happening, and that's what I'm going to do."

My mother looked shocked, but I knelt beside her and my son and said, "Tommy, I am going to take you out the basement door into the backyard. We are going to get away from here, and I'll take you somewhere where Mayra can't find you."

My mother sighed in relief. "Thank you, Royce. What do you want me to do?"

"Wait here for as long as you can. If Mayra starts shouting for me, and she will, then go upstairs and tell her what I explained to Tommy and that I have taken him somewhere safe until I can get my attorney to take care of whatever unethical and illegal things her attorney has done."

Mom hugged me and then Tommy, and he took my hand and let me lead him out of the house. "Where are we going, Dad?" he asked as we quickly worked our way from the backyard and slipped into my vehicle, hoping Mayra didn't see us. Then I drove straight to my attorney's office, praying that he was in.

Tommy held my hand as we hurried into the building where my lawyer had his office. I stopped at a door that said, *Wendell Lawson, Attorney at Law*. I opened the door and stepped into his reception area. He had a new receptionist. I did a double take. I'd seen her at a couple of singles events I'd attended in the stake and had thought she was a pretty girl, but I had never spoken to her. She was very attractive, and she smiled brightly at me. "You are Royce Fleming, aren't you?"

"I am, but you have the advantage of me. Did Mrs. Williams retire?"

"A month ago. My name is Kaci Walters," she said with an ever-widening smile. Her teeth were perfectly formed and very white, giving her smile a glistening effect. She was definitely striking. "Are you here to see Mr. Lawson?"

"Is he in?" I asked.

"He's with a client right now, but I'll let him know you're here. I don't think he will be long."

"Thank you. This is very pressing," I said, my voice strained and my throat tight. "I have a big problem."

"Can I tell him what your visit is about?" Kaci asked.

"It's my ex-wife. She's trying to take Tommy from me," I said. I must have sounded desperate, but I was, and it was hard to hide it. "He's got to help me. I can't lose this little guy."

She looked at me for a moment. I wasn't sure what she was thinking, but I didn't care. Finally, she smiled, picked up the handset, punched a button on the phone, and a moment later said, "I'm sorry to interrupt, Mr. Lawson, but Royce Fleming and his son are here to see you. Mr. Fleming says it is very important." She listened for a moment and then put the receiver down and said, "He said it will be about ten minutes. Why don't the two of you sit down?"

I wanted to pace the floor. I wanted to punch a hole in the wall. I wanted to scream in frustration. But I did none of those things. I simply did as she suggested and sat with Tommy right next to me, attempting to get my emotions under control. Miss Walters came out from behind her desk, went to a magazine rack on the far side of the room, and thumbed through it for a moment. Then she pulled a thin book out and came over to us. She knelt in front of Tommy and said, "Would you like to read this book? I'll bet you are a good reader."

"I am," he said proudly and took the book from her outstretched hand.

She smiled at him, patted his knee affectionately, and then stood up. "Royce," she said, "If you'd like, Tommy can stay out here with me when you go in. I think we will get along very well."

"Thank you," I said as I looked into her eyes. She was even more attractive than I had remembered, and just looking at her helped me bring my emotions under control. The thought crossed my mind that I should consider asking her to dinner sometime. But it was gone as quickly as it had come.

She continued to look into my eyes and said, "It's my pleasure." She smiled. She sat down next to Tommy and said, "Would you like to read the book to me?"

He seemed fine with that. I watched the two of them, thinking how much Tommy needed a sweet mother figure in his life. He did not need Mayra or anyone like her. The door to Mr. Lawson's office opened a couple of minutes later, and he escorted a thin elderly man to the outer door. Then he offered me his hand and said in a deep, commanding voice, "Why don't you come on in, Royce. Would you like Tommy to stay here with Kaci? She's really good with kids."

"That would be great. Thanks."

A moment later, we were seated in his office. "Okay, Royce. I can see that something is bothering you. Take a deep breath and then tell me how I can help."

I took that deep breath. His secretary's smile and friendly manner had calmed me, but I felt all of my anxiety returning as I faced him. I tried to tamp down my rising temper before I spoke. "Mayra showed up at my parents' home a little while ago," I finally said in a reasonably calm voice. "And she informed my mother that she was taking Tommy with her."

Mr. Lawson's smile faded, and he said, "That would be kidnapping. Did you explain that to her?"

"I tried to reason with her, but she wouldn't listen," I said. I then recounted my exchange with Mayra, and he sat back when I'd finished and rubbed his chin with one hand. I watched him. Wendell Lawson was bigger than me, around fifty years old, and, I knew, very shrewd. He gazed at the ceiling for a moment, and then his piercing eyes met mine again. His deep voice rumbled as he asked me the name of the judge and the attorney who were involved in the issuance of the order Mayra had claimed existed. I told him, and he shook his head. A lock of his thick brown hair fell across his forehead. He swept it back and then said, "I don't know the judge, but I have crossed paths with Fred Zietz. Have you ever met a cobra, Royce?"

I jerked slightly in surprise at his question. "I've seen them in zoos," I said hesitantly.

"If and when you meet Fred Zietz, you will have met a cobra. He's in his mid-thirties, is part of a large firm in Salt Lake, and is very smart. But he is not honest, Royce. The day will come that he will be disbarred," Mr. Lawson predicted with a shake of his head. "It would give me a great deal of pleasure if I could be the one to make the complaint to the bar that knocks him off his self-made pedestal. Maybe, just maybe, you have presented me with that opportunity."

"I did not receive anything about a hearing, nor did I get a copy of the order the court made," I said.

"I don't doubt it," he said with a frown. "I fully expected you to say that. Listen Royce, I have to be in court here in Vernal at one this afternoon. I'll make some calls and see if I can find out what this is all about, and then I'll ask the judge here in Vernal to give me a temporary restraining order against your ex-wife and her attorney."

"That would be great," I said.

He relaxed back in his chair and was thoughtful for a moment. Then he leaned forward, drummed his fingers on the desk, and asked, "Are you working the case of the man whose body showed up next to Stu Goldman's house?"

I said, "I am, and I need to get back to work on it before the chief calls me in again. The mayor is pressing him to get the matter solved."

"Yes, the mayor would do that," he said with a smile. "You go to work. I'll take care of things for you. I'll give you a call and let you know what I learn and what happens. Let me just make sure I have your cell number right."

I recited it for him, and he noted it on a pad on his desk. When he looked up, I said, "I'm not sure what to do with Tommy. If I take him back to my parents' house, I'm afraid Mayra might go in and try again to take him."

He stood without replying, walked to his door, and opened it. "Kaci, I have a favor to ask. Would you mind keeping Tommy for the rest of the day?"

"I'd love to," she said. "He's a sweet boy, aren't you, Tommy?"

The little guy nodded and grinned. Tommy was sucking on a sucker Kaci must have given him.

"Are you sure?" I asked. "I don't mean to be a bother."

She smiled that soothing smile again and said, "It's not a bother. I'd love to help."

"Give Royce your number and your address so he can let you know when he gets off work. You can pick him up at Kaci's place, can't you, Royce?"

I agreed with that and hugged my son tightly as the attorney turned and went back into his office. I looked Tommy in the eye and said, "You'll be really good for Kaci, won't you, son?"

"I will, Dad," he said, an exasperated sound in his little voice. But suddenly a shadow crossed his face. "Dad, she won't let that other lady take me, will she?"

"Tommy," Kaci said before I could reply. "I'll make sure no one touches you. Maybe we can make cookies in a few hours. Do you like cookies?"

"Yes," he said.

Then, turning to me, she asked, "What does your ex-wife look like?"

I described Mayra, but I said, "I can't imagine she would come here. So it shouldn't be a problem."

"We'll be just fine, won't we, Tommy?"

He said, "Yes. You can go now, Dad."

After Kaci had given me her address and phone number, she smiled as I thanked her, and I started for the door. But before I opened it, Mr. Lawson stepped back into the reception area. "Royce," he said. "Do you have the name of Mayra's husband?"

"It's Ed Sills," I said.

"Just as I thought," he said with a frown. "He and the cobra are in the same law firm. They were, I believe, raised in the same snake pit." He had some papers in his hand. "I'm sure you have copies of this at home, but just in case, I'll have Kaci make a copy for you before you leave. This is your divorce decree, as well as the papers showing that Mayra gave up any rights to your son and declined visitation rights." He handed them to Kaci and slipped back into his office.

"Ooh," Kaci said. "I've never heard him speak of other attorneys like that. They must not be very good men."

"I'm sure you're right," I said as I thought about what I'd just learned. Mayra was married to a less-than-reputable attorney.

Kaci made the copies for me, and after I had folded them and tucked them into an inside pocket of my sports coat, I patted Tommy on the head, exchanged smiles with Kaci Walters, and strode to the door. As I opened it, she said, "I'll take good care of him for you, Royce."

I was protective about who my son stayed with when my parents were not available, but for some reason, I didn't have any reservations about Kaci. "Thank you," I said.

I headed back to my car. I had barely fired up the ignition when my phone began to buzz. It was my mother. She said, "Mayra is as mad as I've ever seen anyone. She says she'll make you pay for lying to her and stealing her son. I hope that Mr. Lawson can help you." She sounded very worried.

"Tommy is *my* son," I corrected mildly. "And did you explain that I didn't lie to her? She just assumed some things."

"I tried, but she didn't listen very well."

"I'm not surprised," I said.

"She told me to tell you that she is going to report what you did to the police chief. She says she'll make sure you get fired."

"I'll be fine, Mom," I said as my phone began to ring again. I looked and recognized the chief's number. "I have another call; I need to take it," I said as I felt my chest constrict.

I took a couple of deep breaths before I switched to the other call and asked, "Chief, what can I do for you?"

"You can come into my office as fast as you can get here," he said. He did not sound happy.

CHAPTER EIGHT

MAYRA WAS SEATED IN THE chief's office when I entered. It was all I could do to keep from walking right back out. She had a smirk on her face. *What had gone wrong with her?* I wondered. *She wasn't like this when I married her.* I wondered if it had been my fault—if I had somehow caused her to change. That thought had haunted me for more than six years.

Then I saw Chief Collins's face. I felt my throat constrict. He looked incensed. It was pretty clear to me that my ex had worked her considerable charm on him and convinced him that I was a real ogre.

I stood near the door, waiting apprehensively for what the chief was going to say. "Sit down, Detective," he ordered, pointing to a chair beside Mayra's. I sat down, but not there. I took another seat, beneath the window at the far side of his office, as far away from Mayra as I could get. Chief Collins glared at me for a moment, but I guess my return glare convinced him to leave well enough alone. I was seated and, so help me, that was all he was going to get.

Mayra continued to smirk. I thought she would say something, but by the way she kept glancing at Chief Collins, it appeared she thought she had him primed and that he would take care of me in short order. Perhaps he would. I prayed that would not be the case.

He leaned forward in his chair, placed his arms on his desk, looked me squarely in the eyes, and said, "Detective, you do understand, I'm sure, that you can't ignore the order of a court just because you disagree with it."

I decided to play dumb. "Court order?" I asked with a tight throat. "If it has something to do with my ex-wife, I assure you that I have not seen a court order. If she's told you otherwise, she hasn't been truthful."

She shot me a look of pure loathing, making me cringe, and then she said, "Chief Collins, he knows exactly what court order I'm talking about. I don't have a copy with me. I didn't think it would come to this. I was told that he had already received it, which I'm sure he did."

"That's not true," I said hotly.

"I can assure you, Chief Collins, it was issued by a district court judge in Salt Lake, and I am taking my son home with me today like I was told I could." She glared at me and then smiled sweetly at my boss.

Chief Collins, appearing to side with her, said, "It sounds like you should turn him over, Detective. If you don't, your job here could be in jeopardy."

I reached into my pocket and pulled out the papers Kaci Walters had copied for me. Then I stood, walked to Chief Collins's desk, and laid them in front of him. "Speaking of court orders," I said, "you will want to take a look at these before you start siding with my lying ex-wife."

"Those are old," she said haughtily.

"They are binding, Mayra. Chief, please look right here. This paper, signed by Mayra, shows that she voluntarily gave up custody of Tommy."

"You've had him to yourself for over six years. It's my turn," she shouted. "I'm taking him now. And you'd better not keep interfering."

I ignored her as the chief looked at where I'd pointed, and then he sat back in his chair and began to read. I sat back down and waited. He read that document and the divorce decree as well. Then he held the papers up to me. I retrieved them and then once again returned to my seat by the window. His eyes were narrowed as he focused on Mayra. "Mrs. Sills, this looks pretty clear to me. You gave up all rights to your son. According to this, he simply is not your child."

"I've changed my mind, and my attorney and the judge agree with me. It's not my fault Royce chose to ignore a subpoena and in doing so did not present anything in court. Now, please tell him to give me my son, right now." She was glaring at Chief Collins. That wasn't very smart of her.

Because of that, I had a feeling the chief was changing his position. But he didn't state that. When he spoke, it was to me. He asked, "Royce, how old was Tommy when your wife left?"

"A few months," I said. "When I got home from work that day, Tommy was in his crib, crying. His diaper was badly soiled, and he was very hungry. She hadn't even bothered to get somebody to take care of him until I got home. I have no idea how long he was alone, but it may have been several hours. I don't know why she wants him now, but he's not hers. He's mine and only mine."

"He's mine now!" she screeched. "He needs a home with a good mother and a good father. Ed and I can provide that for him. You can't."

"You abandoned him!" I reminded her strongly.

"That's because I couldn't live with you anymore," she hissed.

"You didn't even ask for custody," I reminded her.

"I will be a great mother, and Ed will be a great father," she shot back.

"Is Ed your husband?" Chief Collins asked.

I answered for her. "Ed is her husband, and he's a law partner of her attorney, Fred Zietz." I turned to Mayra and asked, "Why, after all these years, have you decided you want Tommy? You and Ed can have kids of your own."

She bristled. "No, we can't," she said hotly. "He has some problems and can't give me a child."

"Ah," I said, enlightened. "Now I see. Well, Tommy is mine, and nothing is going to change that."

"A judge already has," she said testily.

"I don't believe you, and if he has, it will be overturned. My attorney is working on that now," I said. Then I turned to my boss. "Chief, as you know, I have a lot to do. I need to find a witness in the case I'm working on."

Mayra wasn't through. She said, "You need to fire Royce, Chief. And you need to order him to get my son for me." In the same breath, she said to me, "Where is he, Royce? I'll have you arrested if you try to hide him from me."

I stood. "Is it okay if I get back to work, Chief Collins?"

"Please do. And as for *his* son, Mrs. Sills, it appears to me that his solid papers trump your theoretical ones—for now. You may leave."

She pointed a finger at Chief Collins as she rose from her chair. "You'll wish you hadn't done this, Chief. My attorney will be in touch." And with that, she whirled and stormed to the door. She opened it with such force that it slammed against the wall, and then, thank goodness, she was gone.

"Royce, I'm sorry about this. Were you really married to that woman?" Chief Collins asked.

"I'm afraid so. And people wonder why I'm not in a hurry to marry again. I don't want to make the same mistake twice."

"Is your son where your ex can't find him?" he asked, concern on his face.

"He's safe from her for now," I said.

"I'm sorry I jumped to conclusions. But she had a pretty convincing story. If I can help you in some way, please let me know."

***

I spotted the house number that I was told was Andrew Hutchins's. I parked behind an old yellow Chevy pickup that looked to be in rough shape. There was no doorbell, so I knocked loudly on the door. I waited for a minute and then knocked again. Finally, a wild-looking teenage boy with baggy pants, long greasy hair, and several rings in his ears opened the door and stared at me. When

I identified myself and told him that I was looking for his father, he attempted to slam the door in my face. I stuck a foot over the threshold. He glared at me. "Ain't seen the old man today," he said. "And I don't know when he'll be back."

"Where is he?" I asked.

He shrugged his shoulders and said, "How'd I know?"

"Then I'll talk to your mother," I told him.

"Ain't nobody home but me," he said and pushed on the door, but my foot was still in place.

"Where is your mother?" I asked.

"At work, I guess."

"You don't look too good today," I said as I caught a faint whiff of the odor of burnt marijuana.

"That's cause I been sick," he said.

"And smoking pot helps you feel better?" I asked.

"What's it to you?" he asked. "But for your information, I haven't been smoking. That's my parents' stuff."

"What's your name?" He stared at me, so I said, "That's not a hard question."

Finally he said, "Reggie Hutchins."

"Okay, Reggie, I'm going to get some more officers over here; we'll get a search warrant, and we'll find the marijuana you've been smoking."

He looked at me vacantly. Then he said, "I haven't been smoking."

"May I come in?" I asked him.

"I ain't stupid," he said.

I made no response to that but instead called dispatch. A couple of uniformed officers pulled up within three or four minutes. I explained what was happening with Reggie and that I would let them take it from there. They both grinned, and finally, Reggie seemed to realize that I was serious. "Okay, I guess you can have the pot," he said, swinging the door wide. "But it's not mine. It belongs to my parents."

One of the patrolmen asked him if the old yellow truck was his or if it also belonged to his parents. When he admitted that it was his, he was told that the registration was expired, so he couldn't drive it.

"I don't need to," he said.

The other officers followed him into the house. "Keep him under your thumb, and don't let him touch a thing," I said. "I'll get a search warrant."

I drove back to the office and started on the warrant. Within about thirty minutes, I had it prepared and contacted the on-call warrant judge. As soon as the approval came through on my computer, I printed the warrant and headed back to the Hutchins's house.

We found plenty of marijuana in the house, both in the living room, where I supposed Reggie had been, and in his parents' bedroom. But there was none in his bedroom. I began to wonder if he was telling the truth. I had the patrol officers take him to the station for a urine test.

"I'm okay with that. You'll see that I'm clean," he insisted.

"If you are, they will bring you back here. If not, you'll be going to detention," I said.

I left and began searching the local bars to see if Andrew Hutchins had made an early start on drinking. If I found him, I had every intention of arresting him for the marijuana violation in his house. But I didn't find him, so I drove back to the police station where I met the officers. They explained that they had tested Reggie, that he was clean, and that they had taken him home.

I thanked them and then said, "I'm glad to hear that. Let's go and get arrest warrants for his mother and father."

They agreed with me and went to work. I was working with them when I got a phone call.

"Detective Fleming. This is Kaci Walters. Mayra is here, and she's trying to take Tommy. Mr. Lawson isn't here. Tommy is hysterical."

She didn't have to tell me that. I could hear him screaming. She was almost hysterical herself. "Don't let her touch him," I said urgently as I rushed to the door. "I'm on my way."

"I'll try, but she's being violent," Kaci cried.

"Royce, what's the matter?" Chief Collins shouted as I reached the front door at a dead run. He was walking briskly toward me.

"Mayra is at my attorney's office. She's trying to take Tommy," I shouted over my shoulder and burst through the door.

"She found him?" he asked as he too left the building.

"I'm afraid so," I said as we both ran to the parking lot.

"I'll meet you there," he said.

By the time we got to Wendell Lawson's office, Mayra was out of the building, carrying a screaming little boy. "Daddy, help me!" Tommy screamed as I braked to a stop beside Mayra's Mercedes.

I leaped out of the SUV and blocked the passenger door to Mayra's car. "I'm leaving," she said with a hiss. "Don't you dare touch me."

I didn't have to touch her. Chief Collins grabbed an arm while I pulled my struggling son from her grasp. He threw an arm around my neck and said, "Daddy, you said she couldn't find me."

"I'm so sorry, Tommy. I didn't think she could," I said lamely. I had clearly underestimated Mayra's determination.

A patrol car rushed up, siren blaring and lights flashing. The same officers who had been helping me with the Hutchins' search sprang from the car and assisted the chief, who was being battled by my ex-wife. I left them to it and carried Tommy quickly inside the building and toward Wendell's office. "She hurt Kaci," he said as we hurried through the door into the office.

I spotted Kaci sitting on the floor, her head in her hands. I put Tommy down, and he ran behind Kaci's desk. Blood oozed from the back of Kaci's head. She looked up at me. She was also bleeding from a cut lip and seemed a little dazed. I knelt beside her. "Kaci, are you all right?" I asked.

She looked up at me and said with a sob, "I'm sorry, Detective. She hit me in the mouth, and I fell. I was trying to keep Tommy from getting hurt, and I hit my head on the desk. I blacked out. Did she get away with Tommy?"

"I'm here," Tommy said with a trembling voice as he came back around the desk.

"Oh, thank goodness," she said. "I'm so sorry, Tommy."

I checked the back of her head. There was a large bump there, and though blood was oozing from a small wound, it didn't look too serious. I said, "Let me help you up, and we'll do something about the blood."

I had her sitting in her chair and was dabbing at the back of her head with a wet paper towel while she held another one on her lip when the police chief came in. "Did Mrs. Sills do that to you?" he asked.

"She hit me. I struck the desk when I fell," Kaci said.

Tommy, still trembling and sobbing, was standing beside Kaci. Her free arm was around him. "She is on her way to jail," the chief said with a dark face. "This is unbelievable."

It was beyond unbelievable to me. I would never have guessed that I'd have to defend Tommy from his own mother after she had so coldly deserted him all those years before.

"Kaci, what happened?" Wendell Lawson shouted as he came through the door. But he soon figured it out and asked in disbelief, "Mayra came here?"

"I had no idea she would think of looking for Tommy at your office," I said, feeling overwhelmed by the horror of it all.

"Well, she's facing both kidnapping and assault charges now," Chief Collins said.

"I'd better take Kaci to urgent care to have her checked out," Mr. Lawson said.

I had stepped back to a chair and sat down with Tommy on my lap, holding him tightly. I was feeling overwhelmed. I had once loved Mayra. And to have her do this to me was unfathomable. At the same time, her going to jail hurt me in a way I'd never have guessed it would. What had happened to turn her into the kind of person she had become?

I hadn't thought about Mayra much for a long time. But now, as I did, I was sad. Would she be okay in jail? It was horrible to think of a girl I had once loved and shared my life with sitting in there with all those criminals. What could I have done differently when we were married? I couldn't help but feel responsible for both our failed relationship and her current dilemma. As if reading my mind, Chief Collins sat beside me and said, "It's not your fault, Royce."

I trembled with the sadness of what was happening. "I must have done something wrong for it to come to this," I argued.

"Take your little guy and go home, Royce. Take the rest of the day off and tomorrow too, at least part of the day. Things will look brighter after you take some time off," he said. He stood up. "I'll get back to the office now." He left while I was still sitting there, feeling sorry for my ex-wife and for Tommy and even for myself. I couldn't help but think of what might have been.

"I'm sorry, Royce," Kaci said. "I didn't know what to do when she came in and headed straight for Tommy."

"Thanks for calling me," I said, looking up and into her eyes. My attorney was standing beside her, and he patted her arm as I spoke. "If it hadn't been for you trying to protect him, she would have been gone before I even got here. You protected him."

"I still want to help if you will let me," she said with a touch of anguish in her voice.

"I appreciate it, but I guess I have some time off. Tommy will be okay," I said as I got to my feet, still holding my little guy. "I'm sorry you had to get involved in my trouble and that you got hurt," I added lamely. "I'll take Tommy home now."

"As soon as I make sure Kaci is all right, I'll prepare a protective order for Tommy," Wendell said. "I want it signed by a judge before someone bails Mayra out of jail."

"I'm okay, Mr. Lawson," Kaci protested. "I can stay and help you with it. I don't need to see a doctor. I don't think we should wait to get that done. It would be best if it could be served on her while she's in jail."

"How about if Tommy and I take you to urgent care? Then Wendell can be working on it," I offered. "I owe you. We owe you."

She looked at me and smiled. "If you're sure," Kaci said. She touched the back of her head and winced. "Maybe I should see a doctor. I don't feel very well."

"Go with him, Kaci. I'll get this done," Wendell said.

"Yeah, let's go with Kaci, Dad," Tommy said. "I like her."

CHAPTER NINE

AT URGENT CARE, KACI WAS checked out and told she had a mild concussion and that she should take it easy for the rest of the day.

"I'll take you back to your car so you can go home," I offered.

"Thanks, Royce. But when I get to the office, I think I'll help Mr. Lawson for a little bit. I feel a lot better," she said stubbornly.

"I'm hungry, Dad," my son said as we walked into the bright sunlight a moment later.

I looked at my watch. It was a little past four. "Me too," I said. I looked at Kaci and asked, "Do you feel like eating? The least I can do is buy you an early dinner. I'm hungry. I didn't ever stop for lunch."

She smiled brightly, despite the fat lip she was sporting. "I'd like that," she said.

As we sat in a restaurant a few minutes later, I realized with a pang in my heart that this was the first time Tommy and I had ever eaten out with a woman other than his grandma and my sisters. Once again, I couldn't help but think how it might have been if things had worked out with Mayra and me.

I enjoyed Kaci's company, and I could tell that Tommy was quite enthralled with the attention she gave him. It saddened me to realize what he was missing not having a mother in his life. My eyes caught Kaci's, and her smile made my heart pound. She was really a sweet girl. Perhaps . . .

My phone rang as my thoughts began to drift away. I checked the number and then answered. "How is it going, Mrs. Mavey?" I asked.

"I think you should come by. There is something Ellerie just told me that you should hear," she said.

"Okay, but will she talk to me? She was pretty angry when I left earlier today," I said.

"Of course she will. She was just upset. She *wants* to talk to you. Can you come by?" she asked. "She is with me at my house. The Franklins have gone."

"I can. Give me a few minutes. I'm with someone right now," I said.

After ending the call, Kaci said, "Is everything all right?"

"Yes," I said. "I just need to go talk to someone involved in a case I'm working on. Tommy can come with me. He and I are going to go home, and in the morning we'll go fishing. Would you like that, Tommy?"

"Yeah, let's do it," he said, giving me a high five.

"You are such a good father," Kaci said. "When I have kids, I hope they have a father like you."

Goodness, but that statement startled me. Kaci had no idea what kind of father I really was. She grinned at me. "Thanks for lunch. I'd better go help Mr. Lawson."

The thought, senseless as it was, crossed my mind that it would be nice to have her go fishing with Tommy and me. But I hardly knew her. For all I knew, she had someone in her life. As sweet and pretty as she was, it seemed very likely. Anyway, she would need to work in the morning.

I dropped her off in front of the law office. "Thanks for dinner, Royce," Kaci said again. "And for taking me to urgent care. It's great to know you and Tommy."

I chuckled mirthlessly. "Yeah, I'm sure. How else could you have gotten a split lip and a concussion?" The moment the words left my mouth, I wished I hadn't said them.

A shadow crossed Kaci's face, but then she smiled and said, "It's okay. It was actually nice getting to spend a little time with you and Tommy, Royce. You'll call me if you need help with him, won't you?"

"Sure. Take care."

I watched her as she walked to the door of the office building. When she got to it, she turned, smiled, waved, and then went inside. "She's nice, Dad," Tommy said.

"Yes, she is," I agreed. "Now, Tommy, there is something I need to do."

His face dropped, and fear flashed in his eyes. "Daddy, don't leave me. That lady—"

"Hey, son," I said, quickly cutting him off. Mayra had really scared him. "I'm not leaving you. I need you to be my police partner for a little while, that's all, and then we'll go home and watch a movie or something."

"Okay, I'll help you do your police work," he said as his face brightened and his little chest puffed out.

"Let's go then," I said.

A few minutes later, I pulled up in front of Mrs. Mavey's house. "This is the place, Tommy. We need to go inside, and I need to talk to some ladies. It shouldn't take too long."

"Okay," he said as he unfastened his seatbelt.

Mrs. Mavey met us at the door. "Who's this young man?" she asked, smiling at Tommy. "You sure are a handsome fellow."

"I'm Tommy," he said. And then, puffing his little chest out, he added, "I'm Dad's partner."

"Well, you sure look like a good partner. Your dad is lucky." She looked up at me and smiled. "Why don't you *men* come in?"

Ellerie was sitting on the sofa in the living room. She stood up when we entered. "I'm so sorry for how I acted, Detective," she said. "I know you are only doing your job, and I'm grateful."

"It's fine, Ellerie," I said. "I don't blame you. So let's forget it and get on with things."

"Thanks," she said somberly. Ellerie's eyes went from me to Tommy. "Is he your son?" she asked.

"Yes, he is. I have the rest of the day off, and in the morning we are going to go fishing."

"Oh, I'm sorry. You aren't working," she said. "I guess this can wait."

"No, let's talk," I said.

"Did somebody hurt you?" Tommy suddenly blurted.

"Tommy, it's okay. This is Mrs. Pearson, and she's having a rough time. I'm trying to help her with some things," I explained.

My charming little guy smiled at her and said, "You are pretty. That lady that tried to steal me today, she's not pretty like you. She scared me." Fear crossed his little face at the recall.

Ellerie looked at me with a question in her eyes. Then she stepped over to Tommy and said, "Your dad is lucky to have you. You are such a handsome boy. He'll keep you safe."

"Tommy and I will be in the kitchen, if that's okay with Tommy," Pamela said. "I was thinking about mixing up some cookies. Would you like that, Tommy?"

"Sure, me and Grandma make cookies all the time," he said.

"Thank you," I said to her. She smiled, took Tommy's hand, and left Ellerie and me alone in the living room.

"Detective Fleming," she began awkwardly as she pointed to a chair. "I've interrupted something serious, haven't I?"

"It's okay. Tommy's had a hard day. But he'll be all right," I said.

"Did someone really try to kidnap him?" she asked. Then she dropped her eyes in embarrassment. "Of course, you don't have to tell me about it. It's none of my business. I shouldn't have asked."

"It's okay," I said again as we both sat down. I tried to smile at her, and as I did, I realized that my son was right. As the bruises faded, it was easy to see how pretty Ellerie was. I took a deep breath and then, with a catch in my voice, I said, "It was his mother. I mean, she used to be his mother. My ex-wife. She gave up all rights to him. But he's safe for now. She's in jail."

Ellerie gasped and her hand went to her mouth. "His . . . his mother?" she stammered.

"I'm afraid so," I said. I chuckled cheerlessly. "You and I have something in common. I'm sure you never knew Darien would turn out like he did when you married him. And I certainly had no idea Mayra would do what she did to Tommy and me."

Ellerie had compassion in those striking amber eyes of hers as she leaned in my direction. "Did she hurt Tommy?" she asked. "Or did she just frighten him?"

I reminded myself of the chief's stern warning that Ellerie must be considered a suspect in her husband's murder. But something made me want to share my story with her. I justified it by telling myself that maybe she might have more confidence in me as an officer if she knew what I'd gone through.

"I guess you could say that she frightened him," I said. "When Tommy was only a few months old, I came home from work one evening to find him alone in his crib. He was crying, he was very messy and wet, and he was starving. Mayra's car was gone. I thought she'd taken him to the store when I'd first stopped in our driveway. I hadn't expected the baby to be in the house. But he was, and I have no idea how long it had been since she left. I was totally shocked. My wife was gone, Ellerie. And she never came back. Until today, she hadn't seen Tommy since she left. He has no idea who she is. To him, she is a stranger who was trying to steal him."

"Oh, Royce, I'm so sorry," she said, her hands covering her mouth again. "That is so sad."

"But I have him, and he's an amazing kid," I said in an attempt to lighten the mood. "My parents live here in Vernal, and they watch him when I work. Well, mostly my mother does. Dad's job takes him out of town a lot, but when he's home, he and Tommy hang out. Tommy loves his grandpa and grandma. I don't know what we would have done without them."

"So she came back today after all those years?" Ellerie asked softly.

I nodded. "I'm afraid so. My mother called me. Mayra was there, and she was trying to take Tommy. She said it was her turn to have him." I shook my head. "I guess she's a little crazy. I have total custody. I didn't even have to fight her on it. She simply said she didn't want to see him or have to take care of him. But I guess she and her new husband can't have children of their own, so they decided to take my son."

"She must have married a creep," Ellerie said, with anger in her eyes.

"He's a lawyer, and according to my attorney, he's not an honest one. She claims a judge signed an order giving her back custody, but there's no way. She claims I was ordered to be in court, but I was never notified. If there really was a hearing, which I doubt, I knew nothing about it. No judge would proceed on something like that without making sure the opposing party had been served. And I wasn't."

Ellerie perceptively said, "Unless somebody lied about it, an officer or someone else who could have served you."

My stomach clenched for the hundredth time that day. "That's exactly what I'm afraid of, but my attorney is working on it for me now. He's a good lawyer, and he'll help me straighten things out. In the meantime, Mayra is in jail." I sat back in my chair. "Enough about my troubles," I said. "Mrs. Mavey said you have something to tell me."

"I do, but it can wait if it needs to. You've had a horrible day."

"It's okay, Ellerie. Please, go ahead," I urged. "And if it's okay, I'll record this."

"If you're sure you have time, and yes, go ahead and record it."

I nodded.

"It's about my brother," she said hesitantly. "No, this can wait. Your son needs you right now."

"He's okay. I can hear him in there with Pamela, laughing and talking his little head off. He's fine. Let me get this recording." As soon as that was done, I said, "Now, Ted told me you had a brother and a little about how you both grew up. I'm sorry for what you have gone through. I can't even imagine what it would be like for parents to split up and each take a child. It is so cruel."

"Yes, it was cruel, but no crueler than your wife deserting you and her baby."

"I guess it is about the same thing," I agreed.

"More so than you know," Ellerie said with a sad shake of her head. "My mother raised me. The reason I stayed with her was because my dad despised me. Even though I was a small kid at the time, I still remember him looking at me and saying to my mother that he didn't want me because I would just be another female who couldn't be controlled. I remember his exact words when he said, 'I don't want anything to do with Ellerie. She'll just be another you. I'll take Rico.'

So, you see, Detective, he did to me what your wife did to Tommy. It breaks my heart for him."

"I don't understand why parents do some of the things they do," I said.

"Me neither," she responded, absently rubbing her abdomen. "What Dad said in my presence hurt me more than anything else about my parents' divorce. It still hurts. And maybe that is partly because the man I married didn't want to have anything to do with the child I was carrying, just like my dad didn't want to have anything to do with me. I can't help but wonder if Darien wanted me to lose the baby."

She began to sob. I wanted to put my arms around her and comfort her, but of course, that was not something I could do. So I simply said, "You are probably right," even though I hoped that wasn't really the case. That was too cruel. Homicidal.

She rocked back and forth on her chair for a moment, and then she rubbed her eyes, threw her long brown hair over her shoulder, and looked at me. "It could have been worse. At least Rico and I were allowed to see one another once a month. So we played a lot together and had at least some kind of sibling relationship. It was always at our house because Dad didn't want to see or talk to me. His rejection of me was total. And it still hurts to this day."

"Of course it does," I offered.

"My father wasn't a good man, and even though I've never understood why my mother would let him split Rico and me up, at least she was good to me. She even took me to church sometimes. And when she didn't want to go, she didn't stop me from going with my friends. On the other hand, Dad was mean to Rico, and I'm afraid my brother has turned out to be a lot like Dad," she said and shuddered. "Don't get me wrong—I love Rico. I can't say the same about my dad. Rico was always protective of me. Not once did he ever treat me badly or even talk to me in a cruel way. We still talk on the phone from time to time."

"Did you talk about Darien?" I asked.

"Not much. I didn't want Rico to know about how Darien beat me. But after the time Pamela took me to the hospital, Rico called me like he often did, just to talk. I don't use my landline much, but when he couldn't reach me on my cell he tried that number instead. Anyway, I guess he could tell from my voice that something was wrong. He kept after me until I finally broke down and told him what Darien had done to me."

She looked at the ceiling for a moment, and when her eyes again met mine, she had to blink back the tears. "He was really mad, Detective."

"Ellerie, please call me Royce," I said.

She nodded and gave me a tight smile. "Royce," she said. Then she continued with her story. "He called me again right after Darien kicked me that last time, but it was before the baby came and Darien . . . you know . . . did what he did."

I nodded. "What did your brother say?" I asked.

She shuddered. "He was so angry. I would like to think that he would never kill anyone. I won't let myself believe he's that bad. If he was, he would have shoved me out of his life just like my father did. But he cares about me. I'm sure of it. He is so nice to me. And yet, now, as I think about it, I don't really know much about him anymore. I don't even know what he does with his life now."

"I'm glad he at least cared enough to keep in touch with you," I said.

Ellerie tugged at a lock of her hair for a moment. When she spoke again, her voice was filled with sadness. "If he killed Darien, he did me a favor, I guess."

She paused, and I pressed her with, "Did he threaten to do something to Darien?"

She looked away, and without meeting my eyes, she said, "Yes. He said he'd kill him if he ever touched me again. But I never told him about the baby, that I was pregnant," she added quickly. "I don't think he would really do anything to Darien, and I've fought with myself over the idea of telling you, but I finally knew I had to."

"Yes, it's important that I know. Thanks for telling me, Ellerie. If it really is Darien who was killed, I sincerely hope it wasn't Rico who did it. But I'll need to find out what he was doing at the time. You understand that, don't you?"

"I do. I wouldn't have told you what I have if I expected you to do nothing about it. The fact that you insisted I let you see my shoes, even though I know you didn't want to, tells me that you will do whatever you need to find out who the killer is. And if it is my brother, I'll have to live with it, just like I have to live without my baby. I should have told you sooner. I'm sorry."

"Remember, it could be Donald who's dead," I reminded her.

"Rico could have mistaken Donald for Darien," she said tearfully. "I really didn't want to tell you about Rico, but after I got thinking, you know, after you left this morning, I knew you would work to clear him, just like I know you are working to clear me, even though I doubted that for a little while."

"Ellerie, despite what you've told me about your father, I have to ask: is there any chance he might have killed Darien—or Donald?" I asked.

She shook her head. "No, I don't think so." She looked up at the ceiling again. I almost caught myself doing the same, like there was something up there I should see. When she finally looked down, her eyes once again met mine.

"Rico always defended me to my father. And lately, he's told me that my father actually asked a couple of times what I was doing."

I decided then that I should include her father on my list of possible suspects. Who knew? Even though he didn't do anything good for Ellerie, maybe he took exception to anyone else mistreating her. "Ellerie," I said. "Do you have any idea where your father lives now?"

"You do worry about him being involved, don't you?" she asked. Ellerie was a bright woman.

"I just want to be thorough," I said.

"I can see that," she said, forcing a smile. But it was a fleeting one, and as it faded from her face, she answered my question. "Dad lives somewhere in the Salt Lake area. So does Rico, but I don't have addresses for either of them."

"That's fine. I'll figure it out. What is your dad's name?"

"Hank Starfire. That was my maiden name." I jotted the name down.

"His age?" I asked.

"About fifty."

"Thanks. There is one more thing," I began and paused.

"What's that?" she asked expectantly.

"Does your mother have a current husband?"

"Yes, she remarried after I graduated from high school."

"Do you know him well?"

"Not really. I mean, I've stayed with them a few times. And I talk to my mother on the phone a lot, and she mentions stuff she and Jess have been doing."

"Jess. What is his last name?" I asked.

"Quinn," she said. "And Mom's name is Carmen, in case you need that. But I don't think Jess or Mom would have had anything to do with this. Jess is a lot older than Mom. He's about seventy, and she is only forty-eight. They live clear down in St. George."

"Does your mother know how badly Darien treated you?" I asked.

She slowly shook her head. "I don't think so. I've never told her. I was . . . I was ashamed," she said.

"She doesn't know she was going to be a grandma?"

"I don't think so. I didn't tell her."

"Ellerie, you don't seem sure. Is it possible that someone else told her?" I asked.

A shadow of doubt crossed her face. She played with a long strand of hair again. I waited, not wanting to press her at this point. Finally, she looked my way and said, "I didn't tell Rico I was pregnant, but I think he might have guessed, although I don't know how he could have. And he and Mom got along okay, and maybe he'd tell her something like that if he did somehow figure it out. Like I told you a minute ago, we spent one weekend a month together at Mom's house. And I know he still calls her sometimes. He is a mess in his personal life, and he's been in trouble with the law, but deep down, Rico has a good heart. And he loves our mother. I'm sure of that."

I cocked an eyebrow as I asked, "So she could have known you were pregnant?"

She was again slow in responding, but when she did, it was the answer I expected. "Honestly, I doubt it, and she never asked me about it."

"Okay, just to confirm, you have never told her the way Darien treated you or that you were going to give her a granddaughter?"

"That's right. I probably should have told her, but I was so . . . so humiliated. I married Darien when people, including Mom, warned me against it," she said. "It's always been hard for me to admit it when I'm wrong. And I was wrong for marrying Darien. But that's not the only reason I didn't tell her. Her husband, Jess, doesn't like me and I feel terribly uncomfortable around him. I was afraid he would make my mother think it was my fault that Darien was abusive to me, or even more, I suspected he might think I was making it all up and would convince her of that. It was easier to just not tell her."

I nodded, my heart heavy for her. "Thanks, Ellerie, for telling me what you have today. I know it's not easy."

Tommy came running from the kitchen. "Dad, the cookies are almost done. Mrs. Mavey says we can take some home with us."

"That's great, son," I said, rising from my chair. Turning back to Ellerie, I said, "I guess that Tommy and I better get going. We need to get some rest so we can get up early and go fishing in the morning."

What I didn't mention was that I was going to take a look at the background and current status of her mother and Jess. I was afraid that would anger her again, and I preferred it when she wasn't mad.

Tommy ran back to the kitchen, and I thought of one more thing I needed to clear up with Ellerie. I sat down again and said, "Ellerie, I think your mother needs to know about the baby now. She needs to know you lost her and why."

She teared up again. "I know you're right. I'm just so embarrassed and worried about how Jess will react."

"Ellerie, she's your mother," I said. "Regardless of how her husband feels, she loves you. She raised you. I think she would want to know. And wouldn't you like to have her with you for the baby's funeral?"

She squeezed out a smile for me. "Of course I would. I'll call her in a few minutes. I don't know if her husband will let her come. He's very controlling. But I'll at least let her know she's welcome."

CHAPTER TEN

WE WERE IN THE MOUNTAINS beside a small lake early the next morning. Unlike my current mood, which was still gloomy and dark, the morning was sunny and bright. The fish weren't biting, but Tommy didn't seem to mind. He was having a good time being with his father. I supposed part of the reason we weren't catching fish was because of Tommy's constant chatter. My, how I love that little guy. Even just the thought of losing him to his mother made me ill.

A lot of the time, I was so deep in thought, thinking both about the murder case and my ex-wife's sudden and tumultuous appearance back in my life, that I didn't really hear a lot of what he was saying. But then he asked, "So, Dad, which one do you think is the prettiest?"

"What?" I asked, surprised by his question.

"You know. I think Kaci and Ellerie are both pretty. I just told you that." He gave me a stern look. He obviously knew my mind had drifted.

I focused on his little face. "Which one do you think is?" I asked.

"I don't know. They are both pretty, and I like them both. Which one do you like the best?" he asked.

Where in the world were these questions coming from? Had my folks been planting ideas in his head that he needed a new mother? I suspected that was the case. I was trying to decide how to answer him when he suddenly squealed, "Dad, I've caught something!"

He sure had, and his line was running out fast. I dropped my own pole and helped him. We fought that fish for several minutes. As it came closer to shore, it occasionally broke the surface, its silvery body reflecting the sun. It was a big one. I really wanted to help him land that fish. But when we nearly had it to shore, Tommy's line broke, and the fish swam to freedom, taking a good fly with it.

"It got loose, but it was a big one, wasn't it, Dad?" he asked with excitement, his little eyes gleaming.

"It sure was. Let's reel the rest of your line in, and I'll help you get another fly on so you can try again," I said.

"That's okay. Let's quit fishing and take a hike," he suggested.

"Are you sure that's what you want to do?" I asked.

"Don't you?" he shot back at me.

"If you want to hike, then I want to hike. Let's take this fishing equipment back to the truck first. Maybe we can take my binoculars so that you can look at birds and squirrels and stuff," I suggested.

"Yeah," he readily agreed.

As we walked back to the truck, he chattered happily. I was grateful to the fish that got away and hoped it would be okay. It had gotten Tommy's mind off those uncomfortable questions he'd asked me. Although I kept thinking about them. Ellerie and Kaci were both very attractive women. And they both seemed really nice. But I wasn't interested in women at this point in my life, so what was I even thinking about it for?

Tommy, bless his little heart, got my mind off that train of thought when he asked, "Dad, how big was that fish? I want to tell my friends." So the rest of the way to the truck, we speculated on the size of the fish. The longer we discussed it, the bigger the fish got.

After we'd put our equipment in the truck, we got the binoculars out, put our fanny packs on, and headed up the trail again, this time with hiking in mind rather than fishing. I had thought about leaving my cell phone at home when we left, but even though the chief had told me to take the day off, at least part of it, I was in the middle of a major murder investigation, and I knew that if I was needed, I had to be available—unless I reached an area where I didn't have a signal. I found myself hoping that would be the case. I pulled my cell out and checked it, just to satisfy my curiosity. It had three bars.

The trail was wide, and Tommy grabbed my hand as we headed deeper into the hills. To my dismay, he returned to the uncomfortable topic the big fish had so mercifully interrupted. He looked at me, his face very serious. "Dad, you didn't tell me, and I think it's important. Do you like Kaci the best, or do you like Ellerie? I like them both. Kaci is so fun. She likes me. Ellerie seems sad, but she is really pretty. She has cool eyes, doesn't she?"

Tommy was very observant. I really needed to nip this thinking of his in the bud. Ellerie was a suspect in my case—totally out of bounds. Anyway, for all I knew she wasn't even a widow. And I didn't really even know Kaci, and I figured she probably had a serious boyfriend. I opened my mouth to give Tommy an answer that would not satisfy him but would, I hoped, put an end to the topic.

My phone saved me from the difficult answer this time. "I'd better take this call, son," I said as I pulled my phone out. I didn't recognize the number, but I answered anyway. It could be important.

"Hello," I said.

"Is this Detective Royce Fleming?" a man, whose voice I didn't recognize, asked me.

"It is," I replied.

A stream of words were spat out of my phone, insulting my ear. It was clear that the caller, whoever he was, hated me, and I was glad my son couldn't hear the profanity I was being subjected to. The caller was insulting me in every vile way I could imagine. I was just ready to cut the call off when my caller finally indirectly identified himself. "Do you really think I'm going to let you treat my wife like you did?"

I think he must have run out of breath, because he stopped talking after that question. I gave my phone a moment to recover from the obscenities it had just endured. The caller had to be none other than Ed Sills, scummy lawyer and greedy husband of my ex-wife. I took a moment to cool my anger, and then I said, "Where did you get my number?"

He chuckled, an evil sound if I'd ever heard one. "I called your department. I told the lady who answered I had some important information on a case you're working on. The woman didn't hesitate to give it to me. Now, about my wife—"

I cut him off and said, "Yes, about her. Mayra is the one who is out of line, and I don't appreciate you calling me. She's in jail, which I suppose you have figured out, and that's where she deserves to be."

I had stopped walking when I had answered the call. Fortunately, Tommy had kept walking. He was not far away, but he was far enough that he wouldn't be able to hear what I was saying.

"No, that's where you deserve to be and where you will be, Detective. You are selfishly keeping her son from her, and I will not allow it. No mother should be deprived of her own offspring," he said.

"She has no son!" I said testily into my phone. I lowered my voice as a precaution and watched Tommy as he wandered a bit farther ahead and paused to look up at a nearby tree. "She gave up parental rights years ago. She abandoned him. She didn't want him. Not one time in over six years has she even so much as asked about him. So don't you tell me I'm depriving her of his association. *She* deprived Tommy of *her* association."

"You know very well that she has a right to him now—more right than you do," he said as if it might actually be a fact. "I will come after you. And when

I go after someone, I get them. I am an attorney, and I am highly respected by the courts and very good at what I do. I will come after you in the courts, and you'll wish you'd let her take Tommy. But since I'm a nice guy, I'm giving you one chance to make this right. Release her from jail, give her our son, and I will forget what you've done. If not, well, I'll see you in court. I'll have you found in contempt for disobeying a court order. When that happens, the judge will put you in jail, and you'll lose your job."

I'd had all I could take. He had called Tommy *their* son. He was laying claim to *my* boy. That made him nothing more than a scummy thief. I cut the call off, my hands shaking.

I resumed walking to catch up to Tommy, and as he heard me approach, he suddenly turned, ran to close the distance, and started jumping up and down in front of me. "I need the binoculars, Dad," he said excitedly. "There's a really pretty bird over there." He was pointing to the tree he'd just been peering into.

I slipped the binoculars from around my neck and handed them to him. He skipped back up the trail. I proceeded slowly in his direction, unable to feel the pleasure I should in his excitement. By the time I reached him, he was watching intently through the binoculars. Without breaking his gaze, he said, "Dad, it's yellow and orange and black and red. What kind is it?"

I had no idea, but to him I said, "You make sure you remember what it looks like, and we can look it up on the computer when we get home."

"Oh, oh," he suddenly said. "Something scared it. It flew away." He straightened, a bright smile on his face and his blue eyes sparkling. I fondly tousled his soft blond hair.

"Let's go, Dad," he said, starting up the trail again, the binoculars in his hands. "Maybe I'll see him again."

I thought that highly unlikely but thought, *Far be it from me to dash his excitement.* So I followed behind him, trying to forget the call I'd just had. We went along for five minutes or so. I was trailing slightly behind my son when my phone buzzed again.

I recognized the number this time. This call was from Wendell Lawson's office. "Hello," I said, trying to control my voice, not wanting my agitation to go through the phone.

"Hi, Royce, it's Kaci." For some strange reason, her sweet voice had a calming effect on me.

"Hey," I said. "How are you feeling today?"

"I'm feeling better," she insisted.

"I'm glad. I was worried about you," I said.

I could feel the warmth of her smile over the phone. "I'm fine," she said. "We got the papers completed, and Wendell took them to the judge. He called me a minute ago and said they were signed and that the judge said that no one was to take Tommy without his—I mean the judge's—express permission. I knew you'd want to know, so I called as soon as I could."

"Thanks, Kaci, you're a gem," I told her. "I really needed to hear that after the phone call I just got."

"What phone call?" she asked.

"It was from Ed Sills, Mayra's husband. It was ugly. He threatened me. He called Tommy *his* son. I'm sure grateful you guys got that order prepared and signed. I owe you both."

"I'm sure Wendell will bill you," she said with a chuckle. Then, her voice slightly husky, almost sultry, she said, "Dinner again sometime will be payment enough for me."

"You got it," I said, a smile finally cracking my face. It felt good.

"Are you okay, Royce?" she asked.

"I am now."

"How's Tommy?" she asked.

"He's having a great time. I think he's let the memory of yesterday fade."

"I'm glad. He's such an adorable boy," Kaci said.

"He is a great kid. I don't know what I'd ever do if I lost him."

"You won't, Royce," she said firmly. "Oh, and Mr. Lawson asked me to see if I could find any orders from another judge giving your ex-wife custody. There is nothing like that anywhere. She was lying to you."

"Thanks—that's great news."

"I've gotta get this other line," she said. And her sweet voice vanished. I hoped her voice had been enough to purge my phone of the filth that had passed through it thanks to Ed Sills.

I held the phone for a moment to finish airing it out and then put it back into my pocket and looked up the trail. My heart lurched. I couldn't see Tommy. I ran up the trail, fear pushing me. I rounded a bend in the trail and came to a sudden stop. Tommy was fine. He was sitting on a rock at the side of the trail looking intently through the binoculars. I watched him while my heart settled down. I didn't think he was aware of my presence, and I said nothing to him. I didn't want to break his concentration. Anyway, just watching him was calming. Oh, how I loved him.

A few minutes later, my son and I were walking hand in hand up the trail. He was chattering like a little squirrel, which was what he'd been watching earlier. My stomach still stirred with worry, but my little boy's company was calming.

And then that pesky phone of mine rang again. Tommy looked up at me and said, "People must really like you, Dad. They sure call you a lot."

If he only knew.

"Hello," I said, trying to remain cheerful. I watched as Tommy again ran ahead of me. This time, I didn't let him get out of my sight.

"Detective Fleming?" the caller asked. It was another unfamiliar male voice, an older man, I thought.

"This is Detective Fleming," I said, wondering with no small amount of anxiety exactly who was calling me now.

"Detective, my name is Jess Quinn. I am the husband of Ellerie Pearson's mother. I understand you are helping her," the caller said.

I said, "I am working with her on a case. What can I do for you?"

"My wife got a call from Ellerie a little while ago. We are both in shock, to say the least," he said. He sounded sincere, but I wasn't sure. I hoped he was.

"I'm sorry about what's happened, Mr. Quinn. What can I do for the two of you?" I asked.

"Well, first, since Ellerie had chosen to keep her mother and me out of the loop as far as the struggles she was having with that dangerous guy she married, we don't know what all he's done to her. I suppose you do. We'd like to know how long this has been going on and why you didn't do something to stop the man before he succeeded in destroying our grandchild. We think that you were derelict in your duties."

I felt my chest constrict with sudden anger. "Mr. Quinn, I didn't know anything about your daughter's problems until after the baby was dead. I'd never even met her before that. I do know that she did not report the earlier incidents to the police. That means that no one in the police department knew anything about what he was doing to her. She was afraid to report it. That's often the case in situations like hers," I explained.

"You don't need to bite my head off," Jess retorted.

I guess my anger had come through despite my attempt to control it. "Sorry," I said. "I didn't mean to come across that way, if I did. But you accused me of not doing my job while I didn't even know Ellerie was in trouble."

"You should have known. You're a cop," he said.

I bit my lip until it hurt. Finally, I said, "I wish I would have known. Believe me, if I had, I would have done something. You just need to be careful about casting blame when you know nothing about what has happened."

"We live clear down in St. George," he shot back. "You and your police buddies are right there in Vernal."

As if that meant we could see what was occurring in every home in town. I didn't say that, but I did say, "Maybe if you and your wife would have made an occasional visit to Vernal to see Ellerie, you could have *seen* what was going on. At the very least, her pregnancy would have been quite apparent to you."

"I don't like your attitude, young man," he snapped back at me. "It isn't that easy for us to get away from here."

"I would think that visiting a family member would be worth a little effort," I snapped right back. Ellerie's mother might love her, but like Ellerie had told me, the jerk she married clearly didn't.

"Well, we may have to," he said. "Ellerie asked Carmen if she'd like to come when the little thing is buried."

"I would hope she would, Mr. Quinn. For that matter, I think both of you should come. Ellerie is suffering. She needs some support right now. This has been devastating to her," I said.

For a moment, I listened as Jess Quinn breathed heavily into the phone. He finally said, "Carmen wants to go. I mean, we both do. But there is one problem."

"Problem?" I asked. "She really needs her mother with her right now. I think you need to see that it happens."

"You don't understand, Officer. We can't come if Darien is there. My wife is frightened after what he's done to Ellerie. That's why I'm calling you," he said. "We are counting on you to arrest him and put him in jail. If we know he's locked up, we will try to come."

"Mr. Quinn, Darien won't be a problem," I said.

"Is he in jail?" he asked.

It was clear that Ellerie hadn't told her mother everything, not that I could blame her. Either that, or her stepfather was playing a game with me. What if Jess Quinn had been to Vernal and didn't want anyone to know it? If he was the killer and Darien, not Donald, was the dead man, then there would be no reason not to come, unless of course he was afraid that I would arrest him. I had absolutely no evidence against him or his wife, so they had nothing to fear from me at this point. But the man's attitude made me wonder about him.

"If Darien is not locked up, then I'm afraid I won't be able to let Carmen go up there," he said.

"If I find him, I can assure you he will be locked up," I told him. If I found Darien alive, then it would be his brother who was dead, not him, and that would make Darien my prime suspect. And even if I couldn't make a case against Darien for murdering his brother, I would not hesitate to arrest him for assaulting his wife and killing his unborn baby.

"I expect a call from you when you find him," Mr. Quinn said. "Also, if you do catch him, then you'll need to let us know when the funeral will be, and we will see if we can work a trip to Vernal into our very busy schedule."

"I'll let you know," I said, trying not to sound as cold as I felt toward the guy. I knew it was he who wanted to prevent their attendance to the burial, not Ellerie's mother. What I couldn't imagine was why. Ellerie had said she didn't know Jess very well but that he was controlling. Perhaps he'd tried for a long time to cause a chill between mother and daughter. Again, I couldn't imagine why, but I suspected him of it.

"That's all for now, Detective," he said. "I'll be waiting to hear from you." He ended the call on that note.

I shook my head as I put the phone away. I wondered if Carmen was suffering a similar fate to what Ellerie had suffered—domestic abuse.

Once again, I caught up with Tommy on the trail. "Dad," he said. "Why do you keep getting behind me? All you are doing is talking on the phone." His little chin quivered as he spoke.

"I'm sorry, buddy. People just keep interrupting me. I'll try to do better. You are having fun, aren't you?" I asked.

"I'm having a good day, but I want you to be right here with me. Please, Dad."

I smiled at him fondly, knowing he was right. But before I could even promise to try to stay off the phone, I once more began reluctantly digging a ringing cell phone from my pocket.

CHAPTER ELEVEN

"NOT AGAIN, DAD," TOMMY SAID with a frown.

"I'm sorry. I'll try to make this short." For the third time in the past few minutes, there was a male voice on my phone that I didn't recognize, although I should have. I'd talked to Felipe Salvagi, Donald Pearson's boss, before.

"Detective, this is Felipe Salvagi. You said to call you if I heard from Donald."

"I take it that you have," I said hopefully. Maybe I was about to get a break.

"He showed up to work about an hour ago. I asked him where he'd been. He said he'd been dealing with a family problem in Utah. If he wasn't such a good stuntman, I'd fire him. He's been gone for two weeks or more. But the fact is, I need him. He's on a set as we speak."

"And you are sure it's Donald?" I asked.

"Why do you ask a question like that? Of course I'm sure. I know the people who work for me. He has an identical twin brother by the name of Darien, but this isn't the brother. I would know the difference," he said.

"I just need to be sure," I said.

Felipe laughed. "No, believe me, Detective, this isn't his twin brother. For one thing, I'm sure his brother wouldn't know his way around this facility the way Donald does. And anyway, there's Donald's tattoo."

"Which is identical to his brother's," I informed him.

"Well, that may be, but this is Donald," he said firmly.

"Dad, I need to talk to you," Tommy interrupted, his little face looking up at me appealingly.

"Just a second, Tommy," I said after moving the phone away from my mouth. Then I spoke to Felipe again. "Did he mention what the nature of his family problem was?" I asked, changing focus.

"No, and I didn't ask," Mr. Salvagi said. "Would you like me to ask him?"

"Not at this time," I said as I tried to decide the best way to handle this. Tommy tugged on my pant leg. I ruffled his hair and smiled down at him. If Donald was Darien's killer, I didn't want to scare him off. On the other hand, if he was not, it would be great to finally make a determination of my victim's identity. I finally asked, "Did you tell Donald I'd called about him?"

"No, but I can if you'd like," he said.

"That won't be necessary. Don't worry Donald with it. Thanks for letting me know he's back. That is a relief to me and a great deal of help," I said and terminated the call. It looked like I was going to have to make a quick trip to California.

After that call was over, I said to Tommy, "Bear with me, son. I need to call my boss." I then called Chief Collins. Unlike during other calls, Tommy was sticking close to me now. I felt bad, but I had to deal with my work.

"I thought I told you to take this morning off and spend it with your son, Royce," the chief said sternly.

"Tommy and I are on a hike right now, but my phone won't leave me alone," I said.

"Let me guess—did your ex-wife's husband call you?" he asked.

"He did," I said, surprised that he would ask. "He threatened to have me found in contempt of court and put in jail. He said if I didn't drop the charges and let Mayra out of jail and let my son go with her, he would make me pay."

"Did he threaten you physically?" the chief asked.

"No, but he said he was a highly respected attorney and that he would make my life miserable in court, or something to that effect. Did he call you too?" I asked suspiciously.

"As a matter of fact, he did, and it sounds like I received about the same kind of treatment you did," Chief Collins said with a laugh. I didn't see anything funny about it, but if the chief could laugh about it, then I felt he still had my back. For that I was grateful.

"What should we do?" I asked.

"Just what we are," he informed me. "We prosecute your former wife. And if her husband causes us trouble, we may end up having to arrest him as well."

"I assume he's coming to bail her out," I said.

"Oh yeah, but he thinks he can intimidate us into giving him everything he wants, including *your son*. But that won't happen. There is a protective order in place for both you and your boy," he said. "I have been on the phone with Wendell Lawson, and he had the paperwork signed and asked me if I could have someone serve it to her at the jail. A deputy sheriff picked up a copy from him a few minutes ago and assured me it would be served promptly. When the husband shows up at the jail to bail Mayra out or demand that we release her, he will also be served. So you can relax and enjoy some free time with your son. Let me worry about Ed Sills. He doesn't intimidate me in the least."

"That would all be great, but there are some other things that have come up. Like I said," I told Chief Collins, "my phone has been rather busy the past little while."

"Yeah, too busy," a frowning Tommy said. I smiled at him.

"Is there anything pressing?" the chief asked, his tone cautious.

"I'm afraid so," I told him, and then I brought him up to date on my conversation with Felipe Salvagi. "So I think I'd better get to California, don't you?"

"I do," he said. "I'm sorry you have to leave, but I think it needs to be soon. Let me have my secretary make flight arrangements."

"What about my son?" I asked. "If Mayra's going to get bailed out of jail, despite the protective order, I'm afraid she and her jerk of an attorney husband may still try to grab him."

"Oh boy," the chief said. "You have a point there. Let me think for a moment."

I was silent, watching Tommy as he once again got busy with the binoculars but while standing only a couple of feet away from me. Finally, the chief spoke again. "I hate to spend the money, but I think I'd better also have her get a ticket for Tommy and one other person. He'll need someone to be with him down there while you interview Donald, and that will be especially important if you find that he is the likely killer. Who would you like to take to help with him?"

"Well, I suppose my mother, but I don't think she would enjoy it. She hates flying," I said. "She might simply refuse. And my dad has to work. He is in the middle of an important project that keeps taking him to Colorado."

"May I make a suggestion?" the chief asked.

"Sure," I replied, assuming I would be accompanied by another officer.

"Wendell Lawson told me his secretary got close to Tommy very quickly. He says he'd let her help in any way she could if she were needed. Kaci, I think he said her name is. I'll call him and see if he can get someone to cover for her so she can go with you. Will that work?" I heard a soft chuckle after that.

"I suppose," I said. "Tommy does seem to trust her. And I'm not sure my ex-wife and her husband wouldn't try to intimidate her if she stays in town. She is the only adult witness on the assault Mayra is charged with. I'm pretty sure they would try to coerce her to change her story."

"Then it's settled, if she and Wendell agree," he said. "I'll let you know as soon as the arrangements are made. If for some reason that doesn't work, I think I can arrange for Central Dispatch to let us borrow Connie Bost. From what I'm hearing, she'd jump at the chance." The chief didn't even attempt to hide his mirth at that suggestion.

"Please, Chief, not Connie," I begged. "She'll take it as a marriage proposal and start making wedding plans." I was trying to keep things light, but I meant every word I said.

"That would be a last resort," he agreed with another chuckle. "But I'm sure you could handle her if it came to that. She's a nice lady."

"Just not for me," I said firmly. "Please, Chief, convince Kaci to go with us. At least she doesn't know me well, and she probably has a serious boyfriend anyway," I said. "That way I won't be pressured the way I would be with Connie. She's a friend, but I don't want her to get the idea it might go further than that."

"I get it," he said. "And by the way, I made a short, very generic press release last night about the murder. I don't suppose you've had the radio on and heard it."

"Nope, I've just been enjoying some father-son time. And it's been good," I said.

"Is Kaci going somewhere with us, Dad?" Tommy asked. I'd thought he'd been focused on looking at something through the binoculars. But apparently he'd heard every word I'd said.

I held the phone away again and said, "Maybe, if she wants to."

Tommy's face lit up, and he started jumping up and down and squealing.

The chief laughed again and then said, "I take it your boy likes the idea of going somewhere with Kaci. Head back with him and start getting ready to leave for LA. Frankly, I'd like to have you on your way before Ed Sills tries to get your ex out of jail. I'll get back with you shortly."

I put my phone away—again. "Hey, Tommy," I said. "You and I are going on a trip."

He grinned as he looked at me expectantly. "A long trip?" he asked.

"As a matter of fact, yes, it will be a long trip. We will be flying on an airplane clear to California."

He gave me a high five. "Is Kaci coming with us?" he asked.

"Probably," I responded as he began tugging at my hand, leading the way back down the trail to the truck.

"When can we go?" he asked.

"As soon as we can get ready. So we'll need to head back home and get packed," I said as he handed me the binoculars with one hand while continuing to tug with the other.

"Can Kaci and I both be your partners like I was last night when you had to talk to Ellerie?"

"I think we can work that out," I said.

He pumped his fist again, the one that wasn't tugging at my hand. "That will be fun," he said enthusiastically.

Kaci had really made an impression on him in the short time he'd been with her. His little blue eyes twinkled, and he asked, "So does that mean you like her best of her and Ellerie?"

Good grief. Somebody had gotten to my kid. Who had him thinking like this? I chuckled and patted his head. "I guess it means I don't like her less," I said lamely. "And it also means she likes you."

Letting go of my hand, he gave me another high five and then skipped down the trail ahead of me. At least his two difficult encounters with Mayra didn't seem to have done any permanent damage to his psyche. Maybe a day or two with someone like Kaci would help keep it that way.

As we drove back to Vernal a little before noon, I kept my ears tuned to my son's excited and almost constant chatter. But at the same time, I was thinking about what lay ahead. First, it would be the most time I'd spent with any woman other than my mother or my ex-wife since before she'd so abruptly left us. I guessed it would be good to see if I could stay sane that long. Not that I saw anything wrong with Kaci. But I knew me and my reservations. Mayra had seriously damaged my ability to spend time with ladies. It was an uncomfortable fact that I was trying to face, but it was proving to be very difficult for me to overcome. I carried a load of guilt that I simply couldn't shed.

Second, I was thinking about Ellerie. I guessed it would be a relief to her if I could tell her for sure that Darien could never hurt her again and that her mother might be willing to come to the baby's funeral. I couldn't help but smile at the reaction I figured she would have when I told her. I just hoped I would be able to find who the killer was soon and remove the shadow of suspicion that hung over her. I wanted to be able to confirm beyond doubt that she was innocent. But in the meantime, there was that niggling little doubt that lingered in my mind.

I was just pulling back into town when the chief called. "It's all set," he said. "We tried to get a flight from here to Salt Lake, but the timing wouldn't work. Same with a direct flight to LA. We do have reservations for the three of you on a flight out of the airport in Salt Lake. We are emailing them to you, so check your phone. Then gas your SUV up and get packed. You will need to get on the road pretty soon. Kaci will be ready for you at her apartment in thirty minutes. Do you have the address?"

"I do," I said, heaving a sigh of relief. I had honestly feared Kaci would say no, and I knew Connie wouldn't. "Tommy and I will hurry."

The chief's voice grew very serious. "Royce, good luck out there, but be really careful. I will arrange for assistance from the LAPD. I'll let you know what I work out."

"Thanks. I'll be careful. I just hope I get a break on the case when I see Donald Pearson," I said.

"I'm sure you will," he agreed. "If I wasn't, I wouldn't be spending so much money to send you down there. And you and Tommy and Kaci try to have a good time while you're there. Let me know how it goes."

Tommy was so excited he could hardly contain himself as we hurriedly packed. We were taking nothing but a carry-on bag, so it didn't take long. I realized I needed to let my folks know what was going on, so I called and talked to my mother.

"I can keep Tommy," she volunteered when I told her about my trip and that it had to do with the murder case I was working on. "I can't imagine Mayra will try a trick like that again."

"I think she would. I'm not leaving him," I said. "I won't put you or him in that position." As quickly as I could, I summarized what had occurred since I had picked Tommy up from her house the day before.

My mother was flabbergasted. "I can't believe she actually tried to take him from your attorney's office. And you say she assaulted the secretary?"

"She did, but she's in jail now. However, her husband, who called me and made some threats, is on his way to bail her out sometime today. With Mr. Lawson's help, we now have protective orders against both Mayra and her husband. They aren't allowed to talk to or even approach Tommy or me. Mayra's been served," I explained. "And as soon as Ed shows up to get her out of jail, he will be served too. I know Dad's in Colorado, so with him gone, I'm not taking any chances that you or Tommy could get hurt."

"But if you are working on a murder case, won't that be dangerous for Tommy?" my mother asked.

"We will have someone with us to watch him while I'm working," I said. "And the chief will arrange for someone from the LAPD to help us in the morning."

"I don't dare fly," my mother reminded me, "or I would go with you. I'm glad someone else will be going."

"I would never make you fly, Mom," I said. "Tommy got pretty close to Wendell Lawson's secretary while she was watching him in her office. The chief made arrangements for her to go with us."

"Is she a married woman?" my mother asked.

"No, Mom, she is not married. It will be fine."

I could imagine the gears turning in my mother's mind. "Is she young?" she asked.

"Yes, and she's pretty, but don't start reading things into this that aren't there. She is simply going to help, and since Tommy seems to trust her, Wendell offered to let her go with us," I said.

"Well, that's good, then," she said. "But you be good to her. What's her name?"

"Kaci Walters," I said. "Now, I have to be going. I need to gas my car and pick Miss Walters up in ten minutes."

"Royce, don't you dare call her *Miss Walters*. You call her by her first name," my mother chastened me.

"I'll keep that in mind. I love you, Mom. But please don't worry about us. Flying is not dangerous." I could imagine her shudder at that statement.

We were a couple of minutes late picking Kaci up. She started down the sidewalk from her apartment before I could get out of my SUV. But I did make it to her in time to take her travel bag and put it in the back. Then I held the door while she got in. "Thanks for doing this for us," I said when I was seated and pulling into the street. "I just can't leave Tommy here with Mayra likely getting out of jail."

She lit the car up with her smile. "I understand that, and I'm happy to help," she said. Then she turned and spoke to Tommy. "You and I will have fun, won't we?"

"Yeah, we will," he said.

Tommy chattered until he got tired and fell asleep in the back seat. Kaci looked back at him and said, "You are so lucky, Royce. He's a great kid."

"Thanks. He is a good boy."

"Mayra must have changed. I can't imagine you marrying someone like her," she said.

I turned my head so I could see her and said, "She had me fooled, I guess." Then I turned my eyes back to the road.

"I'm sorry. I hope you have better luck the next time you marry."

I shook my head. "I don't know that there will be a next time," I said morosely. "It's pretty hard to shake off an experience like that. I trusted my wife. I don't know if I dare trust anyone again."

"She's the exception, Royce. You can find someone. Just give yourself the chance."

"I don't know. I must have done something to cause her to leave us. I just wish I knew what it was. It scares me, Kaci. I don't want anyone to have to go through whatever Mayra thinks I did."

"Hey, Royce, don't beat yourself up. I'm sure you did nothing to cause what happened," she said.

"I'd like to think that's true, but it worries me," I said. I couldn't believe I was talking to her so openly, but I guess I just wanted her to know I wasn't a good prospect for a serious relationship.

She abruptly changed the subject. "Are you free to tell me what you have to go to California for?"

"It has to do with the case I'm working," I said. "I need to interview a possible suspect."

"Does this have to do with what I've been hearing about a murder in Vernal?" she asked. "There was a short news release on the radio by your chief."

I nodded. "He kept it generic. We are still trying to identify the victim," I explained.

"He didn't have ID on him?" she asked.

"'No, and we couldn't fingerprint him to identify him that way."

"Why not?" she asked.

"His hands are mutilated," I said, looking over at her again.

Her eyes were like saucers. "Mutilated?" she asked in horror.

"That's right." I paused for a moment, thinking, and then I said, "Kaci, since you are helping me here, and this involves a possible suspect in the case, I probably should tell you exactly what's been going on. But you'll need to keep it to yourself for now."

"I will, Royce. I promise," she said.

I had scarcely started to tell Kaci the story surrounding the murder when my phone rang. "I'll tell you after this call," I said apologetically. I looked at the number and then answered. "Hi, Ellerie. How's it going?'"

"I just talked to my mother again," Ellerie said. "I'm pretty sure she and Jess won't be coming to the burial. She is being really strange about it. She says she's scared of Darien. But I think there's more to it than that."

"I can't believe your mother would do that to you," I said.

"It's Jess. He doesn't like me. If it wasn't the excuse she gave, it would be something else. I wouldn't be surprised if he were to fake being sick or something if we found out Darien really is dead. He doesn't want to come, and he doesn't want Mom to either.'"

"You're probably right. He called me earlier," I said.

"He did?" Ellerie sounded surprised. "I wonder why Mom didn't tell me that."

"She may not know. Frankly, Ellerie, I don't like the guy, and I haven't even met him," I said.

"What did he say to you?" she asked.

"He wasn't very nice. Basically, he said it was my fault that you got hurt, that I should have done something about it a long time ago."

"But you didn't know. Nobody did," she said.

"Try convincing him of that. But I'm not persuaded you can't get your mom to come for the burial. Do you have any idea when it will be?" I asked.

"Soon, I hope. I got a call from the mortician. He said he is going to get her today and that the medical examiner is through. Since Mom isn't going to come, I was thinking maybe tomorrow."

"I'm on my way to California. I have a lead on the case. I'll let you know what I find out. Can you wait to decide until I get back with you tomorrow or the next day at the latest?"

"Okay, because I want you there, if you will come," she said.

"Of course I will. Is your bishop going to conduct the service?" I asked.

"He came by last night. He says he will. He's a good man, Royce. He's been a great support to me," she said.

"Of course he has," I said. "Are you still at Pamela's?"

"Yes. Until I'm sure that Darien is either dead or in jail, I'm staying here."

"'Good."

"Oh, there's somebody at the door," she said. "I panic anytime somebody comes."

"Let Pamela answer it," I instructed her.

"Will you stay on the line until I see who it is?" she asked, a tremor in her voice.

"Of course."

"I wish you were still here. Or have you left Vernal yet? I'm scared."

"It'll be okay."

"Oh, Royce," she suddenly moaned. "It's that other woman, Kallie. Pamela says she wants to talk to me. I don't know what to do."

CHAPTER TWELVE

I GROANED. WHAT IN THE world could Kallie be up to? "Oh, Ellerie, I'm so sorry. Make sure Pamela stays right there with you. I'll call someone from the department and call you right back. Keep your phone in your hand."

"I'm scared," she said again.

"Hey, you'll be okay. I'll get right back to you, I promise."

I ended the call as a stone rolled around in my stomach. "Is something wrong?" Kaci asked.

"It could be," I said. I switched my phone so it was synced to my vehicle and verbally instructed it to dial Chief Collins's number and waited while it rang.

"Was that your girlfriend?"

I shook my head. "I don't have a girlfriend, Kaci. It was the wife of the man I think was the murder victim. Her husband's girlfriend just came to the door and wants to talk to her."

Chief Collins answered. "Royce, is something wrong?"

"I'm not sure. Kallie Briggs, the girl Darien Pearson was stepping out with, is at the house where Ellerie Pearson is staying. I need to call Ellerie back, but can you send a car around in case there is any trouble?"

"I'm on it," he said and terminated the call.

A moment later, I had put my phone on private again and had Ellerie on the line. "Are you okay?" I asked her.

"I think so. Kallie says she wants to tell her side of the story about her relationship with Darien."

"Ellerie, there's a patrol car on the way. But put Kallie on the phone," I instructed.

"Kallie, this is Detective Fleming on the phone," I heard her say. "He wants to talk to you."

"What about?" I heard Kallie ask.

"I don't know. Ask him," Ellerie snapped.

A moment later, Kallie came on the line. "I'm not going to hurt her, Detective," she said.

"I'm not accusing you of it," I replied. "But I do want to know why you are there. And you'd better not lie to me."

"I wouldn't think of it," she said haughtily. "I know there's nothing more you'd like than to arrest me."

"Oh, come on, Kallie, you can quit talking like that," I said. "But please, why are you there?"

"To apologize, all right? I came to explain that I didn't know Darien and Ellerie were married and that I wouldn't have dated him if I'd known."

"Okay, tell her you are sorry, and then you will need to leave. She's hurting right now, as I'm sure you should know."

"Okay, okay, Detective. Ellerie, I'm sorry. I didn't know Darien was already married. That's all I came here to tell you. Here's your phone. I'm out of here."

The next voice was Ellerie's. "She's leaving. Oh, goodness. The cops are here."

"Good. Then she'll know I meant what I said," I told her. "I'll hang on here until she's gone."

I drove in silence for a moment. I was aware of Kaci's eyes on me. I looked over and smiled at her. She smiled back attractively. I was glad, for Tommy's sake, that she was with us.

Ellerie came back on the phone. "She left. The officers followed her out. She was mad. I think maybe she really did come to apologize. I feel stupid now."

"Don't feel that way, Ellerie. I'm not sure she didn't have something to do with Darien's death. I don't think it's very likely, but we can't be too careful," I cautioned her.

"But you told me that you checked her shoes and they didn't match."

"That's right, but that doesn't mean she didn't throw away the ones she was wearing when he was killed," I explained.

I heard a sudden intake of breath. "Like I told you I did," she said with a catch in her voice.

"Yeah, like that," I said with a chuckle. "You be careful, Ellerie. If you'd like, I'll let you know when we get to California this evening."

"I'd like that. Is another officer with you?"

"No, but my son is, and a friend is with us too. I didn't dare leave Tommy in Vernal."

"Oh, of course. But isn't your ex-wife in jail?"

"Not for much longer, I'm afraid," I said. "Her husband is likely on his way from Salt Lake to bail her out this afternoon."

"I'm sorry. He's a cute kid. Give him a hug for me and Pamela," she said. "And I'll talk to you later."

I put my phone back into my pocket and looked over at Kaci. "I'd better let Chief Collins know everything is okay with Ellerie." I made the call and then said, "Let's see, what was I saying when we were interrupted?"

"I can't remember," she admitted.

"Okay. Then, we'll start from the beginning." I told Kaci about the case.

When I'd finished, she had tears in her eyes. "It's complicated and so very sad," she said.

"It is, but I'll sort it out."

"I know you will," she said. "But I feel awful for Ellerie. I can't imagine being married to someone like that. I'm sure she had no idea what he was actually like when she married him."

"Yeah, I know how that feels," I said.

"Oh, Royce, that was a dumb thing for me to say. I'm sorry. And don't go blaming yourself."

"It's okay. I just hope Donald Pearson is there when we get to California and that I can be sure it's him. Then at least I can tell Darien's wife that her husband can't hurt her anymore."

We had a pleasant trip the rest of the way to the airport. Kaci was good company, and I tried to tell myself that there was someone out there whom I could trust. I considered that if we were still friends after this trip, that maybe, just maybe, I might ask her out on a real date. But my doubts about myself started niggling at my mind. *Maybe not.*

The next interruption on my phone didn't come until the three of us were waiting to board the plane at the Salt Lake International Airport. I did not recognize the voice.

"This is Fred Zietz, Mayra's attorney. You have nerve, Detective," the angry voice said into the phone. "If you think that phony protective order you had served on Ed and Mayra will stand up, you are sadly mistaken. Just because she didn't have the order with her doesn't mean she isn't supposed to pick up her son. So here's what you will do. I don't know where you and the kid are hiding, but it doesn't matter. You will take him to your parents' house and leave him there. Ed and Mayra will pick him up, and this little misunderstanding will all work out. If you don't do that, I will ask the judge to find you in contempt, and you will be the one in jail."

"I'm not too worried," I said.

"You'd better be. And you'd better believe I'm serious. You don't want to mess with me. I have the court order in my hand from a judge here in Salt Lake, and you are living dangerously trying to defy—"

I broke in. "Zietz, I don't know how stupid you think I am, but I know there is no such order. So you can knock it off with the bluff."

"You are a fool, Detective. Of course there is an order," the crooked attorney insisted.

"My attorney's secretary checked. There is no such order filed anywhere in the district courts of the state of Utah. If you want to lose your license, just keep this up," I warned him.

"If you are talking about that brainless blonde nitwit who gave Mayra such a hard time, then all I can do is laugh," he said. "She's not smart enough to know which way is up."

I glanced over at Kaci. She was blonde, but that was the only thing Zietz had right about her. "Kaci is a very intelligent girl. Mayra will regret laying a hand on her." Kaci's eyes were wide. I winked at her.

"If you believe her, you are as dim as she is. All Mayra did was defend herself against that crazy little blonde's attack," he said.

"Zietz, you are playing a dangerous game here. Kaci was only doing what I asked her to—keeping my son safe and out of the hands of a kidnapper," I said angrily.

"You'll see which of us is playing dangerous games," Zietz said, his voice full of hatred. There was a pause. Then he said, "It's nearly four now. I'll tell Mayra and Ed to pick Tommy up at five from your parents' house."

Before I could tell him it would be a waste of time, he ended the call. Kaci cocked an eyebrow at me. "That was my ex's attorney," I said. "He's not a very nice man."

"What did he say about me?" she asked.

"You don't want to know, because it was a lie."

Her eyes narrowed. "I do want to know," she said.

"Okay, he essentially claimed you were wrong about there not being an order in place for my ex to take Tommy. Of course, we know he was way off base," I said, trying to get her to relax. She was looking angry. "Don't let it bother you. He's never even met you, Kaci. It's easy for him to say you were wrong, even though he knows that's a lie. I get that kind of stuff all the time from people like him."

The anger faded from her face, and she asked, "So what does he want you to do?"

"I can't believe this. He thinks I'm stupid enough to leave Tommy with my parents and to tell them to let Mayra take him when they go there in an hour."

She shook her shoulder-length blonde hair and grinned at me. "He will be in the air by then," she said, glancing over to where Tommy stood looking through the huge plate-glass window at the plane we would shortly be boarding. Her smile faded, and she shook her head again. "It's good Tommy doesn't know what's going on."

I nodded. "I just want him to forget all about what happed yesterday. My little fishing trip with him this morning and being with you this afternoon seems to be helping," I said. "Thank you for that."

"You are welcome, Royce," she said, with just a touch of rose in her cheeks.

I smiled at her and then I called my mother and suggested she lock her doors and not answer them. I explained about Zietz's call and suggested that if Ed and Mayra were persistent, my mother should call 911.

"I'll be all right, son," my mother assured me. "You and that girl you're with just take good care of Tommy."

Next I called my dad on his cell phone. "Have you talked to Mom?" I asked.

"Yes. I wish I were home. I will be tonight sometime but probably not until seven or eight. Do you think Mayra will really try to find Tommy at our house?" he asked.

"I think so. I just warned Mom. I told her to lock her doors."

"I'll call her. I think she should leave for the rest of the day," he said. "She can go shopping for a few hours or visit a friend. She can come back when I get home."

"That would be best, Dad, but she needs to leave right away. Mayra and her husband could be there pretty soon," I said.

He assured me he would make sure she was safely away from home in the next few minutes. A couple of minutes after the call was over, we were instructed to board our plane. I shut my phone off, and we were airborne before five. I supposed I would get an angry call from Fred Zietz when he learned that I had not left Tommy at my parents' house and that no one would even be home there. But it would just have to go to voicemail. I was not going to speak with him again.

Tommy sat at the window, where he was fascinated by the lights of the city below us. Kaci sat between us. We talked quietly for a little while, just small talk. I had to admit to myself that it was really quite pleasant. After a while, she got tired and fell asleep. When her head fell against my shoulder, I let it stay there. I had to further admit that it actually felt good to be this close to a woman again.

But that did not relieve me of the anxiety I felt at the mere thought of any kind of long-term relationship.

Tommy also fell asleep. My mind was far too active to allow me to indulge in such a peaceful respite. So I sat and thought about the case, mentally reviewing what I knew about each of my suspects. Then I thought more about Donald Pearson, if it really was him in California. I couldn't imagine that it wasn't, but I had to be sure. In my mind, I formed a few questions I would ask him.

Before I knew it, we were landing in Los Angeles. Once the plane had pulled up to the terminal, I turned my phone back on. Kaci did the same. I had some missed calls, as I expected I would. She had none. She grinned and said, "I'm not as popular as you are."

"Count yourself lucky," I said. "It looks like I have some messages too. I'll bet they are fun."

I held the phone so we could both hear as we waited for other passengers to deplane. I clicked on the first message as she leaned closer to me so her ear would be near the phone. Her perfume was nice, as was her closeness. I warned myself to be careful about my emotions, but I couldn't stop the tingle that I felt as her light-blonde hair brushed my cheek.

Fred Zietz's angry voice was on the first message. "You will wish you hadn't done this, Detective. You think you're pretty smart. I told you not to mess with me. You will pay. Don't say I didn't warn you."

Kaci looked at me. "He sounds more like a criminal than an attorney," she said. "My boss sure dislikes him."

"I can't say I care for the man myself," I said. "I guess you could say that Fred is a combination of attorney and criminal. I just wonder how far he'll push this nonsense, faking court orders and threating things that can't be done."

"He'll be stopped sometime," she said. "And if Mr. Lawson has anything to do with it, Fred Zietz will lose his law license."

"That's true. Let's check the next message."

Once again, she leaned close to me. I glanced past her. Tommy was engrossed with whatever was occurring on the tarmac outside the plane window. I clicked on the message and recoiled as Mayra's voice came through, angry, shrill, and full of animosity. "I'll make you pay for this, you and that ditzy blonde girlfriend of yours. I am going to get my son back. You and that . . . that . . . silly girl are not going to keep him. I hate you. And I hate her."

The message ended. Kaci and I both straightened up. "She thinks I am your—" she began, a pretty rose blush creeping to her cheeks.

"Let her think it," I said as I struggled to control the anger I was feeling.

Her blush deepened. "She wouldn't believe us if we told her we were just friends anyway."

"That's true. She says she hates me, Kaci. And I guess she really does. I suppose I should hate her too, but, you know what? I don't. Is that stupid?"

"Not at all," Kaci said, laying a hand on my arm, sending tiny electric impulses through my skin. "It's because you are a good guy." Then she scrunched her eyes and asked, "Do you still love her?"

I shook my head and placed my other hand on hers. "No, I haven't loved her for a very long time, but I don't hate her either. I guess I feel sorry for her. I wish she was the girl I married, or at least the girl I thought I married."

"You're a good guy, Royce Fleming," Kaci said again, squeezing my arm.

"Not good enough," I said, unable to keep a touch of bitterness from my voice. "It looks like we'd better get our bags. Hey, Tommy, old buddy, it's time to get off the plane."

After the three of us were lined up in the aisle, Kaci in the lead and Tommy between us, I leaned forward and said to Kaci, "We'll check the other messages after we get in the terminal."

She turned back toward me and said, "Do you really want to?"

"Good point," I said. "But I guess I should."

As we walked up the Jetway, I carried our bags and Tommy held Kaci's hand. Just watching him with her filled me with regret at what could have been with Mayra. She had no idea what she was missing. Or maybe she did, and that was why she was after him. That thought made my stomach clench.

We were all hungry, so we stopped in a small café before we left the airport. While we were waiting for our food, I opened the next message on my phone. Once again, Kaci leaned her head near me, and we both listened. "Detective Fleming, this is Kallie Briggs. Please call me as soon as you can. I need to talk to you. There is something I need to tell you. It's important, it really is. And I'm sorry if I upset Mrs. Pearson. That was not my intention. Thanks. Please, call me. Please."

"That's weird," I said as I straightened and Kaci leaned away. "I wonder what she wants."

"Is it just me, or did she sound stressed?" she asked.

"She did. I'll call her in the morning," I said, glancing at my watch. It was now close to seven, California time. "I don't want to deal with her right now. But I wonder what she needs. There is still another message." I opened the final one, and once again our cheeks almost touched as we listened.

It was Ellerie this time. "I just wanted you to know I'm doing better, Royce," she said. "I miss having you close by, but I can't wait to hear what you find out in California. Take good care of Tommy. He's such a good boy. Call me when you can. In the morning would be fine."

"She likes you, Royce," Kaci said. "If all cops were as kind as you are, it would be a better world."

"She won't like me so much if I end up having to arrest her for something," I said.

"But you don't really believe you will have to, do you?" she asked as she brushed her hair from her eyes.

"Honestly, I don't think I will. I pray that I'm not wrong. That girl has already suffered more than anyone should have to."

It was nearly eight o'clock when we finally checked into a hotel near the airport in Los Angeles. I was holding Tommy's hand and held our bag in the other one. I would have offered to carry Kaci's bag too, but I didn't have any more hands. Her room was just two doors down from ours. She unlocked her door, but before she went in, I said, "Would you like to go down for breakfast with us in the morning?"

"Sure. I'll be ready at seven, if that works," she said brightly. She didn't look nearly as tired as I felt, even though she was the one who'd suffered a mild concussion. I admired her. I needed rest. Tommy, bright and chipper now, had already gotten his on our flight. We'd gotten up really early that morning after a night in which I hadn't slept well. I was as mentally exhausted as I was physically.

CHAPTER THIRTEEN

DESPITE THE STRESS IN MY life, I slept fairly well for a change. Tommy was awake early and raring to go. To him, this was a big adventure. To me, it was a day that could turn into a big fat zero or one that could turn my whole murder investigation around. I hoped that it would not prove to be a wasted trip.

When I tapped on Kaci's door, she emerged looking bright and pretty in a dark-red blouse and tight blue jeans. I felt a catch in my throat when Tommy said the very thing that I was thinking. He said, "You are pretty, Kaci. Isn't she, Dad?"

"She sure is," I said awkwardly.

Kaci tousled his hair and said, "Thank you, both of you. And you, Mr. Tommy Fleming, look very handsome indeed."

"Thank you. Does my dad look handsome too?"

Wow, that son of mine said exactly what he thought. I hoped he didn't make Kaci feel too uncomfortable. I would guess that my blush was as deep as hers by that point. She looked at me, grinned, and then said, "Yes, Tommy, your dad looks handsome. That's where you get it from."

"What are we going to do today?" Tommy asked.

"Well, first let's go downstairs and have a really good breakfast. How does that sound?" I asked him.

"Good, and then can we go to Disneyland?" he asked innocently.

Kaci and I both laughed. "That would be fun, but Dad has to do some work. Will it be okay if you hang out with Kaci while I go talk to a man?"

He looked a little crestfallen, but it didn't last. He grasped Kaci's hand and said, "We'll have fun, Dad."

"Yes, we will," Kaci added.

We were eating when my phone rang. It was Chief Collins. "I trust you three are ready to get after things this morning," he said.

"Yeah, we are just having breakfast."

"I told you I'd get you some local law enforcement help. I have arranged for an officer to pick you up at the hotel to help you if you need it and to shuttle you around. Will that work?"

"That will be fine," I said. "What time will he be here?"

"I told him eight; is that okay?"

"Yes, we will be through eating by then."

"His name is Detective Devonte Brockwell," the chief said. "He knows basically what your case is about. He said to meet him out front. He'll be in an unmarked gray sedan. He will, of course, not be in a uniform, but he said you'll know him when you see him. Just look for a tall black man with a shaved head."

"Got it," I said.

"And while you and he are working, another officer is going to show Kaci and Tommy around. Her name is Detective Lucia Sanchez. She is Brockwell's partner. She'll try to be there at the same time as Detective Brockwell. She'll keep in touch with you until you have finished. Keep your hotel rooms. You have a flight back to Salt Lake at eight in the morning. So if you have time, you three can have a little fun. Maybe go to the beach or something. Rent a car if you need to," he offered.

"Thanks, Chief. I appreciate it," I said.

"Okay, go get him," he said and ended the call.

I explained what the chief had just told me. "Is that okay, Kaci?" I asked.

"That's great. It will be better than hanging around in my room watching TV," Kaci said, winking at Tommy, who grinned at her.

"We'll have lots of fun," Tommy said. "Thanks for letting us come with you, Dad."

We ordered, and while we waited for our breakfast to arrive, I pulled out my iPhone and Tommy busied himself coloring a place mat they had given him with some colorful crayons. "I have some calls to make," I said and started with my parents. After telling them that we were fine and what the day held for Tommy and Kaci, I dialed Ellerie's number.

"You made it?" she asked.

"We sure did," I said. "Are you okay this morning?"

"I'm doing fine, all things considered. I will know later this morning when the service will be. The bishop told me to let him take care of things," she said.

"That's good. Text me when you know the time of the graveside service; I may be in an interview and unable to take a call. But I'll call you back when I can," I said.

"Thanks, Royce," she said. "Can you tell me about your lead?"

"Not yet, but I'll let you know when I can," I said.

I didn't bother returning the calls from my ex or her lawyer, so my next call was to Kallie Briggs. This one had me tense. Before Kallie answered, Kaci said, "Is it okay if I call Mr. Lawson and tell him what Mayra and her lawyer said?"

"Yeah, that would be great," I said.

Then I heard Kallie say, "Hello."

"Hi, Kallie, this is Detective Fleming. Are you doing okay this morning?" I asked.

"I'm just nervous. Thanks for calling me back," she said, a tremor in her voice.

"Why don't you tell me what the problem is," I suggested.

"I got a text message that scared me. I don't know how she got my number," she told me.

"It was from a woman?" I asked. I hadn't expected that. I glanced over the table at Kaci, who was now talking quietly to Wendell Lawson. Tommy was still engrossed in his coloring.

"Yes. The text said, *If you killed my ex-husband, you will pay with your life.*"

"That was all of it?" I wondered what it was all about.

"Yeah, who could it be from?" she asked. "I mean, you know, I have a number that it came from, but it's not a number I recognize. I don't know what to do."

"For starters, give me the number," I said.

I wrote it down in my notebook and then read it back to her. "Is that right?" I asked.

"Yes," she answered. "I didn't kill anybody. It's frightening. What should I do?"

"Do you have to go to work today?" I asked.

"No, thank goodness. It's my day off," she replied.

"Then lock your doors and stay in your apartment. Don't answer the door. I am out of town and won't be back until tomorrow afternoon, but I will see if I can learn something about this number," I promised. "I'll also let the police know and have them check by your apartment every once in a while. Call 911 if anybody knocks on your door. Will you do that?"

"Okay, but can't I call you too?" she asked.

"You can, but I may not be able to answer right away, and you may have to leave a message. I'll call you back when I can, okay?" I asked.

"Okay," she said, sounding shaken. "Thank you, Detective."

I had barely put my phone away when it announced an incoming text message. I read it, my stomach clenching. It was from Ellerie. *Royce*, she'd typed. *Somebody knocked on the door a minute ago. When Pamela answered it, there was no one there, but she saw a note taped to the door.*

I quickly called her and asked, "What does the note say?"

"It was kind of like that message that was written on the wall with red paint," she said.

"Read it to me," I said. "But try not to handle it any more than you have to, and put it in a plastic bag. I'll need to check it for fingerprints."

"That's what I thought. It's still on the door," she said. "I told Pamela not to touch it, and I haven't touched it either."

"Good thinking, Ellerie. Are you standing by the door now?"

"We both are."

"After you read it to me, find some gloves, remove the note, put it in a bag, and seal it shut, okay?"

"Okay," she agreed. "It says, *I think you killed my ex-husband and his baby. I will make you pay, you and that Kallie Briggs who was at your house last night.*"

I got goose bumps and shivered as she read it. "Was Darien married before you met him?" I asked.

"I don't think so. I mean, he never told me he was, but I guess he could have been. I mean, I guess he *must* have been. I wonder if she was referring to my baby or if she's accusing me of killing a baby she thinks he had with someone else. Whoever it is was in my house the other day, and she was watching Pamela's house last night." She sobbed for a moment. "I am so frightened. I wish you were here, Royce."

"I do too," I said. "Kallie also got a threat, so whoever this woman is might not really know anything. She might just be trying to figure out what's going on. Here's what we'll do: I've changed my mind. Don't touch the note at all, even with gloves. Leave it where it is and I'll have someone from my department come and get it. If you can, though, maybe you could take a picture of it. Whoever left it there hasn't hurt you so far, and we don't even know for certain if Darien is dead. It could be Donald, as you know."

"Maybe he has a baby I never heard about," Ellerie said.

"Maybe. Take that picture if you can, and then you and Mrs. Mavey stay right there in the house while I get some help for you."

Our food was sitting in front of us now, and Tommy was busy eating for all he was worth. My own food was getting cold, but I ignored it as I called Chief Collins. "Chief," I said the moment he answered. "Whoever wrote that message in red in Ellerie's house has struck again." I quickly explained about the text and the note, and then I said, "I told Mrs. Pearson and her neighbor that someone from the department would be there to get the note. I also told Miss Briggs that we'd have an officer drive by occasionally to check on her."

"This is strange," Chief Collins said. "Did you know that Darien Pearson was married before?"

"No, and according to Mrs. Pearson, she didn't either. But I'm wondering if maybe it was Donald the threats refer to. I hope to know something more about him soon."

"Okay, Royce. I'll take over from here. You do what you're down there to do. I think I might need to move all three ladies to someplace safe until we get to the bottom of this. But don't you worry about it. I'll get other officers on it," he said. "I'll let you know what happens."

I put the phone away. Tommy was still eating with gusto, and he smiled at me with bulging cheeks. My own food was cold, and Kaci's probably was too. She was looking at me, her face creased with worry lines. "Royce, what's going on?" she asked.

"We'd better eat. I'll fill you in while we do," I told her. "Tommy's nearly done," I added with a forced grin. "If we don't eat, he'll be after ours."

That brought a smile to her face, and she took a tentative bite of her stack of hotcakes. I tasted my bacon, and then I told her what was going on as I continued to force my breakfast down. "This is awful," she finally said. "And I don't mean the food."

"Yes, it is," I agreed. "So what did Mr. Lawson say?"

"He said to tell you not to worry, that he's on it at his end. I guess all you can do is trust him. I know he'll do everything he can," she said.

"Without his secretary," I added.

"He got Mrs. Williams to come in. You know her," she said.

"The woman you replaced. Well then, I don't feel quite as guilty about stealing you away."

"I'm glad I'm here," she said with a shy smile. I was glad she was too.

A few minutes later, we were met in front of the hotel by the LAPD officers. Detectives Brockwell and Sanchez smiled at Tommy when they spotted us.

After introducing ourselves, Detective Sanchez dropped to one knee and spoke to Tommy. "I get to show this little man and his mommy around the city. That should make for a fun day."

Tommy, outspoken as always, said, "Kaci is my friend. I don't have a mommy, do I, Dad?"

"That's right. It's just the two of us," I replied.

Detective Sanchez was a pretty, shapely woman of about five-and-a-half feet, with coal-black hair that was tied back in a short ponytail. She had flawless, glossy olive skin, dark eyes, and a cheerful smile. She looked about my age, thirtyish. She stood up and said, "I'm sorry. I assumed. I should know better."

"It's okay," Kaci said awkwardly.

"Well, let's load up in my car and let these handsome guys get to work," she said with a wide smile. Then she turned to Detective Brockwell. "Keep in touch. I'll meet you back here whenever you're ready."

A moment later, they drove off, Tommy grinning widely. Then the tall, dark, slick-headed detective said, "Let's go see if we can find your man, Donald Pearson. That's his name, isn't it?"

"Yes, that's right."

I filled in the holes of the case for him, although the chief had given him a pretty good overview. "So if we can determine this stuntman really is Donald Pearson, then you'll at least know that your victim is his twin brother. And we will then want to determine if Donald is his brother's killer?" he asked.

"Exactly," I said. "I hope to either get him to admit to the murder or provide an iron-clad alibi and possibly even point me in the direction of the guilty party."

"You don't ask for much, do you?" the big officer said with a smile.

"Not much," I agreed with a chuckle.

We were about forty-five minutes from the hotel when we pulled into the parking lot of the large facility where the stuntmen and women were headquartered. We walked into a small but clean lobby and approached a middle-aged woman seated behind the reception desk. Detective Brockwell introduced us and then he said, "We need to speak with Felipe Salvagi and Donald Pearson. But we need to see Salvagi first without Pearson knowing we are here. Can you arrange that?"

She asked us to take a seat, and a couple of minutes later a short, wiry Italian man of about forty entered the lobby. We stood as he approached us. "You fellows looking for me?" Salvagi asked.

"We are," I said. "This is Detective Devonte Brockwell of the LAPD, and I'm Detective Royce Fleming of Vernal, Utah."

"Yes, you are the officer I spoke to yesterday," he said as his eyes lit with recall. "You didn't say you were coming here."

"I wasn't sure until I talked to the police chief. So, where can we find Donald Pearson?" I asked.

"He's in the back working out. My guys have to stay in top shape. It's dangerous work we do," he said.

"I can imagine," I responded. "Would you mind leading the way, and we'll follow you back there."

"I can just have him come up here and meet you," he said.

"No, we'll follow you back there," Devonte said with a voice that left no room for argument.

"What exactly is the problem?" he asked.

"This is a murder investigation, Mr. Salvagi. We are wasting time," my partner said. "Lead the way. And don't give any advance notice to Pearson that we are here."

Salvagi gave no further resistance. I couldn't help but think that he might have argued with me, but Devonte Brockwell wasn't someone most people would argue with. His was a commanding presence.

Felipe spoke to his receptionist. "Did you hear these officers? Do not call to the back. They want to surprise Donald."

She nodded in agreement, and we followed Felipe through a set of double doors. The room we entered first was huge and filled with all kinds of tools of their trade. The second room was also large, and several men were practicing some kind of jump from an improvised ledge onto some mats that were a long way below them. "That looks kind of risky," I observed.

Felipe chuckled. "Only to those who don't know what they're doing. My guys and gals are good. I hire only the best, and I train them well. We seldom get any serious injuries."

We went through a couple of other rooms before entering a large state-of-the-art exercise room that was loaded with equipment. Felipe pointed across the room and said quietly, "That's Donald on the treadmill. He didn't do too well on his stunts yesterday. He went too long without working out. But he is normally very good. I'd hate to lose him. I'll be at my desk. Let me know when you're ready to go."

He turned to leave, but then he turned back. "I hope you don't have to arrest him."

"I hope we don't either," I said, and Detective Brockwell and I started across the room. There were several other men working out on various pieces of equipment. Donald had his back to us, running at high speed on the treadmill. His tank top was soaked, and sweat poured from his head. We were right behind him before I said, "Donald Pearson."

He looked over his shoulder and Devonte and I presented our credentials. Donald slowed down, stepped off the machine, approached us, and then without warning, dashed past us, knocking me to the floor with his shoulder, and fled in the direction of an exit that was about fifty feet away.

CHAPTER FOURTEEN

I WAS SHOCKED AT THE speed at which Devonte moved. He had Donald by the back of his shirt and on the ground ten feet short of the door. Donald struggled against the big detective but to no avail. Devonte pulled the man to his feet and slapped cuffs on his wrists before I even had time to get back on my feet.

Devonte grinned at me. "He shouldn't have done that. Now he will have to talk to us on my turf," he said. Then he advised Donald that he was under arrest for assault on a peace officer. He said, "Detective Fleming, why don't you call Felipe and tell him he is out a stuntman for a while."

As I pulled out my phone, Devonte read Donald his rights. The prisoner struggled, but even though he was a big man, he had no chance against the powerful detective. When Felipe answered his phone, I said, "I'm afraid we are going to have to take Mr. Pearson with us. Detective Brockwell just arrested him." I did not elaborate.

"I'll meet you as you leave," Felipe said in clipped tones. I could tell by the sound of his voice that he was not happy. What I couldn't tell was if he was mad at Devonte and me or at Donald.

We met Donald's boss in the main lobby. The wiry Italian was seething. "What did you do, you idiot?" he shouted in Donald's face. Okay, he was mad at Donald. I suppressed a smile.

"Nothing," Donald said. "This is a false arrest."

"What are the charges, Detective Brockwell?" Felipe asked.

"So far, assault on a police officer," he said with a face that betrayed no emotion.

"You hit this man?" he shouted again to Donald. He was indicating Devonte.

"I didn't hit anybody," Donald protested. "Detective Fleming stepped in my way, and I accidentally knocked him down. It was not my fault." It was true: I had stepped in his path, trying to block him from getting away.

Felipe was apparently not a dummy, and he read correctly what had really happened. "You tried to run, didn't you?" he asked. "Well, Donald, we'll see if you still have a job when these men finish with you."

"You gotta come get me out of jail," Donald begged. "I didn't do anything in Utah. But I know this cop is going to try to tag me for murder. But it wasn't me who killed my brother."

Felipe raised an eyebrow. His unspoken question was clearly directed to me.

"He is a suspect in his twin brother's murder," I said.

"You'd think you'd learn. The last time you got yourself in a jam like this, you got a knife to the gut. Get him out of here, detectives," Felipe said angrily, his fists clenched.

"Who's going to get me out of jail?" Donald cried.

"Not my problem, Pearson," Felipe said and walked away.

A few minutes later, Donald sat cuffed in an interview room. Detective Brockwell and I watched him through the one-way glass as he squirmed and looked around the room. "He's scared," Brockwell observed. "Let's give him a few more minutes, and then we'll go in. Maybe he'll be ready to confess."

I chuckled mirthlessly. "That would be too easy," I said. "The first thing we need to do when we go back in with him is have him take his shirt off. If he has a scar on his stomach from the knife wound Filipe mentioned, I'll know my victim is Darien Pearson." I had already explained to Brockwell about the problem of the mutilated hands. "Then I'll need to let Darien's wife know that her husband is for sure the dead man."

"Let's do that right now, and then we can let him squirm for a while longer," Detective Brockwell said. "That will give him more to think about before we question him."

So the two of us entered the interview room. "I'll handle this," Devonte quietly said to me, and then he turned to our prisoner. "Stand up," he ordered.

Donald sat glaring at us. Devonte said, "I mean right now, or I will stand you up myself." He stepped next to the chair that Donald was sitting on, towering over him. This time Donald complied. "Face me," Devonte ordered.

Donald slowly did as he was told. Then the detective reached down and grabbed the front of his shirt and pulled it out of his pants and up high enough for us to see a dark, jagged scar across his stomach. He let go of the shirt and said, "Okay, you can sit down. We'll be back."

He headed to the door, with me right behind him. "I guess that clinches it," Devonte said when the door closed.

"I'll talk to Darien's wife right now if I can reach her," I said and pulled out my phone.

"Would you like some coffee?" the detective asked me.

"No, I'm fine."

He grinned at me. "You're from Utah. You must not drink coffee because you're a Mormon."

"That's right," I said.

"A soda then?"

"A bottle of water would be fine, if you have one."

"Water it is. Go ahead and call the widow," he said. "I'll be back in a minute or two."

I dialed Ellerie's number. It rang four times before she picked up. "Hi, Royce," she said, sounding slightly out of breath.

"Are you all right?" I asked.

"Oh yeah, I'd been cleaning Pamela's spare bedroom and came down to get a drink of water. I left my phone upstairs, so I ran back up to answer it. I hoped it was you."

"I have news for you. I'm not sure how to say this, but—" I began.

"You found Donald, so it's Darien who's dead," she interrupted.

"That about sums it up, but just to be absolutely sure, I need to ask you one question. I know we talked about scars before, but again, does Darien have any scars?"

"Only the small one on his hand that I told you about," she said. "Why?"

"The man we have here at the station has a big scar on his stomach."

"Then that's not Darien, Royce," she said with a sigh that I could hear on the phone. "I am so relieved. Now I can quit looking around for Darien every time I hear a sound."

"I'm relieved for you," I said. "I will call the medical examiner and let him know what I've learned."

"Oh, Royce, thank you, thank you, thank you. I know it's awful to be glad my husband is dead, but I can't help it. Nobody knows the terror I've lived with. I'm sorry if you think I'm a horrible person."

"I think no such thing," I said. "I think you are a wonderful, kind, and special girl." Even as I complimented her, I remembered the admonition of Chief Collins. Ellerie was still a suspect. I hoped that in the next hour or so with Donald I could change that, but for now, I needed to keep it in mind.

"Thank you, Royce," she said in a sweet voice. "Now I have a question for you. Is Donald under arrest?"

"He is."

"So he confessed to killing Darien?" she asked.

"No, let's not get ahead of ourselves," I cautioned. "He's been charged with assault. We have yet to question him about Darien's death."

"Sorry, I just thought . . . I mean . . . well, you know," she stammered. "Who did he assault?"

"It's nothing serious, but he knocked me down when I tried to block him from getting away when we confronted him at his place of employment." I went on to give her a short account of his arrest. Then I said, "I need to go now, Ellerie. We are about to interrogate Donald. You hang in there. I'll call you later and let you know what we find out."

When Detective Devonte Brockwell entered the observation room, I was calling the medical examiner. I was unable to talk to him directly, but I left him a message concerning the identity of our murder victim. Devonte handed me a cold bottle of water. I opened it and drank half of it. I hadn't realized how thirsty I was.

"It's confirmed, then," he said.

"It is." At that moment, another thought popped into my head. I glanced through the window at Donald. His head was resting on the small table in front of him. "Do you mind if I make one more call?" I asked.

"No, go ahead. Our suspect looks like he's deep in thought. We can keep him waiting a little longer. Anyway, I need to finish my coffee first. Does he look thirsty to you?" He suddenly asked me.

"I was, so I'm sure he is as well," I said.

"I think I'll run and get him a water too. Sometimes simple acts of kindness help a suspect to be more cooperative. I'll be right back," Devonte said.

He stepped out, and I called Kallie Briggs. "Hello," she said tentatively.

"It's Detective Royce," I said. "I should have asked you this earlier, but I neglected to. Does Darien have any scars on his body?"

She was silent for a moment. Then she said, "He has a large scar on his stomach."

I nearly dropped the phone. "Are you sure?" I asked, my head spinning.

"Yes, I am. He said he got it in a bar fight a few years ago. He said the guy tried to kill him."

"I see. Kallie, you told me that the blue Dodge in the parking lot was his, isn't that right?"

"Yes, but the only time I saw him drive it was the day he disappeared. Most of the time he was in a car—a Mustang. A nice one. Black, with a white stripe over the hood."

"Did he tell you the truck was his?"

"Yeah, I asked him, and he said he was buying it from a friend. Did he lie to me about that?" she asked.

"Perhaps. Tell me again how long you'd been dating him," I said.

"Well, I might have said it had been for a while, but that's not exactly true. We knew each other for about a week. But we were in love, I can tell you that. He told me about Ellerie, but like I told you before, he didn't tell me he was married to her. He referred to her as a girl he'd been dating," she explained.

I shook my head. "Kallie, I'm still out of state, but I'm going to have one of my fellow detectives come over and talk to you. I will need him to record the interview with you. I need you to tell him exactly what you just told me," I said as Devonte once again came into the room.

I held up a finger and said, "One more call." I dialed the chief's number. "We have Donald Pearson in custody on a local charge. Our dead man is Darien Pearson. I let the medical examiner know. We have yet to question Donald, but I'll let you know what we learn. In the meantime, I need a favor."

"And what would that be?" the chief asked.

"Someone needs to go to Kallie Briggs's apartment and take a recorded statement from her. Whoever does it needs to avoid any mention of me having Donald in custody. But it needs to be done right away," I said. Then I explained why.

"My, that's a new twist," he said. "She didn't even know who she was seeing. I'll do it myself right now. By the way, instead of moving the ladies, I've had an officer posted at each of their places. There has been no sign of whoever left the threatening notes. I'll talk to you later."

"Thanks, Chief."

"Do I gather that your murder case has a few interesting wrinkles?" Devonte asked.

"You could say that," I said and brought him up to date.

"That should make our session with Donald interesting. Shall we begin?" He motioned to the door.

"Sure," I said. "Now if he just doesn't lawyer up right away, maybe we'll figure my murder case out."

Donald lifted his head from the desk when we walked in. Detective Brockwell held out the water. "I'll take the cuffs off you now and let you have a drink if you'll promise to behave yourself," he said.

"I won't try anything—as if I could," he said, standing up.

Devonte grinned as he slipped the cuffs off and handed Donald the water. He sat back down and drank thirstily, finishing the entire bottle before he placed it on the table. "Hey, thanks, Detective. I was parched."

I then pulled out my recorder, turned it on, and set it between us. Donald eyed it but didn't say anything. Then I said, "I am going to record this interview." He nodded and I gave the necessary information and advised him again of his rights.

"I don't want a lawyer mucking this up," he said. "Let's get on with it. I got nothing to hide. I didn't kill my brother."

"But you do know he's dead."

"Yes, but I didn't do it."

"Explain how you heard about it," I said.

He leaned back in his chair, rubbed his wrists where the cuffs had been, and said, "I had words with Darien in a bar, but I suppose you know about that already."

I nodded and said, "Yes."

"Okay, then you know I told him he owed me money."

"I heard that."

"And he did, but I guess I'll never get it now. He owed me five grand. I helped him pay for that blue truck he drove." He stopped speaking.

"Go on," I said.

"Okay, so anyway, I told him to pay me back. That I was tired of waiting." He snorted. "I wasn't the only one he owed money to. You need to talk to those other guys, the ones Darien and I were playing pool with. They were very mad. Anyway, Darien told me to go back to California or he'd kill me and feed me to the fish in, I think it was the Green River. It is the Green River that runs past Vernal, isn't it?"

"It is," I confirmed. "What happened next?"

"I told him we should go tell his wife that he owed me money and that he should pay up so I could leave. I was missing work, and I didn't want to lose my job."

"Did that happen?"

"Not right then. I left the bar, but I waited for him outside."

"Donald, isn't it true you threatened that he would be the one who ended up in the Green River if he didn't pay up?" I asked.

"Did I? I suppose I might have said something like that," he admitted. "But why would I kill him? I wouldn't ever get my money if I did that. No, I waited for him, and when he came out, I talked to him again. I'd been thinking. I told him that there was a way he could pay me back, and he asked what it was. I told him he could give me the truck."

"What kind of truck was it?"

"A blue Dodge pickup."

"And what was his response to that?"

"This may surprise you, but he agreed. He said the truck was worth more than he owed me, but that if I would help him get into an old beater car that he could drive, I could take the truck," he said.

"Did you work that out then?"

"We did. He gave me the title to the truck. I helped him get a car—a cheap, battered old thing, but it ran. So you see, I didn't have a motive to kill him after that since I had my money back, or at least I got the truck that I could sell."

"Where did you get the car?" I asked as I realized that his motive may have, as he said, dissolved.

"It was listed in the local Nickle Ads. I don't remember the name of the guy we got it from, but I only had to give him a couple grand for it," he said.

"Describe the car," I instructed.

"It was white, a Ford of some kind. Small, with a lot of dings. Escort, I think is what it was called. Yeah, that's it. A Ford Escort."

"Can you remember where the guy you bought it from lived?"

"I don't know the address, but it was right there in Vernal. If you can get a copy of the Nickle Ads from a few days ago, you can probably figure it out," he suggested.

I had already thought of that. So I asked, "Tell me about the truck. When did he turn it over to you?"

"We did this all the next morning," he said.

"So now Darien was driving the Ford Escort, and you had two vehicles. Is that right?"

"Yeah, I had my Mustang. But I didn't intend to take the Dodge back to California. I was going to try to sell it first," he said.

"But that didn't happen?" I asked.

"No, he gave me the title, took the plates off it, gave me the keys, and drove away in the Escort."

"Drove away from where?" I asked.

"From the guy's house," he said. "The one we bought it from."

"So how did you and Darien get to that house in the first place?" I asked.

"In his truck. I guess it was my truck then," he answered.

"And where was your Mustang while you were getting him the Escort?"

He grinned. "It was over by the apartments where this really hot chick lives. I'd spent some time with her. Darien picked me up there, and we drove across town to buy the Escort."

"You paid cash for it?" I asked.

"I did," he answered.

"Okay, so what did you do then, after Darien left in the Escort?"

"I drove the truck to the apartments where Kallie lives and parked it there."

"The hot chick?" I asked with a grin.

"Yep, that's her name."

"Did she ever see the truck?"

"Oh yeah, I showed it to her and told her I was going to leave it there for a day or two while I tried to sell it."

"Did she wonder where you got it from and why you bought it if you were just going to turn right around and sell it?" I asked.

"Well, sort of, but I didn't ever answer her directly. She thought I was Darien. I used his name," he said with a grin. He seemed quite relaxed now, and I was anxious to move forward.

"Why did you do that?" I asked.

He shrugged his shoulders. "Because I could. And that way, when I headed back to California, she wouldn't know who I really was, and I wouldn't have to worry about her trying to chase me down."

"So you were not in love with her?" I asked.

"No way. She was cute and all, but you know, I'm not one for long-term relationships," he said.

"Did you wonder what this little deception would do to Darien or his wife?"

"That wasn't my problem. My brother was a jerk. I figured if it made her leave him, if she ever found out about Kallie, that it would be in her best interest," he said. "He was not good for Ellerie, but I think you know that."

"I do know that. But I'm confused about one thing. You were going to sell the Dodge truck, but you didn't. Why not?" I asked.

"Okay, so this takes us back to your earlier question. You wanted to know how I knew Darien was dead," he said.

"I was coming back to that," I said. "So tell me about it now, if you are ready to."

"Well, after I got the truck, I discovered that some of Ellerie's stuff was in it," he said.

"What stuff?" I asked.

"Cell phone, keys, credit card, debit card, checkbook, purse. You know, stuff she needed. I figured Darien must have taken them from her. I decided to take them back to her, surprise her, so to speak. So I drove over to her house in my Mustang to give her the keys and stuff. I knocked on the door, but no one answered. The door was unlocked, so I opened it. I thought I'd just leave her stuff there. As it turned out, someone else was in the house, and I recognized her. It was Darien's ex-wife, and she had just sprayed some words in red on the wall. She saw me, and she had this shocked look on her face. She said, 'You! You're dead!'

"So then I was shocked. I wasn't dead. I wasn't even hurt. So I told her she could see that I wasn't dead and that I needed to get back home.

"That was when she realized I wasn't Darien. She said, 'You're Donald.' I said I was and asked her what she was doing in Darien's house. She told me she was leaving a message for his wife, that Ellerie had killed Darien and she wanted the cops to know it, and that was why she wrote what she did on the wall. And then she said, 'Maybe you did it.'"

"What happened then?" I asked.

"That made me mad, and I must have raised my hands—you know, clenched my fists like I was going to hit her. I wasn't, though. I'm not like Darien. I never hit women. Anyway, I started to walk toward her, but I guess I scared her. She ran out the back door, and I decided not to chase her down. I went out the front door, threw Ellerie's things back in my car, and took off."

"Why did you do that?" I asked.

"I figured if Darien's first wife suspected me and if Darien really was dead, the cops might also think I killed him. That scared me, so I put her stuff back in the truck and left the state," he said.

"This isn't making sense," I said. "I didn't find any prints on the phone or the cards or other items."

"I wiped them down," he admitted. "I was running scared. I didn't want anyone to think I killed Darien, and I swear to you, I didn't. I had no reason to. I mean, you know, he paid his debt, although I don't have the truck now. I suppose the cops do."

"That's right," I said. "Were you going to go back and get the truck?"

"Only after the cops caught whoever killed him," he said.

"You have the title, don't you, Donald?"

"Yes, I have it, with Darien's signature. I have the keys too. I never left the keys with the truck."

"So I noticed," I said. "What is Darien's ex-wife's name?"

"Harley. I don't know her last name. I mean, it was Pearson, but she might have remarried," he said.

"Describe her for us," I directed.

"She is about as tall as you, not quite. She is slender but full-figured. She has short black hair, at least when I saw her in his house she did," he said. "I think it used to be longer."

"What's her eye color?" I asked.

"I honestly don't know. She had kind of dark skin, so maybe they're brown. Dark, that's for sure," he said.

"Okay, Donald, where were you on the night Darien was killed?" I asked.

"I was at Kallie's for a little while, but I left there fairly early. I told her I had something I needed to do."

"And what was that?" I asked.

He shook his head. "I just wanted away from her. Kallie was getting awfully clingy. I don't like it when women get clingy. I felt like drinking. I thought about going to a bar, but I didn't want to take her with me."

"Did you go to a bar?" I asked.

"No, I went back to the place I was staying, a hotel over in Ballard—I think that's the name of the town. I guess it's a town. It doesn't look like one. It's near Fort Duchesne. Anyway, I ended up buying a six-pack of beer and stayed in the room and watched a movie and drank."

"Where did you buy the beer?" I asked.

"At a convenience store in Fort Duchesne. Ute Plaza or something like that," he said.

"What is the name of the hotel?" I asked.

He told me and then said, "They might remember me there."

"I'll check," I told him. "Now, Kallie says you were told by her apartment manager not to go to her place again."

"Yeah, but that didn't mean I couldn't. I just had to be sneaky about it. I know the guy didn't see me when I snuck in that evening or when I left. Like I already said, I was tired of her. She thought I liked her, and I didn't. She was being really pushy. But I didn't kill Darien. I think I might know who did though," he said.

"Oh yeah? Who?" I asked.

"The guy I had the fight with in the parking lot at Kallie's apartment complex. He thought I was Darien. He might have gone looking for him and killed him. He was mighty jealous. He thought of Kallie as his girl," he said.

"You are talking about Max Hermo?" I asked.

"Yup, that's the guy. He probably did it. Have you talked to him?" he asked.

"I haven't been able to find him," I said.

"That kind of figures, doesn't it?" he asked with a chuckle. "Well, you need to find him."

CHAPTER FIFTEEN

I CONTINUED TO QUESTION DONALD for the better part of an hour after that. He denied sending any emails to Ellerie using Darien's account. He also denied using her phone, saying he wouldn't have been able to access it, as he didn't have her password. I asked him every question I could think of. Detective Brockwell threw in a few of his own. Finally, I ended the interview and went back into the observation room with Devonte.

"I don't think he's your man," Devonte said. "If he did kill his brother, he had to have had a woman help him, accounting for the small feet, and that would likely have been Kallie."

I was shaking my head. "Yeah, it was probably not him, but what about this Hermo guy? Could she have helped him for some reason, like maybe he threatened her if she didn't?" I suggested.

"I agree. You need to find Max Hermo," Devonte said.

"What do we do with Donald now?" I asked.

"Well, do you want to see him charged for assaulting you?" Devonte asked. "Or should we let him go and see if he still has a job? But if we do that, I think you will want to make sure he understands that he should not leave the area."

"Let's take him back and speak on his behalf with Felipe Salvagi, make sure he still has a job, and leave it at that for now," I suggested.

"That's what I was thinking. Then you and that boy of yours and your beautiful friend can spend some quality time together before you have to fly home," the detective said with a grin.

Donald did not lose his job. I was glad we'd spoken on his behalf, because I think he would have had we not. And Donald was grateful the charges had been dropped.

We met up with Kaci, Tommy, and Detective Sanchez a few minutes later. I offered to buy both officers a late lunch, but they declined. They left us at the hotel, with an offer to help again if I needed it. Then my son, Kaci, and I ate in the restaurant at the hotel. Tommy was his usual talkative self. He told me all about driving around Los Angeles and all the things they had seen, and then he asked, "Dad, can we go to Disneyland now?"

"Son, I don't think we have time. But maybe we could go to the beach."

"I don't have my swimsuit," he said.

"I think we can take care of that problem. What do you think, Kaci?" I asked.

"Let's do it," she said with a wink. "I need a new suit anyway." I rented a car, and then we bought suits and spent the rest of the day, until late in the evening, at one of California's warm, sandy beaches. While Kaci and Tommy were running in and out of the water, I stepped away and watched them while I made some calls. Kallie, I learned from the chief, had told him the same thing she'd told me.

"I still wonder about Max Hermo," I said. "I haven't been able to find him yet. I suppose Kallie could have helped him. If so, she threw the shoes away that she used that night."

"I'll have someone swing by and see if Hermo's home yet. If he is, we'll call you right away," he promised.

The next call I made was to my parents. I assured them that all was well and that we would be home sometime the next day. They quizzed me about Kaci. I watched her as she was running along the beach with Tommy. She was really quite stunning, and she was certainly good to my son. But I didn't tell them that. I didn't want them pressing me further. I liked her. I was attracted to her, but I wasn't ready for a commitment. And I would *not* be pushed into it.

Finally, I called Ellerie. I told her as much as I felt was appropriate about the interview with Donald. I mentioned that Darien had given Donald his truck to pay off a debt and that somewhere around Vernal we should find the Ford Escort Donald had bought him to make up for the value of the truck that was above what Darien had owed him. I also told her I did not think Donald was guilty of killing her husband but that I had some things to check on when I got back to Vernal, just to make sure. I also told her he denied sending her an email using Darien's account.

I told her that it appeared Darien had been married before. She again said she'd had no idea. She asked me, "How do you know he was married before?"

"Donald told me. He says he saw her when he was in Vernal."

"When?" she asked.

"He went to your house to give you back your phone and stuff. He said you weren't there and that the door was unlocked, so he opened it. He was just going to leave your things inside, but Darien's ex was there spray-painting your wall."

I heard her gasp. "That's who left that awful message?"

"Donald knew about her and recognized her. He said she accused you of killing Darien. There was no mention of your baby. She also accused Donald and ran out the back door. That was when he decided to leave town. He was afraid that if Harley—that's her name—suspected him as well as you of killing Darien, the cops might too. He took time enough to take your stuff back to the truck, where he figured we would find it and make sure you got it back, and then he left Vernal."

I watched Kaci and Tommy while I talked to Ellerie for a while longer. I still had to find a way to make sure she wasn't involved in the murder, although I was more certain of it than I ever had been. I hoped it wasn't her. In my opinion, she deserved a new start in life. I wondered if she would go back to Salt Lake and work for Ted in his business again. I didn't ask her about that. But I supposed that someday, once I had cleared her of any suspicion, she might. I couldn't think of anything that might make her want to stay in Vernal.

"Ellerie, I did learn something I haven't mentioned to you that I think you should know," I said.

"What?" she asked. "I hope it's not something bad."

"It's not," I assured her. "Kallie Briggs did not have an affair with Darien. She was actually dating Donald."

"No, that's not right. She told me she did. She said she didn't know that we were married," Ellerie said.

"I know. What Kallie didn't know, and what I found out today from Donald, is that it was Donald, not Darien, whom she had been seeing," I explained.

"But, I mean, how could that be? Why would he make her think he was Darien?"

"Donald told me it was just because he could. He knew they looked so much alike that he could get away with it."

"Just because he could?" she asked. "What does that mean?"

"It seems he really didn't like Darien very much, and he thought you would be better off without him. So he pretended to be Darien, thinking that if it got back to you about Kallie that maybe you'd leave him," I said. "He thought he might have been doing you a favor."

For a long time, Ellerie didn't say anything. I could hear her steady breathing in the phone, but finally, she spoke again. "That's crazy, but believe it or not, it makes me feel a little better," she admitted.

I ended the call as Kaci and Tommy headed toward me. Tommy was skipping and laughing. Kaci was following along behind him, looking quite stunning in her new red swimsuit. I tried to keep my eyes on Tommy, but they kept slipping back to her. She was smiling and watching him. She seemed to be quite fond of Tommy. Then she looked up, saw me, and ran past Tommy. He sped up, and they were both out of breath by the time they reached me.

Even though I knew I should be cheered up to be with such an attractive girl and to see my son so happy, I wasn't. No, I felt that familiar sadness at what could have been, what should have been. That should have been Mayra laughing and playing fondly with our son. Once again, I found myself wondering where I had gone wrong. Was it because of something I had done that caused Mayra to leave me? And if I allowed myself to fall in love with someone like Kaci, would I make the same mistake again and drive another wife off? If I knew what I'd done, I could try to change to make sure it would never happen again. But I didn't. And it drove me crazy. I couldn't get Mayra's words out of my mind when she said that she'd been an emotional wreck when she'd walked out on Tommy and me. But what had I done to cause that damage to her? I had no idea, so once again, I reminded myself not to fall for anyone, not for Kaci or anybody else.

"Royce, what's wrong?" Kaci asked. "You look troubled."

"I'm sorry, Kaci." I sat down on a towel. "I have too much on my mind, I guess." I wasn't about to tell her about my gloomy thoughts, so I led her to believe it was about the case. I said, "I have to figure this murder out. It's driving me nuts."

That was not helpful. She came over, sat down beside me, and took hold of my hand. Then, leaning against me, she said, "You will figure it out, Royce. I know you will. You are a great detective. I wish I could do something to help. I would if I could."

Tommy sat down beside me and started talking about how much fun he was having. He said, "When are you going to come in the water with us?"

"In a minute," I said as I tousled his wet hair.

Kaci snuggled closer to me on the opposite side of where Tommy was. Oh, boy. I wanted to put my arms around her. Her touch sent pleasant shivers through me. But I couldn't do it. I shouldn't do it. I should pull away from her. I didn't. That seemed like it would be unkind. Or was letting her think I was starting to care for her be even more unkind? In the end, I did neither. But I did say, "You already have helped a lot, Kaci. You came with us. You helped me with Tommy and kept him safe. Thanks."

"You're welcome," she said, suddenly touching my cheek gently with her lips. Then she let go of me and sprang to her feet. "Hey, come on. Tommy wants you to get in the water with us. Let's go," she said, laughing.

I got up, attempting to dash my melancholy mood away. "Let's do it," I said with as much fake enthusiasm as I could find. The kiss to my cheek was great. Her touch was great. Her very nearness was great. *But it was all wrong.*

I did manage to enjoy myself for the next hour or two. And Tommy had a ball. He kept telling me how much fun he was having. And I kept telling him that I was glad. But after we finally decided it was time to head back to the hotel, Tommy grabbed my hand and said, "Dad, I wish Kaci was my mom."

Fortunately, she was a little way behind us still gathering up her things and didn't hear him. At least I didn't think she did. I leaned down toward him and said, "She's nice, but don't you think you and I are doing just fine by ourselves?"

He seemed to consider that, and then he said, "Yeah, we're doing okay. But I like Kaci."

I could possibly get serious about her if I let myself, but I wasn't about to. *It's for her sake*, I tried to tell myself. I was flawed, and it would be unfair to hurt her by letting a relationship begin. It simply couldn't be. She didn't deserve the baggage I carried.

We were just getting ready to leave the beach when I got a text from Ellerie. She informed me that the graveside service for her baby would be at ten o'clock A.M. the day after tomorrow. So I would have time to do a little work after we got back to Vernal the next day and make the service without any problem the following morning. I texted her back and thanked her and told her I would be there.

I was more careful for the rest of our time in California to not get too close to Kaci. That resolve fell apart when we boarded our plane for the flight home early the next morning. It had been my intention to have Tommy sit between me and Kaci. But he wanted the window, and I gave in. Kaci was again in the center seat, and I was in the aisle seat. She chatted with me much of the way home. I couldn't help but enjoy her company. At least she didn't fall asleep and let her head rest on my shoulder.

We arrived back in Vernal in the early afternoon. To my dismay and delight, when I let Kaci out at her apartment, she leaned close and kissed me again on the cheek. "I have had a wonderful trip, Royce. You and Tommy are so fun to be with," she said.

I shivered pleasantly from her touch. Why did I have to be so flawed? She was such a sweet girl. She proved that even more when she knelt beside Tommy, held him close for a moment, and then kissed him on the cheek as well.

As we were driving to our house, Tommy was deep in thought. I couldn't help but wonder what he was thinking. He let me know before we reached the house. "I really like Kaci, Dad. And she likes both of us. I think she'd be a really good mom."

How could I explain to my sweet boy that even though he may be right, I might not be able to be a good husband? I didn't try. I just brushed off his comment and said, "There are a couple of things I need to do at the house, and then I guess I'd better take you to Grandma's and get to work. I have a lot to do."

I spent a few minutes with my mother. Then I asked her if she was comfortable with me leaving Tommy there for a few hours. "Of course," she said. "Tommy and I will be just fine. Chief Collins says Mayra and her husband went back to Salt Lake. He says he watched them leave town and made a call to an officer he knows who lives near them and asked him to let him know if they showed up, and they did."

"That's good to hear. If you have any trouble, call me. I'll come as quickly as I can," I said.

"What kind of trouble could we possibly have? Mayra is gone. You go catch a murderer. Tommy and I will be fine," she assured me. "I have some grocery shopping to do. I think we'll do that, and then we'll get busy here with some baking I have to do."

It was hard to feel assured, but I didn't see a lot of choice. I wished my dad could be there, but his job kept him terribly busy. So I hugged my little guy and headed for the office. A copy of Chief Collins's interview with Kallie was on a thumb drive in my inbox. I took it out and listened to it on my computer. She didn't vary from what she had told me in her statement to the chief. I put the thumb drive away and pulled out my ever-growing file on the Darien Pearson murder.

After reviewing it and making some notations on my interview with Donald, I closed it and jotted down some things in my notebook that I needed to do that day. The two most pressing items were to locate Max Hermo and try to interview Andrew Hutchins. I was on my way to Andrew's house when my mother phoned. From the second she spoke, I knew something was wrong. "Royce, you need to meet me somewhere," she cried into the phone.

"Mom, is Tommy okay?" I asked as my heart began to pound and adrenaline streamed through me.

"Yes, so far," she said. "But you need to take him. Mayra is back in town."

"How do you know she's back?" I asked urgently.

"I just saw her. She was at my house. She was at the door when I turned the corner into my street. Her car was parked in front of the house," she said. "I turned around and drove away as fast as I dared."

"Did she see you?" I asked.

"I don't think so, but I'm not sure," she said.

"Okay, come to the police station. That's probably the safest place," I suggested.

I met her in the parking lot and held Tommy's hand while Mom and I tried to decide what to do. As we were talking, my phone rang again. I looked at the screen. It was Kaci. I considered letting it go to voicemail, but my curiosity got the best of me and I answered.

"Royce, Mayra is at my door," she said quietly but with a touch of anxiety. "She must think I have Tommy again. What should I do?"

"Do not answer the door," I instructed her.

"She's pounding on it and shouting," she said. "Can you come?"

"She just left my mother's place," I said. "But she didn't get Tommy," I said as my brain searched for ideas. Finally, I said, "Okay. I'll come right now. Don't let her in. But talk to her through the door," I said. "Tell her I'm coming, if you have to. She might leave when she hears that. If she doesn't, she'll be back in jail within the hour."

I clicked the call off and turned to my mother. "Mayra's at Kaci's now. Will you take Tommy inside and ask for Chief Collins? Tell him what's happening and ask him if you and Tommy can stay there for a few minutes," I said, watching as she took Tommy's hand.

"Okay," she said, and I jumped into my SUV and tore out of the parking lot.

I made it to Kaci's apartment in record time. Mayra was leaning against her silver Mercedes when I drove up. I jumped out of my vehicle and ran right past her to Kaci's door. Kaci must have been watching through the window, because she opened the door the second I got to it and slammed it behind me after I went in. She locked it and turned to me. She was trembling and fear shone on her face. She fell into my arms and sobbed for a moment.

"It's okay. She'll wish she hadn't done this," I said as a fierce pounding on the door commenced, accompanied by Mayra's shrill shouts for me to come out.

"If you don't give me Tommy today, you will be the one in jail. I'd love to see you in handcuffs," she shrieked. "Come out right now."

"What are you going to do?" Kaci asked as she pulled back from me, her eyes as wide as saucers.

"I'm going out. Lock the door behind me," I said and reached for the door.

CHAPTER SIXTEEN

I HALF-EXPECTED MAYRA TO PHYSICALLY attack me when I went out the door. But to my surprise, she backed away a few feet and smiled. She was holding one hand behind her back. "What do you think you are doing?" I demanded.

"I'm giving you this," she said as she pulled her hand from behind her back and reached toward me with an envelope. "You are served," she said, slapping it against my chest and letting go. The envelope fell to the ground. "Now, take me to where you are hiding Tommy." I bent down, picked up the envelope, and opened it. "Now you can't say you haven't seen the order from the judge."

I made no comment as I pulled out a sheaf of papers. They looked official enough, and I felt my chest constrict. I scanned through it just as two patrol cars screamed up and slid to a stop in the street. Chief Collins was riding with Sergeant Merten in the lead car. A pair of uniformed officers was in the second one. Sergeant Merten stepped between me and Mayra and informed her that she was under arrest for violating a protective order.

She smiled sweetly at him and said, "I don't think so. I just served Royce with an order to turn my boy over to me. If he doesn't, you'll be arresting him."

Chief Collins joined him and said, "Mrs. Sills, you will need to come with us."

She began to throw her arms around. She kicked the chief and spat in the sergeant's face. The other officers helped, and in a minute she was secured and on her way back to jail. The chief relieved me of the papers as Kaci stepped out the door and stood beside me. He looked them over and then he said, "Take these to your attorney, Royce. There is something fishy going on here."

"What does it say?" Kaci asked.

"That Tommy is to be turned over to her," I answered.

"I'll meet you at the office," she said decisively. "Mr. Lawson will know what to do. And I'll do what I did before and check to see if anything has been filed since then. This just can't be right."

"I agree with you," Chief Collins said to her. Then he turned back to me. "As soon as you finish up with Mr. Lawson, meet me back at the station."

"What about Tommy?" I asked.

"He's safe," the chief said with a smile. "Your mother is with him in the office right now. We'll work something out as soon as we figure out what your ex is up to."

Ten minutes later, Kaci was sitting at her computer, searching for the order online. I was with Wendell Lawson in his office. He was studying the order Mayra had served me. He slowly shook his head. "This can't be right. Let me make a phone call. Why don't you see how Kaci is coming on her search while I do this?"

I joined Kaci and Mrs. Williams in the reception area. Mrs. Williams was sitting next to Kaci and watching what she was doing. Kaci looked up as I joined the two of them behind her desk and peered at her computer screen. "Nothing so far," she said.

I watched as she continued to search. Before she had finished, Wendell joined us. "I just talked to the judge's chief clerk. She says she's almost positive she's never seen this document. She would like us to fax it to her, Kaci." He handed her a slip of paper. "Fax it to this number, attention Heidi."

Kaci took it from his hand and said, "I can't find a record of it on here. I'll get this sent right now."

Ten minutes later, we heard back from the clerk of the judge whose signature appeared on the order. She stated in no uncertain terms that the order had not come from the court. She said it was fraudulent. "That does it," Wendell Lawson said. "I am reporting Fred Zietz to the state bar. I won't rest until his law license is revoked. And furthermore, I am going to make some calls to the District Attorney's office in Salt Lake and see if they will initiate criminal action against him."

"What about Mayra's husband, Ed Sills?" I asked. "He is in the middle of this."

"I can't see where he's referenced on the paperwork," Wendell responded. "But you make a good point. He had to have known it was a fraud. I'll ask to have him included in the investigations."

"Thank you," I said. "I suppose Ed will be here to get his wife back out of jail pretty soon."

"That will be a little more difficult this time," my attorney said with a grin. "I think as soon as I call the county attorney's office, they will ask the judge to revoke the former bond since the latest arrest is a violation of the terms of her release."

A short while later, after getting Tommy and my mother settled at my parents' home, I went back to work on the homicide case. The first thing I did was go to the home of Andrew Hutchins, the drinking buddy of Johnny Torello. The two had played pool with the Pearson twins, and Andrew would have heard the two threaten each other. Even though I had pretty well cleared Donald of suspicion, I still needed to interview Andrew. He might have seen or heard something that would help me.

Young Reggie Hutchins's old yellow Chevy pickup was parked in front of the house. I parked behind it. I smiled to myself when I saw that there was a new sticker on the rear plate. Apparently, Reggie had renewed the registration. I saw no other cars around the house, either in the driveway or in the carport that was attached to the house.

I knocked and waited. It was Reggie who answered the door. He frowned, but this time he did not attempt to shut the door in my face. "What are you doing here? There is no pot in the house anymore," he said.

I smiled at him. "Looks like you've got your truck registration renewed."

"Yup," he said. "I did that as soon as you guys left. Why are you here?" he asked again.

"I still need to speak with your father," I responded. "Is he at home?"

"He isn't, but you can come in and look," he said.

I accepted his offer and stepped into the house. The only scent of marijuana that I picked up was old. "When do you expect your dad to come home?" I asked as I glanced around the living room.

He shrugged his shoulders. "I have no idea. I don't even know where he is. Do you want to look in the other rooms?" he asked, waving his hand toward the back of the house. "Mom's not here either."

"I'll take your word for it," I said, and he looked surprised.

"I'm sorry Dad isn't here. I have no idea where he's at," he said.

"Tell me about your mother. Does she go to the bar with him?" I asked.

"No, she smokes pot, but she doesn't drink very much. She does go and pick him up at the bar at night a lot of the time so he won't get arrested for drunk driving. When she's at work at night, then I go get him." He actually grinned at me as he added, "And they can't get me for an expired registration."

"Reggie, maybe you can help me," I said. "I was told that a man by the name of Darien Pearson owes your father some money."

"Yeah, he does," Reggie said. "I heard Dad telling Mom about it."

"How much?" I asked.

"Quite a lot, I think," he said. He shrugged his shoulders. "I'm pretty sure it's more than a thousand dollars."

"Do you have any idea why he owes your dad money?" I asked.

Reggie shook his head. "I dunno," he said. "I think it's really something about my aunt, but I don't know."

"Your aunt?" I asked.

"Yeah, Dad's sister. I just remember Dad saying something about it. But I don't know any more than that. She lives in Florida. I haven't seen her for a long time. She never comes around here."

"What's her name?" I asked.

"All I ever remember Dad calling her is Jean. I don't know for sure what her last name is, but it might be the same as mine. I don't think she's married."

"Thanks, Reggie," I said. "What are you doing today?"

He shrugged his shoulders, a gesture that was becoming very familiar to me. He pointed into the kitchen and said, "I got behind in school. So I'm having to do some work online. It's math. I'm having a hard time with it. I'm stuck right now, and I don't know what to do."

"I was good at math in school," I said. "Would you like me to take a look? Maybe I can help you."

He seemed taken aback. "Why would you do that?"

"Why not?" I said. I had a lot to do, but if I could help this young man, it wouldn't hurt. Who knew? Maybe someday he could help me in some way. I'd learned that it never hurt to make friends with some of the less upstanding people in the community.

Once again, he gave his trademark shrug, followed by, "Sure then." He led the way into the kitchen.

I tutored him for the next thirty minutes. He wasn't a dumb kid; he just hadn't paid a lot of attention in school. At least, that was what I figured, because he caught on fairly quickly to what I was showing him. I watched him as he worked some problems on his own. When he got them right, I said, "I think you'll be okay now, Reggie. If you get stuck again, call me." I handed him my card.

He accepted it and stood up from the table. "Thanks. I might," he said. "If you don't mind."

"Hey, no problem. I can tell you're a smart guy. I'd like to see you succeed in school. I mean it, Reggie."

He smiled and said, "For a cop, you're okay."

"Thanks," I said. "And Reggie, if you'd call me when your dad comes home, I'd appreciate it."

"Sure, I'll do that," he said. I left Reggie, fairly confident that he would keep his promise.

My next stop was the apartment complex where both Kallie Briggs and Max Hermo lived. I walked through the parking lot after leaving my vehicle on the street. Kallie's yellow Mazda was there, but a black Durango that Kallie had told me Hermo drove was not. I went to his door first anyway. After knocking and waiting for a full minute, I gave up and went to Kallie's apartment.

She answered the door after only a brief wait and me answering her shouted inquiry as to who was there. "Not working again today?" I asked as she signaled for me to enter her apartment.

"I got switched to the evening shift," she said. "But until you tell me that whoever threatened me and Ellerie is caught, I'm not too sure I dare go to work."

"I'm sorry, but we really don't even know where to look for her. I know her first name is Harley, but that's about all I know. She hasn't bothered Ellerie again. Maybe she left town," I said, but I didn't say it with any conviction.

I spent the next several minutes reviewing with her my interview with Donald. "He was just leading me on," she said as she wiped at a tear. "I guess I'll never see him again."

"Probably not," I agreed. Then I asked, "Have you seen Max Hermo?"

She scowled. "I don't want to see him. He's such a creep." I took that as a no.

"He doesn't answer his door, and his Durango is not in the parking lot," I told her.

"I still think he might be a murderer. He might have been fooled by Donald just like I was and killed Darien, thinking he was Donald," she said.

"I wonder the same thing," I said, but I still wasn't satisfied. The tracks at the murder scene were small. I couldn't think of any reason Kallie might have wanted Darien dead, but I wasn't ready to scratch her name off my list quite yet. "Will you let me know if you see Max?" I asked.

"I will, but I don't think I'll see him. I don't want to see him." She shuddered when she said that, and it appeared that she really didn't want to have anything to do with Max Hermo. But when I left, I was still uncertain. All I could do was keep checking back—that and alert all the local police departments to be on the lookout for his vehicle.

I went back to the station and put out the request for information on Max's Durango. Then I called my mother and checked with her on Tommy. "He's doing fine," she told me. "But I'm not letting him go outside. I guess it's a good thing, but he doesn't seem to understand how serious this thing with Mayra is."

"I'm glad. And of course, he really doesn't know she's his mother. To him she's just some crazy woman," I said. "It's getting late enough that I think I'll call it a night. I'll be over to get him in a few minutes."

Tommy was in what Mom called his playroom, one of the spare bedrooms in her house, with my father when I got there. "I think Tommy and I will spend a quiet night at home," I told her.

She chuckled. "Quiet? With Tommy? He likes to talk. He sure has talked a lot about Kaci this afternoon. It sounds like the three of you had a good time in California. He's been telling me all about how much fun you all had at the beach."

"He did have fun," I agreed. "And I think Kaci did too."

"He says Kaci likes you, Royce. Are you going to ask her out soon? Tommy sure wants you to."

"Mom, Kaci is a great girl, but I'm not ready to take the risk yet. After what happened and is still happening with Mayra, I don't want to take a chance on anyone," I said.

"Royce, Kaci is a very different girl from Mayra. You can't let her treatment of you keep you from spending time with girls like Kaci," she said.

I'd heard all this before, but there was something I had never confided to my mother or my dad. Maybe if I did, she and Dad wouldn't constantly pressure me about getting married again. Dad came in just then and asked how things were.

"They're fine," I said. "Did Mom call you about what Mayra did today?" I asked.

"Yes, of course. That girl is just getting herself deeper and deeper in trouble. I can't imagine what she's thinking," Dad said.

Mom grinned. "You should hear Tommy talk about Kaci, the young lady Royce took to California."

"Oh, he's been telling me all about her," my dad said with a grin.

I needed to stop this before it got worse. And since my father was there now, I decided to tell them my concerns. So, plunging in, I said, "Mom, Dad, I have no interest in getting serious with anyone. I should have told you this a long time ago. It's not so much about Kaci and what kind of girl she is—or anyone else for that matter. This is about me."

"What do you mean it's about you? Any number of women would think you were a great catch," my mother said. "Don't be hard on yourself."

"I thought Mayra was a great girl. And at first she was, but then something happened. She says it was because of me," I confessed.

"No, son. It is not about you. It's about Mayra," my dad broke in sternly.

"That's right. She was never the girl we all thought she was," my mother insisted.

"Maybe, but what if it was something I did that caused her to leave?" I asked. Before either of them could answer, I pressed on. "If I was doing something that caused Mayra to do what she did, I might do it to another girl. That wouldn't be fair to Kaci or anyone else."

"I can't imagine what you are thinking, Royce. You treated her very well," my dad said as my mother nodded in agreement.

"I thought so, but maybe not. Please, you guys. Don't push me. Tommy and I are doing just fine. Maybe someday I'll figure myself out," I said. "In the meantime, I am not interested in getting close to anyone. You probably don't understand this, but it's how I feel. I love both of you, and I understand your concerns, but you've got to let me work things out. Maybe someday I'll feel differently. Until I do, I'm not letting anyone, not Kaci, not anyone else, think I am interested in getting married." I left after that, knowing that neither one of them understood how I felt, but a weight lifted off me from having told them.

Tommy and I had a great evening together. We went out to eat and then to a movie. By the time we got home, he was ready for bed, and so was I. After he had said his prayers and I had him tucked in, I headed for my bedroom. As I did, it occurred to me that Tommy had not said a word about Kaci. I was relieved. He'd be okay. We'd both be okay.

I dropped Tommy off the next morning, spent a little time with Mom, and was grateful that she didn't mention Kaci. I finally hugged Tommy and told him to have a good day. Then I headed for the door.

"I need to go now, Mom. Let me know if there is any kind of problem at all. I need to take care of some things at the office, and I also plan to attend the graveside for Ellerie Pearson's baby at ten. You never know who might show up there. Killers have been known to do stupid things. Who knows? Maybe I will get a lead on this case."

My cell phone rang and I answered. "Royce, it's Ellerie. I'm sorry I keep bugging you all the time."

"You aren't bugging me," I said. "What can I do for you? Are you about ready for the service?"

"I'm as ready as I will get. I don't look forward to it, but I know I can't move ahead with my life until my baby is at rest," she said. "But that's not what I'm calling about. I just got another email. It's from Darien again. This is crazy, Royce."

"I'll come over and read it. Are you at Pamela's?"

"No, I came home to get dressed for the graveside. Pamela, the sweet thing, is getting ready too. She's going to take me to the service."

"She is a good neighbor," I said. "I'll see you in a few minutes."

CHAPTER SEVENTEEN

ELLERIE MET ME AT THE door. Despite the worry in her eyes, she looked nice. The bruises were fading, and it appeared that what was still there she'd succeeded in covering quite effectively with makeup. She was a good, kind woman and didn't deserve the abuse she had endured. Once again, I wondered how Darien could have been so cruel.

"You look great," I told her as she signaled for me to come in. She certainly did not look like a murderer. But . . . I shook my thoughts aside and entered the house.

"I got ready and had a little time before I needed to go, so I decided to check my emails," she said as she led me into her kitchen where the laptop was open on her kitchen table. "I know it's not actually from him, because he's dead—that is for sure, isn't it?" she asked me, looking just a little doubtful.

"It's for sure. Someone is trying to play with your head," I said. "Let me have a look."

She sat at her computer and brought up the email. I knelt beside her and examined it. "It is from his email address, is that right?" I asked.

"Yes, it is."

"So someone has that address and knows how to use it," I said as I leaned forward. My head was close to hers. She smelled great. I shook off the distraction and read the message.

Ellerie,

I am still in California. I have a problem. Well, both of us have a problem. My ex-wife is demanding I pay her back-alimony. I owe it. I can't make it home for a while. She will be in touch with you. She won't leave us alone until it's paid. You will need to sell the house to pay it. We need to leave Vernal anyway if I get this job down here. Don't argue with her. She might try to hurt you if you do. I wish I could be there, but I can't. Put the house up for sale today. Don't wait.

Darien

I leaned back after I had finished. Then I stood and pulled a chair from the far side of the table and sat facing her. "Ellerie, in my opinion, this email was written by Darien's former wife."

"I still can't believe he was married before. You'd think I would have known," she said with a shake of her head.

"He deceived you in lots of ways, didn't he?" I asked.

She tucked a lock of her long shiny brown hair behind her ear and then said, "Yes, I guess he did. I don't think I ever knew the real Darien Pearson. But could this be true? Could he owe his ex-wife, if she really is his ex-wife, past alimony? I know this can't be from him, but it says he owes her a lot of money."

"If he does have an ex like Donald says, then she could easily enough be using his email address. But regardless of that, if it's true he owed this woman past alimony, he's dead. You are not responsible for what he owed her," I said. "Let's print this, and I'll take a copy of it."

"We owe a lot on the house. I don't know how I can afford to keep it. I can't make the payments. And I don't know if I could sell it for more than we . . . I owe. But are you saying I shouldn't try to sell the house?" she asked.

"Of course not," I said. "Don't even think of it. There is time to consider what you want to do with it in the future. This whole thing with this email is phony. I'm sure that woman is messing with your mind. Maybe she thinks you'll panic and sell the house and give her what she wants. Anyway, forget about it for now and think about your baby's service."

She nodded her head, ran her fingers through her hair, and smiled. "Okay."

I left, went to the station, and added the email to my growing file. I made some more notes, reviewed a few items, and then shut down the computer and headed for the cemetery.

There were more cars there than I had expected. The hearse carrying the tiny body was beside a small open grave. Mrs. Mavey's car was nearby, but I couldn't see Ellerie through the crowd gathered around the grave. I parked where I could easily get out if I had to and then walked toward the crowd.

I stood a ways back and began to study the people there. I recognized a few of them, including Ellerie's bishop. But there were a lot I did not know. I assumed most of them were members of Ellerie's ward. Women outnumbered men by about three to one. I spotted Ellerie standing on the far side of the grave from me. She was surrounded by people, all of whom appeared to be extending sympathy and support to her.

Ellerie looked up, and her eyes seemed to be scanning the gathering. When she saw me, she smiled through her tears and raised a hand in greeting. I nodded my head toward her, smiled, and then resumed my search of the crowd.

I really didn't expect to see anyone or anything suspicious, but I wasn't about to miss something if it was there. A few more cars drove up and parked. Ted and Fiona Franklin were among the people I spotted in the vehicles. As soon as they got out, Ted spotted me and veered in my direction, his wife following slightly behind him.

"Hello, Detective Royce," he said when he reached me, extending his hand. "I'm glad I saw you here. I was hoping to get an update on the case today. I haven't talked to Ellerie for a while. Is she doing okay?"

"I think so," I said without elaborating.

"Can you tell me what's happening? The last I knew, there was a question of whether the dead body you found was Darien's or his brother's," he said.

I didn't want to be distracted, so I made my answer short. "It's Darien," I said. "Maybe after the service we could go over what I've learned so far."

"Is the service about to start?" he asked.

"I think so. It's almost ten. I'll meet you afterward," I said again, in an effort to get him to move on.

"Sure thing, Detective," he said, and he and his wife looked toward the gathering. "There's Ellerie," he said. "Let's see if we can speak with her before the service begins."

They walked toward the grave, and I continued to watch the few people who were still approaching. One woman caught my eye. She seemed to be alone and was acting furtive, her eyes darting around. For a brief moment, she looked straight at me, but then she looked away and walked slowly toward the ever-growing crowd.

She was fairly tall, maybe five-eight or five-nine. She was slender but full figured. A slight breeze had begun to blow, and her short black hair blew into her eyes. She raised a hand and brushed it away as she walked past me. Once again, she looked at me, her dark eyes sparking. She looked angry. She went on past me, but then she slowed down. I was pretty certain she had spotted Ellerie when she came to a stop but kept her head facing forward. I suspected that those dark eyes of hers were glaring at Ellerie. Her fists were bunched at her sides. That sign of anger concerned me.

I recalled the description Donald had given me of Harley. The description fit. I was almost certain this was her. I continued to look around the group, but mostly I watched her. I had no idea what she planned to do, but she was here, and she was angry, so I had to expect the worst. I moved toward the crowd, keeping an eye on both Ellerie and the angry black-haired woman. Ellerie was speaking now with Ted and Fiona. She looked up and caught my eyes. I smiled and nodded at her, and then she turned her attention back to her boss. The bishop then spoke to her, and she nodded. Then he raised his hand, trying to get the attention of the crowd. He paused while everyone quieted, and then he began to speak.

I could hear his voice, but I was still far enough back that I could not understand what he was saying. The woman I assumed was Harley was at the outskirt of the people gathered there. Her face was directed at Ellerie. I slowly moved around until I was directly behind Ellerie. Then I watched the woman closely. She had a large purse slung over her shoulder, and that made me nervous. Who knew what that purse held? I felt inside my jacket for my pistol. I kept my hand there as I continued to observe the woman.

The service took only about ten minutes. Then the bishop again addressed the crowd. I had eased closer and could hear him tell them they could go back to the church, where a meal was prepared. After that, the crowd began to disperse. Ted and Fiona spoke for a moment to Ellerie, hugged her, and then started toward me. Mrs. Mavey was standing near her. I remembered that she had brought Ellerie to the cemetery.

The woman I assumed was Harley began to inch forward. The crowd, which was headed in the other direction, parted to let her through. Ted and Fiona reached me. "Is now a good time to bring me up to date?" Ted asked.

I shook my head and said, "I think Ellerie is in danger. I need to walk back to the car with her and Pamela."

Fiona's eyes widened, and Ted's mouth grew tight. "From whom?" he asked as he looked back toward me.

"The woman with black hair who's walking toward her," I said as I moved away from them and hurried through the thinning crowd. I reached Ellerie only a moment before Harley stopped in front of her. I whispered to Ellerie, "Stay with me. We are going to walk away now. I'm sure Pamela will be right behind us. I want to get the two of you away from here."

But we had only begun to move when the angry woman reached out and grabbed Ellerie by the arm. "You aren't going anywhere right now," she growled. "I need to talk to you."

Ellerie glanced at me, fear in her eyes. I spoke for her. "Mrs. Pearson has nothing to talk to you about," I said. "Let's go, Ellerie. You too, Pamela."

Harley said, "No you don't," as she reached her free hand into the large purse hanging at her side.

Not taking any chances, I stepped in front of Ellerie, broke the other woman's grip on her arm, and swiftly snagged the purse from her shoulder. She turned her wrath on me as her hand came out of the purse—empty. "This woman stole my husband from me, and she owes me a lot of money," she said with a sneer. "Not that it's any of your business. Now give me back my purse."

"What were you reaching for in your purse?" I asked.

"That's none of your business," she said.

"Do you mind if I look in it and make sure you don't have a gun in there?" I asked, swinging the purse out of her reach as she grabbed at it.

Ted Franklin had circled around us, and at that moment, he took hold of Ellerie's arm and tugged. She looked at me. I nodded, and they moved toward the parked cars at a brisk rate. Fiona walked beside Mrs. Mavey. Harley looked at her purse and at Ellerie, seeming to be undecided about what to do. I helped her decide when I took hold of her arm and spun her toward me. She again made a grab for her purse, but I held it firmly.

"Who are you?" she asked as she once again glanced at Ellerie and Ted. They were almost at a trot now. Fiona and Pamela were struggling to keep up. "I need to talk to that woman."

"I don't think so." Then I told her, "My name is Detective Royce Fleming. And I know you are Harley Pearson."

"So what if I am?" she asked as she struggled to get away from me.

"You have been harassing Mrs. Pearson. I have evidence that you broke into her house," I said. "I am placing you under arrest for burglary and for criminal mischief."

She narrowed her eyes at me and said, "You can't prove anything. That woman owes me money, and I intend to get it."

"Maybe your ex-husband owed you," I said, "but Ellerie doesn't. Let's go. I'm taking you to the police station."

She argued with me for a moment, but finally, when she could see I wasn't backing down, she reluctantly walked with me to my vehicle. I placed her in handcuffs and put her into the SUV. I called in to dispatch and told them I had made an arrest and was heading to the police department with one female subject.

When I escorted Harley inside the police station, she again demanded her purse. "Not until I make sure you don't have a gun in it."

"You don't have a warrant, so you can't do that," she haughtily informed me.

"Actually, since you are now under arrest, I can. It's for officer safety." I'd been joined by Sergeant Merten. We stepped into my cubicle, and then I handed the purse to him and said, "Would you check and make sure there isn't a weapon in there?"

He nodded, took the purse from me, stepped to my desk, and put the purse down. He opened it and reached inside, his hand coming out with a small .38-caliber pistol. "It looks like you were right, Detective," he said.

I turned to Harley and asked, "Do you have a concealed carry permit for that pistol?"

She held her mouth tightly shut and turned her head away from me. Her refusal to answer was an answer in itself. But to be sure, I had Merten check further in her purse. He took everything out of it and scattered it on the desk. There was a lot of stuff in there, including a driver's license and credit cards. But Merten did not find a permit. I told her I was adding that to her charges. I invited the sergeant to assist me, and we prepared to interview Harley.

Before we began, my phone rang. I looked at Sergeant Merten and said, "I need to take this. Will you stay here with Harley?"

I stepped out into the hallway and took the call. "Royce, this is Ellerie. Are you going to come eat with us at the church?" she asked.

"I'm afraid I'll have to pass," I said. "I arrested Harley and need to interview her now."

"Did you look in her purse?" she asked.

"She did have a pistol in there," I informed her. "Are Ted and Fiona still with you?"

"They are, but Ted really wants to talk to you. I didn't feel like I should tell him what you've learned. That's why I wondered if you were coming down here," she said.

"Have him come here when he's through there," I said. "I'll talk to him then."

Before I went back to my cubicle, Chief Collins came down the hallway. "Royce, are you busy?"

I told him what I was doing. "Do you have something I need to know before I interview her?"

"As a matter of fact, I do. While you were out, the report came in on the phones you confiscated. The calls from Ellerie's phone," he reported, "were to a number that has been identified as Harley Pearson's. It seems Darien had called her from Ellerie's phone as well as from his own."

"I guess I'll see if I can get her to tell me what they talked about," I said.

"What are your impressions, Royce? Could she be the killer?" he asked.

"I don't know, but I certainly won't rule her out at this point."

"Is she a tough cookie?" he asked with a wry grin.

"You could say that," I replied. "As I think about it, I wonder who made the biggest mistake on a first marriage—me or Darien Pearson."

The chief shook his head and said with a tight smile, "Let me know how the interview goes."

Back in my cubicle a minute later, I began the interview. But as soon as I spoke to her about her right to an attorney, she said, "I want my attorney. I won't talk to you without him here with me."

That was the end of that. My hands were tied for the time being. I turned my phone toward her and told her to make her call. "I don't know any attorneys here in Vernal," she said, "and mine is in Las Vegas. It'll take him a long time to get here. So I guess you'll just have to wait."

"I guess so," I said. "And so will you. Sergeant Merten, would you take her to jail and book her for me?" I asked. "She is going to be doing her waiting there. She can call her lawyer from the jail too."

Harley's face went pale. "You can't put me in jail," she said with a catch in her voice.

"I can, and I will," I said as I rose from my chair. "I have a lot to do."

"Please, don't lock me up. I need to go home," she begged.

I walked out of my cubicle without another word. I intended to let her stew for a while. In the meantime, I wanted to see Ted Franklin. And since Harley refused to talk, I could do that at the church rather than waiting for him and his wife to come to the police department.

I was in my car and driving toward the church where the luncheon was being held when my phone rang. "Detective Fleming, I just saw Max Hermo," Kallie said as soon as I answered. "He's packing stuff out to his car. I think he's leaving town."

CHAPTER EIGHTEEN

By the time I got to the parking lot, Max Hermo was getting into his car. It was packed to the ceiling in both the passenger seat and the back clear to the back windshield. I parked directly behind him and got out just as he was getting his black Durango in gear. He slammed on his breaks and jumped out of his car, swearing at me as I walked toward him.

I let him rant for a moment before saying, "Are you Max Hermo?"

"Of course I am. Who are you?"

I produced my shield. "Detective Fleming, Vernal City Police," I said.

Who I was did not daunt him in the least. "I ain't got time for whatever you want," he said. "Now get out of my way before I ram your car."

"I would suggest you don't try that," I said as I approached him. "I need to speak with you about Darien Pearson."

"That jerk? What does he want?" he asked. "He hit me. I should press charges against him for assault."

"The way I hear it, he got the worst end of the fight. I'll need you to come downtown with me," I said.

"Who told you that? Was it him, or was it that two-timing girlfriend of mine?"

"Who would that be?" I asked.

"I'm sure you know. Kallie Briggs. But she ain't worth my time. If she wants Pearson, she can have him. Am I under arrest?" he asked, the veins in his thick neck bulging.

"Not yet. I just need to ask you a few questions. Were you planning on going somewhere?"

"Yeah, as a matter of fact, I am. I got a new job. I need to start in the morning. It's in Salt Lake, so I need to leave now."

"This shouldn't take too long. Why don't you jump in here with me?"

"What is this about? Is it about the fight?" he asked belligerently.

Watching closely for his reaction, I said, "No. It's about a murder."

There was no hesitation in his answer. "I didn't kill nobody, cop. So don't go trying to pin something like that on me."

"Then maybe you can help me figure out who did," I said as I opened the passenger door of my SUV.

"Okay, I'll talk to you," he said after staring at me for a moment. "But let me drive my Durango down there. I'll follow you. I gotta go as soon as we're done."

"That's fine," I said. "But don't try getting away, or I'll have to throw you in jail."

I wasn't confident that I was making the right decision, but he followed me to the department and parked right beside me. We went straight to my cubicle. I got my recorder out as I told him I was going to record this interview.

"I didn't do no murder," he said. "And I don't know anything about one, so I don't see why you have to record this."

"It's procedure," I said.

He settled back in the chair across from me and said, "Okay, go ahead."

As soon as the introductory information was recorded, I said, "Max, tell me about your relationship with Darien Pearson."

"I thought this was about murder," he said.

"This will go quicker if you don't keep stalling," I said.

He swiped a hand across his forehead and then said, "Me and him had a fight. He was stepping out with my girl. I told him to back off. He took a swing at me. I swung back. That's about all there is to it."

"Are you sure it was Darien?" I asked.

"Well, that's what the guy said his name was. And Kallie said it was too."

"Could it have been his brother, Donald?" I asked.

He looked confused for a moment. "Brother?" he finally asked. "I don't know nothing about a brother."

"The man Kallie was seeing is a man by the name of Donald Pearson. He's a twin brother to Darien," I said.

"What's this about? I still don't know nothing about a murder," he protested.

"Max, did you threaten the man you thought was Darien?"

"Yeah, but you already know that. He was messing with my girl."

"That was Donald. Did you threaten him?"

Max looked at me for a moment, a shadow crossing his face. "I don't know what this is all about," he finally said.

"When was the last time you saw the man you thought was Darien?" I asked.

"When we had the fight," he responded. "Did something happen to him?"

"Donald is fine. He's back at his home in California. He was pretending to be his brother. And that brother is Darien. Somebody killed him," I said.

Max threw both hands in the air and said, "Hey, I didn't touch the guy. And I don't know who did."

I asked Max to tell me where he'd been since the last time he saw Donald. By the time I got through, he'd pretty well established an alibi for the night of the murder. In fact, if what he'd told me about his travels checked out, I could rule him out as a suspect, unless, of course, he'd hired someone else to do it. That was something he denied, and I finally had to let him go. He gave me an address where he'd be living in West Valley City and the name and address of his new employer. I also got the name of his recent employer in Vernal.

After he left, I called his former boss, who told me that Max had been planning to move to the city for some time and that he'd finally gotten a job there. After a few more calls, I was satisfied that he'd been where he'd claimed.

I had just concluded the last call when the receptionist called me on the intercom and told me that there were some people there to see me. I glanced at my watch. The dinner at the church would be over by now. I asked her who it was, and when I was told it was Ted and Fiona, I told her to send them back.

"Did Ellerie and her neighbor get home okay?" I asked.

"Yes, we made sure before we came here," Ted said. "She told us about the supposed ex-wife. I'm not sure the woman isn't a phony. I'm convinced Ellerie had no idea her husband had been married before. If I'd known that, I'd have argued stronger for her to not marry the guy."

"I think she really is an ex-wife," I said. I proceeded to tell him what I'd learned. Twenty minutes later, I had explained everything I knew so far.

"Is Ellerie a suspect in Darien's murder?" Ted asked. But before I could formulate an answer, he said, "I can assure you she isn't capable of such a thing. She is as sweet and innocent a girl as I've ever known. Isn't she, dear?"

"She is," Fiona agreed. "Darien simply lied to her, led her on, and made her believe he was something he wasn't."

"I agree with that," I said.

"Is she a suspect?" Ted pressed.

"Not much of one," I finally said lamely. "But we can't rule anything out until I can catch the killer. She had motive and opportunity."

Ted looked at me for a moment, shaking his head. "She thinks very highly of you, Detective," he said. "She trusts you to find out who did this horrible thing."

"And I will," I said firmly. "Believe me, I won't quit working on this until I've solved it."

"You don't really think Ellerie had anything to do with it, do you?" he asked.

I took a deep breath and then said, "No, I really don't. But you've got to understand that—"

Ted cut me off. "I understand. And I'm trusting you to take care of that girl. She is like a daughter to Fiona and me."

"We only had sons," Fiona said. "We love Ellerie. And we know her heart. She was naïve and made a mistake, but she would never hurt anyone."

"This woman, the one you say was married to Darien—she can't really make her sell the house and give her the equity, can she?" Ted asked.

"I'm pretty sure she can't," I agreed.

"I told her she should sell the house and come back to Salt Lake. I told her I would help find her a place to live," he revealed.

"Really?" I said. For some reason I couldn't define, that bothered me. "What did she say?"

"She said that as soon as she can, she probably will list it. And as soon as it sells, she will come back to Salt Lake."

I could see no reason she shouldn't. But it bothered me all the same. I visited with them for a few more minutes, and then they left. I called Kallie and told her about my interview with Max Hermo. "I don't have any reason to hold him," I said.

"Are you sure?" she asked me.

"All I can tell you is that I've checked out his alibi. It's legitimate," I told her.

"Is he leaving Vernal?" she asked.

"He has a job in Salt Lake that starts tomorrow," I said.

"Good, then I guess I won't have to worry about him bugging me anymore. That's one good thing."

After hanging up, I once again reviewed the entire case. I was coming up empty. That bothered me a lot. I had to clear this up, and soon. The chief was going to be on me again, as I was sure the mayor would be on him as well. I buzzed the chief's office. I told him where I was at on the case, and then I said, "I wonder if we should make a press release and let the public know more about the murder than you did before. We could at least let them know the identity of the victim now."

"I've been thinking about that myself," the chief said. "The mayor has been bugging me to release more information. I'll take care of it. You keep plugging away. You'll get a break."

I hoped so. I worked longer, and when I finally looked at the clock on the wall, I saw that it was nearly five. I decided to call it a day and go pick up my son. My mother met me at my parents' door and said, "Tommy's doing fine. But he did ask me about that woman who wanted to take him the other day. I think it's starting to worry his little mind."

"I was afraid of that. I'm finished for today," I said. "I'll spend some time with him tonight. We both need it."

"What he really needs is a—" she began.

"Don't go there, Mom," I said a little sharply.

"I'm sorry," she said. "But I worry about you."

"Don't. Like I told you and Dad, when I get things straight in my mind, then I'll think about it. But for now, Tommy and I are doing just fine."

"I guess you have tomorrow off," she said. "It is Saturday."

"Unless something comes up, I will spend the day with Tommy," I told her.

"Your dad and I are going to Salt Lake in the morning. We won't be home until late, so we won't be here if you need help with Tommy," she said. "Maybe Kaci will help if you need someone."

"I'm sure she would," I agreed. But I didn't want to ask her. She was a sweet girl, but, well, I just wasn't going to ask her if I could help it.

"Do you want Dad to fix dinner, or should we go to McDonald's again tonight?" I asked Tommy as we pulled out of the driveway a little while later. We'd eaten out the night before, but I didn't feel much like cooking this time either.

"McDonald's," he said with a grin.

My son and I had a relaxing evening. I hoped we could have a good day on Saturday, just me and him. But it wasn't to be. I had just ended a call to see if Ed Sills had been able to bail Mayra out of jail when Ellerie called me Saturday around ten in the morning. "Some guy just left. I didn't talk to him, but Pamela did. She told him I couldn't come to the door. So he unloaded on her. The guy claims he's Harley's brother and that he was going to help her collect from me. Pamela told me he said he didn't care if Darien was dead, that he deserved to be. But he said it wasn't his sister's fault and that he would see that she got what Darien owed her."

"Did he give his name?" I asked.

"Pamela wrote it down. I have it here."

"I will be right over and get it from you," I said. After she hung up, I said to Tommy, "Come on, Tommy. I need you to be my partner again."

He was all for that, so ten minutes later, we were seated in Pamela Mavey's living room. I held a paper in my hands. The name Mrs. Mavey had written on it was August Jeppson. She had gotten a phone number and an address in Magna. I studied the name for a moment, and then I turned to Ellerie. "Do you have your laptop here?"

"Yes, of course. Would you like to use it?" she asked.

"Please," I said.

"What are you going to do?"

"I'm going to see what I can find out about this August Jeppson guy."

She disappeared for a minute. Mrs. Mavey smiled at Tommy. "It looks like your daddy is going to be busy for a few minutes. Would you like to go to the store with me? I have to get a few things. And maybe we could get some ice cream while we're there."

"Can I, Dad?" Tommy asked.

"I guess." Then I looked at Mrs. Mavey. "I don't expect to be too long here."

"We'll hurry," she said. "Come on, Tommy."

They were just leaving the house when Ellerie returned with the computer. She plugged it in at the kitchen table, booted it up, and logged in. Then she pulled up a chair next to me. Again I noticed how nice she smelled. And she looked really good. Every day she was further healed, and having the baby at rest seemed to have lifted a load from her shoulders. "Where are Tommy and Pamela going?" she asked.

"To the grocery store. She said she needed to go and get a few things and that they would get some ice cream," I told her as I typed in August Jeppson's name and began a search.

"Is Mayra still in jail?" she asked.

"She was a little while ago," I said. "I checked before you called me."

"Good. I would sure hate to have her try to grab Tommy again," she said as she hunched closer to me and studied the screen.

"So would I," I said. But the thought of Harley and August made my chest tighten. I wondered if I shouldn't have let Tommy go. But it was too late now. I was sure they would be back soon.

"Maybe Harley's brother is going to get her out," Ellerie suggested, worry in her voice.

That didn't do anything to relieve my own worry. But I tried to reassure myself and set it aside while I studied the computer. It took me a few minutes, but I found someone by the name of August Jeppson listed. "Oh, boy," I groaned as she gasped. We were both reading the same thing. If this was the same August Jeppson, he was a thirty-eight-year-old ex-convict. "Aggravated assault, a litany of drug charges, and, oh no," I moaned. "He's a registered sex offender."

"Oh," she said with a whimper.

I glanced at her worried face but made no comment. I continued my search for information as my gut churned. I should never have let Tommy out of my sight. I kept searching. According to the latest information I could find from his record with Adult Probation and Parole, he had a job at a body shop in Magna. I found the number for the body shop and dialed it, hoping it would be open despite it being Saturday.

It was, and I shortly confirmed that August worked there. But the fellow wouldn't tell me anything else when I began to try to learn more from him about August. So I turned back to the computer and began searching again. "Let's see if either he or his sister has a Facebook account."

"I wish Pamela would get back," Ellerie said, sounding like she was worrying as much as I was.

"She'll be here shortly, I'm sure," I said, as much to reassure myself as her. "Ah, here we go. This is Harley Pearson. Let's look at some of her pictures. Maybe we'll find a brother."

Sure enough, we did find pictures of a guy who fit the description Mrs. Mavey had given me. Then I found one that confirmed that I had the right guy. There was a picture of him standing in front of the body shop I had just confirmed he worked at.

I sat back. "Does Mrs. Mavey have a cell phone?" I asked as I felt myself getting sick to my stomach.

"Yes. I'll call her," Ellerie said. A moment later, she said, "Pamela, are you about finished?"

She put the phone on speaker, and we both listened as her neighbor said, "No. I'm worried. Tommy and I were just leaving Jubilee when we saw that guy who was at the house. I grabbed Tommy, and we ran back into the store," she said. "He hasn't come in, but I can see him just standing out there beside a pickup. It's an older truck with a nice paint job," she said. "It's green."

I was on my feet. "Tell her to stay there, Ellerie," I said. "And tell her I'm coming."

I left the house at a dead run. As I got in my pickup, I was surprised to see Ellerie getting in on the other side. "I'm going too," she announced. Then into her phone she said, "Don't hang up, Pamela. We're on our way."

CHAPTER NINETEEN

I SPOTTED THE GUY IN the parking lot as soon as I drove in. He was leaning nonchalantly against his green pickup. I parked a short distance away from him and then said to Ellerie, who was still on the phone with Pamela, "Go in and meet them. Take them to her car, and go to her house. Lock the doors. If this guy even so much as makes a move toward you, I'll stop him," I said.

There was doubt in those amazing amber eyes of hers. "I don't know. Why don't you come with us?"

"I need to talk to this guy. This will give me that chance," I said.

She ran her fingers through her hair and looked at me for a minute. "Go," I said. "And keep my little guy right with you."

"You trust me with him?" she asked.

"Of course I do. Now go," I said again.

"Thank you, Royce," she said with a catch in her voice. "I'll take care of Tommy. I promise."

"I know you will," I said, and she was gone.

As I watched her walk to the store, still talking on her cell phone, I realized that I had just entrusted the most important person in my life to her. And I didn't have a twinge of regret. From that moment, I knew somehow that Ellerie was a good person, that she was not capable of hurting others. Yes, I trusted her. I offered a prayer, telling the Lord how I felt and asking Him to watch over both of them. Then I stepped out of my truck and leaned against the door.

A minute later, Ellerie, Pamela, and Tommy left the store. Ellerie, though she was not a big woman, had Tommy in her arms. Pamela was right beside them. They hurried into the parking lot. August pushed away from his truck and followed them. I waited until he was right in front of me, and then I stepped out and blocked his path. "That's far enough, August," I said with anger in my voice.

"Get out of my road," he said. "I'm going in the store."

I stood my ground and pointed toward the entrance. "The store is that way," I said.

Fortunately, I was watching him closely, and I saw the punch coming, quickly enough to avoid it. I stepped back and said, "I am a police officer. Don't try that again, or you will be in jail again."

His eyes narrowed to dangerous slits. "Get out of my way," he growled.

"Go that way, to the store, and I'll let you walk away," I said.

"I'm going that way. I need to talk to that woman," he said, pointing at Ellerie.

"She's off limits to you," I said as I glanced and saw the three of them get into Pamela's car.

August tried to shove me aside, but I stood firm. He threw another punch, and when he did, my karate training kicked in. I fended off the blow with my left arm and struck him in the throat with a hard right knife-hand strike. He choked and grabbed at his throat, his eyes bugging out. Then he slowly sank to the ground.

He was coughing and spluttering as he attempted to get to his feet again a full two minutes later. "I'll kill you for that," he said. As he spoke, I wondered if I had just found another suspect in the death of Darien. Clearly, Harley's brother didn't like Darien, or he wouldn't be trying to extort money from his widow.

I heard a siren, and a moment later a marked car pulled up and Officer Kolton Henderson leaped out. "I just got a call and was told you needed backup," he said as he eyed the man who was still trying to stand but wasn't having a lot of luck.

"Help me cuff him," I said. "Assault on a police officer."

August struggled, but we soon had his hands secured behind his back. Once again, August spoke. "You'll regret the day you ever met me," he said with a broken voice. He was still struggling for air.

I didn't waste my breath on a reply. But I said to Officer Henderson, "Take him to the emergency room. Have them check him out before you book him," I said. "I didn't hit him as hard as I could have. He should be okay in a few minutes."

"It was Ellerie Pearson who called," he told me as he shoved August toward the patrol car.

"Ellerie and her neighbor have my son. I'd better go and make sure they made it home okay. I'll get back with this guy at the jail in a little while," I said.

As I drove off, I thought about what I'd just said—that I'd go to the jail in a little while. I was without someone to care for Tommy. There was no way I would take him with me to the jail, and I had to go there. I needed to speak with August, and I didn't want him getting bailed out before I got the chance.

Ellerie and Pamela had the door locked, like I'd asked. I rang the bell and waited. Pretty soon my phone rang. I answered it and saw that it was Ellerie. "Is that you at the door, Royce?" she asked.

"It's me," I responded.

In a moment, the door opened, and I slipped in and locked it behind me. I turned to face Ellerie. She had a haunted look on her face. "Will it ever end?" she asked, her tearful eyes pleading for a positive response.

So that's what I gave her. "Sure it will," I said, trying my best to sound confident.

She smiled and responded with, "If you say so." Which, by the tone of her voice, meant, *Not in a million years.*

"Is Tommy okay?" I asked, looking around and not seeing him.

"He's helping Pamela in the kitchen. They are dishing up some ice cream, and there's plenty for you too," she said. "I know your son will not leave until he's had some."

"In that case, I guess I'd better join you."

Before she moved in the direction of Mrs. Mavey's kitchen, Ellerie's face grew long, and she asked, "Where is Harley's brother?"

"An officer is having him checked out at the emergency room, and then he'll be going to jail," I responded.

"What happened?" she asked. "The last thing I saw was you blocking his way from coming after me."

"He took exception to that," I said. "He took a couple of swings at me."

She cocked her head to the side and wrinkled her forehead. "And then what? You look okay."

I smiled and said, "He forgot to ask if I had any training and experience in self-defense."

She grinned. "I take it you have had some."

"I was in a karate club growing up. I'm not very good, but I guess I was better than him."

"Are you a black belt?" she asked.

I really didn't want to brag, so I said, "It's been a while since I was active in it."

She grinned again. "So you do have a black belt." It was not a question. I didn't deny it. She then asked as a shadow crossed her face, "He'll be out soon, won't he?"

"That would be my guess. Let's go have that ice cream."

Nothing more was said about August Jeppson as we ate our ice cream with some cake on the side. As we ate and made small talk, I thought about my dilemma with Tommy. I had no one to tend him. I pulled out my phone and said, "I need to make a call." I stepped back into the living room. I really hated to call Kaci, but I honestly didn't have any other choice. I just hoped she didn't take it as a romantic overture on my part—I didn't want her to think that.

Her phone rang several times, and I was just about to end the call when she answered. She sounded out of breath and was laughing as she said, "Hello. This is Kaci."

"Hi, Royce here," I said. "I have a little problem."

"I'm sorry. What's the matter?" she asked. "And how can I help?"

"Well, my parents are out of town, and I've had something come up on the murder case," I began.

"You need someone to help with Tommy," she speculated. "Just a second. I need to step away for a minute. There are others around." I waited, and in a few seconds she came back on the phone. "I wish I could take him, Royce, but I'm in Denver. We won't be home until tomorrow. I would be glad to help then if you need me to."

"No, that's okay. I'll work something out," I said, wondering what that something would be.

"I'm really sorry," she said again. "I'm on a date right now, but if I had my choice I would rather be with Tommy."

"It's okay. Maybe some other time," I said. "I'll let you get back to your date. I'm sorry for interrupting."

"Really, Royce. Call me again. I want to help," she said with a plaintive whine to her voice.

"Thanks," I said, embarrassed and anxious to end the call. "I'd better go."

I was slipping the phone back into my pocket when I saw Ellerie standing in the doorway. "If you need someone to watch Tommy for a little while, Pamela and I can help," she said. "I gather your regular sitter is unavailable."

"Yeah, I'm afraid so. But I can't impose on you."

"Please, I'd love to spend some time with him. He seems like a good kid."

"He is that," I agreed.

Mrs. Mavey and Tommy joined us just then, and Pamela said, "Yes, we'd love to keep him for you if you need to go for a while."

I was torn. Ellerie was part of a case. It didn't feel right to leave my son with her, even though I had pretty well ruled her out as a suspect. I had a prime candidate who would be in jail in a few minutes.

Tommy did not miss what was going on, and he said, "It's okay, Dad. I want to stay with Ellerie and Mrs. Mavey. Please, can I?"

"There you go," Ellerie said, grinning at my son. "You heard Tommy."

Yes, I'd heard Tommy. But it didn't relieve my anxiety. I felt like I was between a rock and a hard place. "Will you be okay here?" I asked Ellerie.

"We will lock the door, and nobody gets in but you," she said firmly.

I shook my head, and Mrs. Mavey spoke up. "Tommy, go get yourself another cookie from the kitchen." He skipped away. Then she said to me, "My late husband was a hunter. I still have a whole gun case full of his rifles and pistols. And I have shot them all. You just go, and don't worry about us."

I looked back and forth between the two women, and they both smiled at me as I silently asked the Lord for guidance. Ellerie took it one step further as she closed in on me and laid a hand on my arm. "We'll be fine, and I promise, so will Tommy."

I felt a surge of emotion toward her, and I made my decision. I hoped I wouldn't regret it. "I'll hurry," I said. "And I'll have my phone on. Call me if you need me."

"Bye, Dad," Tommy said as he emerged from the kitchen with a half-consumed cookie in his hand. "Me and Ellerie and Mrs. Mavey will have fun."

Dismissed, I left the house, drove to my home, picked up my police SUV, and then headed for the jail. August was still in booking when I got there, and I told the jailers I needed to speak with him. So they took him to an interview room and left me with him. August stood looking at me, his dark eyes glaring with anger.

I pointed at a chair and said, "Sit down. I need to talk to you."

He touched his throat and said, "I can hardly talk, thanks to you."

"Sorry, but when someone swings at me, I react. That's how I was trained," I said.

His look hardened, and he said with a hoarse voice, "You are lucky I didn't have my knife with me. I won't make that mistake again. I'm really good with a knife."

I pictured in my mind Darien's bloody hand with the missing fingers and elevated August and his sister to the very top of my suspect list. I said, "I'll keep that in mind."

"Best you do," he said, nodding his head and finally taking the seat I'd indicated.

I pulled my digital recorder from my pocket, placed it on the table, and sat down across from him. I told him I had a few questions I needed to ask and wondered if he would mind answering them.

"I got nothing to hide," he said. "I haven't done anything. Darien's latest fling, the short girl with long hair and weird-colored eyes, owes my little sister some money. I'm just helping her collect it."

I flipped the recorder on and said, "This is Detective Royce Fleming. I am in the Uintah County jail and am interviewing August Jeppson." Then I told him that what I was going to speak to him about had nothing to do with the scrape he and I had been in. "I am working on a murder case," I said.

"Darien?" he asked.

"That's right."

"I heard on the news he was dead. That's why I'm trying to help my sister. Darien owes her a bunch of back-alimony. And since he's dead, we figure his wife will need to pay her."

"Well, I'm not quite sure it works that way," I said. "For her to be required to pay, you'd have to get a court order."

"Then, that's what we'll do," he said, his voice still raspy. "About the death of Darien, there's really nothing I can say to help you, because I don't know anything about—"

I cut him off then and said, "I guess I'd better follow procedure and advise you of your rights."

I did that and he said, "I got nothing to hide. I don't need an attorney. I don't even like Darien. I have nothing to do with him."

"Why don't you like him?" I asked.

"Well, it's like this, Detective," he said. He stopped and cleared his throat. "I hope this clears up. You throw a pretty dangerous karate chop. But anyway, Darien wasn't very nice to my little sister. In fact, he was real mean to her."

"What did he do to Harley?" I asked.

"He'd get mad and kick and punch her. At first, she didn't say anything to me. Course, I was in prison for a while, and I couldn't have helped her then. But after I got out, she called me one night, crying. She said he'd knocked her down and kicked her."

"So what did you do?" I asked as I thought about the fact that what Darien had done to Ellerie wasn't new. He was an experienced abuser.

"I took him aside and explained the facts of life to him. He wanted to fight me, so I let him take a swing. That's the only swing he got in," he said with a smirk. "When I got through, he'd had an education."

"You didn't use your knife on him?" I asked.

"I didn't need to that time. I'd been working out in the joint, and I could throw a pretty mean punch," he bragged. "And Darien wasn't like you. He didn't know how to put up a real fight."

"So did that stop him from beating Harley?" I asked.

"For a while. At least, she didn't call me again for quite some time. The next time it happened was several months later, as far as I know. She called me again," he said. "I went looking for Darien, but I never did find him. He'd taken off. The next time I saw him was in court. She was divorcing him. I couldn't very well confront him then, and anyway, Harley asked me to let it go—said he was out of her life, that she would be getting alimony, and that she didn't want to take a chance on making him mad and messing that up."

"So when was the last time you saw him?" I asked.

He fidgeted in his seat and finally said, "I haven't seen him for a long time."

I needed to get more from him. It felt like he wasn't being honest with me. "Did he do anything else after the divorce to make you angry?" I asked.

His eyes narrowed. "You bet he did," he said. "He paid alimony for a while, and then he quit. She didn't hear from him for a long time—almost a year—so I helped her see if we could figure out where he'd gone. That was when we found that he'd married again. Anyway, to make a long story short, we figured out he was living in Vernal. We found a phone number, and my sister called him," he said. He stopped for a moment. He seemed deep in thought.

I tried to jar him out of his thoughts, hoping he would say something incriminating. I asked, "Did you talk to him?"

August shook his head. "No, but after several tries, Harley finally found him at home. All his bimbo wife would say when she answered the phone was that she didn't know where he was. Harley didn't ever leave her number because she figured Ellerie wouldn't give him the message, and if she did, she knew Darien would never call her back."

"I take it Harley told Ellerie who she was," I suggested.

August laughed. "She's not stupid," he said. "No, she just told her she was an old friend and needed to ask him about one of the kids they went to school with."

"But she finally reached him on the phone," I prodded.

"Yeah, finally. She told him she wanted him to pay her the alimony he owed," he said. He frowned and then continued. "Darien just laughed at her and told her that if she wanted the money, she would have to come get it. Then he laughed at her some more, and he told her he didn't make enough money to pay her and keep his new wife fed too, so she wasn't going to get another dime, that he figured he didn't owe it."

"So the two of you came to Vernal," I speculated.

"That's right," he confirmed. Then he stopped and thought for a minute. When he spoke again, he seemed to be carefully considering what he was saying. "Actually, I didn't, but Harley did. I only came after she called me and told me Darien was dead. That's when I told her she would need to go to Ellerie and demand the money he owed."

I was thoughtful for a moment, and then I asked, "Isn't it true that you emailed Ellerie using Darien's email account and tried to convince her that Darien was in Los Angeles?"

He grinned. "That was pretty smart, wasn't it?"

I didn't think it was, so I did not agree with him. Instead I asked, "How many emails did you send?"

He didn't even hesitate. "Two," he said. "We were trying to get her to put her house up for sale and then pay what she owed to Harley from the proceeds." He laughed. "We figured she'd know we meant business."

"Did she agree to sell the house?" I asked, knowing she had not responded to the emails.

"No. She didn't say anything," he answered. "She was probably wondering how her dead husband could send emails." He laughed out loud.

"August, you said you didn't come to Vernal until after we released the information on his death. Is that right?" I asked.

"Yup. That's how it was." Frankly, I didn't believe him. I was quite certain that Harley had told him. I must have looked skeptical, because he said, "You don't believe me."

"Your sister came before you knew he was dead," I said. Not that I needed to remind him. I paused for a moment before going on. "Let's talk about when she entered Ellerie's home and sprayed threats on the wall, saying that Ellerie would pay for killing Darien. And don't tell me she didn't, because I have a witness who confronted her in the house."

The color seemed to drain from August's face, and he fidgeted with his hands.

"I think you've been lying to me. You were here before Darien was killed, weren't you?" I asked.

He didn't speak for a minute. But when he did, all he said was, "I got nothing more to say. I want a lawyer."

CHAPTER TWENTY

WHEN I WENT TO PICK up Tommy, I gave Ellerie a thumbnail account of what had occurred in my interview. But I didn't tell her much. When I informed her he'd demanded an attorney, I saw the lights come on in her eyes. That's when she asked me, "He did it, didn't he?"

"It certainly makes him a serious suspect," I agreed. I had not told her about his bragging that he was good with a knife, but in my mind, that was what made me most interested in him as a suspect. I knew my work was cut out for me. I had to hit the streets and find out if anyone had seen him or Harley here the night of the killing.

But for right now, I needed to clear something up with Ellerie. "August told me Harley called you several times but that she didn't talk to Darien until he finally answered the phone. Do you remember those calls?" I asked.

She slowly shook her head and then suddenly said, "Wait. I wonder if that was who kept calling and saying she was an old friend of Darien's and was trying to find a former classmate. Oh my goodness. I had no idea that was who was calling. Of course, I didn't have any reason to think it was his ex-wife because I didn't know he had one."

Satisfied with her answer, I nodded and said, "I guess I'd better gather Tommy up. We can still spend some quality father-son time today."

Ellerie went into another room and came back with Tommy. He was as chipper as he could be. "Ellerie is fun," he said. "I like her a lot."

"She's a great lady, isn't she?" I said.

"Yep, she is, Dad. I like her as much as Kaci. Do you?"

I didn't have a ready answer for that curveball question. I glanced at Ellerie. She smiled and said, "Oh, I know all about Kaci. I guess you guys had a pretty nice trip to California."

"It was okay," I said. "Except for the part where I had to confront Donald, although that made the confrontation worth my time."

"Was it Kaci who couldn't help you with Tommy today?" she asked perceptively.

"She was on a date in Denver," I said. "Did Tommy tell you how we met her?"

"No, but he sure seems to like her," she said.

"She is my attorney's secretary," I said. "She had a little confrontation with someone."

"Yeah, she tried to keep that crazy lady from stealing me. She knocked Kaci down. But Dad saved me," Tommy said. Then his little chin began to quiver. "Dad, will she try to take me again? She is scary. I don't ever want to go with her. I want to stay with you." I knelt on the floor and took him in my arms. "Tommy, no one is ever going to take you from me."

"Do you promise?" he asked.

"Yes, Tommy. I promise."

"What about that lady?" he persisted.

"That was all a big misunderstanding on her part. You don't need to worry about her," I assured him. I wished I felt as much assurance as I was trying to convey to him.

I stood up with him in my arms and looked over at Ellerie. Mrs. Mavey had entered the room during our frank little conversation and was standing with her hand on Ellerie's arm. To my surprise, both women had tears in their eyes. Pamela said, "Detective Fleming, I will help with Tommy anytime you need." She glanced at Ellerie, who was wiping her eyes. "We both will, won't we Ellerie?"

"Yes," she said firmly. "Tommy, I promise I won't let anyone hurt you. You are a special boy."

I should have been out the door by then, but I wasn't, and as a consequence, my son once again spoke his mind. "Do you think Dad's special too?" Ellerie blushed a deep shade of crimson. But she held her head high, looked at Tommy, and said, "Yes, I think your dad is special. He has been a big help to me."

Pamela grinned. I thanked the two of them for their help and made a quick getaway. Once we were in my sheriff's vehicle, I said, "Tommy, sometimes you shouldn't say everything that is on your mind. It might hurt people's feelings."

He put a little pout on his face and said, "What did I say?"

So I spent the rest of the ride home discussing with him the fact that sometimes we should keep our thoughts to ourselves so we wouldn't make someone else feel bad. I thought I had made some headway until I pulled into our driveway. He looked over at me and asked, "Dad, do you like Ellerie the best, or do you like Kaci the best?"

Okay, so I wasn't doing so well. I looked at him, smiled, ruffled his hair, and said, "I like you the best. And don't you ever forget it."

***

Sunday was the first day since the murder that I didn't get called out to work on the case. Tommy and I attended meetings at our ward. I'd missed the week before, as I'd been working on the murder. He'd gone to church with my parents that day. I was glad I could take him today. Afterward we went home, and I was preparing lunch when my doorbell rang. I hurried to the door, making sure my pistol was still in my shoulder holster. I wasn't taking any chances until I got all the recent problems behind me.

I opened the door, and there stood a smiling Connie Bost, dispatcher, with a plate of warm cookies in her hand. "Hi, Royce," she said. "I thought you and Tommy could use a treat. May I come in?"

What could I do? Connie was a very pretty, sweet girl, but I felt very little attraction to her. I had no intention of asking her out again, but I was not a rude person, so I invited her in.

"Thanks, Royce," she said, batting her eyelashes seductively. I wasn't affected, but I accepted the plate of cookies from her and sat it on an end table. Tommy wandered in, saw the cookies, and helped himself.

"Hey, only one now. You can have more after we eat dinner," I said.

"So this is Tommy," Connie said, smiling at my little guy. Even though we'd gone out together, she'd never met Tommy. I would have been content to leave it at that. "I'm Connie, your dad's friend," Connie told him with a wink.

"You're pretty," my little Casanova said. He was rewarded with a bright white smile. He could have left it at that, but not my Tommy. He was becoming as much a matchmaker as my parents. "Don't you think she's pretty, Dad?" he asked.

I couldn't lie, so I said, "Yes, she is." Of course, I couldn't explain to him in front of Connie that there was more than a pretty face to be considered. That conversation would have to be saved for another day, and even then, I wasn't sure if that would be too much information for him. I could just picture him explaining what I'd told him to someone like Kaci.

"We were just about to sit down to dinner," I said with the intent of encouraging Connie to excuse herself and leave. "Thanks for the cookies."

"Could you use help getting dinner on the table?" she asked presumptuously.

"I think I've got it," I said.

"Dad." I glanced at Tommy. I could read his mind, but I couldn't zip his lips. "We have enough for Connie too, don't we?"

He already had her name down pat, and now what could I say? We did have plenty. "Sure, I think we do," I said, trying to keep the irritation from my voice.

I wasn't a bad cook. I'd had to learn. As a single parent, I wanted my boy to eat well. So I had worked at it. Dinner today was meatloaf, mashed potatoes, and creamed peas and carrots. I hadn't made any dessert, but of course, we now had cookies. To make matters worse, my cooking, simple though the meal was, impressed Connie.

She pitched right in and helped me clean up after we'd finished eating. We were not quite finished when my cell phone rang. It was not a call out on the homicide, but it was close enough. It was Reggie Hutchins on the phone. I still had to catch up with his father and interview him about what he remembered from the night he'd played pool with the victim and his brother.

"Hi, Reggie," I said. "Has your dad finally come home? I sure would like to talk to him."

"No," he said. "He called and said he and Mom had decided to take a few days and go on vacation. I guess I wasn't invited. But that's okay. They both work hard and deserve a vacation. So I'm not complaining."

"So what can I do for you, Reggie?" I asked, disappointed and relieved at the same time. I was disappointed that I still couldn't get the interview out of the way, although with Harley and her brother, August, as my prime suspects, I wasn't sure how much Andrew Hutchins could add. I was relieved because I didn't need my Sabbath spoiled with my work like the one last week had been.

"You said if I needed help on my math, I could call you. I've done pretty good ever since you were here, but I'm stumped again," he said. "I'm sorry, but would you mind coming over for a few minutes? I know it wouldn't take you long to explain what I'm missing."

I considered it for a moment, decided that I could take Tommy with me, and told Reggie, "Sure, my son and I can come in a few minutes. Will that work?"

"Is your son good at math too?" Reggie asked as I watched Connie pull Tommy aside and whisper in his ear.

I chuckled. "Actually, he is, but not at your level, Reggie. He's only seven years old. We'll be right over."

"He can play with my new puppy while you help me," Reggie said.

"Sounds good to me. See you shortly," I promised and ended the call.

"I guess I need to go," I told Connie, grateful for the excuse from Reggie, because I had a feeling Connie would have figured out a way to spend the rest of the afternoon, and—who knew?—maybe even the evening with us.

Her little whispered discussion with Tommy, it turned out, was a conniving one. "You go ahead, Royce. Tommy and I will be fine here until you get back."

I had no doubt Connie wanted to get me cornered. I think she had marriage in mind, but I could imagine what a marriage to her would be like. She was a tricky girl. I could almost imagine all the things she'd slyly get me into. *No way!* But for now, what should I do? Then I remembered that Reggie mentioned he had a brand-new puppy. I couldn't count the times Tommy had begged me for a dog. "Or do you want to go play with the puppy?" I asked him.

"What puppy?" he asked.

"The fellow who just called me is a friend I'm helping with some math problems. He has a new puppy, and he says you can play with it," I said, desperate to entice him into going with me and keeping my Sunday afternoon from being ruined by a well-meaning girl who I honestly didn't want to spend more time with.

"A puppy?" he asked, his eyes lighting up. "Can we bring it home?"

"No, it's Reggie's, but you can play with it while we're there."

Tommy thought for a moment. Then he looked at Connie. She was grinning. "We can have popcorn while Dad goes?" he asked.

"Yes, and punch if you have some," Connie said slyly.

"We have some Kool-Aid," he said brightly.

I was afraid my son's stomach trumped playing with a puppy he couldn't have. "I'd love to watch him for you," Connie said. "You go ahead."

"Keep the door locked behind me," I said in defeat. "It's been a rough few days."

"I will take good care of him, Royce. You know you can trust me."

Yeah, I did. I could trust her to push her way into my life. I gave in. "Thanks. I'll be right back," I said.

Reggie's puppy, a gorgeous little Alaskan malamute, greeted me enthusiastically the moment Reggie opened the door. I petted the puppy, or wrestled with him would probably be more accurate. He wiggled and jumped and acted like life was the most wonderful thing he could imagine. "He's beautiful, Reggie," I said. "Where did you get him? You don't see a lot of malamutes around here."

"My uncle is from Alaska. He brought him to me yesterday."

"I see. How much did you have to give him?" I asked.

"Oh, nothing," he said. "He gave him to me."

"And he brought him all the way here from Alaska just to give him to you?" I asked.

"No, he's thinking about moving here. He says he's getting to where he can't take the cold weather in Anchorage. He's looking for a job," he explained.

"Is he your dad's brother?" I asked.

"No, my mom's," he said. "He's her little brother. He's not married, and he was given Ranger by a neighbor when Ranger's mother died a few days ago. The guy gave the whole litter away. But when my uncle decided to come to Utah, he called me about the dog. He said he was going to have to give him away because he'd probably be living in an apartment. When he said I could have him, I took him up on his offer."

"Well, he's a beauty, that's for sure," I said as I stood up. The pup continued to jump at me. But Reggie told him to quit jumping. He looked at his new master and then, to my surprise, obeyed.

I spent the next thirty minutes working with Reggie on his math. "I got it now," he said. "I don't know what I'd do without your help. Thanks."

"You are welcome. Like I said, I'll help you anytime I can."

"How come you didn't bring your son?" he suddenly asked. "I thought you said you were bringing him. Did he stay with his mother?"

"He doesn't have a mother," I said. "I had intended to bring him. But there was lady who was there having lunch with us, and she offered to watch him for me."

"A girlfriend, huh?" he said with a grin.

"No, Reggie, she's not my girlfriend. Although I think she wants to be."

"Does your son like her?" he asked.

"Unfortunately, yes, but he likes every woman I meet. He fancies himself a matchmaker."

"Sounds like he wants a mother," Reggie said with surprising perceptiveness.

"I think so, but his dad isn't real anxious to have a wife," I said.

"Why not?" he asked.

"My first marriage ended in disaster. I don't think I want to take a chance on having that happen again," I said.

"I bet it wasn't your fault," he said. "You are a really nice guy. My dad would never go out of his way to help a stranger the way you've helped me."

I don't know why I was so willing to talk frankly to Reggie, but I was. I explained about how Mayra had left when Tommy was a baby. "She blamed me," I said. "But she didn't want her own son. She gave up her parental rights. But I worry that whatever it was about me that made her turn on me is something that would cause another marriage to fail. Anyway, Tommy and I get along just fine by ourselves."

"I'm sure you're a great dad," he said as I once more gave some attention to Ranger, his beautiful puppy. "Bring him over and let him meet my dog sometime. Will you do that?" I promised that I would.

As I left Reggie's house a few minutes later, I couldn't help but wonder what he'd be like if he had parents who spent more time with him and less time smoking pot or drinking at the bars. I really quite liked the kid. He had a good heart if one just looked beyond his rings, his long hair, and his sloppy pants. I hoped that by helping him with his math I could influence his life in a positive way. Maybe he'd even go to church with Tommy and me if I invited him. I resolved to think and pray about that.

At home, I found Connie and Tommy deeply involved in a game of Candy Land. It was one of his favorite games, and I felt a twinge of jealousy watching someone else playing with him. A bowl with a few popcorn kernels in it and a couple of empty glasses on the table were now being ignored as the two of them concentrated on the game.

"I've beat Connie twice," Tommy bragged as I approached the kitchen table. "But I think she let me."

She looked up and smiled. "Honestly, Royce, this kid is good. I didn't let him win. We're almost finished here. Do you want to join us for the next game?"

I looked at her for a moment, and as I thought that I would rather she left, I felt like a jerk. Tommy was having a great time. And in all honesty, I had to admit once again that Connie was not only attractive but she was also a nice girl. "Sure," I said. "But, you know, I'm pretty good."

"I can beat you, Dad," Tommy said. "I bet Connie can even beat you." He laughed, his eyes bright. They fell fondly on Connie, and I gulped. He really did need a mother. Maybe I should give myself some slack and think about what was best for my son.

Connie helped us fix tuna sandwiches that evening. Reggie called me again at about seven o'clock with one question about his math. "Are you still at it?" I asked.

"Yes. I want to do well," he said.

"Thanks for calling me," I told him, my heart touched at his new perseverance. I talked him through the problem, and then I said, "Call again if you get stuck."

Connie was studying me as I ended the call. "That's neat, Royce. You are a great guy." Her eyes were shining, and I gulped again.

We continued to play games until, finally, a little after eight, she said, "I haven't had this much fun in forever. Thanks, Royce and Tommy. I think I'd better go. I go back on shift tomorrow. Thanks for inviting me to stay, Royce," she said as I saw her to the door. "We need to do this again."

To my surprise, the word, "Sure," slipped out. She really was a nice girl.

CHAPTER TWENTY-ONE

I HADN'T BEEN AT THE police station for long before I got a call from the county attorney's office requesting that I be in court that morning for the arraignments of Harley Pearson and her brother, August Jeppson. I wasn't sure until then that they hadn't been bailed out. So I met with a prosecutor for a minute before court began and then went into the courtroom. As expected, both of them pled not guilty to the charges I had brought against them. Then, to my dismay, they were appointed counsel.

When they were taken back to the jail, I met their court-appointed attorney, Mark Lanning, and told him I wanted to meet with his new clients in the jail. He agreed that it would be okay, and we set a time for that at one o'clock in the afternoon.

Mark was about my age, but from the interactions I'd had with him, he seemed to be a conscientious attorney. I quite liked him. I spent the morning in the office doing further research on Harley and August. Harley had a DUI conviction, but other than a couple of speeding tickets, that was it. August, as I'd already learned, was a sex offender and had a history of violence.

I phoned a couple of officers who had handled previous cases against him and was told in each case that August had severe anger problems. Was he capable of murder? Both men said that in their judgment, it was only a matter of time. A call to his most recent parole officer confirmed what the officers had told me. I considered everything I had learned so far. He was violent. He was an angry man. And he was most likely capable of murder. Add to that the facts that he loved knives and claimed to be proficient in their use and that he had motive. He disliked Darien, and he was angry that he had refused to pay the alimony owed to his sister. But there was one major drawback. August had big feet. He could not have left the footprints at the murder scene.

His sister, Harley, on the other hand, had small feet. I needed to interview the two of them. And then I would probably need to get with officers from where they lived and see if I could get search warrants. I needed to find the shoes, a knife that might match the wounds on my victim's hand, and whatever else I could come up with.

I still had some time before I needed to meet Mark Lanning for the interviews at the jail, so I decided to go talk to the man who had discovered the body, Stu Goldman. I didn't bother to call ahead. He was sixty-eight, a widower, and retired. I thought there was a good chance he would be home. As I was leaving the building, Chief Collins was just coming in. "Hey, Royce," he called out. "Got a minute?"

I was not in any hurry, and anyway, who told their boss they didn't have time for them? I liked my job, so I followed him back to his office. He wanted an update on the case. He pumped his fist when I told him what I had on Harley and August. "Great work," he said. "Keep me posted. Go see Mr. Goldman now."

I found Goldman in his front yard weeding some pretty flowerbeds. When he saw me, he stood up, brushed his hands off against his pants, and extended a slightly dirty hand. We shook, and then he asked, "Have you got the killer yet, Detective?"

"I'm getting closer," I said. "That's why I'm here. I have a couple of viable suspects in jail. I will be interviewing them right after lunch. I just wanted to talk to you before I speak with them again."

"Whatever I can help you with, I'd be glad to. I want the killer caught," he said. "Let's go in out of the heat."

He offered me a cold glass of water, which I accepted. Then, sitting on a soft brown sofa in his living room, I said, "One of my suspects, a man, drives an older-model green Ford pickup. The other one, his sister, drives a white Ford Fusion. Did you see any vehicles matching those descriptions the day of the murder?"

Stu rubbed his chin, closed his eyes, and was thoughtful for a moment. Then he opened his eyes. "Not on the day of the murder or the night of the murder, for that matter, but I'm pretty sure I saw a green Ford pickup the next day. I was nervous, and I sat out on my porch much of the day. I'm sure a truck like that came by."

"You are very observant," I said. "Did you get a look at the driver?"

He again closed his eyes and rubbed his chin. Then he said, "Small person. Black hair, I think. Came to about the shoulders."

Harley Pearson had black hair of about that length. I leaned forward and asked, "Was it a man or a woman?"

He slowly shook his head and said, "I figured it was a man. You know, you expect a guy to be driving an old but spruced-up truck like that."

"But could it have been a woman?" I pressed.

"Yeah, I suppose it could," he said.

I kept questioning him, but he couldn't describe the clothes and hadn't noticed the license plate. He didn't remember seeing a white Fusion, but he admitted that he didn't know what a Fusion looked like. I found a picture of one on the Internet on my cell phone and showed it to him. "Nope, that doesn't look familiar," he said. "I'm sorry. I'm not much help."

"Actually, you have been a great deal of help," I said. I looked at my watch. "I'd better go. If you think of any more details, call me."

My visit had taken me into the lunch hour. There was not enough time to grab a sandwich before going to the jail, so I stopped at the office. I spent a few minutes telling Chief Collins what I had learned from Mr. Goldman.

He smiled and said, "You know, Royce, it's not unheard of to have someone drive by the scene of the crime after the fact. If I had to guess, I'd say the Pearson woman was driving her brother's truck. It all fits. See what they tell you, and then it will be time to check into any alibis they might give you. I just don't want them to get out of jail before you get enough that we can hold them for murder."

His assessment mirrored mine. I was feeling pretty confident when I got back into my vehicle to drive to the jail. Just like every other time I had checked on the air that day, it was Connie that responded. For some reason, I didn't bristle at her overly friendly voice the way I had before the previous evening. I could picture her face as she watched my son. He liked her. Perhaps I should consider taking her out again sometime. When I checked off the air at the jail, I had about made up my mind to call her again and give myself a chance to get to know her better. But by the time I walked inside, I had reminded myself that my personal issues were not resolved. It wouldn't be fair to Connie to lead her on at all when I couldn't correct whatever flaws had turned Mayra against me.

I met Mark Lanning when I walked in. "Which one do you want to question first?" he asked.

"I think I'll start with Harley," I responded.

"Okay, that'll be fine. Let's lay some ground rules before they bring her in," he said. "If I tell her not to answer a question, you have to back off. Is that okay?"

"I guess it has to be," I said. "Have you talked to her yet?"

"I got out of court early, so I came over at eleven. I spoke briefly with both of them."

"Nice people, aren't they?" I said with a grin.

He looked at me, his expression neutral. But then he said, "Just because they aren't very pleasant doesn't mean they are killers. Keep that in mind, Detective."

"I will," I responded.

We followed a correctional officer back into the jail and she showed us to a room. "Bring Harley Pearson first," the attorney said.

A few minutes later, the officer ushered Harley into the interview room. She had a smile for her attorney, a glare for me. The officer left the handcuffs on, but she handed a note to me.

I read it. She'd written that another inmate, Mayra Sills, was asking to see me. I looked up. "When we get through here, I'll see her," I said even as I wondered what my ex could possibly want.

I set my recorder on the table and introduced, for the purpose of my recording, who the participants in the interview were. Then we began.

"You are the ex-wife of Darien Pearson, is that right?" I asked.

"He was my biggest mistake," she said with a growl.

I couldn't help but remember that I'd said the same thing about my marriage to Mayra on several occasions. "So you no longer have feelings for him?" I asked.

"Are you kidding me?" she asked. "I hate the guy. He wouldn't even pay me the alimony he owed me, but you already know that."

"Yes, I know that. Did you and your brother, August, have discussions about Darien and what you could do to get the money you believe he owed you?"

"Of course we did," she said. "I called Darien and asked him to pay me, but he laughed at me. Can you believe that? He laughed at me and said if I wanted the money, I'd have to come get it from him. But after that, he told me he didn't have the money and that he didn't think he owed it, so I could just forget about it. He said I wouldn't get another dime."

"Tell me about the emails you sent to Ellerie Pearson on Darien's email account," I said in a quick change of topic.

"That was my brother's idea," she said, surprise in her gaze.

"But you are the one who knew how to get into his email and use it?" I asked.

"Yes. I still can't believe he hadn't changed his email password," she said. "What an idiot."

I decided that was enough on that subject. "Okay, Harley. After he refused to pay you, is that when you and August came to Vernal to try to collect the money?" I asked.

"Yes. We didn't know how else I was going to get it."

"Both of you came?" I asked.

"Yeah, I wasn't going to face Darien by myself. He'd beaten me up enough times that I wasn't going to risk it again," she said.

I thought for a moment. August had told me Harley had come alone to Vernal, discovered that Darien was dead, and he had come later. I had believed that he was lying to me about her coming first. Now I was quite certain of it. I decided to leave that for now. "Harley, you entered Ellerie's house and wrote on her wall with red paint, isn't that true?" I asked.

She looked at her attorney. He nodded at her to answer. He'd read my report by now, I suspected, so he probably knew I could prove that she'd done it. "Well, after I found out he was dead, it made me mad," she admitted. "I went to their house to tell his wife I still wanted my money. She wasn't there. I left and bought a can of paint and came back. She still wasn't home, so I went in and left her a message."

"You accused her of killing Darien, didn't you?" I asked.

"Yeah, and I still think she did. He'd hurt her," she said.

"How bad had he hurt her?" I asked.

"Pretty bad. She lost her baby. At least, that was what I was told," she said.

"Who told you that?" I asked.

She looked at her attorney. "You can tell him," he said.

"I heard it on the news," she said.

I narrowed my eyes and tried to look intimidating. "Harley, that was not on the news. Is that where you heard that Darien had been murdered?"

She looked confused. Finally she said, "Yeah, I'm pretty sure I heard it on the news."

"Harley, his death wasn't on the news either, not until way after that. Why don't you think about it for a second and tell me where you heard it," I said.

I leaned back and stared at her. She squirmed. Finally, her attorney spoke. "Did someone tell you about it?" he asked her.

"Yeah," she said quickly. "Someone told me."

"Who told you?" I asked.

She looked at her lawyer. He nodded and said, "It's okay. He needs to know."

She hung her head for a minute. I let the silence work on her. Finally she said, "My brother told me."

"August?"

"Yeah, he told me."

"When did he tell you?" I asked.

She hesitated but finally answered. "Okay, it was that same day—the day I went in and wrote on the wall."

"So you admit you went into her house and that you painted on the wall?" I asked.

"Don't answer that," her lawyer advised her. *Too late*, I thought. He'd already let her admit it only moments ago.

She looked at me with a sneer, like she'd shown me. "Did you talk to Darien's twin brother, Donald, that day?" I asked.

I could see that Mark was about to object to that question, but she answered before he could speak. "I saw him in the house. He broke in just like I did."

Mark frowned and shook his head. "Harley, you don't answer until I give you the go ahead," he admonished her.

"Mr. Lanning," I said, trying to keep the smugness I was feeling from my voice. "Don't you think we should go ahead and clear the matter up now?" I asked. "She's already admitted she was in the house and that she saw Donald Pearson there."

He leaned back in his chair and took a deep breath. After he'd exhaled, he said, "I think enough has been said about that. Let's move on, Detective."

"Very well," I said. "Harley, does your brother usually carry a knife?"

"Don't answer that," Mark said.

"Okay, is he good with a knife?" I asked.

"That's all I will allow about a knife," Mark said sharply. "Move on to something else, unless you are done."

"I'm not finished," I said. Then I asked Harley where she was between the hours of six and eleven on the night Darien was murdered.

As I expected, she hedged. Then she looked at her lawyer. "I don't have to answer that, do I?"

He nodded his head and said, "I think you should. Where were you?"

"I . . . ah . . . oh yeah, I was in a hotel that night. My brother and I shared a room with two beds," she finally stammered.

"What hotel?" I asked.

More hesitation, and then she said, "I can't remember."

"Whose name did the two of you check in under?" I asked.

She was having a really hard time answering without spending a lot of time thinking. I glanced at her attorney, and he had that, *Oh, boy, I think I have a guilty client* look. I was pretty sure he knew he had his work cut out for him.

Harley finally said, "I think it was in August's name."

I then asked her where she was each day and each night from the night of the murder until I put her in jail before the weekend. She had a tough time. She tried several times to say she was at her home in Salt Lake, but then I reminded her that she had been in Vernal the day she'd broken into Ellerie's house. She stammered and tried to say she'd been in a hotel again, but she didn't know which one. But then she said, "No, I was at home in Salt Lake. I wasn't in Vernal then, and I didn't ever go into Ellerie's house." *Good grief.* What kind of dummy did she think I was?

Her poor attorney was having as hard a time as I was keeping up with where she'd been on specific dates. Of course, I knew, and I'm sure he did, that she was lying. Finally, I asked, "How often do you drive your brother's truck?"

"My brother's truck?" she asked, looking slightly dazed.

"Yes, his old green Ford," I said.

"I don't know. I drive it sometimes, I guess, but not very much," she answered. She rubbed her forehead and said, "Are we about done here? I don't feel very good."

"I guess we need to wrap it up, Detective," her attorney said.

"I have just one more question, Mark. Then I'll call it good."

"Okay, but only one more."

"Did you kill Darien Pearson?"

"Don't answer that!" Mark shouted. "That's it! We are done here."

I ended the recording and shut it off. Mark signaled for an officer and had her take Harley back. "And when you do, we'll need to speak with August Jeppson," I said.

But Mark Lanning said, "Just a moment. I don't think so."

"Why?" I asked, irritated, as the officer removed Harley from the room.

"Well, I don't think I can represent him. After listening to your interview with Harley, I'm convinced it would be a conflict to handle him too."

I was not surprised. In fact, I'd been expecting him to come to that conclusion earlier. "I guess you're right," I said. "But I think I'll speak to him anyway. He might decide to proceed without counsel at this point." I knew I was pushing the limit here, but it was worth a try.

"No," Mark said abruptly. "I'm still his counsel of record. And I simply am not going to allow it. I will contact the court tomorrow and ask to have conflict counsel appointed, but for now, I simply cannot allow you to talk to him."

I knew when I was beat. And it was frustrating, but there was nothing I could do about it. I was pretty sure I had the right people in jail, but I didn't have enough yet to charge them with murder. To Mark, who was gathering up his papers, I said, "I'll be doing some follow-up investigation. I'll let you know when I need to speak to Harley again."

"We'll see," he said and left.

The officer returned a minute later, and she had my ex-wife in tow. She explained that Mayra had insisted she needed to speak with me, that she had something critically important to talk to me about.

She sat down. "Hello, Mayra," I said.

"Hi, Royce."

To the officer, I said, "Would you mind taking the cuffs off her?"

She looked questioningly at me. I nodded, and she removed the cuffs and then left the room.

CHAPTER TWENTY-TWO

I HAD NOTHING TO DISCUSS with her at this point, so I simply waited for her to begin. She hung her head, and tears sprang from her eyes. "I'm sorry. I'm being a boob," she said. "Give me just a minute. I have some important things to tell you."

I said nothing, but watching her hurt me. I had loved this girl once. I had planned to spend forever with her. And as badly as she had hurt me, and despite the way she had so brazenly tried to steal Tommy away from me, I could not find it in my heart to hate her. In fact, I had to fight to keep from letting my own emotions spill over.

Still, I said nothing. Finally, she wiped her eyes and her wet cheeks with the back of her hand, looked up at me, and said, "I didn't know. Honest, I didn't know."

"Didn't know what?" I asked, trying to be firm.

"I thought the court really had ordered Tommy to be given to me," she said. I made no comment. I wasn't sure where this was all going. Finally she spoke again. "Ed's boss, the senior partner in the firm, came to see me yesterday afternoon."

"He came on Sunday?" I asked.

"It was important. He had some things he said I deserved to know—that I needed to know." I waited while she again rubbed her eyes. She'd always been such a beautiful girl. Right then, she looked pretty rough. She finally continued. "He told me Fred Zietz had raped a teenage girl and then given her parents a bunch of money to keep it quiet."

Once again, she stopped talking. She looked at the ceiling and then at the wall, and finally at her hands that she now held folded on the table in front of her. Without looking up, she said, "Ed figured it out. I don't know how he did, but he did."

Suddenly, I could see exactly where this was going. But I didn't interrupt her. I needed to let her tell her story in her way and at her pace. When she again spoke, her voice was so low I had to strain to hear her. "Ed wanted a child badly. He wanted a son, actually. He and I couldn't have children. We went to a doctor. We both had tests. The problem was his. Anyway, he is the one who suggested we should get Tommy."

She finally looked up at me and said, "I still love him, Royce. I know I left, but my heart has ached for him ever since."

I wasn't sure I believed that. I said, "You should have thought about that before you left and before you gave up all parental rights to him."

"I know. You're right, Royce. I was wrong. I hate myself for what I did," she said as she once again looked down at her folded hands. "Ed told me there was a way to get him. I told him you would never give him up."

"You told him right," I said with a growl.

She nodded her head, and then she went on. "He said he asked Fred to represent us."

"At what cost?" I asked, pretty sure what she was going to say.

And she said it. "Fred told Ed he would get Tommy for us through the courts if he would not disclose what he knew about the rape. Ed had threatened to turn him in, and this was Fred's way of keeping him quiet. He knew how badly Ed wanted a son."

"And your husband agreed," I said. "Mayra, that's blackmail, pure and simple. It makes him no better than Fred."

"I know, and I am divorcing Ed because of it," she stated flatly. "He and Fred both lost their jobs. They are also going to lose the right to practice law, and they could both go to prison."

I had no sympathy for either of them. But I was just a tiny bit sympathetic to my former wife. "They belong in prison. They both knew how serious what they were doing was."

"Royce," Mayra began again, trying to fight back more tears. "I didn't know the order I had was false. I would never have come to get Tommy if I'd known. And I believed those guys when they said you had been served and didn't bother to come to court. They made me believe you didn't care if I took Tommy."

"How could you think that?" I asked. "He is my whole world."

"I don't know. I mean, I hadn't seen you in years, and for all I knew, you needed a break from being a single father. I'm sorry, Royce. I'm more sorry than I can say."

"I'm glad you are. You frightened Tommy, Mayra. And you scared me too," I said.

She hung her head and was quiet again for a little while. After a minute or more she said, "I still love you, Royce."

That rocked me. I didn't even know how to respond to that. So I didn't. "And I really did want to get Tommy back," she added. "I made myself think Ed would be a good father, but I knew deep down he wouldn't. There is only one man who can be a good father for him. That's you, Royce."

"I'm glad to hear you think that," I said coldly.

"Royce, I wish I'd never left you," she said. "That was so stupid of me. You have no idea how badly I've felt all these years."

I rubbed my hand across my face. I didn't know what to believe and what not to about what she was saying. The only thing I was certain of was that she had left me, had left Tommy, had given up her rights to be his mother. But there was something I wanted to know. "Mayra, I need for you to explain something to me," I said.

She looked at me. The look was tender, painfully reminding me of how it had once been with her. "I'll tell you anything you want to know," she said. "No more lies. I promise."

"When you filed for divorce, you claimed that it was because of how I acted toward you, how I treated you. You said you simply couldn't take me anymore. For the life of me, I don't know what it was about me that hurt you so badly. I'd like to know that now. Will you tell me?"

Tears erupted from her eyes. They ran down her cheeks and fell onto the table. I felt my stomach clench. Whatever I had done must have been really bad. How could I have not known? But I had to now. I prayed she would tell me. "Please, Mayra, it has haunted me ever since. What did I do?"

With a face so stricken that it actually made me feel sorry for her, she finally managed to talk again. "I lied," she said. And again, tears poured like a fountain. I handed her my handkerchief, and she wiped at her face and her eyes.

"What do you mean, you lied?" I pressed after she finally seemed to have her emotions under control.

"It was never you; it was me. You didn't do anything to hurt me," she said. "I couldn't have asked to be treated better. You were a wonderful husband. I loved you then, and I love you now."

I hoped she was telling me the truth, that I really was not flawed in some way I'd never recognized. But she loved me? That I wasn't so sure about. "Thanks for telling me. I hope that's the truth."

"It is, Royce. Honest. It was all my fault. I was scared of raising a baby. Whenever he'd cry, I'd panic. But you were always so sweet with him. You would settle him down when I couldn't," she said.

Thinking back, I realized that was true. But I had never faulted her when she'd hand him to me, howling like a wolf. "You were doing okay. You were the one who was with him most of the time," I said. "You would have been a great mother."

She shook her head, and suddenly she looked angry. "No, I couldn't. That day, the day I left, he was crying terribly. I tried everything I could to calm him down. Nothing worked. I wanted you to walk in and take him and calm him for me. But I knew it would be a while before you could come home." Mayra shuddered. "So you wonder why I left that day? I'll tell you why. It was for Tommy's sake. I wanted to hurt him. I wanted to shake him and make him be quiet." She was shaking herself as she spoke those words. "Royce," she said, looking at me with those dark-green eyes of hers that I had thought were so beautiful. "I loved him. I didn't want to hurt him. I was about to. So I put him in his crib, packed some stuff, and left. I did it for him, Royce. Don't you see?"

"I'm sorry," I told her. "I had no idea it was that rough on you. Why didn't you tell me? Why didn't you ask me to help you get some counseling or something? I would have done anything to help you," I said. And I knew that to be true. I had loved her dearly.

"I've changed now, Royce. I was only nineteen when we got married. I wasn't mature enough to be a mother. You had served a mission and gone to college for a while. You were so sure of yourself. You were so strong. I loved you for that, but I hated myself for being so weak."

"Oh, Mayra, I wish I'd known," I said as I felt my emotions coming to the surface. I didn't want to cry in front of her, but I felt like it. My heart was breaking for the beautiful girl I had once loved so deeply.

"I've grown up since then," she said softly. "I'm a different person. I married Ed because I knew I'd blown it with you. But he wasn't you. He wasn't the kind of man you are. I never really loved him. Oh, I tried to. I tried really hard. And I wanted us to have a baby so that I could prove to myself and . . . and to God that I could raise a baby." Her eyes were focused on the tabletop. Slowly she looked up. "I wanted to prove to the only man I have ever loved that I could do it. I wanted to prove it to you, Royce. But Ed and I couldn't have a baby."

"I'm sorry. You would probably have done better a second time," I said. I didn't know if that was true or not, but I wanted to believe it was.

For a full minute or more, neither of us spoke. I felt the urge to reach out and put my hand on hers, to try to give her a small amount of comfort. I resisted the urge. She finally spoke again, softly, her voice filled with emotion, her eyes soft and shining. "Royce. We could try again if you will take another chance on me. I know I could be a good mother for Tommy. And I know I could be a good wife for you. I want to make it up to you for all the hurt I've inflicted. I want you back. I want my family back. Please, that's what I want."

Once again, she had stunned me. I did what I had resisted just moments before. I put one of my hands on hers. It felt so familiar, so soft. I was shaken to the very core. She put her other hand on mine and looked at me in the way she had from across the alter in the temple when we were married, when I'd thought we were forever.

But reality hit me, and I jerked my hand free. She looked at me in surprise. "I won't hurt you again, Royce. I promise. I love you. Don't you understand that?"

"I need to go," I said.

"Don't. Not yet. Can't we talk about this?" she begged. I saw no anger on her face—only pain. I wanted to leave, and yet I didn't. Not quite yet. "Please, I'm begging you," she said. The look in her eyes now was almost more than I could bear.

"Mayra, I have to think about more than myself. I have to think about Tommy. You scared him when you tried to steal him. I don't want to scare him again," I said.

The hurt in her eyes was real. She couldn't fake what I was seeing. But I had to resist. I had to have time to think. My love for her had long since grown cold. I didn't know that I could ever get it back. But to her, I said, "I need to think about it, Mayra," and stood up.

I signaled for the officer. She entered the room. Mayra was sitting with her hands folded in front of her. She looked so afraid, so vulnerable, so fragile, so hurt. "I want you out of this jail," I said, my voice cracking. "I'll see what I can do."

She did not look at me. But she said, "Thank you. And, ah, will you pray about what we talked about?"

The officer looked from her to me and back to her again. "I will," I promised, and then I made my escape.

My stomach was churning. Hot bile rose into my throat. I felt physically ill. And it wasn't because I hated Mayra. Far from it. I just had received a jolt I had never expected. Her sudden desire to return into my son's and my lives was as shocking as her sudden, unexplained departure had been more than six years ago. I veered to the men's room and emptied my stomach. Then I sat there in that stall and cried. I hadn't cried like this since she left me. I heard two or three other people come into the restroom and then leave. I had to get back to my car. I had to get home. I needed to put myself together. I eased out of the stall and washed my face. My eyes were red and swollen. There was nothing I could do about that. So I left the restroom and walked quickly toward the door, my eyes veering neither left nor right. I prayed I wouldn't meet anyone while I was hurrying to my car. My prayer was answered. I had more prayers to offer, but I wasn't ready to do that yet. My mind was whirling around. Confusion reigned. I was a wreck.

I had a hard time keeping my voice steady as I checked on the air and again as I checked out at home. Connie was dispatching. She called me by my call number and said, "Are you okay?"

The concern in her voice only added to my confusion. I wasn't okay, but I told her I was, and then I hurried into my house and collapsed onto my sofa. I don't think I moved for at least an hour. I prayed at lot, but not on my knees. I needed to do that, but I just stayed on the sofa. When I did finally sit up, it was to answer my cell phone. I had a murder case to wrap up. I couldn't spend more time right now worrying about what I should do. I glanced at the screen on my iPhone. It was central dispatch. I answered it, my voice as steady as I could make it. "Royce, it's Connie. I know something's wrong. What can I do for you?"

"I'm okay, Connie," I said. "I need to get back to work. I wasn't feeling too well. I'm okay now. I do need to check with my mother and make sure Tommy's okay. So don't worry about me when I check off there. I won't be long."

"Okay, but if you need me, I'm here for you," she said. And after the enjoyable time we'd had the evening before, I knew it was true. And for the first time, I began to wonder if maybe I could make marriage work again. Maybe I wasn't to blame for my failed marriage. At least not *totally* to blame. I should have recognized what Mayra was going through. By not realizing she was in so much pain over her own inadequacies, I had failed her. So maybe I *was* to blame.

I tried to clear the cobwebs from my mind. I did want to check on Tommy, but more than that, I needed to talk to my mother. She had always been there for me. Dad had too, but it was Mom who seemed to understand my injured feelings, and she was always able to make me feel better. Right now, I needed my mother.

I was jarred as that thought was followed by another. Did Tommy also need his mother?

"Royce," Mom said as I stepped into the home I'd grown up in, a place that I still, after all these years, felt safe in. "Something's wrong. Tommy is okay. He's watching a cartoon in the family room right now. Do you need to talk?"

"I do, Mom. I didn't think I'd ever receive a shock that compared to the day Mayra walked out of mine and Tommy's lives," I said.

She stepped close, gave me a quick hug, and said, "I can't imagine anything worse than what happened to you then. What has you so upset today?"

"This will be a shock to you too, Mom," I said as the two of us sat down, I on the love seat, she facing me on her sofa.

"I suppose it will. You are such a strong man, Royce. But go ahead, if you want to," she said. "I'm here for you."

"I know you are. That's why I'm here. I spent some time at the jail today interviewing a suspect on my murder case," I said.

"You mean you may have it solved?" she asked brightly.

"Yes, I may have," I said, "but I'm not sure. But that's not what I want to talk to you about. The jailer told me Mayra wanted to talk to me. So I had her bring her up to the interview room." I choked back a sob.

My mother, using the very technique I so often employed in interviews, sat quietly, letting me tell her what I had to say and to do so in my own good time. I took a deep breath, cleared my throat, and said, "Mayra is getting divorced. She found out her husband had lied to her." I went on to explain all that Mayra had relayed to me concerning Fred Zietz's and Ed Sills's arrangement. "Zietz forged those court papers, but Mayra believed they were real," I said.

Mom nodded and spoke briefly. "That makes me feel a little better about her. And it should you, too. You have forgiven her, haven't you?"

"I thought I had," I said. "It was the hardest thing I'd ever done. But now, I'm not sure," I admitted.

"Son, you must. The Lord requires us to forgive. Always. Without strings." She smiled at me. I had just been lovingly reproved.

"I know, Mom," I said, and then I dropped on my mother the bombshell Mayra had dropped on me. "She wants Tommy and me back."

My mother's face went totally white. She stammered as she said, "What is she thinking? Forgiveness is one thing, but . . . but you and Tommy have moved on."

"Yes, we have, but she explained why she left me. It was my fault," I said. I then explained what Mayra had told me.

When I finished, Mom said, "I don't see how that makes anything your fault. It makes my heart ache for Mayra, but there is no way it's your fault."

"Isn't it?" I asked. "I should have recognized that she was struggling. I should have helped her more. I should have got her into counseling. I failed her, Mom," I said, wiping at my eyes.

She slowly shook her head. "Royce, you can't blame yourself. You were a good husband and a good father. Don't let that stop you from marrying again," she said. "It wouldn't be fair to Tommy."

"Do you think I should marry Mayra?" I asked, surprised.

My mother stood up, walked over, and sat down beside me. She put an arm around my shoulder and pulled me against her like she used to do when I was a child. "That isn't what I was saying, but tell me this, son: Do you still love her?"

"I don't think so. But I don't hate her. I can't hate her. I don't even want to. But what about Tommy?"

"Royce. Right now, he is terrified of Mayra. I'm not sure that can be overcome, but maybe it could," she said.

"So what should I do?" I asked.

"You should fast and pray, Royce. No one can make a decision as important as this one but you, and you can't do it without the Lord's help. But make sure the decision you make is the right one, not one that emotionally feels right but maybe isn't. You loved Mayra, but has she really changed? Only the Lord knows the answer to that. And if she has, does that mean you can turn the clock back? Again, only the Lord knows."

"Thanks, Mom," I said. "I won't decide until I know for sure. There is one other thing. I was thinking about going to the county attorney and asking that the charges against Mayra be dropped. I can't bear thinking about her sitting in jail any longer."

"You have a big heart, Royce. Do what you think is best. But you do need to keep the feelings of one other person in mind," she said.

"Tommy?" I asked.

"Him too. He's got to feel good about anyone you choose to marry, when you do decide. But no, I was thinking of Kaci. Royce, she was physically attacked by Mayra for protecting Tommy. I hardly know her. But she likes you and Tommy a lot. You need to talk to her before you talk to the prosecutor. I'm sure," she said as she removed her hand from around my shoulders, "that she will see it your way. She is a very sweet girl. Go talk to her."

CHAPTER TWENTY-THREE

I DID AS MY WISE mother had suggested, and I drove to the office of Wendell Lawson. Kaci Walters smiled when I walked in. "It's good to see you, Royce. How are you?"

"I'm doing okay," I said.

"Any more progress on the murder?" she asked.

"I think so. But I've got a lot more to do to be sure I'm not overlooking something," I said.

"You'll get it done. You're a good officer. How's my little friend, Tommy?" she asked.

"He's doing really well. He's with my mother right now," I said.

Kaci frowned. "Royce, I'm really sorry I couldn't help you when you called me. I really would like to help with Tommy. This guy—he's been calling me a lot. I've turned him down enough times you'd think he'd get the hint. I finally accepted a date with him because I, ah, I guess I felt sorry for him."

"You don't have to explain to me," I said.

She smiled that beautiful smile of hers and said, "I know. Mr. Lawson isn't here. He had to run to Provo this morning."

"It wasn't him I came to see," I said

Her face lit up. "You came to see me?"

"There's something I need to get your feelings on," I said. "It's about Mayra."

Her face fell. "What about her?" she asked.

I spent the next couple of minutes explaining about what Mayra's husband and her attorney had done to her. I did not tell her Mayra was hoping she could once again be part of a family with Tommy and me. As I talked, Kaci seemed to be feeling a great deal of sympathy. When I had finished, she said, "Royce, you need to help her get out of jail. She shouldn't be in there. This wasn't her fault. I can forgive her."

Kaci, whom I already liked and admired, grew in stature in my eyes. She could forgive, but could I? I mean, could I really? "That's what I wanted to talk to you about. She hurt you trying to get to Tommy. And I thought that—"

Kaci cut me off as she said, "After what you've just told me, I can't keep being angry with her. She needs to have the charges dropped so she can rebuild her life. She must be feeling just horrible right now. I don't hold it against her."

"She is pretty depressed," I said. "Of course, it's not up to me if the prosecutor drops the charges, but I was hoping he would if I talked to him. But there was no way I could talk to him without talking to you first."

"Do it, Royce. Tell him I don't want to testify against her, that I want the charges dropped," she said firmly.

I had never sat down, and Kaci had not stood up, but she did so now, and she walked over to me and threw her arms around me. She hugged me tightly, kissed me lightly on the cheek, and said, "I'm glad you came in." She stepped back. "You and Tommy are both great guys. You are special," she said.

"Thanks, Kaci. I think I'll go over to the county attorney's office right now."

I was in my sheriff SUV when my cell phone rang. I answered. It was Ellerie's mother. "Ellerie just called," she said. "She says she feels bad that my husband and I didn't come to the burial. She was not happy with me. She said that since Darien was dead, he couldn't hurt me now. I tried to explain that we had decided to come, but Jess got sick. I had to put him in the hospital. I don't think Ellerie believes me. You've got to convince her that I couldn't leave Jess."

"Do you also want me to convince her you couldn't call her and explain why you weren't coming?" I asked her coldly.

"Jess wouldn't let me. He said it was best to just leave things as they were. We argued, but he's my husband," she said. "I must honor his wishes."

I wanted to remind her that Ellerie was her daughter, but I decided that would not do any good. Carmen Quinn had made her choice. She was feeling guilty now, or she wouldn't be calling me. I decided I'd let her continue to feel guilty. "I'll talk to Ellerie the next time I get a chance," I said and ended the call. I wasn't going to drop everything and just run over there because her mother had made a mess of their relationship. It could wait.

I spoke to the prosecutor, and he agreed with me and told me he'd contact the judge and see if he could get my ex-wife released that day. The actions of Ed and Fred disturbed him. He told me that it was lawyers like the two of them who gave all lawyers a bad name. I left his office feeling relieved. I had done what I felt I should do. Any future there might be for Mayra and me remained to be seen.

I then visited with the prosecutor about Harley and August. He told me he thought we were getting close, that if I could get a little more, he'd consider bringing murder charges against both of them.

I spent the next two hours checking at hotels. Vernal had a lot of them. But I hit them all. None of them had any record of either Harley or August having registered there. I wondered if I should check outside of Vernal, just to be sure. But I decided against it. I was convinced Harley had lied to me. But I was not convinced I had gained enough to talk to the prosecutor again. I needed to do more.

I was driving back to the office in the late afternoon when Ellerie called me. "Royce, I need to talk to you," she said. "When can you come over?"

I assumed that it was about her mother, so I decided it wouldn't take long and headed toward her house. Her mother wanting me to talk to her was one thing, but when it was Ellerie herself—well, that was different. Ellerie's car was in her driveway, so I went to her door. She answered within a few seconds of when I rang the bell. Her long brown hair was neatly brushed, hanging to her waist. Her amber eyes sparkled. And she smiled warmly as she invited me in. It came as a total shock to me as I looked at her and felt my heart flutter. I had grown to like her, to trust her, and to enjoy being around her, but the feelings she stirred in me now had come unexpectedly.

She took me by the arm and led me to her living room. My skin tingled at her touch. She asked me to sit on her sofa, and then she sat beside me. "I wasn't sure where I'd find you," I said. "I thought you might still be staying with Pamela."

She shook her head and looked at me with determination on her face—her attractive face. "I think it's time I quit being afraid. I will grieve for my baby for a very long time. But I can do that and still get on with my life. Royce, I won't sell the house to pay that woman anything. I am determined to get my life in control again."

"You are a strong woman, Ellerie," I said. "You can do whatever you set your mind to. And frankly, I'm glad you want to stay." Surprisingly, I was more than glad; I was relieved. I left that thought hanging and said, "Now let's talk about your mother. That is why you called me, isn't it?" She grinned at me and laid a soft hand on my arm. It tingled again. I didn't jerk it away.

"Did she call you?" she asked. "That's not what I called about."

"Yes, she did," I said. "She didn't think you believed her and wanted me to convince you she would have come if Jess hadn't been in the hospital."

She frowned. "She chose not to come. She didn't call and tell me she wasn't coming. But I can't let the fact that I am no longer important to her affect me.

She probably lied anyway, and Jess was behind it. But that's okay. I can live with it."

I pulled my phone from my pocket and looked up the number for the hospital in St. George. I entered the number and waited while it rang. Five minutes later, I closed the phone. I said, "Pneumonia. She didn't lie to you, Ellerie."

She frowned and then said, "I'm glad, but it still doesn't explain why she didn't at least call and tell me what was happening and why she couldn't come."

"I asked her about that," I said. "Jess wouldn't let her."

She nodded and said, "That I can believe. It's like he's jealous of me. If he thinks I would ever try to break them up, he couldn't be more wrong." Then the sparkle returned to her eyes. "That's not why I called, Royce. I've been doing a little detective work."

"Oh, really?" I said. "From the way your eyes are shining, I have to assume you have something good to report."

"Maybe you already know," she said. "But it's about my father and my brother."

"I have had some officers checking. But no one has gotten back to me yet. I don't think it's a high priority to them," I said. "So, tell me what you found out."

"Dad couldn't have done it," she said firmly

"Why do you say that?" I asked.

"Because he's in jail in Las Vegas," she said with a triumphant smirk.

"Why are you happy about that?" I asked.

"It means he couldn't have killed Darien. He's been in jail for two weeks. He beat up an old man on the strip," she said. "He's where he needs to be. But he couldn't have been here in Vernal. I'm glad he didn't do it."

"Me too," I said, smiling at her.

"There's more," she said. "I also have checked on Rico."

"You've been busy," I said. She paused and smiled again, warming my heart. "Have you discovered he couldn't have done it either?" I asked.

"I have," she said. "He is in New York with some friends."

"And you know that because . . . ?"

"He called me. He bought a motorcycle, and he and a bunch of guys went there together. They left Friday morning, the day before Darien was killed," she said. "So I think it was Harley and her brother who did it."

"I sort of think the same thing," I said. "But I can't prove it yet. Back to Rico. How can you be sure where he is?"

She grinned. "I played detective some more. He could tell I didn't believe him, that I wondered if he'd done something to Darien. He swore he didn't, and he told me the places they'd stayed along the way. I made a bunch of calls today, and he was telling the truth. The night Darien was killed, Rico was in Denver."

"Thank you, Detective Pearson," I said. "You've just made my job a whole lot easier."

"It's the least I can do," she said. "So can you tell me anything about Harley and August?"

I gave her a brief outline, and she seemed relieved. I needed to go. I still wanted to check on a couple more things before I picked Tommy up. Tonight was family home evening night, and I had tried very hard to spend my time with Tommy on those nights. When my work made it impossible, as it often did, I always made it up to him another time.

As I got up, Ellerie stood too. "Thanks for coming," she said. "I knew you would want to know."

"I did, and thank you. But I'd better get going now." I headed to the door. But my feet had grown unbelievably heavy. They didn't want to leave Ellerie. I didn't want to leave Ellerie. She stood beside me and smiled. "You seem very chipper today," I commented as my heavy feet came to a stop.

"The bishop and his counselors came by last night. We had a really good visit. And before they left, the bishop gave me a blessing," she said.

"That's great. Blessings help," I said.

"Yes, they do, but it's been a long time since I had one." She looked beyond me at the door. Then she looked back and took hold of my arm again. Tingle, tingle. *Slow down, my heart.* "He said the most amazing thing."

"What's that?" I asked as I turned to face her directly.

"He said in the blessing that there was going to be a huge change in my life and that when it came, I should not resist it. And that wasn't all. He said there would be someone else I would learn to love, someone who would treat me the way I deserved."

She looked deeply into my eyes. "I prayed after they left and asked the Lord to help me know when it happened."

"I'll pray for you too. I've got some praying of my own to do. I have to make some tough decisions," I said. I stopped short of telling her about my ex-wife and what she had in mind. That was something I needed to deal with—me and the Lord.

Once again, I started for the door, dragging my feet. She pulled on my arm, I turned again, and she threw her arms around me and hugged me tightly. "Good things will happen for me. I just know it. And I have you to thank," she said. I got another pleasant peck on the cheek, and my clumsy feet finally made it to the door. As I touched the doorknob, that pesky phone of mine rang again.

"Hi, Royce." It was Connie the dispatcher. Her pleasant voice served only to add to my confusion. But even though she spoke with a sultry note in her voice, her call was about police business. "You are needed at a house on South Vernal Avenue," she said. "Sergeant Merten is there. He says he thinks there is something there you need to see."

"Give me the address, and I'll be on my way," I said.

The sultry was gone from Connie's voice when I spoke to her on the radio moments later. She was all business. I couldn't help but think about the day before. And then I thought about Mayra. Right now, if I wanted to get married, there were two women who would agree to it. But I also thought about Kaci and, to my surprise, I saw those gorgeous amber eyes of Ellerie's in my mind. I shook my head to clear it of the confusion and concentrated on my driving. It didn't take me long to get to where Connie had directed me. Sergeant Merten met me at the front door. A local realtor I recognized was talking animatedly to him, waving her hands around like she was directing a symphony. Before I got to him, she rushed down the sidewalk and right past me without so much as a word, although I could hear her muttering under her breath.

"Was that woman upset?" I asked.

"I'll say she was," he told me. "She wanted to show this house to a prospective buyer. I told her that for now, it was a crime scene and that she'd have to wait until it was cleared."

"A crime scene?" I asked. "What have you got?"

"Come on inside, and I'll show you," he explained.

It didn't take me but a moment to determine that this empty house, one that was currently on the market, had been used by squatters. "There has been someone living here," I said.

"That's what I concluded," Sergeant Merten said with a nod of his head. "And I would say from the mess of food wrappers and cans that whoever it is has been here for several days," he said. "I was wondering if this is where a couple of your suspects may have been staying."

"Good work," I said. "And thanks for calling me. You might be onto something. Let me tell you what I've been doing today." I then once again recited some of what Harley had told me. "I've checked all the hotels in town. Neither she nor August have been registered there."

"Unless they used aliases," he reminded me.

"Yeah, I thought about that. But if they did, the question would be why," I said. "And the answer could be that they didn't want anyone to know they'd been here in Vernal for several days."

"And that could be true of why they might have been staying here," he stated. "This way no one really could know they were staying in town."

"I think we'd better look around. Do you have time to help me?" I asked.

He said he did, and we both pulled on gloves and went to work. The late afternoon wore on, but we made progress. We worked together in the living room first. It appeared that the squatters had used candles for light. And for food, they had eaten mostly fast foods, and the wrappers were scattered about along with a few cans and plastic spoons and forks. We found both beer and pop cans. More of beer than of pop. The power was off, but there was still water, and the squatters had made use of it.

I picked up several items and bagged them to be fingerprinted later. We were careful not to touch doorknobs and other surfaces our squatters may have used, just to be on the safe side until we could dust for prints.

The house had three bedrooms. There was a lot more to do. I called the chief and asked for some assistance. When I told him why I was interested in the house, he said he would come himself and bring a couple more officers with him.

It was obvious that a woman had been staying in one bedroom and a man in another. We both started next in the woman's room, searching slowly and meticulously. I found a laptop computer in a dresser drawer. "Ah," I said. "Here's something that might be very useful. We'll need a search warrant, but I'll sure be interested in knowing what's in it." I bagged it and continued to search.

The reinforcements arrived. We divided up rooms, and back to work we went. I kept glancing at my watch as the afternoon wore into early evening. I really did not want to disappoint my son, but searches such as these were tedious and slow. Chief Collins called to me from the bedroom where the man had been staying. "Detective Fleming. I think you need to come see this."

Beneath the mattress, he had found a long, very sharp knife. The back side of the blade was serrated. "It looks clean, but if it was used to cut the fingers off Darien Pearson's right hand, he may have cleaned it. But that doesn't mean a lab can't find blood," he said.

"This is where August and Harley were holed up," I said conclusively. "I think we should get a prosecutor over here. I don't want those two getting out of jail. They will skip the country if they do."

"I'll work on that, Royce. You keep at it here," he said and pulled his phone out.

Ten minutes later, I found a grocery receipt from Jubilee. The date was the very day Darien was killed. "This means whoever was staying here was in town the day of the murder," I told Sergeant Merten.

When the chief came back in to report that the prosecutor was on his way, I showed him the receipt. "All we have to do is find their prints here or prove the computer belongs to one of them," I said.

As soon as the prosecutor saw what we'd found, he left again to draw up information outlining the charges on each of them and have them served in jail. He promised to ask a judge for no bail and thought that if he didn't get it, at least the bail would be very high. After he left, we soon finished up by dusting for prints.

Back at the sheriff's office, we were able to pull more prints off some Pepsi and beer cans. We ran them; some came back a match on Harley and some on August. I pumped my fist. "We've got them," I said jubilantly. It was almost eight when I left. I picked up Tommy and hurried home. We still had time to have our family home evening.

CHAPTER TWENTY-FOUR

WE WERE JUST FINISHING A short lesson on forgiveness when the doorbell rang. The lesson was more for me than for Tommy. I opened the door, and Kaci was standing there smiling and holding a hot loaf of what smelled suspiciously like fresh banana bread. "I hope you guys like banana bread," she said. "I meant to have it here earlier, but Mr. Lawson got back from Provo at about five, just as I was ready to leave, and needed me to stay late to type some documents for him. By then I'd missed my own family home evening group. So I hurried and baked some banana bread. I was afraid I would be too late getting it to you."

"Thanks, Kaci," I said as I held the door wide and invited her in. She handed the warm loaf to Tommy.

He grinned and said, "I love banana bread. Grandma makes it for me all the time."

"Your timing was fine. We are also running late," I said as I accepted a hug. "We got a major break on the case today, so I also had to work late. We have some ice cream in the freezer that we were going to eat for refreshments. But now we will have ice cream, fresh banana bread, and lovely feminine company. You will stay, won't you?" I asked.

"I'd love to," she said. "If you two don't mind."

"Yeah, stay," Tommy said with unfeigned enthusiasm.

She knelt down, hugged him tightly, and said, "I will, then."

We were just finishing with the second helping of refreshments when the doorbell rang again. My stomach lurched. *Surely it couldn't be,* I thought. But it could. I opened the door, and there stood Mayra, smiling and looking so pretty it hurt. She stepped in and looked around, spotting Tommy and Kaci instantly. Tommy saw her, and with a scream of terror, he burst from the room. Kaci raced after him.

"Oh," Mayra said with a long sad face. "I really did blow it, didn't I?"

"Well, the timing wasn't the best, that's for sure."

"I didn't know you had a girlfriend. Isn't that your lawyer's secretary?"

"It is," I said awkwardly.

"She is probably not happy to see me out of jail. I don't blame her," she said, the sadness in her eyes making my own fill with moisture. I quickly blinked it away.

"Kaci suggested it," I said. "I explained to her about Ed and Fred and what they did, and she said you shouldn't be in jail."

"She sounds like a good person," Mayra said. "Do you plan to marry her?"

"I'm not making plans to marry anyone at this point in my life. Kaci is just a friend. She brought some banana bread for Tommy and me," I said just as Kaci, with Tommy holding her pant leg, came out of the kitchen with a serving of banana bread and ice cream.

"Please, sit down and eat this," Kaci said.

"Are you sure?" Mayra asked, looking like a deer in the headlights. I think she was about ready to bolt. "I don't think I should stay."

"Please do," Kaci said, gaining respect in my eyes. "Tommy is okay with it. I just explained to him that you were not here to take him or to hurt him, that it was all a big misunderstanding."

Mayra's troubled eyes fell on Tommy's frightened face. "I promise, Tommy. I won't hurt you. Some bad men told me to do what I did. They are in trouble tonight, and I just came over to say I'm sorry before I go back to Salt Lake. Will you forgive me, Tommy?"

I'm pretty sure he didn't want to. But the lesson we'd had just minutes before was fresh on his mind. I believed I'd taught him well about how important it was to forgive, as I personally struggled with that principle when it came to what Mayra had done. "Yes," he said, his little eyes downcast as he still clung to Kaci's leg and peeked around at the woman who had been his mother but who was a total stranger to him.

"It's kind of late to drive. You are probably tired," Kaci said.

"I'll be okay. I've had plenty of rest in . . . where I've been staying." Mayra had still not accepted the plate. I honestly didn't think she would.

"Please stay," Kaci said as she thrust the plate toward Mayra.

Mayra looked back at the door, then she looked at the plate, and finally her eyes settled on Tommy. "Only if it's okay with you, Tommy," she said in such a kind voice that I could see my sweet, tenderhearted son melt.

"It's really good," he said. "You'll like it. Kaci made it, and she's a really good cook."

The ice was broken, and though Tommy never left Kaci's side, the fear was gone from his little face. To make Mayra feel a little less uncomfortable, Kaci and Tommy cut each of us another small piece of her banana bread and spooned a small portion of ice cream on each plate, and the four of us ate together.

"I spoke to your dad and mom," Mayra said after an uncomfortable period of silence. "I wasn't sure your dad wasn't going to punch me when he opened the door, but he invited me in. I apologized to both of them and then left. They were very gracious." She cocked an eyebrow. "Did you tell them what we talked about?" she asked.

"I did. At least I did talk with my mother. She never keeps anything from Dad, so they both know, I'm sure," I said.

She gave me a very weak smile and said, "Thanks for doing that. Was your mother okay with it?"

"My mother, as you know, is a very good person. She lets me make my own decisions. And that's what I'll do," I said.

Mayra nodded her head and said, "Thank you. That's all I can ask."

I didn't comment on that. I couldn't tell her how torn I was. That was something I had to work out, and with God's help, I would.

Mayra finished her banana bread and ice cream, stood and handed the plate to Kaci, and then said, "Thanks. I'd better take off. I have a three-hour drive ahead of me."

Kaci stood and elevated herself one large notch higher in my estimation by saying, "Mayra, I have a spare bed. You would be welcome to stay tonight."

Mayra smiled at her. "Thank you, Kaci. You are a wonderful person. But I'd better decline. I'll be okay driving late. Tommy, can I have just a tiny little hug before I leave?"

I held my breath. But to my amazement, my little guy stepped forward and held out his arms. It was brief, and then with tears in her eyes, the woman I once loved turned to the door. I followed her and opened it. She looked at me with that look I had fallen in love with so many years ago. "What about his father?" she asked.

I held out my arms, and she stepped into my embrace. It felt right, and it felt wrong. When she left a moment later, I felt as empty inside as I'd felt that day I came home to find that she'd left. Despite all that had transpired, I realized with a jolt, the love I'd felt for her was not entirely gone. There was still a small portion of it lingering in some small spot in my heart.

Kaci's eyes were misty when I shut the door and turned back to face her and Tommy. "I'd better go too," she said.

"Kaci, you are a wonderful person. Thank you for what you did tonight. Please, I know it's late, but Tommy and I wanted to watch a movie tonight. You would be welcome to join us."

She smiled at Tommy. He said, "Yeah, stay."

"I think I just might do that," she said. When she got ready to leave two hours later, we were all tired. She helped me get Tommy to bed. She listened to his prayer, tucked him in, and kissed his cheek.

"Thanks," I said as I walked her to the door. "I'm not sure what Tommy would have done when Mayra showed up tonight had it not been for you. You got him through it," I said. "Thank you," I said again. I kissed her lightly on the lips, and she left.

I checked in on Tommy a moment later. He was sound asleep. For me, no such luck. Even after a long prayer for guidance, I didn't feel an answer come. I was not sure what I expected. It would have been helpful if an angel had appeared and said, "Royce, you should marry Mayra again." Or perhaps say, "She had her chance. Move on, Royce."

But of course, it wasn't that simple. God would make me work it all out for myself and then ask him for his blessing on whatever decision I made. And it was not going to be easy. I tossed and turned, and finally sometime in the wee hours of the morning, I fell asleep.

Tommy woke me up. "Dad, it's time for breakfast," he said. "How come you're still in bed?"

That was not something I could explain to him. So I simply said I was tired and that I would hurry. By the time I dropped him off at my parents' house, he was chipper, talkative, and ready to make my mother's day hard. It started out as soon as he saw her. "The mean lady came last night. She hugged me. She's not mean anymore." But he didn't stop at that. He added, "Kaci was there. She brought banana bread. It was almost as good as yours. She stayed and watched a movie with us and tucked me in my bed. I like Kaci a lot."

Mom looked at me. "Looks like you have some decisions to make."

"You have no idea," I said.

"Oh, I think I do. Tommy told me all about Connie's visit Sunday night." She smiled. "You'll work it out."

"The mean woman is pretty, Grandma. But she's not as pretty as Kaci." Mom grinned at Tommy's words. "And she's not as pretty as Ellerie."

"What about Connie? Is the mean lady as pretty as her?" my mother asked, winking at me.

"Nope, but she's really pretty. I think she likes me. She didn't try to take me away last night."

"Good luck," I said to my mother. "I need to get back to work."

"No, good luck to you," she said. "Remember, the Lord will help you sort it out."

I shook my head as Tommy ran into the house. "I'm not sure yet I should even think about marriage. That might be the right answer."

Mom just smiled. "I trust you to do the right thing," she said.

The first thing on my agenda today was to make sure the murder charges had been filed and that both Harley and August were being held without bail. I drove to the police station. As soon as I got to my desk, I called the jail. I heard what I had hoped to hear. I was not finished, though. I had to continue to build my case. I still hoped to talk to August, but I had to wait for a new attorney to be appointed. Hopefully, that would occur this morning and then I could contact his new attorney and interview August.

I got a call on the office phone and picked it up. "Detective, this is Mark Lanning. I just learned you convinced the prosecutor to file murder charges against Harley and August. Don't you think you're jumping the gun a little bit?"

"Not really," I said.

"Then you must know something I haven't been told about," he said. He sounded angry. That didn't sit well with me. "Why don't you tell me what's going on."

"That's not my place," I said. "Call the county attorney's office. You know what you need to do to get discovery."

"So there is something new," he said.

"I didn't say that. Do your homework, Counselor." I ended the call on that note.

A few minutes later, I was summoned to Chief Collins's office. I hurried over there. "Good morning, Detective," he said with a smile on his face. "You have done a great job."

"Thanks, but I still don't have enough to make it stick," I said. "I've got more work to do."

"Yes, you do," he agreed. "But when we get into the computer and get the knife back from the lab, I suspect we'll have what we need. So you need to get a search warrant for the laptop. Do it this morning," he said.

"I'll get right on it," I promised.

"Does the victim's wife know about the arrests yet?" he asked.

"Not that I know of," I answered.

"Then that is your first job. Get over there and give her the good news. Then you can work on the warrant," he said.

"Thanks, Chief. I'll go right now," I said.

As I drove toward Ellerie's house, my stomach started to churn. I was anxious to give her the good news, and yet I was nervous. Something had shifted yesterday in my relationship with Ellerie. I was suddenly seeing her less as a victim and a witness in a case and more as a woman. A beautiful, sweet, desirable woman at that. I needed to watch what I said and what I did on this visit. I needed to stay focused and professional.

It took her a while to answer the door when I rang the bell. When she finally did, she almost took my breath away. "Hey, you," she said with a grin that lit her face and made her amber eyes look more beautiful than ever.

That greeting, all by itself, unnerved me. I felt like a teenager asking the most popular girl on campus on a date. I was tongue-tied and starstruck. She was gorgeous.

"Come in, don't just stand there," she said, reaching for my hand.

I felt a jolt of electricity run up my arm at her touch. *What in the world is wrong with me?* I wondered as the smell of something sweet baking teased my nose.

She led me in and didn't let go of my hand until she'd shut the door with her free one. Then she stepped in and hugged me. My knees turned to jelly. This wasn't the same woman who had come into the police department just last week, bruised and beaten and broken. No, this was a woman who was sure of herself and who was determined to move forward from the tragedies of the recent past. "You look warm," she said. "Could you use a drink of water?"

Yes, as a matter of fact I could. I felt like I was about to melt in her presence. "That would be nice," I said.

"Please, Royce, sit down," she said. I did so, and as she walked toward her kitchen, I couldn't take my eyes off her. She was damaged, but she did not look it. I was damaged myself, but could I hide it like she did? I wondered. In a strange way, she and I had something in common. The big difference was that the person who had hurt me wanted me back. The person who had hurt her was lying stiff and cold in the morgue.

I sat stiffly, anxious to deliver the good news and then to get out of there before I had a complete meltdown. Because that was what I felt like was happening. She was gone for longer than it took to fill a glass with water, but when she came back in, I understood why. She had ice in the glass with the water and was carrying a plate of cookies, freshly baked. That was what I had smelled when she opened the door.

She handed me the glass and then said, "Have a cookie. I hope it tastes okay."

I took one, and then she placed the plate on the end table nearest to me. She sat down next to me on the sofa and smiled. *Oh my!* I pictured the dead body with the mutilated hands, and I wondered what in the world had been wrong with that man. This girl had been his, and he'd shattered her world. It was beyond my limited comprehension to understand how something like that could have ever happened.

"I hope you've come with good news," she said softly.

"I have," I said. Then I took a bite of the cookie. It was still soft and warm and tasted heavenly. "This is really good," I said.

"Thank you," she said. "I'm glad you like it. So what is the good news?"

"Harley and August have been charged with murdering Darien," I said.

She slumped. Not the reaction I had expected. "I wonder what he did to them to turn them into killers," she said. "Maybe he treated her the way he treated me. Maybe when she didn't get her money, it tipped her over the edge. But that's not right what they did."

"No, it's not, but I guess it is what it is," I said.

"Can you convict them?" she asked.

"I don't know. I need more evidence, but let me tell you what we found last night." When I had given her the Reader's Digest version of last night's search, she slowly shook her head. Then she stood and moved toward her window and stood looking out of it, her hands clasped behind her back.

"It sounds like it was them, all right," she said after a moment. She turned to face me, the shine gone from her face and the sparkle from her eyes. "Why did they do it? As bad as he was to me and to my baby, it never once occurred to me that I should kill him. I wanted to leave him. I really did, and eventually, after losing my little girl, I would have left him. But take his life? That's for God to decide, not me, and certainly not them."

"I'm sorry," I said as I sat my glass down, the partially eaten cookie beside it, and stood and joined her at the window.

She stepped toward me, the sunlight that was streaming through the window making her long hair glow. "Why do people do these kinds of things?" she asked. "Who does to a woman what Darien did to me? And why does a woman do to a man what Mayra did to you?"

"I don't know. Mayra tried to tell me why she left."

"She did?" she said as her hand flew to her mouth. "Why, or can you tell me? I know it's none of my business. You don't have to tell me. I shouldn't have asked."

"No, it's okay, Ellerie," I said as I looked deeply into her eyes. I trembled. Then I told her.

For a long time, she just stared at me. Finally she said, "It wasn't out of meanness, was it?"

"I don't think so now. I always thought it was because of something I did to her. But I had no idea what it was. Ellerie, all these years I have been haunted by what I must have done. And I'm still not sure it wasn't my fault. I should have known she was struggling. I should have seen it. Why didn't I see what she was going through, how frightened she was, how insecure? I should have gotten help for her, but I guess I was so wrapped up in my own life I didn't see what she was going through. I blame myself, and I guess I always will."

For the life of me, I couldn't keep the mist from building in my eyes. She reached up and wiped a tear that had begun to make its way down my cheek. "Royce, you are like no one I've ever met. Please, don't blame yourself. It breaks my heart to see the pain you're feeling."

I took hold of the hand that had wiped the tear away and squeezed. "What I have gone through is nothing like what you went through. My experience is as different from yours as night is from day."

"Royce, you are so sweet. You are a cop, a detective. I would have expected you to be cold to me, to treat me as just another victim. But you didn't. Oh yeah," she said with a grin. "I know you had to wonder about me for a while. *Could she have done it?* I know you thought about it, and that is as it should have been. But you were sweet to me. You treated me like I was an important person—like I was a lady. I wasn't used to that. You made me feel like I mattered. And I will always be grateful to you for that."

"Thank you. There is something special about you." For a moment, I looked at her lips. They were no longer swollen. And the urge to kiss them caused me to lean forward just a little. But I caught myself in time. "I have work to do," I said awkwardly. "I have to compare Harley's shoes to the tracks. And I'll have to go to the jail to do that. I should go now."

But just like the day before, my feet became terribly heavy, and it was with a great deal of effort that I turned away from Ellerie and started toward the door. She stepped lightly beside me. Her feet were just fine. "You didn't finish your water or even one cookie. Don't you like them?"

I started to laugh. "Oh, Ellerie, of course I like them. And I like you. Can I take a couple of them with me?"

She stepped close and hugged me. It was a long hug, an intense hug. And when she finally pulled back, she said, "I hope you won't be a stranger now that you've caught your suspects. I kind of like seeing you once in a while."

I dragged my heavy feet to the door, with two cookies in my hand and chewing on the one I'd started eating earlier. I left.

CHAPTER TWENTY-FIVE

THE SHOES HARLEY WAS WEARING when she was taken to the jail were not the ones the killer had worn at the scene. I needed to find those shoes. Perhaps they were in her car or her brother's truck. I had completed the search warrant for the computer we'd found in the house she and August had camped in. Now I needed to prepare another warrant for the cars. The truck we had already impounded. I didn't know where the car was. Two important things I still hoped to find and search were their cell phones. My work was cut out for me.

So I set to work, and in doing so hoped I could clear my mind of Ellerie. She had affected me in a way I had not expected. My sudden attraction to her had been a shock, and I was determined to fight it off. In doing so, I experienced dark thoughts of her. She was damaged. She had been hurt in ways I wasn't sure I could live with. But then, as I sat at my desk, trying unsuccessfully to get those amber eyes and beautiful smile off my mind, another thought came to me. *I was also damaged.* I had less to offer her than she had to offer me, if I was honest about it.

I had prayed much. I felt again an attraction to my former wife, but as I thought about her, I wondered if I could face the possibility of once again being rejected after months or years of marriage. That was not appealing.

I thought of the other two women who seemed interested in me. They were both pretty women, strong and without baggage. Which would make it unfair to either of them if I allowed a relationship to develop with either one. Yes, I had a lot of baggage. They had none. They deserved better.

Finally, another thought entered my mind, slipping in quietly but firmly. It began to develop without me even giving it permission. Ellerie Pearson and I had more in common than we had differences. Yes, we had both been hurt, but what if we committed to helping each other through those pains? Maybe we could be right for each other. I started to try to shake that thought off, but

I found I didn't want to let it go. Perhaps my prayers were being answered. I felt a weight lift from my shoulders. I felt a hope for my future. Was there any chance she would feel the same? As crazy as it was, I hoped so. I honestly hoped so.

"What are you working on, Detective?" The voice of my chief came from over my shoulder. *I was working on my future.*

"I was just going to prepare some more search warrants," I said. *Was going to* were the key words in my response. But I hadn't started yet. So now I did. He watched and visited with me for a moment as I proceeded. "I'm starting with Harley's car, if I can find it, and August's truck."

"You've got to find the shoes if you can, Royce," he said. "Since you already found August's prints on the knife, all we need is for that knife to be found to have even a minute trace of the victim's blood on it, and we've got him. But we clearly need more than that to nail her."

The chief wasn't telling me anything I didn't know, but he did his job by helping me feel the urgency of it. I had an old search warrant affidavit open on my screen. All I had to do was take out the parts that didn't apply now, add those that did, and then do the same to a warrant, and I'd be ready to send it to the on-call judge.

"Good luck, Royce. You are doing a great job," he said. And then in parting, he added what he'd said more times than I could count. "Keep me advised."

An hour later, I began my search of August's green Ford pickup. The only things I found were a meth pipe and a small amount of white powdery substance, which I was sure was meth. There were two more charges the prosecutor could tack on. But there was nothing in the truck to add to my murder case. I could dust for fingerprints, but I already had Harley's admission that she had driven her brother's truck, so it would be a waste of my time.

The next thing I did was drive around town looking for the white car. It was not at the house where they had been staying. So where could it be? Near that house? Say, within walking distance? That made sense, so I concentrated on an ever-widening search of the area and finally found a Ford Fusion parked behind some trees on a vacant lot. I called the plates in to dispatch. A moment later, I got the results I had expected. The car was registered to Harley Pearson. I got out of my vehicle, stepped over to it, and peered inside. There on the passenger seat, I spotted a cell phone. I had no more than congratulated myself over that find before my own cell phone indicated I had just received a text.

I pulled the phone from my pocket and looked at the text. It was from Reggie Hutchins. I quickly opened my phone and accessed the text without reading it from the front screen. I expected that Andrew Hutchins and his wife were home from their vacation. I was not nearly as anxious to speak with Andrew as I had been because I didn't see how he could be of much help now that I had Harley and August in custody. But of course there were warrants out for both of them for marijuana possession, which I should serve. But it was not what I expected. His parents were still not home. Reggie was telling me he had just aced an online math test and said he could never have done it without my help. Then he thanked me.

I sent him a quick text in return, congratulating him on his achievement and reminding him that I was available to help at any time. He fired one right back telling me that he would for sure ask for help when he needed it.

I had Harley's Fusion towed and commenced to search it as soon as it was in the impound yard. I had to jimmy the lock to get in. When I opened the door, I bagged the cell phone and put it in my pocket.

I had been very busy the entire morning, but my mind did not rid itself of thoughts of Ellerie. I kept getting the impulse to leave the search for later and drive to her place. I succeeded in tamping that impulse down. But my desire to see her again, to see if the spark we'd both felt the night before and this morning was real. It had not faded on my part. It only grew brighter. I wondered how she felt. I found myself smiling as I searched the white Ford Fusion. Even though I once again failed to find the shoes or anything other than the phone that might help prove Harley's involvement in the murder, my spirits remained high.

It was a few minutes past lunchtime when I finished the latest search, and I gave in to the urge to see Ellerie and drove to her house again. I was disappointed when her car was gone and no one answered her doorbell. As I was walking glumly back to my car, I heard someone call my name.

I looked over my shoulder to find Pamela Mavey hurrying toward me. I turned and met her at the end of her sidewalk. "Good afternoon, Pamela," I said. "You don't happen to know where Ellerie is, do you? I need to talk to her." *Wanted to* was more like it, but Pamela would never understand that.

"She was over here for a while this morning," Pamela said as a smile crossed her elderly face. "She just went to the grocery store. She'll be back soon, I'm sure. Why don't you wait for her? You can come in my house while you do."

I accepted her kind offer. "Have you had lunch?" she asked when we were seated in her small but tidy living room.

"I haven't, but I came to ask Ellerie the same thing," I said.

Mrs. Mavey's face lit up. Then she narrowed her eyes while continuing to smile. "Were you by any chance planning to ask her to go to lunch with you?" I felt my face go red. Before I could admit that I had planned exactly that, she said, "You were. I knew it." She laughed.

"Yes, I was, but there are some things we need to talk about," I said. Things like seeing more of each other when this case was over. And things like how our respective broken pasts might help us to help each other. *Just little things like that.*

"I am going to let you in on a little secret," she said, looking very conspiratorial. "That girl talks about you whenever she and I are together. You might be the policeman that solved the case of her horrible dead husband's murder. But you are also the policeman who has burrowed a place right into that girl's heart. Don't hurt her. She needs your support and your friendship."

"And she will have it," I promised as I heard a car drive up next door.

"Ah, here she is," Pamela said, grinning broadly. "Go make that girl's day. She deserves it. And so do you."

I thanked her and hurried out the door. Ellerie was just leaning into the back seat of her car when I walked up. She came out with her hands empty, but her beautiful eyes shone and her face lit up when she saw me. "Royce, I was just thinking about you," she said as she stepped toward me. Then, as natural as taking a breath, I took her in my arms, right there in front of anyone who happened to be watching. It felt right.

"Royce," she said as she drew back. "Did you come to tell me you found Harley's shoes?"

"I haven't found them, but that's not why I'm here. I came to ask you if you would like to go to lunch with me."

Her eyes popped wide, and she put one of her small hands over her mouth. "Why?" she finally asked.

"Why not?" I countered. "I enjoy your company."

"And I enjoy yours," she said, blushing. "Yes, I'll go." But then a panicked look crossed her face. "But what will people think?" she asked.

"Who cares? You are single now. I'm single. I think you are gorgeous, and if you don't mind being seen with me, then what does it matter what other people think?" Then another thought, an unhappy one, came to me. "Of course, if you don't want to be seen with me, I'll understand. It's only been a little over a week since you lost your husband."

She turned away from me, and my heart lurched. I shouldn't have said that. I touched her arm, and she turned back to me, her eyes misty. "Darien and I lived in the same house, but he has not been a husband to me for many months. I have been so sad, so afraid, and so . . . so lonely," she said.

"We can do this another time," I said.

She shook her head, and gradually her face softened. "I'd love to be seen with you. I'll go with you. If you'll help me take these groceries in the house and put them away, then we can leave."

It had been more than six years since my world had been shattered. But as I walked beside Ellerie with our arms full of groceries, I felt a joy I had not felt in all those years. Maybe this friendship would go nowhere beyond that—just friendship—but I was going to give it a chance, no matter what anyone else thought.

When we left the house a few minutes later, I held her hand. I helped her into my SUV, and as I circled it to get to my door, Mrs. Mavey called out, "Detective."

I looked back at her. She just grinned and pumped her fist. Well, there was one person who was not going to judge us. With a light heart, I joined Ellerie, and we drove into town. "Where to?" I asked.

"You asked me to lunch. You decide, Royce."

"American, Chinese, or Mexican?" I asked.

"I like them all. It's up to you."

"Café Rio?" I asked.

"Sure," she said. "I guess that would be Mexican."

"Have you never been there?" I asked.

"For all intents and purposes, I have been a prisoner in my own home. Darien never took me out. I mean, you know, after we married and moved to Vernal. It was my job to cater to him," she said as her lips began to quiver.

"Well, it's my job to cater to you now. Let's go to Café Rio."

As we parked, she looked over at me and said, "Thanks for doing this for me. I had assumed you would not want to be seen in public with me after all that has happened."

I smiled at her. "Ellerie, assumptions are bad manners. So let's both resolve to have good manners from here on out. You see, I have also had bad manners. I assumed you would never go out with me after the rejection that was thrown at me by Mayra. No more bad manners. Deal?"

"Deal," she said, leaning across the console and touching my face with a tenderness that was foreign to me. My face tingled at her touch.

We were eating, making small talk, and just enjoying one another's company when someone I recognized walked in. I hadn't heard Connie's voice on the police radio today, so apparently she wasn't working. She and a young lady I recognized as her roommate were together. She looked around the room, spotted Ellerie and me, and visibly gasped. To my knowledge, she had not seen Ellerie before. So she likely didn't know who I was with.

I looked quickly back at Ellerie and smiled at something she said. Then I took another bite of my burrito. I made an effort not to look Connie's way. I had enjoyed her company the other night and had flirted with the idea of asking her out again. But I had no such intentions anymore. Maybe it was a good thing she was seeing me with someone else, someone very attractive and who appeared to be enjoying my company. It couldn't hurt, so I didn't worry about Connie.

However, Ellerie kept looking in that direction. "Is something the matter?" I finally asked her.

"Don't look now, but there's a lady over there who keeps looking at us. She looks angry," she said.

I smiled at her, reached across our table, and patted her hand. "I saw her come in. That's Connie Bost. She is a dispatcher. In fact, she was the one who was on duty when I was sent to the scene of Darien's murder."

"Is she your girlfriend?" she asked, her lips quivering again.

"No, but I think she'd like to be," I said. "I took her out a while back. I think she viewed that as more than I intended."

"Do you like her?" she asked, appearing to be very vulnerable.

"I like her, but I am not interested in her beyond our professional association," I said. "Frankly, I'm glad she's seeing us here together. Maybe she'll get the message. So quit worrying about it."

"Are you sure?' she asked quietly.

"Yes, I'm sure. I wouldn't be here with you if it wasn't something I wanted to do," I said.

She didn't appear to be satisfied. "When did you go out with her?" she asked.

"Several weeks ago. You need to understand that I haven't dated much. I've honestly been afraid to."

"But you are a very good-looking man," she said.

"But I was burned once."

"Yeah. I understand. We have that in common," she said as she began to be more cheerful.

There was one thing I would not do, I resolved at that moment, and that was that I would not hide things from Ellerie or lie to her. And since I knew my son was not one to beat around the bush or hide things from anyone, I decided it would be best if she heard from me about Connie's visit before she heard it from him. "Now, don't take this wrong, but Connie did come to my house Sunday night. She brought cookies and spent the afternoon and the evening. But it wasn't by my invitation that she came."

"Does Tommy like her?" she asked.

"Yes, but he likes you too," I said. "We both like you."

She smiled at that and seemed to relax again. However, I noticed her glancing Connie's way every so often. We didn't talk a lot the rest of the meal. However, just as we were getting ready to leave, she said, "Royce. I have a favor to ask."

"Whatever you would like," I said cheerfully.

"I haven't been back to the grave since my baby was buried," she said, her eyes misting. "Would you mind taking me there for just a minute before you go back to work?"

"I'd be happy to," I said.

She smiled. "You are a great guy. Thanks. I didn't want to go alone."

As we walked out of Café Rio, arm in arm, I was sure I could feel Connie's eyes following us. I noticed that Ellerie glanced back once. But she didn't say a word about Connie until we reached my SUV. Then she said, "She doesn't like me."

"Connie?"

"Yes."

"Don't worry about it. I like you."

When we got to the cemetery, I parked near her baby's burial plot and opened the door for Ellerie but made no effort to go to the little grave with her. I sensed she needed her space. After maybe two or three minutes, she turned back to me and said, "Why don't you come over for a moment?"

I joined her there and put an arm around her shoulders. After a moment, she began to sob. I pulled her close. She didn't resist. Finally, she turned toward me and let me hug her. "Royce, I feel so guilty. If it weren't for me, she would still be inside of me, waiting to come into my world," she said

"Woah, Ellerie. This was all Darien's fault. Don't blame yourself."

"But I do," she said as her tears flowed harder. She took a Kleenex from her purse and dabbed at the tears. "If I had found the courage to leave him, to go far away, to hide from him, my little girl would not have died. So it is my fault. I was a coward and stayed and did what Darien told me to." Her chin quivered. I touched her face.

"Don't do this to yourself," I said.

"Royce, don't you see?" she said, her eyes suddenly flashing with anger. "She died because I caved in to my fear."

"No, she died because her father had become a beast," I said as I felt my own temper rise.

"You can say what you want, but I know what I should have done, and I didn't do it. I thought I could just put this behind me and go on and build a new life. But I can't. She deserved more from her mother," she said, and then she broke down and fell into my arms.

For several minutes, the tears flowed and she sobbed hard. I let her cry. No one but I knew the times after Mayra left me that I cried half the night. I was a man. *Men aren't supposed to cry*, I'd been told. But I had, and I had never admitted it to a soul. So I let her grief flow. She needed for it to. And I was glad I could be there for her.

It seemed like an hour, but it had only been a few minutes when she finally pulled back from me and turned back toward the little grave with the small temporary marker. She stepped over, fell to her knees, and poured her heart out to her little girl. "I'm so sorry. I let him hurt you. I let him hurt me. I let him kill you. Oh, my little one, can you ever forgive me?"

Her words cut me to the core. I had to speak. "Ellerie, she has already forgiven you. Now you need to forgive yourself."

She didn't look up, and I wasn't sure she'd heard me. But after another minute or two, she once again got to her feet and stumbled toward me. "Do you really think so?" she asked.

"Oh, Ellerie, of course I do. Her exaltation is assured. She was too good for this cruel world. Yes, she has forgiven you, even though I still don't think you are to blame at all," I said.

"But you, you blame yourself for what happened to your marriage. You blame yourself that Tommy doesn't have a mother. What's so different from how I feel to how you feel?" she asked.

"I guess it's about the same. Ellerie, you and I both have to forgive ourselves and move on. I will try harder if you will," I promised.

She touched my cheek and then she stepped into my arms. I held her tight again as she said, "I will try too, but only if you will help me."

At that point, I knew the Lord had answered my prayer. I knew what I had to do. I knew what I wanted to do. "We can help each other."

"Yes, I think we can," she said as her endless tears flowed onto my shirt. "I will do my best. But I can't do it without you."

"You won't have to," I promised.

After a couple of silent minutes, she said, "Okay, we can go now. Thanks for bringing me here. And for being the best person I've ever known."

She had elevated me far beyond where I deserved, but I let it go. We got back into the SUV. As I drove from the cemetery, my phone began to ring.

CHAPTER TWENTY-SIX

"I'M SORRY IF I'VE KEPT you too long, Royce," Ellerie said as she wiped her eyes. "I'm sure someone else needs you now."

"Probably," I said as I glanced at the screen. "Oh, it's Reggie Hutchins. He's a kid I've been trying to help with his remedial math."

"You tutor?" she asked.

"Not usually. I just decided to help this kid. I'll tell you more about him," I said as my phone continued to ring. I answered it. "Hi, Reggie," I said.

"Detective, you've got to come right now!" he said, sounding like he was seriously shaken about something.

"I'll be right there. I need to take—"I began, but he cut me off.

"Please hurry. Right now. It's horrible!"

"Hang in there, Reggie. I'm coming. What's wrong?"

"My puppy. He was digging . . . it's awful," he said. And then his phone was apparently away from his face, and I heard him say, "No, Ranger! Naughty dog. Drop it. Right now."

Then he spoke to me again. "I'm behind the house." And with that, the call was cut off.

"I need to get you home. Reggie sounded frantic. Something about his dog," I said as I flew from the cemetery and onto the road.

"I'll go with you," she said. "You don't have to take time to take me home."

"Are you sure?" I asked.

"Yes, I'm sure," she said.

When I reached Reggie's house, his old yellow truck was sitting in its usual spot on the street. I checked out with dispatch as I parked behind Reggie's truck. Then I piled out and ran for the back of the house. Ellerie was right behind me.

Reggie seemed to have gotten his emotions somewhat under control. His beautiful Alaskan malamute puppy was sitting on the lawn whining, his dark eyes on the can Reggie was holding. "It's in here," Reggie said, holding the can out to me. His eyes were red, and his hand was shaking. "Ranger dug it up in the garden, I guess. He was playing out there, and when he came back, he had this in his mouth. I had a hard time getting him to drop it."

I accepted the can, and my stomach nearly revolted at the putrid smell that flowed out. Reggie's eyes were still wide, and he stepped back. I looked into the can and gasped at what I saw. "Reggie," I said as the significance of what his dog had found hit me. "I need to know exactly where this came from."

"I'm not sure. But it was somewhere back there. Mom and Dad grow a few things in a garden," he said as he pointed.

It took only a glance to see that what Reggie's parents grew was mostly weeds. The garden was a tangle of weeds and wild grasses. I guessed there could be some vegetables in there somewhere. There was a high shelf on the back porch, and I put the can there and then said, "Show me where he found this."

"What is it, Royce?" Ellerie asked, her gorgeous eyes still red from all the grief that had poured out of her at the cemetery. "It sure smells awful."

I wished I'd taken the extra time to take her home, but it was too late now. "Later," I said to her. "Reggie, put a leash on the dog. We'll let him lead us to where he found this."

He did that, and then to Ellerie I said, "You may want to stay here," as I signaled for Reggie and the big puppy to lead the way into the garden.

Either Ellerie didn't hear me or she didn't want to be left alone with the awful object the can held. "Reggie," I said as we started across the top of the garden, Ranger pulling hard on the leash. "What's in the little building over there?" I was pointing across the garden at what looked like an enclosed windowless shed of some kind, but the door was shut.

"Dad won't let me go in there," he said. "But I know he buys rusty old tools and cleans them up—puts new handles in them and things like that. Then he sells them on the Internet. But I don't know why he won't let me go in there. He keeps it locked."

Ranger was heading around the garden and toward the shed. I hoped he would lead us to where he had found the object. But I had expected it to be somewhere in the weedy garden. He went right past it and started around the shed. Behind it was a small garden of a different kind. It was well tended; the only weeds there were of the marijuana variety. Reggie tugged on the dog to stop.

He turned back to me and said in anguish, "I can't believe this. Dad is growing weed back here. That's why he keeps me away from the shed."

"Yes, it looks like he is," I said as I looked beyond the foot-tall plants where the ground was disturbed. "Don't let the dog come any closer, Reggie. I can see where he was digging."

I stepped around the small patch of several-dozen marijuana plants. There, beside a hole that the puppy had dug, were two muddy shoes and a partially decayed finger, just like the one in the can. And there was also a wristwatch, muddy and corroded.

I heard a stifled scream behind me and turned to find Ellerie staring at the hole and what it contained, her hand covering her mouth. There was no doubt she knew as well as I did what Reggie's puppy had dug up. "I'm sorry you saw this," I said. "I shouldn't have let you come back here."

"That's Darien's right ring finger," she said as she fought to stifle threatening sobs. "That turquoise ring. I told you about it. He always wore it." Her eyes shone with horror. "And that watch is his too. Is there another finger in that can Reggie gave you?"

"Yes, there is," I said.

"So those are Harley's shoes?" she asked, her hand still near her mouth.

"I don't know who Harley is, but those shoes are my dad's," Reggie said. "Did he kill someone?" There was horror in his voice and on his face that matched Ellerie's.

"Possibly," I said. "But those shoes are quite small."

"My dad's feet are small. You've never seen him, but he's not very big. His feet aren't any larger than Mom's," he said. "I'm a lot bigger than either of them."

Ellerie looked from Reggie to me, her face puzzled. "I thought his ex-wife killed him."

"So did I," I said. "It looks like I was wrong."

I pulled out my iPhone and keyed in the chief's cell number. "I'm in a meeting," he said when he answered. "I'll call you back, Detective."

"Sorry, but I need you out here," I said calmly. "I have Darien Pearson's missing fingers, his wrist watch, and his killer's shoes."

"I guess my meeting is over," he said both to me and whoever was with him. "Where are you, Detective?"

I gave him the address and then said, "We'll need some other officers as well," and ended the call.

I looked at Ellerie and Reggie. They looked like they could both pass out. "You two need to go to the house," I said. "Ellerie, are you going to be okay?"

She nodded her head. "I'll try. Come on, Reggie," she said.

"Wait just a second," I said as my mind caught up with the evidence. "Do you have any idea where your father's at, Reggie?"

"He called last night. He asked if an arrest had been made for the murder," he said, choking up for a minute. "And when I told him two people had been arrested, he said that was great news. After that, he said they'd be home today."

"We'll watch for him," I said.

"He killed that man," he said. He looked at Ellerie and asked, "Was it your husband?" She nodded. "I'm sorry my dad did that. He must have been really mad about the money your husband owed him."

The chief showed up shortly after Ellerie and Reggie went back to the house. Ranger, the young malamute, was tied up outside. I started by showing the chief the finger in the can. Then I showed him the spot where the other two fingers, the wristwatch, and the shoes had been buried. And I explained about Andrew Hutchins and his small feet.

"We'd better get a search warrant for the house and for this shed," he said. "Do you have your laptop in your car?"

"I do," I said as more officers arrived.

"Take it in the house and work on the warrant," he instructed me.

Ellerie sat next to me as I worked. I kept glancing at her. She wore fatigue and shock like a second skin. I wanted to take her in my arms and try to comfort her, but now was neither the time nor the place.

An hour later, with the warrant approved, I searched the shed out back. It had been locked, and Reggie had no idea where the key was. So we broke the door open. In the shed were some old rusty shovels, picks, and other tools piled in a corner. And there on a wooden workbench was a bloody knife and a large bottle that had contained hydrochloric acid. The bottle was broken, and acid had been spilled on the bench and the floor, where there was also a little of what could have been blood. A small rope that looked like the rope that had bound Darien's hands sat on the workbench.

How Andrew Hutchins got Darien to go into the shed was a mystery, but the evidence showed that it was here that his fingers had been severed and his hands burned with acid. I figured Darien's hands had been bound behind his back and that Andrew had forced him to his car and from there took him to the area where he'd walked him into the abandoned field. And it was there that Darien had died after his head struck the large, jagged rock, according to the preliminary report from the medical examiner.

I eventually took Ellerie home, but not until I'd explained to Chief Collins why she had been there in the first place. He just smiled and said, "Maybe you can take her home now and then come back. She's probably had about all she can take for one day."

Ellerie was quiet for most of the ride home. When I walked her into the house, I said, "Would you like me to ask Pamela if she would come over and keep you company?"

"Will you come back after you're done?" she asked, sidestepping my question.

"I will, Ellerie," I said as I took her in my arms.

She smiled weakly and then said, "As long as I know you'll be back, I'll be fine here alone. It's you I need."

"I have an idea," I said suddenly. "I would normally be picking Tommy up from my folks in a couple of hours. Maybe you could get him and bring him here. But only if you don't want to be alone."

Ellerie smiled. "I'd like that a lot, if you think he'd be okay with it."

"He adores you," I said. I gave her the address to my parents' home and then said, "I'll let my mother know you're coming."

"It'll be a half hour or so," she said. "I need to clean myself up."

"I'll let her know."

"Would it be okay if I fixed dinner for you and Tommy?" she asked.

"You don't have to do that," I said.

"I'd like to," she responded. "I need to keep busy or I'll go crazy."

"Then I'd like that. I'll see you later."

Once I was in the car, I phoned my mother. "Mom, it's been a rough day," I said.

I told her briefly about the real killer. Then I said, "Ellerie was with me. She's pretty shaken up. But she wants something to do. She's going to pick up Tommy in about thirty minutes, and then she'll take him to her house and fix dinner for the three of us. She looks pretty rough. But don't tell her so," I said.

My mother was the most spiritual person I knew. She was in touch with the Spirit in ways I could only hope to be one day. She said, "You know I would never do that." She paused and then asked, "Has the Lord answered your prayers?"

"I think so, but not in the way I expected," I said.

"It's often that way," she said. "I'll watch for Ellerie."

An hour later, we arrested Andrew Hutchins, who had acid burns on his hands, for the murder of Darien Pearson. It fell to me as the investigating officer to interview him. He was stubborn at first, but later, after I had presented him with a list of the overwhelming amount of evidence we had against him, he said he didn't need an attorney and finally admitted that he was responsible for Darien's death.

When I asked him why he did it, he looked at the tabletop in front of him and said simply, "I didn't mean for him to die. But I did what I did to him because he owed me money, and he was just arrogant enough to believe I'd let him get by without paying it back." Andrew looked up before going on.

"Even then I might not have hurt him, Detective, but he bragged to me about beating his wife and making the baby come early," he said. "He told me he was glad it died. I am a lot of things, but I have never struck my wife. What he did to his wife was horrible. That made me really angry, and I lost it with the guy."

"So you dumped acid on his hands, cut some of his fingers off, and took him to a vacant lot where you shoved him down and he struck his head on a rock? Then you left him there to die?" I asked.

For a moment, he was silent, but when he finally spoke again, he said, "It wasn't quite like that, but I guess it's essentially true. But all I did was avenge her. He was drunk and I got him drunker, and I was going to try to convince him he should give me back my money and admit what he did to his wife to the cops. I wanted him to pay for it. I used my pistol to make him go with me from the bar to my shed. He was very drunk, and I gave him some whiskey that I kept in the shed and got him a lot more drunk, but not enough that he didn't try to fight me there in the shed. He grabbed that bottle of acid and broke it and tried to stab me with it. He got acid on his hands, lots of it. He got some on mine too." He held out his hands. They were red and starting to scar, but he hadn't gotten much acid on them.

"How did Darien lose his fingers?" I asked.

"That was not intentional either, I swear. I could have just shot him, but I didn't want to kill him, so I dropped the gun and grabbed the knife. I swung it just as he jabbed at me with the broken bottle. When I swung it down at his hand to keep the bottle from cutting me, it took off those three fingers," he explained. "I didn't mean to, but I had to defend myself without killing him."

"How did you get him tied up?" I asked.

"He started howling about his fingers and dropped the bottle back on the workbench. I cut off a piece of rope I had hanging there and tied his hands behind his back. By then he wasn't resisting much," Andrew told me.

"What did you do after that?" I asked.

"I gagged him so he would quit screaming and forced him to my car. Then I took him out there on the edge of town and made him walk to where you found him. I told him he could walk home from there. He stumbled and fell onto his back. I did not push him. I know this sounds crazy, but I figured he'd walk home or to the hospital or something. I guess he hit his head, and that killed him. And you know what, Detective?"

"What?" I asked.

He slapped a hand on the table and said, "I don't care that he died. He deserved it. No man has the right to do to his wife what that monster did to his."

Andrew Hutchins was not a good man, but I had to agree that men have no right to abuse their wives. And I swore that if and when I married again, I would never lay a finger on my wife in anger.

"Andrew, most people don't have bottles of acid and extremely sharp knives sitting around," I said. "Can you explain that to me?"

"I use the acid to clean tools. I collect old tools and restore them. I do it in the shed. Then I sell them online. I make some decent money at it. As for the big knife," he said, "I use it for lots of things, but I always keep it razor-sharp." He grinned a bit sheepishly. "I also use it to cut my weed with. I grow good weed, and my wife and I both like it."

I had no doubt about that. But there was something else I needed to know. I asked, "Let's talk about your gun. You said you dropped it when he jabbed at you with the bottle. Did you pick it up again?"

Andrew said, "Yeah, I used it to make him go with me again, although by then I guess I didn't need it much. He was in a lot of pain and very drunk."

"Where's the gun?" I asked.

"In a gun cabinet in the bedroom," he said.

"He had a car—a white Ford Escort. What did you do with it?" I asked. "He must have driven it to the bar."

"I hid it later that night, after I left him in that vacant lot."

"Where?" I asked.

He shook his head. "I, ah, I honestly don't remember."

After he was booked, it fell to me to tell Harley and August that they were no longer charged with murder, although they still had other crimes they would have to pay for. I called Mark Lanning, her defense attorney, explained what was happening, and asked him to meet me at the jail. "You screwed up," he said with a chuckle when he sauntered into the jail lobby.

"Maybe," I admitted. "But you've got to agree I had a lot of evidence that pointed to the two of them."

He didn't argue with that. We sat Harley down, gave her the good news, and then I said, "Harley, there are a couple of things I don't understand." She stared at me. So I said, "How did you know Darien was dead before it was ever on the news?"

"I heard that old lady tell Ellerie," she said. I must have looked puzzled, so she clarified for me. "I was in the bushes by the house when you and Ellerie came home. The old lady came out, and I heard what the three of you talked about."

That cleared that up. She had come to confront Ellerie, found that she wasn't home, and then hid and listened to our conversation. "I see," I said.

"When you left with them to go have the old lady look at some pictures, I decided to go buy the paint and send her a message. Darien owed me a lot of money, and she messed it all up for me."

I asked her a few more questions, and she admitted that she and August had broken into and stayed in the vacant house. I didn't even bother to talk to August after that. I told Mark he could tell him if he wanted. He said he would.

***

Tommy and Ellerie had had a nice time, despite the horrors of the day. She had prepared a simple but tasty dinner. After we finished eating and had cleared up her kitchen, I asked if she wanted Pamela to come over so she wouldn't be alone when we left. "No, I'll be okay. I have a lot to think about," she said.

The next morning, as soon as I dropped Tommy off with my mother, I drove right back to Ellerie's house. She let me in, hugged me, and said, "Thanks for coming back this morning. I've missed you since last night. It was a long night. I think I'll have nightmares for the rest of my life."

"I think I can help," I said.

"You still aren't afraid to be seen with me, are you?" she asked.

"I am proud to be seen with you. I think you and I will make a great team. We can start out slow and see what happens, if that's okay," I said.

"I would like that a lot," she replied, her amber eyes glowing.

EPILOGUE

I DID MARRY AGAIN. IT was six months later in the Vernal Temple. Mayra was not the happiest woman in the world, but I simply could not go there again. Kaci had a hard time understanding the choice I'd made, but it was okay, because she then got serious with the man she'd told me was chasing her and whom she didn't really care to date. Go figure. Connie was angry with me. I guess she figured I should have married her. She never did seem very friendly to me on the radio after that, but she still did her job. And I appreciated her for that.

Ellerie Fleming was now my wife. We both carried tainted pasts as we entered the temple that day. But we both were determined to never allow what had happened to us before to happen again. We were what each other needed. She was my rock, and I'd like to think I was hers.

Another year passed. Tommy had been adopted by Ellerie. He had a mother now. He loved her, and she loved him. I loved them both. We again entered the temple, and when we came out, we were an eternal family, us three—and the little one who was growing inside the woman I adored.

ABOUT THE AUTHOR

CLAIR M. POULSON WAS BORN and raised in Duchesne, Utah. His father was a rancher and farmer, his mother, a librarian. Clair has always been an avid reader, having found his love for books as a very young boy.

He has served for more than forty years in the criminal justice system. He spent twenty years in law enforcement, ending his police career with eight years as the Duchesne County Sheriff. For the past twenty-plus years, Clair has worked as a justice court judge for Duchesne County. He is also a veteran of the US Army, where he was a military policeman. In law enforcement, he has been personally involved in the investigation of murders and other violent crimes. Clair has also served on various boards and councils during his professional career, including the Justice Court Board of Judges, the Utah Commission on Criminal and Juvenile Justice, the Utah Judicial Council, the Utah Peace Officer Standards and Training Council, an FBI advisory board, and others.

In addition to his criminal justice work, Clair has farmed and ranched all his life. He has raised many kinds of animals, but his greatest interests are horses and cattle. He's also involved in the grocery store business with his oldest son and other family members.

Clair has served in many capacities in The Church of Jesus Christ of Latter-day Saints, including full-time missionary (California Mission), bishop, counselor to two bishops, Young Men president, high councilor, stake mission president, Scoutmaster, high priest group leader, and Gospel Doctrine teacher. He currently serves as a ward missionary.

Clair is married to Ruth, and they have five children, all of whom are married: Alan (Vicena) Poulson, Kelly Ann (Wade) Hatch, Amanda (Ben) Semadeni, Wade (Brooke) Poulson, and Mary (Tyler) Hicken.

They also have twenty-five wonderful grandchildren and a great-granddaughter.

Clair and Ruth met while both were students at Snow College and were married in the Manti Utah Temple.

Clair has always loved telling his children, and later his grandchildren, made-up stories. His vast experience in life and his love of literature have contributed to both his telling stories to his children and his writing of adventure and suspense novels.

Clair has published more than thirty novels. He would love to hear from his fans, who can contact him by going to his website, clairmpoulson.com.

Please enjoy these bonus free chapters of Gregg Luke's suspense novel

"MOTHER NATURE IS A SERIAL killer." Dr. Brandon Udy couldn't remember where he'd heard that quote, nor did he know why it popped into his mind just then, but nearly a decade of experience had taught him it wasn't quite right. A serial killer targets a specific caste of victim—hence the term *serial*. Mother Nature, on the other hand, kills with indiscriminate wantonness. She was a mass murderer of unparalleled accomplishment. No one was more insidious, more creative.

Mother Nature. A mass murderer. No one is more creative . . .

Brandon sat back and removed his disposable gloves. He rubbed his bloodshot eyes, no longer able to concentrate on those prophetic words or on the fungus displayed on his dissection microscope. He'd worked on the new specimen straight through the night, taking only one outhouse break and pausing only once for a snack. He wasn't hungry; he simply needed the energy.

The image in the microscope was sharp and detailed, but the specimen's morphology no longer felt significant to him. Neither did its uniqueness, suspected virulence, or unquestionable deadliness. All he could think about was Goliath, a 150-foot-tall kapok tree, roughly three kilometers from their remote research lab. He had to seek it out, had to reach it before it was too late. Nothing else mattered.

Without shutting down his microscope or storing the specimen in its sealed container, he stood and headed toward the plywood door of their large tent.

"Crikey, you're at it early," yawned his research partner, Julia Fatheringham. "You off to the dunny?"

Brandon didn't answer. It wasn't that he didn't want to. He couldn't. He knew she had asked a direct question; he could see her in his peripheral vision, stepping from their sleeping area. But she registered as an object of minimal importance, nothing more. His immediate focus was on the door. After that it'd be on the narrow trail that led through the rain forest to the thorny trunk of Goliath.

He opened the thin door to a drab morning that seemed to have come without preamble; the ubiquitous cloud cover was opaque and somber. No wind blew along the creek-bed swale. The precipitation fell in a slow, silky cascade. Looking up, he saw the treetops above the canopy swaying to a steady breeze. That was a good sign, though he didn't know why. Dressed in his usual garb—a T-shirt, cargo shorts, and flip-flops—he headed straight for a trail he'd walked a hundred times before, a trail he was now *compelled* to follow.

"Oy. Hold up a tick, will ya?" Julia said, her Aussie-accented voice somehow no longer humoring him.

Her voice sounded close, but he was so intent on his destination that her words didn't slow him a bit. His eyes focusing on the entrance to the shadowy, rain-soaked trail, he let his legs carry him forward automatically, almost as if without sentient command. His mind sparked with snippets of information at every step: the distance to the tree, the ambient temperature and wind direction, the current time of morning, what he had to do when he reached Goliath. Its enormous trunk would be damp from rain and incessant humidity. Regardless, climbing the tree was vital. He would find a way.

"Wait up, B. Where're you headed?"

Julia was just a few paces behind him. He could hear her pushing through the underbrush, trying to keep up. She clearly did not feel the same urging, the same unrelenting compulsion to climb the kapok—hence her banal question. Wasn't it obvious? He was heading to climb the tallest tree in the vicinity. He *had* to. Even if he wanted to stop, he couldn't.

"Come on, Brandon, give it a rest a sec."

He paused when she grabbed his shoulder, although his body strained to continue forward.

"Talk to me, please."

"No . . . time," he heard himself say with considerable effort. Jerking his shoulder from her grip, he resumed his trek in earnest. Time was of the essence—although, curiously, he didn't feel the need to run. A steady pace would get him there soon enough, and walking would conserve energy. Julia continued pleading for answers as he wended his way into the gloomy interior. He wished she understood his need to do this. It should make perfect sense to her, a fellow scientist.

By the time Brandon reached Goliath, the urge to climb was overpowering. Looking up, he could see where the giant kapok disappeared into the canopy.

The emergent layer—his destination—stretched another fifty feet beyond the treetops. Once he was there, all would be well.

"What's going on, mate?" Julia asked urgently, coming up behind him. "You're acting very bizarre."

The base of the kapok was supported by numerous buttressed plank-roots radiating out in several directions. The buttresses rose anywhere from three to ten feet above the ground and sloped away up to twelve feet across the forest floor. They would have made good handholds were it not for the thick, sharp thorns protruding from the bark to ward off would-be grazers.

As Brandon grabbed the top of a buttress to hoist himself up, he felt a dull stab of pain. He thought he heard Julia gasp, but it sounded distant, dreamlike. Removing his hand, he saw blood seeping from a small hole in his palm. His hand throbbed . . . but it didn't seem to matter. Somehow the pain wasn't important. Grabbing the buttress with both hands, he pulled himself over the top and lay across the large plank root. Thorns pierced the skin of his belly. Again, the punctures registered as hurting, but they seemed secondary to his need to reach the top of the tree. Using the trunk for stability, he stood, balancing on the massive root. Multiple thorns punctured the soles of his feet; one sank deep into his heel. Somewhere along the way he'd lost his flip-flops. Pain pulsed up his legs, but his mind overrode the reflex to jerk away from the source. Instead, he wrapped his arms and legs around the enormous trunk and began to shimmy upward. The hard thorns along the bole tore at his chest and arms, his belly and thighs. His flesh shredded; blood ran freely. With morbid efficiency, the thorny protrusions helped him stick to the otherwise slippery trunk.

Julia's calls turned to cries, fearful and desperate. His mind tuned them out, paying no attention to the emotion they may once have engendered.

It took nearly sixty minutes to reach the first branch, some eighty feet up. The thorns were smaller and less dense higher up but still very sharp. He swung over the branch and looked down. In the shadowy gloom below, he saw Julia staring up at him with wide, horror-filled eyes. She'd soon understand his need to climb; in a few minutes it'd be obvious. Steadily ascending from branch to branch, Brandon finally broke through the 120-foot canopy.

Birds left their roosts in raucous annoyance at his appearance; monkeys screeched in protest. At that height, a steady breeze caressed the treetops, drying the sheen of blood covering his face and frame. He climbed a dozen feet higher before the branches of the wide crown became too thin to hold his weight. He needed to get as high as possible. The wind was stronger higher up—that was important. But he could climb no farther.

Constrained to that elevation, he straddled two stout boughs, wrapped his arms and legs around the last section of emergent trunk, and squeezed tightly. Resting the right side of his face against the trunk, he placed a thin, horizontal branch between his teeth and chomped down, resulting in a strange half smile on his face. He sighed and closed his eyes. He'd made it. The steady, late-morning breeze was perfect. He was as high as he could get. All was well.

The soughing wind and gentle swaying of branches was calming. Gradually, his mind dulled; no stimuli triggered response or emotion. His breaths became sluggish, shallow. Steadily, painlessly, his heart slowed to one or two beats per minute. His murky thoughts slipped into a state of emptiness, totally disassociated from his consciousness.

As he released a seemingly endless, wispy lungful of air, an eerie hush fell across the landscape of the canopy.

CHAPTER 2

TORN BETWEEN WAITING FOR BRANDON to climb down or returning to the research tent for help, Julia anxiously paced at the base of Goliath for close to an hour. The weighty emptiness of abrupt solitude pressed down on her, making it hard to breathe.

She had no idea what condition Brandon was in, but it wasn't good. She'd never seen him act this way—like he was hypnotized or something. He never left the tent without saying where he was headed. Neither did she. It was a precautionary measure. Sure, Brandon had often joked about going to the beach or to Burger King, but he made sure he always said *something*. He was insatiably fun, witty, and full of positive energy, rarely doleful, never lugubrious. Sometimes he was a shameless practical joker, but his boyishly unkempt hair and easy smile made it impossible to stay angry at him for long. Besides, underneath his unremitting lightheartedness was a serious researcher, quick of mind and deep of thought. When he latched on to an idea, he'd see it to fruition, often irrespective of food or sleep but never to the point of carelessness.

That's why she knew this was more than a quirky jest. She'd watched him deliberately drive kapok thorns into flesh without so much as a grimace. She'd seen his skin tear, seen his blood pour. *That* was no joke. Instinct told her this was something she couldn't handle alone; she needed to call their coordinator.

"Oy, Brandon! I'm going to radio for help," she called up to the rain forest canopy. "Don't do anything stupid!" As if free-climbing a kapok wasn't already rife with stupidity.

The trek back to the research tent seemed to take forever. Along the way, the angst of the situation bunched on her like floodwaters pushing against a dam.

Once inside the tent, Julia toggled the transmit switch on their two-way radio, signaling the research coordinator at the CIST: The Centro Investigación de la Selva Tropical located in Caicara del Orinoco, a small city some 330 miles northward. "CIST HQ, this is Ascom base, come in!"

The static hiss undulated with a sinuous, high overtone. She shuddered. It was an eerie, spectral noise she'd heard countless times but had never before considered foreboding.

"CIST HQ, this is Ascom base. I'm calling in an emergency. I repeat: this is an emergency! Felipe, are you there?"

No response.

"Criminy!" She tweaked a couple of dials. "Caicara, this is Ascom. Please respond."

A few electric crackles punctuated the unnerving static before a man's voice filtered through. "This is CIST. Good afternoon, Doctor. How can I help you?"

"Oh, thank heavens you're there, Felipe. Brandon's acting very strange. I think he's in trouble."

"You interrupted my afternoon *siesta* just to tell me Dr. Udy is acting strange?" Felipe asked through a chuckle. "He's always acting strange."

Afternoon siesta? Only then did she realize it was almost one o'clock. Where had the time gone? "No, mate. I think he's in *real* trouble. He free-climbed a kapok—without gloves or shoes. There's blood everywhere."

"Geez, are you serious?"

"Too right."

"Okay, listen. Take a deep breath and tell me what happened exactly."

She quickly rehearsed the events of the morning, trying to include every detail but realizing sadly there weren't many. When she finished, there was a lengthy pause over the airway.

"Is this a joke?" he asked with minimal humor.

"No, Felipe. I'm dead serious. He's . . . I don't know. This isn't one of his typical larks. I'm . . . it just doesn't *feel* right, you know?"

Felipe's voice took on a serious edge. "All right, listen, Doc, just stay calm. It's going to be okay. Is he still up there? Up the tree?"

"As far as I know, yes."

"Copy that. Hold on a moment." More empty static followed. The second pause felt like eternity. "Is he studying a fungus that only grows in the canopy?"

"No. Well . . . I don't know. Not recently. I'm worried because he's not responding when I call to him."

"Are you going up after him?"

"I don't know. I think I should, but we don't have any gear on that tree."

"Copy that."

There was more static hiss while she awaited his counsel. Every empty second was agonizing.

"Okay, look, I'm sorry, but I've already got another flight scheduled this afternoon. It's a government thing, so there's no backing out. You understand. But I'll come out at first light tomorrow. I promise."

The finality of his words was like a knife plunging into her gut. "Felipe, *please.*"

"Just take it easy, Julia. Listen, Dr. Udy's pretty strong, and he's pretty dang smart for a goof-off. He's probably just . . ." His words trailed off, confirming that he couldn't explain Brandon's bizarre behavior either. "I doubt it's anything serious."

"It's as serious as a heart attack, mate! I saw thorns puncture his skin. He stepped on them with bare feet, for cripe's sake. I . . . I don't know what to do." Julia hated the fact that she was acting so flighty. She was a winner not a whiner. She'd been valedictorian of her class at the University of Queensland and had been Dr. Brandon Udy's first pick as research partner for this expedition. Besides, she'd been in tough situations before and handled them with the stoicism and methodical aplomb of a seasoned field researcher. She'd even captured and tagged saltwater crocks for crying out loud. But *this*! This was unlike anything she'd ever seen before—unlike anything she'd ever *heard* of. "Can't you come right after your other flight?"

"That's a negative, Doctor. Flying into your neck of the rain forest is pretty brutal even in daylight. There's no way I can make it there before nightfall. Sorry. I'll stay by the radio, but there's little more I can do right now."

And there it was: her lifeline had just been severed. She was on her own. Maybe he was right; maybe there wasn't anything he could do just then. But *she* could.

"Fair enough," she said. "You're right, of course. But *I'm* going back out."

"Okay, but be careful. You know that rain forest is no place for a casual stroll—especially with the scent of fresh blood in the air. Be sure to get back in before dark."

"He'd do the same for me," she said with certainty.

Felipe's next pause felt contemplative, as if he was mulling over a way to talk her out of her decision. But she was determined. And doing *something* was better than simply sitting around waiting . . . wondering.

His next transmission began with a long sigh. "Copy that. Please be extra cautious, okay? You hear what I'm saying? The weather looks moderate over Amazonas right now, but there's a big storm on the radar. It looks like a bad one."

"No worries." Julia left the transmitter on in case the CIST called back. She downed a protein bar and a bottle of water and traded her shorts and sneakers for cargo pants and hiking boots. Then, stuffing a small backpack with every essential she could think of, she shrugged it on and went outside. Pausing, she breathed deeply, as much to clear her head as to steel her determination. She set her jaw and narrowed her eyes at the forest. She'd been at this remote location long enough that it no longer seemed strange or alien. That bolstered her confidence.

Ascom base sat in a dense section of Venezuelan rain forest in the state of Amazonas. Lush vegetation abounded. From the emergent layer on top, through the profuse canopy, and down the towering understory to the forest floor, the dark, dank environs were ideal for their field of research: mycology. The moist, spongy biomass of the rain forest floor reeked of decay. Fungi thrived there. Ascom's eighteen-month objective was to isolate the basic biochemical properties of as many new fungal species as possible. They had a small gas chromatograph and colorimeter which gave them a good idea if the isolated biologic compound was new or unique. From there, they would store the sample to be studied later in a full biochemical lab before it was tested on animal cells.

The river swale in which the base sat opened to a narrow yet unobstructed length of sky. The morning's rain had passed, leaving a thin, gauzy layer of clouds veiling the heavens. She knew it was the calm before the storm. If Felipe said a storm was coming, it was.

Six meters away, the perimeter was walled by a dense, dark wall of vegetation. Jagged, gray-green silhouettes harried by a fresh afternoon breeze scratched against each other, sounding like the raspy breathing of some unseen predator.

Julia quickly shook the image from her head. Pushing all fears aside, she unsheathed her knife, set her jaw, and marched into the shadowy undergrowth.